THE LEWIS MAN

Also by Peter May

The Blackhouse

THE LEWIS MAN

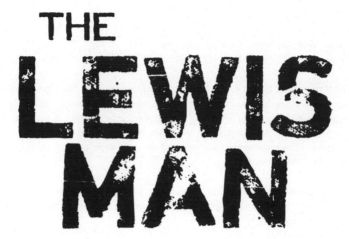

PETER MAY

New York • London

Quercus

New York • London

© 2012 by Peter May, represented by Rouergue
First published in the United States by Quercus in 2014

ISBN 978-1-62365-448-1

Library of Congress Control Number: 2014931822

Distributed in the United States and Canada by
Hachette Book Group
1290 Avenue of the Americas
New York, NY 10104

Manufactured in the United States

10 9 8 7 6 5 4 3 2

www.quercus.com

In memory of my dad

That is where they live:
Not here and now, but where all happened once.

From "The Old Fools" by Philip Larkin

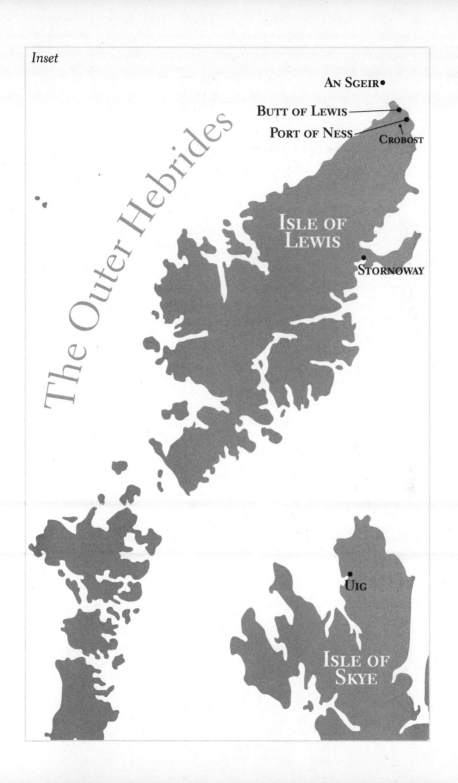

AN SGEIR•

BUTT OF LEWIS

PORT OF NESS

CROBOST

ISLE OF
LEWIS

•STORNOWAY

The Outer Hebrides

•UIG

ISLE OF
SKYE

PRONUNCIATION

Here is a simple guide to the English pronunciation of some of the Gaelic names and words in the book. ch is pronounced as in the Scottish word loch, and the emphasis is placed on the underlined syllable:

Gaelic name	Pronunciation	Gaelic name	Pronunciation
An Sgeir	An <u>Skerr</u>	Iain	Yan
Beag	Beg	Mairead	<u>My</u>rad
Ceit	Kate	Mamaidh	Mammy
Coinneach	<u>Coin</u>yach	Marsaili	<u>Marsh</u>ally
Dubh	Doo	Niseach	<u>Nee</u>shuch
Eachan	<u>Ya</u>chan	Ruadh	<u>Roo</u>agh
Eilean	<u>Yay</u>lan	Seonaidh	<u>Shaw</u>nay
Eilidh	<u>Ay</u>lay	Seoras	<u>Shaw</u>rass
Fionnlagh	Fee<u>on</u>lach	Sine	<u>Shee</u>nuh
Gaelic	<u>Gah</u>lick	Slàinthe mhath	Slange e vah
		Uilleam	<u>Will</u>yam

Machair, pronounced macher, is the Gaelic word for the fertile sandy soil around the coastal areas of the Western Isles of Scotland. It has passed into the English language as a result of international concern over the problem of "machair erosion." Much of the machair is gradually being reclaimed by the sea.

PROLOGUE

On this storm-lashed island three hours off the north-west coast of Scotland, what little soil exists gives the people their food and their heat. It also takes their dead. And very occasionally, as today, gives one up.

It is a social thing, the peat-cutting. Family, neighbours, children, all gathered on the moor with a mild wind blowing out of the south-west to dry the grasses and keep the midges at bay. Annag is just five years old. It is her first peat-cutting, and the one she will remember for the rest of her life.

She has spent the morning with her grandmother in the kitchen of the crofthouse watching eggs boil on the old Enchantress stove, fired by last year's peat. Now the women head out across the moor carrying hampers, Annag barefoot, the bog's brown waters squishing between her toes as she runs ahead over prickly heather, transported by the excitement of the day.

The sky fills her eyes. A sky torn and shredded by the wind. A sky that leaks sunlight in momentary flashes to spill across dead grasses where the white tips of bog cotton dip and dive in frantic eddies of turbulent air. In the next days the wild flowers of spring and early summer will turn the brown winter wastes yellow and purple, but for the moment they remain dormant, dead.

In the distance, the silhouettes of half a dozen men in overalls and cloth caps can be seen against the dazzle of sunlight flashing across an ocean that beats against cliffs of black, obdurate gneiss. It is almost blinding, and Annag raises her hand to shade her eyes to see them stoop and bow as the tarasgeir *slides through soft black peat to turn it out in sodden square slabs. The land is scarred by generations of peat-cutting. Trenches twelve or eighteen inches deep, with fresh-cut turfs laid along the tops of them to dry on one side and then the other. In a few days the cutters will return for the* cruinneachadh, *the gathering of the peats into* rùdhain, *small triangular piles that allow the wind to blow between them and complete the drying.*

In time they will be collected in a cart and taken back to the croft, dry brittle peats laid like bricks, one upon the other, in a herring-bone pattern, to construct the stack that will keep the family warm and cook the food that will fill their bellies all next winter.

It is how the people of the Isle of Lewis, this northernmost island in the Scottish Hebridean archipelago, have survived for centuries. And in this time of financial uncertainty, as the cost of fuel soars, those with open hearths and stoves have returned in droves to the traditions of their ancestors. For here the only cost of heating your home is the expenditure of your labour and your devotion to God.

But for Annag it is just an adventure, out here on the wind-blasted moor with the soft air filling her mouth as she laughs and calls out to her father and grandfather, the voices of her mother and grandmother in shouted conversation somewhere behind her. She has no sense at all of the tension that has caught the little clutch of peat-cutters ahead of her. No way, from her limited experience, of reading the body language of the men crouched down around the stretch of trench wall that has collapsed about their feet.

Too late her father sees her coming and shouts at her to stay back. Too late for her to stop her forward momentum, or respond to the panic in his voice. The men stand suddenly, turning towards her, and she sees her brother's face the colour of cotton sheets laid out in the sun to bleach.

And she follows his eyes down to the fallen peat bank and the arm that lies stretched out towards her, leathery skin like brown parchment, fingers curled as if holding an invisible ball. One leg lies twisted over the other, a head tipped towards the ditch as if in search of a lost life, black holes where the eyes should have been.

For a moment she is lost in a sea of incomprehension, before realisation washes over her, and the scream is whipped from her mouth by the wind.

| ONE |

Gunn saw the vehicles parked at the roadside from some distance away. The sky was black and blue, brooding, contused, rolling in off the ocean low and unbroken. The first spits of rain were smeared across his windscreen by the intermittent passage of its wipers. The pewter of the ocean itself was punctuated by the whites of breaking waves ten or fifteen feet high, and the solitary blue flashing light of the police car next to the ambulance was swallowed into insignificance by the vastness of the landscape.

Beyond the vehicles, the harled houses of Siader huddled against the prevailing weather, expectant and weary, but accustomed to its relentless assault. Not a single tree broke the horizon. Just lines of rotting fenceposts along the roadside, and the rusting remains of tractors and cars in deserted yards. Blasted shrubs showing brave green tips clung on with stubborn roots to thin soil in anticipation of better days to come, and a sea of bog cotton shifted in ripples and currents like water in the wind.

Gunn parked beside the police car and stepped out into the blast. Thick dark hair growing back in a widow's peak from a furrowed forehead was whipped into the air, and he gathered his black quilted anorak around him. He cursed the fact that he had not thought to bring a pair of boots, and stepped at first gingerly through the soft ground, before feeling the chill of the bog water seeping into his shoes and soaking through his socks.

He reached the first of the peat banks, and followed a path along the top of it, skirting the clusters of drying turfs. The uniforms had hammered metal stakes into soft ground to mark off the site with blue and white crime-scene tape that hummed and twisted, fibrillating in the wind. The smell of peat smoke reached him from the nearest crofthouses some half a mile away out towards the edge of the cliffs.

A group of men stood around the body almost leaning into the wind, the fluorescent yellow of ambulance men waiting to take it away, policemen in black waterproofs and chequered hats who thought they had seen it all before. Until now.

They parted wordlessly to let Gunn through, and he saw the police surgeon crouched down, leaning over the corpse, delicately brushing aside crumbling peat with latexed fingers. He looked up as Gunn loomed overhead, and Gunn saw for the first time the brown, withered skin of the dead man. He frowned. "Is he . . . coloured?"

"Only by the peat. I'd say he was a Caucasian. Quite young. Late teens or early twenties. A classic bog body, almost perfectly preserved."

"You've seen one before?"

"Never. But I've read about them. It's the salt carried in the wind from the ocean that allows the peat moss to thrive here. And when the roots rot it creates acid. The acid preserves the body, almost pickling it. His organs should be virtually intact inside."

Gunn gazed with unabashed curiosity at the almost mummified remains. "How did he die, Murdo?"

"Violently, by the looks of it. There appear to be several stab wounds in the area of the chest, and his throat has been cut. But it'll take the pathologist to give you a definitive cause of death, George." He stood up and peeled off his gloves. "Better get him out of here before the rain comes."

Gunn nodded, but couldn't take his eyes off the face of the young man locked in the peat. Although there was a shrivelled aspect to his features, they would be recognisable to anyone who knew him. Only the soft, exposed tissue of the eyes had decomposed. "How long's he been here?"

Murdo's laugh was lost in the wind. "Who knows? Hundreds of years, maybe even thousands. You'll need an expert to tell you that."

| TWO |

I don't need to look at the clock to know the time.

It's odd how the brown stain on the ceiling seems lighter in the mornings. The crystalline traces of mould that follow the crack through it seem somehow whiter. And strange how I always wake at the same hour. It's not the light that creeps in around the edges of the curtains that does it, because there are so few hours of darkness at this time of year. It must be some internal clock. All those years rising with the dawn for the milking, and everything else that would fill the waking daylight hours. All gone now.

I quite enjoy looking at this stain on the ceiling. I don't know why, but in the mornings it resembles a fine horse, saddled, and waiting to take me away to some brighter future. While at night, when it gets gloomy, it has a different mien. Like some rampant and horned creature ready to carry me off into darkness.

I hear the door open and turn to see a woman standing there. She seems familiar, but I can't quite place her. Until she speaks.

"Oh, Tormod . . ."

Of course. It's Mary. I'd know her voice anywhere. I wonder why she looks so sad. And something else. Something that turns down the corners of her mouth. Something like disgust. I know she used to love me, although I'm not sure that I ever loved her.

"What is it, Mary?"

"You've soiled the bed again."

And then I smell it, too. Suddenly. Almost overpoweringly. Why didn't I notice it before?

"Couldn't you have got up? Couldn't you?"

I don't know why she's blaming me. I didn't do it on purpose. I never do it on purpose. The smell is worse as she pulls back the covers, and she puts a hand over her mouth.

"Get up," she says. "I'll have to strip the bed. Go and put your pyjamas in the bath and take a shower."

I swing my legs over the side of the bed and wait for her to help me to my feet. It never used to be like this. I was always the strong one. I remember the time she twisted her ankle up by the old sheep fank when we were gathering the beasts for the shearing. She couldn't walk, and I had to carry her home. Almost two miles, with arms aching, and never one word of complaint. Why does she never remember that?

Can't she see how humiliating this is? I turn my head away so that she won't see the tears gathering in my eyes, and I can feel myself blinking them furiously away. I draw a deep breath. "Donald Duck."

"Donald Duck?"

I glance at her and almost shrink from the anger I see in her eyes. Is that what I said? Donald Duck? That can't have been what I meant. But I can't think now what I did mean to say. So I say again, firmly, "Aye, Donald Duck."

She pulls me to my feet, almost roughly, and pushes me towards the door. "Get out of my sight!"

Why is she so angry?

I waddle through to the bathroom and slip out of my pyjamas. Where did she say I was to put them? I drop them on the floor and look in the mirror. An old man with a scribble of thin white hair and the palest of blue eyes stares back at me. I wonder for a moment who he is, then turn and look from the window out across the machair towards the shore. I can see the wind ruffling the heavy winter coats of the sheep grazing on the sweet, salty grass, but I can't hear it. Neither can I hear the ocean where it breaks upon the shore. Lovely white foaming seawater full of sand and fury.

It must be the double glazing. We never had that at the farm. You knew you were alive there, with the wind whistling through the window frames and blowing peat smoke down the chimney. There was room to breathe there, room to live. Here the rooms are so small, sealed off from the world. Like living in a bubble.

That old man is looking at me from the mirror again. I smile and he smiles back. Of course, I knew it was me all along. And I wonder how Peter is doing these days.

| THREE |

It was dark when finally Fin turned out the light. But the words were still there, burned on to his retinas. There was no escape in darkness.

Apart from Mona's, there were two other witness statements. Neither of them had possessed the presence of mind to note the registration number of the car. That Mona hadn't seen it was hardly surprising. The car had thrown her in the air, to come down on the bonnet and windscreen with sickening force before being flung aside and rolling several times over the unyielding metalled surface of the road. That she hadn't been more seriously injured was miraculous.

Robbie, with his lower centre of gravity, had gone down and under the wheels.

Each time he read the words he imagined himself to have been there, to have seen it, and each time he felt the nausea rising from his stomach. It was as vivid in his mind as if it were a real memory. As was Mona's description of the face she had seen behind the wheel, imprinted so clearly in her recollection, although it could only have been the merest of glimpses. A middle-aged man with

longish, mousy-brown hair. Two or three days' growth on his face.
How could she have seen that? And yet there was no doubt in her
mind. He'd even had a police artist do a sketch from her description.
A face that remained in the file, a face that haunted his dreams, even
after nine months.

He turned over and closed his eyes in a vain search for sleep.
The windows of his hotel room lay ajar behind the curtain, opened
for air but also letting in the roar of traffic along Princes Street. He
drew his knees up to his chest, tucking his elbows in at his sides,
hands clasped together at his breastbone, like a praying foetus.

Tomorrow would be the end of everything he had known for
most of his adult life. Everything he had been and become, and was
likely to be. Like the day so many years before that his aunt had told
him his parents were dead, and he had felt, for the first time in his
short life, utterly and completely alone.

Daylight brought no relief, just a quiet determination to see this
day through. A warm breeze blew across The Bridges, sunlight
falling in shifting patterns across the gardens below the castle. Fin
pushed his way determinedly through chattering crowds sporting
light spring fashions. A generation who had forgotten the warnings of their elders to *ne'er cast a clout till May is oot*. It never
seemed quite fair that other people's lives should go on as before.
And yet who would have guessed at the pain behind his mask of
normality? So who knew what turmoil was hidden behind the
facades of others?

He stopped at the photocopy shop in Nicolson Street, slipping
copied pages into his leather bag before heading east to St. Leonard's Street and the "A" Division police headquarters where he had
spent most of the last ten years. His farewell party had been drinks
with a handful of colleagues at a pub in Lothian Road two nights
earlier. A sombre affair, marked mainly by recollection and regret,
but also by some genuine affection.

Some people nodded to him in the corridor. Others shook
his hand. At his desk, it took him only a few minutes to clear his

personal belongings into a cardboard box. The sad, accumulated detritus of a restless working life.

"I'll take your warrant card off you, Fin."

Fin turned around. DCI Black had something of the vulture about him. Hungry and watchful. Fin nodded and handed him his card.

"I'm sorry to see you go," Black said. But he didn't look sorry. He had never doubted Fin's ability, just his commitment. And only now, after all these years, was Fin finally ready to acknowledge that Black was right. They both knew he was a good cop, it had just taken Fin longer to realize that it wasn't his métier. It had taken Robbie's death to do that.

"Records tell me you pulled the file on your son's hit-and-run three weeks ago." Black paused, waiting perhaps for an acknowledgement. When it didn't come he added, "They'd like it back."

"Of course." Fin slid the file out of his bag and dropped it on to the desk. "Not that anyone's ever likely to open it."

Black nodded. "Probably not." He hesitated. "Time you closed it, too, Fin. It'll just eat you up inside, and fuck with the rest of your life. Let it go, son."

Fin couldn't meet his eye. He lifted his box of belongings. "I can't."

Outside, he went around the back of the building and opened the lid of a large green recycling bin to empty the contents of his cardboard box, and then chuck it in after them. He had no use for any of it.

He stood for a moment, looking up at the window from which he had so often watched the sun and the rain and the snow sweep across the shadowed slopes of Salisbury Craggs. All the seasons of all the wasted years. And he slipped out into St. Leonard's to flag down a taxi.

His cab dropped him on the steep cobbled slope of the Royal Mile, just below St. Giles' Cathedral, and he found Mona waiting for him in Parliament Square. She was still in her drab winter greys, almost lost among the classical architecture of this Athens of the north, sandstone buildings blackened by time and smoke. He supposed it reflected her mood. But she was more than depressed. Her agitation was clear.

"You're late."

"Sorry." He took her arm and they hurried across the deserted square, through arches beneath towering columns. And he wondered if his lateness had been subliminally contrived. Not so much an unwillingness to let go of the past, as a fear of the unknown, of leaving the safety of a comfortable relationship to face a future alone.

He glanced at Mona as they entered the portals of what had once been the home of the Scottish Parliament, before the landowners and merchants who sat here had succumbed three hundred years before to the bribes of the English and sold out the people they were supposed to represent to a union they didn't want. Fin and Mona's, too, had been a union of convenience, a loveless friendship. It had been driven by occasional sex, and held together only by the shared love of their son. And now, without Robbie, it was ending here, in the Court of Session. A piece of paper bringing to a close a chapter of their lives which had taken sixteen years to write.

He saw the pain of it in her face, and all the regrets of a lifetime came back to haunt him.

In the end it took only a few minutes to consign all those years to the dustbin of history. The good times and bad. The struggles, the laughs, the fights. And they emerged into brilliant sunlight spilling down across the cobbles, the rumble of traffic out on the Royal Mile. Other people's lives flowing past, while theirs had been shifted from pause to stop. They stood like still figures at the centre of a time-lapse film, the rest of the world eddying around them at high speed.

Sixteen years on and they were strangers again, unsure of what to say, except goodbye, and almost afraid to say that out loud, in spite of the pieces of paper they held in their hands. Because beyond goodbye, what else was there? Fin opened his leather bag to slip the paperwork inside, and his photocopied sheets in their beige folder slid out and scattered around his feet. He stooped quickly to gather them up, and Mona crouched down to help him.

He was aware of her head turning towards him as she took several of them in her hand. It must have been clear to her at a glance what they were. Her own statement was among them. A few hundred words that described a life taken and a relationship lost. The sketch of a face drawn from her own description. Fin's obsession. But she said nothing. She stood up, handing them to him, and watched as he stuffed them back in his bag.

When they reached the street, and the moment of parting could no longer be avoided, she said, "Will we stay in touch?"

"Is there any point?"

"I suppose not."

And in those few words, all the investment they had made in each other over all these years, the shared experiences, the pleasure and the pain, were lost for ever like snowflakes on a river.

He glanced at her. "What will you do when the house is sold?"

"I'll go back to Glasgow. Stay with my dad for a while." She met his eye. "What about you?"

He shrugged. "I don't know."

"Yes, you do." It was almost an accusation. "You'll go back to the island."

"Mona, I've spent most of my adult life avoiding that."

She shook her head. "But you will. You know it. You can never escape the island. It was there between us all those years, like an invisible shadow. It kept us apart. Something we could never share."

Fin took a deep breath and felt the warmth of the sun on his face as he raised it for a moment to the sky. Then he looked at her. "There was a shadow, yes. But it wasn't the island."

Of course, she was right. There was nowhere else to go, except back to the womb. Back to the place that had nurtured him, alienated him, and in the end driven him away. It was the only place, he knew, that there was any chance of finding himself again. Among his own people, speaking his own tongue.

He stood on the foredeck of the *Isle of Lewis* and watched the gentle rise and fall of her bow as she ploughed through the unusually still waters of the Minch. The mountains of the mainland had vanished long ago, and the ship's horn sounded forlornly now as they slipped into the dense spring haar that blanketed the eastern coast of the island.

Fin peered intently into swirling grey, feeling the wetness of it on his face, until finally the faintest shadow emerged from its gloom. The merest smudge on a lost horizon, eerie and eternal, like the ghost of his past come back to haunt him.

As the island took gradual shape in the mist he felt all the hairs stand up on the back of his neck, and was almost overwhelmed by a sense of homecoming.

| FOUR |

Gunn sat at his desk squinting at the computer screen. Subliminally he registered the sound of a foghorn not far out in the Minch, and knew that the ferry would be docking shortly.

He shared his first-floor office with two other detectives, and had a fine view from his window of the Blythswood Care charity shop on the other side of Church Street. *Christian care for body and soul.* If he cared to crane his neck he could see as far up the road as the Bangla Spice Indian restaurant with its luridly coloured sauces and irresistible garlic fried rice. But right now the subject matter on his screen had banished all thoughts of food.

Bog bodies, also known as bog people, were preserved human bodies found in sphagnum bogs in northern Europe, Great Britain and Ireland, he read on the Wikipedia page on the subject. Acidic water, low temperatures and lack of oxygen combined to preserve the skin and organs, so much so that it was even possible in some cases to recover fingerprints.

He wondered about the body laid out in the cold cabinet in the autopsy room at the hospital. Now that it was out of the bog, how quickly might it start to deteriorate? He scrolled down the page and looked at the photograph of a head taken from a body recovered sixty years ago from a peat bog in Denmark. A chocolate-brown face remarkably well defined, one cheek squashed up against the nose where it had lain in repose, an orange stubble still clearly visible on the upper lip and jaw.

"Ah, yes, Tollund Man."

Gunn looked up to see a tall, willowy, lean-faced figure with a halo of dark, thinning hair leaning down to get a closer look at his screen.

"Carbon dating of his hair placed him from around 400 BC. The idiots who performed the autopsy cut off his head and threw the rest of him away. Except for his feet and one finger, which are still preserved in formalin." He grinned and held out a hand. "Professor Colin Mulgrew."

Gunn was surprised by the strength of his handshake. He seemed so slight.

Almost as if he had read his mind, or detected his wince as they shook, Professor Mulgrew smiled and said, "Pathologists need good hands, Detective Sergeant. For cutting through bone and prising apart skeletal structures. You'd be surprised how much strength is required." There was just the hint of cultured Irish in his accent. He turned back to Tollund Man. "Amazing, isn't it? After two thousand four hundred years, it was still possible to tell that he'd been hanged, and that his last meal had been a porridge of grain and seeds."

"Were you involved in that post-mortem, too?"

"Bloody hell, no. Way before my time. Mine was Old Croghan Man, pulled out of an Irish bog in 2003. He was nearly as old though. Certainly more than two thousand years. Helluva big man for his day. Six foot six. Imagine. A bloody giant." He scratched his head and grinned. "So what'll we call your man, then, eh? Lewis Man?"

Gunn swivelled in his seat and waved the professor towards a free chair. But the pathologist shook his head.

"Been sitting for bloody hours. And the flights up here don't give you much leg room."

Gunn nodded. Slightly smaller than average height himself, he had never found that a problem. "So how did your Old Croghan Man die?"

"Murdered. Tortured first. There were deep cuts under each of his nipples. Then he was stabbed in the chest, decapitated, and his body cut in half." The professor wandered across to the window and peered up and down the street as he spoke. "Bit of a mystery really, because he had beautifully manicured fingernails. So not a working man. There is no doubt he was a meat eater, but his last meal was a mix of wheat and buttermilk. My old pal Ned Kelly, at the National Museum of Ireland, thinks he was sacrificed to ensure good yields of corn and milk in the royal lands nearby." He turned back to Gunn. "The Indian restaurant up the road any good?"

Gunn shrugged. "Not bad."

"Good. Haven't had a decent bloody Indian for ages. So where's our man now?"

"In a refrigerated drawer at the hospital morgue."

Professor Mulgrew rubbed his hands together. "We'd better go and take a look at him then before he starts decomposing on us. Then a bite of lunch? I'm bloody starving."

The body, laid out now on the autopsy table, had an oddly shrunken look about it, well built, but diminished somehow. It was the colour of tea and looked as if it might have been sculpted in resin.

Professor Mulgrew wore a dark-blue jumpsuit beneath a surgical gown, and a bright yellow face mask covering mouth and nose. Above it perched a ridiculously large pair of protective tortoiseshell glasses that seemed to shrink the size of his head, and turn him, incongruously, into a bizarre caricature of himself. Without any apparent awareness of how absurd he looked, he moved nimbly around the table taking measurements, his white tennis shoes protected by green plastic covers.

He crossed to the whiteboard to scrawl up the initial statistics, talking all the time above the squeak of his felt pen. "The poor bugger weighs a mere forty-one kilograms. Not much for a man of

173 centimetres in height." He peered over his glasses at Gunn.
"That's just over five feet eight to you."

"Was he ill, do you think?"

"No, not necessarily. Although he's well preserved, he will have
lost of lot of fluid weight over the years. He looks a pretty healthy
specimen to me."

"What age?"

"Late teens, early twenties, I'd say."

"No, I mean, how long had he been in the peat?"

Professor Mulgrew raised one eyebrow and tipped his head
scathingly in Gunn's direction. "Patience, please. I'm not a bloody
carbon-dating machine, Detective Sergeant."

He returned to the body and turned it over on to its front, leaning in close as he brushed away fragments of brown and yellow-
green moss.

"Were there any clothes found with the body?"

"No, nothing." Gunn moved nearer to see if he could discern
what it was that had attracted Mulgrew's attention. "We dug over
the whole area. No clothes, no artefacts of any kind."

"Hmmm. In that case I would say he'd probably been wrapped in
a blanket of some sort before being buried. And he must have lain
in it for quite a few hours."

Gunn's eyebrows shot up in astonishment. "How can you tell
that?"

"In the hours after death, Mr. Gunn, the blood settles in the
lower portion of the body causing a purplish red discoloration of
the skin. We call it post-mortem lividity. If you look carefully at his
back, buttocks and thighs you will see that the skin is darker, but
there is a paler, blanched pattern in the lividity."

"Meaning?"

"Meaning that he lay for at least eight to ten hours on his back
after death, wrapped in some kind of rough blanket whose weave
left its pattern in the darker coloration. We can clean him off and
photograph it and, if you like, have an artist make a sketch to repro-
duce the pattern."

Using a pair of tweezers, he recovered several fibres still clinging to the skin.

"Could be wool," he said. "Shouldn't be hard to confirm that."

Gunn nodded, but decided not to ask what point there would be in identifying the pattern and fabric of a blanket woven hundreds or even thousands of years before. The pathologist returned to an examination of the head.

"The eyes are too far gone to determine the colour of the irides, and this dark red-brown hair is no indication at all of what colour it might have been originally. It's been dyed by the peat, the same as the skin." He poked about in the nostrils. "But this is interesting." He examined his latexed fingertips. "A fair amount of fine-grained silver sand in his nose. Which would appear to be the same as the sand apparent in the abrasions on his knees and the tops of his feet." He moved up to the forehead, then, and gently cleaned away some dirt from the left temple and the hair above it. "Bloody hell!"

"What?"

"He's got a curved scar on the left front-temporal scalp. About ten centimetres in length."

"A wound?"

The professor shook his head thoughtfully. "No, it looks like a surgical scar. At a guess I would say that this young man has had an operation performed at some time on a head injury."

Gunn was stunned. "Well, that means this is a much more recent corpse than we thought, doesn't it?"

Mulgrew's smile conveyed both superiority and amusement. "Depends what you mean by recent, Detective Sergeant. Brain surgery is probably one of the oldest practised medical arts. There is ample archaeological evidence of it dating back to Neolithic times." He paused, then added as an afterthought for Gunn's benefit, "The Stone Age."

He turned his attention now to the neck, and the broad, deep wound that incised it. He measured it at 18.4 centimetres.

"Is that what killed him?" Gunn asked.

Mulgrew sighed now. "I am guessing, Detective Sergeant, that you have not attended many post-mortems."

Gunn blushed. "Not many, sir, no." He did not want to confess that there had only been one before.

"It is bloody well impossible for me to determine cause of death until I have opened him up. And even then, I can't guarantee it. His throat has been cut, yes. But he has multiple stab wounds in his chest, and another in the right scapular back. There are abrasions on his neck that would suggest the presence of a rope around it, and similar abrasions on his wrists and ankles."

"Like his hands and feet had been tied?"

"Exactly. He may have been hanged, hence the abrasions on his neck, or else he may have been dragged along a beach using that same rope, which would explain the sand in the broken skin on his knees and feet. In any event, it is far too early to be submitting theories on the cause of death. There are multiple possibilities."

A darker patch of skin on the right forearm was attracting his attention now. He wiped at it with his swab, then turned to lift a scrubbing sponge from the stainless-steel sink behind him, and began roughly rubbing away the top layer of skin. "Sweet fucking Jesus," he said.

Gunn canted his head to try to get a better look at it. "What is it?"

Professor Mulgrew was silent for a long time before looking up to meet Gunn's eye. "Why were you so keen to know how long the body might have been in the bog?"

"So I can clear it off my slate, Professor, and hand it over to the archaeologists."

"I'm afraid you might not be able to do that, Detective Sergeant."

"Why?"

"Because this body has been in the peat for no more than fifty-six years—at the very most."

Gunn felt his face colour with indignation. "You told me not ten minutes ago that you were not a bloody carbon-dating machine." He enjoyed putting the emphasis on the *bloody*. "How can you possibly know that?"

Mulgrew smiled. "Take a closer look at the right forearm, Detective Sergeant. I think you'll see that what we have here is a crude tattooed portrait of Elvis Presley above the legend *Heartbreak Hotel*. Now, I'm pretty certain that Elvis wasn't around in the time before Christ. And as a confirmed fan I can tell you, without fear of contradiction, that 'Heartbreak Hotel' was a number one hit in the year 1956."

| FIVE |

Professor Mulgrew took almost two hours to complete the autopsy after breaking for a lunch of onion bhaji, lamb bhuna with garlic fried rice, and kulfi ice cream. George Gunn had a cheese sandwich in his office, and was having trouble keeping it down.

The leather-like quality of the skin had made it impossible to open up the chest using a simple scalpel, and in the end the pathologist had resorted to the use of a pair of heavy scissors to cut through it before switching to his accustomed scalpel to reflect the remaining skin and muscles away from the ribcage.

Now the body lay opened up, like something that might be found hanging from a butcher's hook, internal organs removed and bread-loafed. But this had been a strong, healthy young man, and nothing found internally had detracted from the notion that his death had been caused by anything other than a brutal murder. A murder perpetrated by someone who might, just conceivably, still be alive.

"Bloody interesting corpse, Detective Sergeant." Beads of sweat had gathered in the creases on his brow, but Professor Mulgrew was enjoying himself. "Didn't have quite as interesting a last meal as I did. Flakes of soft meat, and minute translucent fibre-like material resembling fish bones. Fish and potatoes probably." He grinned. "Anyway, happy to give you a hypothesis now on how he might have died."

Gunn was mildly surprised. From everything he had heard, pathologists were almost invariably reluctant to commit themselves to anything. But Mulgrew was clearly a man supremely confident of his own abilities. He closed up the ribcage, folded the skin and tissue back across the chest towards his initial incision, and poked with his scalpel at the wounds.

"He was stabbed four times in the chest. From the downward angle of the strokes I would say that his attacker was either very much taller than him, or the victim was on his knees. I favour the latter, but we'll come to that. The wounds were inflicted by a long, thin, double-bladed knife. Something like a Fairbairn-Sykes, or some other kind of stiletto. This one here, for example"—he indicated the topmost wound—"is about five-eighths of an inch in length and pointed at both tips, which almost certainly indicates a thin, double-bladed weapon. It is five inches deep, passing through the apex of the left lung, the right atrium of the heart and into the ventricular septum. So it's quite long, and typical of the other three wounds."

"And that's what killed him?"

"Well, any one of them would almost certainly have been fatal given a few minutes, but I suspect that it was this deep incised wound crossing the front of the neck that did for him." He turned his attention to it. "It's more than seven inches long, extending between the mastoid area on the left, just below the ear, to the ster- nocleidomastoid area on the right." He looked up. "As you can see." He smiled and returned to the wound. "It completely transects the left jugular vein, severs the left carotid artery, and nicks the right jugular. It's about three inches at its deepest, and even cuts into the spinal column."

"Is that significant?"

"In my opinion the angle and depth of the cut would suggest that it was made from behind, and almost certainly with a different weapon. Which is backed up by the stab wound in the back. That wound is one-and-a-half inches long and has a squared superior tip, and a pointed inferior tip. Which would suggest a large, single-edged knife, better suited to cutting so deeply into the neck."

Gunn frowned. "I'm having trouble getting the picture here, Professor. Are you saying the killer used two weapons, stabbed him in the chest with one, then grabbed him from behind and cut his throat with another?"

A smile of mild condescension settled on the pathologist's face behind his mask, visible to Gunn only in eyes that glimmered on the far side of the giant tortoiseshells. "No, Detective Sergeant. I am saying that there were two attackers. One holds him from behind, forces him down to his knees while the second stabs him in the chest. The stab in the back was probably accidental as the first assailant prepared to draw his knife across the victim's throat."

He moved around the table to the dead man's head, and began peeling the skin and flesh back over the face and skull from an initial incision.

"Here's the picture you should probably keep in your mind. This man was bound by the wrists and ankles. He had a rope tied around his neck. If it had been used to hang him, the abrasion would have canted up towards the suspension point. But it doesn't. So I'm suggesting to you that they used it to drag him along a beach. There is a fine silver sand in his nose and mouth, and in the broken skin on his knees and the tops of his feet. At some point they forced him on to his knees and repeatedly stabbed him before cutting his throat."

The picture that the pathologist painted with his words was suddenly very vivid to Gunn. He wasn't sure why, but somehow he pictured it at night, with a phosphorescent sea breaking over compacted silver sand glowing in the moonlight. And then the blood turning white foam crimson. But what shocked him almost more than anything else was the thought that this brutal slaying had taken place here, on the Isle of Lewis, where in more than a hundred years there had been only two previous murders.

He said, "Would it be possible to take fingerprints? We're going to have to try to identify this man."

Professor Mulgrew did not answer immediately. He was focused on reflecting the scalp away from the skull without tearing it. "It's so bloody desiccated," he said. "Brittle as hell." He looked up. "The fingertips are a bit wrinkled from fluid loss, but I can inject a little formalin to rehydrate them and you should get perfectly acceptable prints. Might as well take a DNA sample, too."

"The police surgeon already sent off samples for analysis."

"Oh, did he?" Professor Mulgrew did not look pleased. "Unlikely to provide any enlightenment, of course, but you never know. Ah . . ." His attention was suddenly taken by the skull, revealed finally by the peeling back of the scalp. "Interesting."

"What is?" Gunn reluctantly moved a little closer.

"Beneath our chap's surgical scar here . . . a small metal plate sewn in to protect the brain."

Gunn saw a rectangular, dull grey plate about two inches long, sewn into the skull with metal sutures looped through holes at either end of it. It was partially obscured by a layer of lighter grey scar tissue.

"An injury of some kind. And very probably a little mild brain damage."

At Mulgrew's request Gunn stepped out into the corridor and watched through the window that gave on to the autopsy room as the pathologist took an oscillating saw around the top of the skull to remove the brain. When he went back in, the professor was examining it in a stainless-steel bowl.

"Yes . . . as I thought. Here . . ." He poked at it with his finger. "Cystic encephalomalacia of the left frontal lobe."

"Meaning?"

"Meaning, my friend, that this poor bugger didn't have much bloody luck. He had some kind of head injury that damaged the left frontal lobe, and probably left him . . . how can I put it . . . one sandwich short of a picnic?"

He returned to the skull, and with a delicate scraping of his scalpel, pared away the film of tissue growing over the metal plate.

"If I'm not mistaken, this is tantalum."

"What's that?"

"A highly corrosion-resistant metal pioneered in the first half of the twentieth century in cranioplasty. Quite often used during the Second World War to repair shrapnel wounds." He leaned closer in as he scraped deeper into the metal. "Highly biocompatible, but tended to produce terrible headaches. Something to do with electroconductivity, I think. The development of plastics in the sixties superseded it. Now it's used mainly in electronics. Aha!"

"What?" Gunn overcame his natural reticence to get even closer.

But Professor Mulgrew simply turned away to rummage in his pathologist's toolkit, which sat up on the counter beside the sink. He returned with a three-inch-square magnifying glass which he held between thumb and forefinger to hover it over the tantalum plate.

"Thought so." There was a hint of triumphalism.

"Thought what?" Gunn's frustration was evident in his voice.

"The manufacturers of these plates often engraved them with serial numbers. And in this case a bloody date." He stepped back, inviting Gunn to take a look.

Gunn took the magnifying glass and held it gingerly above the skull, screwing up his face as he leaned in close to see for himself. Beneath a ten-digit serial number were the Roman numerals MCMLIV.

The pathologist beamed. "That's 1954 in case you hadn't worked it out. About two years before he had his Elvis tattoo. And judging by the amount of tissue growth, three years, maybe four, before he was murdered on the beach."

| SIX |

At first Fin was completely disorientated. There was an intermittent beating in his ears above the sound of wind and water. He was hot, sweating profusely beneath the covers, but his face and hands were cold. A strange blue light permeated the brightness that dazzled him when he opened his eyes. It took a full thirty seconds before he remembered where he was, and saw the white lining of his tent breathing erratically in and out like a runner gasping for air at the end of a race. All around him was a shambles of clothes, a half-unpacked canvas satchel, his laptop, and a scattering of papers.

In the failing light he had chosen a patch of ground which had seemed relatively flat for the pitching of his two-man tent. But now he realized that it sloped with the land down towards the cliffs and the sea beyond. He sat upright, listening for a moment to the guy ropes creaking and straining at their pegs, then slipped out of his sleeping bag and into some fresh clothes.

Daylight blinded him as he unzipped the outer shell and crawled on to the hill. There had been rain during the night, but already the wind had dried the grass. He sat in it, barefoot, pulling on his socks, and screwing up his eyes against the glare of sunlight on the ocean, a burned-out ring of luminescence that flared briefly before the gap in the clouds above it closed, like turning off a light switch. He sat, knees pulled up to his chest, forearms resting on top of them, and breathed the salt air, and smelled peat smoke and damp earth. The wind tugging at his short, fair curls stung his face and sent a wonderful sense surging through him of simply being alive.

He looked back over his left shoulder and saw the ruins of his parents' crofthouse, an old whitehouse, and beyond it the remains of the blackhouse where his forebears had lived for centuries, and where he had played as a child, happy and secure, never once imagining what life might hold in store for him.

Above that the road wound down the hill through the strung-out collection of disparate dwellings that made up the village of Crobost. Red tin roofs on old loom sheds, houses whitewashed or pink-harled, irregular fenceposts, tufts of wool snagged on barbed wire fluttering in the wind. The narrow strips of land known as crofts ran down the slope towards the cliffs, some cultivated to raise basic crops, grains and root vegetables, others supporting nothing but sheep. The discarded technology of distant decades, rusted tractors and broken harvesters, littered overgrown plots, the rotting symbols of a once hoped-for prosperity.

Beyond the curve of the hill, Fin could see the dark roof of Crobost Church dominating both the skyline and the people over whose lives its shadow fell. Someone had hung out washing at the manse, and white sheets flapped furiously in the wind like demented semaphore flags urging praise and fear of God in equal measures.

Fin loathed the church and all it stood for. But there was comfort in its familiarity. This, after all, was home. And he felt his spirits lifted.

He heard his name carried on the wind as he pulled on his boots, and he turned, scrambling to his feet, to see a young man standing by his car where he had abandoned it at the gate of the crofthouse the night before. He set off, wading through the grass, and as he got closer, saw the ambivalence in his visitor's smile.

The young man was about eighteen, a little less than half Fin's age, with fair hair gelled into spikes, and cornflower-blue eyes so piercingly like his mother's that they raised goosebumps on Fin's arms. For a moment they stood in awkward silence sizing each other up, before Fin reached out a hand and the boy gave it a brief, firm shake.

"Hello, Fionnlagh."

The boy thrust his jaw in the direction of the pale-blue tent. "Just passing through?"

"Temporary accommodation."

"It's been a while."

"It has."

Fionnlagh paused for a moment, to give his words emphasis. "Nine months." And there was a definite accusation in them.

"I had a whole life to pack up behind me."

Fionnlagh canted his head a little. "Does that mean you're back to stay?"

"Maybe." Fin turned his gaze over the croft. "This is home. It's where you come when you've nowhere else to go. Whether or not I stay . . . well, that remains to be seen." He turned green eyes back on the boy. "Do folk know?"

Their eyes locked for several seconds in a silence laden with history. "All that anyone knows is that my father died out on An Sgeir last August during the guga hunt."

Fin nodded. "Fair enough." He turned to open the gate and walked down the overgrown path to what had once been the front door of the old whitehouse. The door itself was long gone, a few remaining pieces of rotten architrave still clinging to the brick. The purple paint with which his father had once lavished every wooden surface, including the floors, was still discernible in odd, flaking patches. The roof was largely intact, but the timbers were decayed and rainwater had streaked every wall. The floorboards were gone, leaving only a few stubborn joists. It was a shell of a place, no trace remaining of the love that had once warmed it. He heard Fionnlagh at his shoulder and turned. "I'm going to gut this place. Rebuild it from the inside out. Maybe you'd like to give me a hand during the summer holidays."

Fionnlagh shrugged noncommittally. "Maybe."

"Will you be going to university in the autumn?"

"No."

"Why not?"

"I need to find a job. I'm a father now. I have responsibilities to my child."

Fin nodded. "How is she?"

"She's fine. Thanks for asking."

Fin ignored the sarcasm. "And Donna?"

"Living at home with her parents, and the baby."

Fin frowned. "What about you?"

"Mum and I are still at the bungalow down the hill." He nodded his head vaguely in the direction of the house that Marsaili had inherited from Artair. "The Reverend Murray won't let me go up to see them at the manse."

Fin was incredulous. "Why not? You're the baby's father, for God's sake."

"With no means of supporting either his daughter or her mother. Occasionally Donna can sneak her up to see me at the bungalow, but usually we have to meet in town."

Fin swallowed his anger. No point in directing it at Fionnlagh. Time enough for that. Another place, another person. "Is your mother at home?" It was an innocent enough question, and yet they both knew how charged it was.

"She's been away in Glasgow, sitting exams for university entrance." Fionnlagh registered Fin's surprise. "She didn't tell you?"

"We haven't been in touch."

"Oh." His eyes wandered back down the hill towards the Macinnes bungalow. "I always thought that you and Mum might get back together again."

Fin's smile was touched by sadness, and perhaps regret. "Marsaili and I couldn't make it work all those years ago, Fionnlagh. Why should it be any different now?" He hesitated. "Is she still in Glasgow?"

"No. She came back early. Flew in this morning. A family emergency."

| SEVEN |

I can hear them talking in the hall as if I'm deaf. As if I wasn't here. As if I was dead. Sometimes I wish I was.

I don't know why I should have to wear my coat. It's warm in the house. No need for a coat. Or my hat. My lovely soft old cap. Kept my head warm for years.

I'm never sure these days when I come through from the bedroom which Mary I will find. Sometimes it's the good Mary. Sometimes it's the bad Mary. They look the same, but they are different people. It was the bad Mary this morning. Raising her voice, telling me what to do, making me put on my coat. Sitting here. Waiting. For what?

And what's in the case? She said it was my stuff. But what did she mean? If she means my clothes, I have a wardrobe full of them, and they would never fit in there. Or all my papers. Accounts going back years. Photographs. Everything. It certainly wouldn't all go in a case this size. Maybe we're going on holiday.

I hear Marsaili's voice now. "Mum, that's just not fair."

Mum. Of course. I keep forgetting that Mary's her mum.

And Mary says, speaking English of course, because she never did learn the Gaelic, "Fair? You think it's fair on me, Marsaili? I'm seventy years old. I can't take it any more. At least twice a week he soils the bed. If he goes out on his own he gets lost. Like a damned dog. He's just not to be trusted. Neighbours bring him back. If I say white he says black, if I say black he says white."

I never say black or white. What is she talking about? It's the bad Mary talking.

"Mum, you've been married forty-eight years." Marsaili's voice again.

And Mary says, "He's not the man I married, Marsaili. I'm living with a stranger. Everything's an argument. He just won't accept that he's got dementia, that he doesn't remember things any more. It's always my fault. He does things then denies it. He broke the kitchen window the other day. I don't know why. Took a hammer to it. Said he needed to let the dog in. Marsaili, we haven't had a dog since we left the farm. Then five minutes later he asks who broke the window, and when I tell him *he* did he says no he didn't, I must have done it. Me! Marsaili, I'm sick of it."

"What about daycare? He goes three days a week, doesn't he? Maybe we could get them to take him for five, or even six."

"No!" Mary's shouting now. "Sending him off to daycare just makes it worse. A few hours of sanity each day, the house to myself, and all I can think of is that he'll be back again in the evening to make my life hell again."

I can hear her sobbing. Terrible racking sobs. I'm not sure now if that's the bad Mary or not. I don't like to hear her cry. It's upsetting. I lean to see through into the hall, but they are out of my line of sight. I suppose I should go and see if I can help. But bad Mary told me to stay here. I suppose Marsaili will be comforting her. I wonder what's upset her like this. I remember the day we got married. Just twenty-five I was. And her a slip of a lass at twenty-two. She cried then as well. A lovely girl, she was. English. But she couldn't help that.

Finally the crying has stopped. And I have to strain to hear Mary's voice. "I want him out of here, Marsaili."

"Mum, that's not practical. Where would he go? I'm not equipped to deal with him, and we can't afford a private nursing home."

"I don't care." I can hear how hard her voice is now. Selfish. Full of self-pity. "You'll have to sort something out. I just want him out of here. Now."

"Mum . . ."

"He's dressed and ready to go, and his bag's packed. My mind's made up, Marsaili. I won't have him in the house a moment longer."

There is a long silence now. Who on earth were they talking about?

And suddenly, as I look up, I see Marsaili standing in the door-way looking at me. Didn't hear her come in. My wee girl. I love her more than almost anything in the world. Someday I must tell her that. But she looks tired and pale, the lassie. And her face is wet with tears.

"Don't cry," I tell her. "I'm going on holiday. I won't be away for long."

| EIGHT |

Fin stood surveying his handiwork. He had decided to start by stripping out all the rotten wood, which lay now in a huge pile in the yard between the house and the old stone shed with the rusted tin roof. If the rain stayed off long enough, the wind would dry it, and he would cover it and keep it for the bonfire in November.

The walls and founds were sound enough, but he would have to take off and renew the roof to make the building watertight and allow the interior to dry out. The first job would be to remove and stack the slates. But he would need a ladder for that.

The wind whipped and pulled at his blue overalls, tugging at his checked shirt, and drying the sweat on his face. He had almost forgotten how relentless it could be. When you lived here, you only noticed it when it stopped. He glanced down the hill towards Marsaili's bungalow, but there was no car, so she wasn't back yet. Fionnlagh would be at school in Stornoway. He would go down later and ask if he could borrow a ladder.

The air was still mild, blowing out of the south-west, but he could smell rain on its leading edge, and in the distance saw the blue-black clouds gathering on the far horizon. In the foreground, sunlight flashed across the land in constantly evolving shapes, vivid and sharp against the brooding darkness to come. The sound of a car's engine made him turn, and he saw Marsaili in Artair's old Vauxhall Astra. She had pulled in to the side of the road, and was looking down the hill towards him. There was someone else in the car with her.

He seemed to stand for a very long time, looking at her from a distance, before she got out of the car and started down the track towards him. Her long fair hair blew in ropes around her face. She seemed thinner, and as she approached he saw that her face was devoid of make-up, drawn and unnaturally pale in the unforgiving daylight.

She stopped about a yard from him, and they stood looking at each other for a moment. Then she said, "I didn't know you were coming."

"I didn't decide until a couple of days ago. After the divorce came through."

She pulled her waterproof jacket around her as if cold, folding her arms across the front of it to keep it closed. "Are you staying?"

"I don't know yet. I'm going to do some work on the house, and then we'll see."

"What about your work?"

"I quit the force."

She seemed surprised. "What will you do?"

"I don't know."

She smiled, that old sardonic smile that he had known so well. "Here lies Fin Macleod," she said. "He didn't know."

He returned her smile. "I have my degree in computer studies."

She raised an eyebrow. "Oh? That'll get you far in Crobost."

This time he laughed. "Yes." She had always been able to make him laugh. "Well, we'll see. Maybe I'll end up working at Arnish, like my dad, or Artair."

At the mention of Artair her face clouded. "You'll never do that, Fin." Somehow it had always been the last resort of island men who couldn't get a job on a fishing boat, or escape to university on the mainland. Even although it paid well.

"No."

"So don't talk shit. You did enough of that to last a lifetime when we were young."

He grinned. "I guess I did." He nodded towards the Vauxhall. "Who's in the car?"

"My dad." Her voice sounded brittle.

"Oh. How is he?" It was an innocent enough question, but when he looked back at her he saw that it had provoked a disturbing response. Her eyes had filled. He was shocked. "What's wrong?"

But she kept her lips pressed firmly together, as if not trusting herself to speak. Before finally she said, "My mum's kicked him out. Says she can't take it any more. That he's my responsibility now."

Fin frowned his confusion. "Why?"

"It's his dementia, Fin. He wasn't so bad last time you saw him. But he's gone downhill rapidly. There's almost a daily deterioration." She glanced back towards the car, and her tears flowed freely now. "But I can't look after him. I *can't*! I just got my life back after twenty years of Artair. And his mother. I have more exams coming up, Fionnlagh's future to think about . . ." She turned desperate eyes back on Fin. "That sounds terrible, doesn't it? Selfish."

He wanted to take her in his arms and hold her, but it had been too long. "Of course not," was all he could say.

"He's my *dad*!" Her pain and her guilt were all too clear.

"I'm sure the social services will be able to find something for him, at least temporarily. What about a nursing home?"

"We can't afford that. The farm wasn't ours. Just rented." She wiped her cheeks with the flats of her hands and made a determined effort to take back control. "I phoned the social from my mum's. I explained it all, but they said I had to come in and talk to them. I'm just going to drop him off at daycare to give myself time to think." She shook her head, on the verge of losing it again. "I just don't know what to do."

Fin said, "I'll get changed and come into town with you. We'll take your dad for a pub lunch then drop him at daycare while we go and talk to the social work."

She looked at him with searching, watery blue eyes. "Why would you do that, Fin?"

Fin grinned. "Cos I need a break, and I could do with a pint."

The Crown Hotel sat up on the spit of land called South Beach that separated the inner and outer harbours of Stornoway. The lounge bar was on the first floor, and from up here there were views of both. The fishing fleet was in, at anchor in the inner harbour, rising and falling gently on the incoming tide, rusting trawlers and raddled crabbers, painted over in primary colours like elderly ladies vainly trying to hide the ravages of time.

Tormod was confused. At first he didn't appear to know Fin at all. Until Fin spoke to him about his childhood, when he had visited Marsaili at the farm, already smitten, as if future pain had been pre-destined. Tormod's face had lit up with recognition then. He had a clear recollection, it seemed, of the young Fin.

"You've grown fast, boy," he said, and ruffled his hair as if he were still a five-year-old. "How are your folks?"

Marsaili glanced, embarrassed, at Fin, and said in a low voice, "Dad, Fin's folks were killed in a car crash more than thirty years ago."

Tormod's face was washed by sadness. From behind round, silver-framed spectacles, he turned moist blue eyes on Fin, and for a moment Fin saw his daughter in them, and her son. Three genera-tions lost in his confusion. "I'm sorry to hear that, son."

Fin sat them at a table by the window and went to the bar to get menus and order them drinks. When he got back to the table Tormod was struggling to take something out from his trouser pocket. He twisted and wriggled in his chair. "Damn, dammit," he said.

Fin glanced at Marsaili. "What's he doing?"

She shook her head despondently. "He's started smoking again. After giving up more than twenty years ago! He's got a pack of cigarettes in his pocket, but he can't seem to get them out."

"Mr. Macdonald, you can't smoke in here," Fin told him. "You have to go outside if you want to smoke."

"It's raining," the old man said.

"No," Fin corrected him gently. "It's still dry. If you want a cigarette I'll stand outside with you."

"Can't get the damn things out of my pocket!" Tormod's voice was raised now. Almost shouting. The bar was filling up with townsfolk and tourists in for lunch, and heads turned in their direction.

Marsaili's voice was a stage whisper. "Dad, there's no need to shout. Here, let me get them for you."

"I'm perfectly capable of doing it myself!" More heads turned.

The barman arrived with their drinks. A young man in his early twenties with a Polish accent.

Tormod looked up at him and said, "Get a life!"

"I think he means a light," Marsaili said by way of apology. She turned to Fin. "He'll want matches. My mother's been hiding them from him."

The barman just smiled and left their drinks on the table.

Tormod was still struggling with his hand in his pocket. "It's there. I can feel it. But it won't come out."

There was some muted laughter from nearby tables. Fin said, "Let me give you a hand, Mr. Macdonald." And while he wouldn't accept Marsaili's offer of help, Tormod was quite happy to let Fin try. Fin flicked her a glance of apology. He knelt down beside her father, aware of heads in the bar turned in their direction, and slipped his hand into Tormod's pocket. He could feel the packet of cigarettes there right enough, but like Tormod he couldn't seem to take it out. It was as if the cigarettes were beneath the pocket rather than in it. But Fin couldn't figure out how that was possible. He lifted the old man's pullover to check the waistband for some hidden pocket, and what he saw made him smile, in spite of himself. He looked up.

"Mr. Macdonald, you're wearing two pairs of trousers." Which elicited a ripple of laughter from those at the closest tables who could hear.

Tormod frowned. "Am I?"

Fin looked up at Marsaili. "The cigarettes are in the pocket of the pair underneath. I'd better take him to the loo and get one of them off him."

In the toilet Fin steered Tormod into a cubicle. He managed with difficulty to remove the top pair of trousers after persuading him to take off his shoes. Then once he had the shoes back on, Fin made him sit on the pedestal while he kneeled to retie the laces. He folded the trousers and got Tormod to his feet again.

Tormod let him do everything without resistance, like a well-trained child. Except that he insisted on expressing excessive amounts of gratitude. "You're a good lad, Fin. I always liked you, son. You're just like your old man." And stroking Fin's hair. Then he said, "I need to pee now."

"On you go, Mr. Macdonald, I'll wait for you." Fin turned to run the water in the sink until it was warm for the old man to wash his hands.

"Ahh, shit!"

He turned at the sound of Tormod's cursing as the old boy's glasses slipped off the end of his nose and fell into the urinal. The mishap did nothing, however, to lessen or divert the stream of yellow urine issuing from Tormod's bladder into the trough. If anything he seemed to be aiming for his glasses. Fin sighed. It was clear to him who was going to have to retrieve them. And when finally Tormod finished peeing, Fin leaned past him to reach down delicately and pick the urine-drenched glasses out of the runnel.

Tormod watched in silence as the younger man rinsed them thoroughly under running water from the tap before lathering his hands with soap and rinsing them, too. "Wash your hands now, Mr. Macdonald," he said, and he leaned into the cubicle to retrieve some soft toilet paper to dry off the glasses. When Tormod had finished drying his hands Fin replaced his glasses, planting them

firmly above the bridge of his nose and behind his ears. "You'd better not let that happen again, Mr. Macdonald. We don't want you
peeing down your legs now, do we?"

For some reason Tormod found the notion of peeing down his
legs quite hilarious. And he laughed heartily as Fin led him back out
into the bar.

Marsaili looked up expectantly, a half-smile rising on her face at
the sight of her father laughing. "What happened?"

Fin sat the old man down. "Nothing," he said, and handed her
the spare pair of trousers neatly folded. "You're dad's still got a great
sense of humour, that's all."

As he sat down he saw the grateful look in Tormod's eyes, as if
the old man knew that for Fin to have recounted the truth would
have been a humiliation. There was no knowing what he thought,
or felt, or how aware he was of anything around him. He was lost in
a fog somewhere in his own mind. Perhaps there were times when
the fog cleared a little, but there would also be times, Fin knew,
when it would come down like a summer haar and obscure all light
and reason.

The Solas daycare centre was to be found on the north-eastern outskirts of Stornoway in Westview Terrace, a modern, single-storey
building angled around car parks front and back. It stood next
door to the council-run Dun Eisdean residential care home for the
elderly, surrounded by trees and neatly manicured lawns. Beyond,
lay white-speckled peat bog shimmering briefly in the last sun of
the afternoon before the rains would come. In the slanting yellow
light they looked like fields of gold, stretching away to Aird and
Broadbay. From the south-west, dark clouds rolled in on the edge
of a stiffening wind, bruised and ominous and pregnant with rain.

Marsaili parked around the back, opposite a row of residential
caravans brought in to augment already overstretched facilities,
and the first fat drops of rain began falling as she and Fin hurried towards the entrance with Tormod between them. As they
reached it, the door swung out and a dark-haired man in a black

quilted anorak held it open for them. It wasn't until they were in out of the rain that Fin realized who it was.

"George Gunn!"

Gunn seemed just as surprised to see Fin. He took a moment to collect himself, then nodded politely. "Mr. Macleod." They shook hands. "I didn't realize you were on the island, sir." He glanced acknowledgement in Marsaili's direction. "Mrs. Macinnes."

"It's Macdonald now. I took back my maiden name."

"And it's not 'sir' any more either, George. Just plain Fin. I handed in my jotters."

Gunn raised an eyebrow. "Oh. I'm sorry to hear that, Mr. Macleod."

An elderly lady with a faded blue rinse through silvered hair came to take Tormod by the arm and lead him gently away. "Hello, Tormod. Didn't expect you today. Come away in and we'll make you a cup of tea."

Gunn watched them go then turned back to Marsaili. "Actually, Miss Macdonald, it was your father I wanted to talk to."

Marsaili's eyes opened in surprise. "What on earth would you want to talk to my dad for? Not that you'll get any sense out of him."

Gunn nodded solemnly. "So I understand. I've been up at Eòro-paidh to see your mother. But since you're here it would help if you could confirm a few things for me, too."

Fin put a hand on Gunn's forearm. "George, what's all this about?"

Gunn carefully moved his arm away from Fin's hand. "If I could just ask for your patience, sir . . ." And Fin knew that this was no routine inquiry.

"What kind of things?" Marsaili said.

"Family things."

"Such as?"

"Do you have any uncles, Miss Macdonald? Or cousins? Any relatives, close or otherwise, outside of your immediate family?"

Marsaili frowned. "I think my mother has some distant relatives somewhere in the south of England."

"On your father's side."

"Oh." Marsaili's confusion deepened. "Not that I know of. My dad was an only child. No brothers or sisters."

"Cousins?"

"I don't think so. He came from the village of Seilebost, on Harris. But as far as I know he's the only surviving member of his family. He took us once to see the croft he was brought up on. Derelict now, of course. And Seilebost School where he went as a child. A wonderful little school sitting right out there on the machair with the most incredible views over the sands of Luskentyre. But there was never any talk of relatives."

"Come on, George, what's going on?" Fin was having trouble complying with Gunn's request for patience.

Gunn flicked him a glance and seemed oddly embarrassed, running his hand back through the dark hair that formed the widow's peak on his forehead. He hesitated a moment before reaching a decision. "A few days ago, Mr. Macleod, we recovered a body from the peat bog out at Siader on the west coast. It was the perfectly preserved corpse of a young man in his late teens. He'd died violently." He paused. "At first it was assumed that the body could be hundreds of years old, perhaps from the time of the Norse occupation. Or even older, as far back as the Stone Age. But an Elvis Presley tattoo on his right forearm kind of blew a hole in that theory."

Fin nodded. "It would."

"Well, anyway, sir, the pathologist has established that this young man was probably murdered in the late 1950s. Which means that his killer might just still be alive."

Marsaili was shaking her head in consternation. "But what's any of this got to do with my dad?"

Gunn sucked in a long breath through clenched teeth. "Well, the thing is, Miss Macdonald, there was no clothing or anything else that might help us identify the dead man. When we first found the body the police surgeon drew off some fluid and took tissue samples to send for analysis."

"And they checked the DNA against the database?" Fin said.

Gunn flushed slightly and nodded. "You'll remember," he said, "last year, when most of the men in Crobost gave samples to rule them out as suspects in the Angel Macritchie murder . . ."

"Those should have been destroyed by now," Fin said.

"The donor has to request that, Mr. Macleod. A form signed. It seems Mr. Macdonald didn't do that. It should have been explained to him, but apparently it wasn't, or he didn't understand." He looked at Marsaili. "Anyway, the database came up with a familial match. Whoever that young man in the bog is, he was related to your father."

| NINE |

The rain is hammering against the window. It's making some din! When you were out on the moor you never heard it, of course. You heard nothing above the wind. But you felt it all right. Stinging your face when a force ten drove it at you. Horizontal sometimes. I loved that feeling. Out there in the wild, just me and that great big sky, and the rain burning my face.

But they keep me cooped up inside these days. Not to be trusted outdoors, bad Mary says.

Like now, sitting here in this big empty lounge, chairs drawn up. Everyone looking at me. I don't know what they expect. Have they come to take me home? I recognize Marsaili, of course. And the young man with the fair curly hair looks familiar. The name'll come to me. It usually does.

But the other *gille*. I don't know him at all, with his round red face and his shiny black hair.

Marsaili leans towards me and says, "Dad, what happened to your folks? Did you have any uncles or cousins that you never told us about?"

I don't know what she means. They're all dead. Surely everyone knows that?

Fin! That's it. The young man with the curls. I remember him now. Used to come round the farm winching my wee Marsaili before either of them was even old enough to count. I wonder how his folks are. I liked his old man. He was a good, solid sort.

I never knew my dad. Only heard tell of him. He was a sailor, of course. Any man worth his salt was a sailor back then. The day my mum gathered us in the front room to break the news was a pretty black one. It wasn't that long before Christmas, and she'd put in some effort to make the house seem festive. All we cared about were the presents we would get. Not that we expected much. It was just the surprise of it.

There was snow in the street. There hadn't been much of it, and it had turned to slush pretty quickly. But there was that grey-green gloom in the air that comes with snow, and there wasn't much light came down between the tenements anyway.

She was a lovely woman, my mum, from what I remember of her. Which isn't much. Just the softness of her when she held me, and the smell of her perfume, or her eau de cologne or whatever it was. And that blue print apron she always wore.

Anyway, she sat us down on the settee, side by side, and knelt on the floor in front of us. She put her hand on my shoulder. She was a terrible colour. So white her face would have been lost in the snow. And she'd been crying, I knew that much.

I could only have been four years old, then. And Peter a year younger. Must have been conceived on a home leave before my father was finally sent off to sea.

She said, "Your dad won't be coming home, boys." And there was a catch in her voice. The rest of the day was lost to me. And Christmas was no fun that year. Everything is sepia-brown in my mind, like a light-exposed black-and-white print. Dull and depressing. It was only later, when I was a bit older, that I learned his ship had been sunk by a German U-boat. One of those convoys they were always attacking in the Atlantic between Britain and America. And

I had the strangest sense of sinking with him, endlessly through the water into darkness.

"Do you have any relatives left at all down in Harris, Mr. Macdonald?" The voice startles me. Fin is looking at me very earnestly. He has lovely green eyes, that lad. I don't know why Marsaili never married him instead of that wastrel Artair Macinnes. Never did like that man.

Fin's still looking at me, and I'm trying to remember what it is he asked. Something about my family.

"I was with my mother the night she died," I tell him. And suddenly I can feel tears in my eyes. Why did she have to die? It was so dark in that room. It was hot, and smelled of sickness and death. There was a lamp on the bedside table. An electric lamp that shed a dreadful pale light on her face in the bed.

What age would I have been then? It's not clear to me now. Early teens, maybe. Old enough to understand, that's for sure. But not old enough for the responsibility. And not ready, if you ever can be, to get cast adrift alone in the world. A world I could never have dreamt of. Not then, not when the only thing I had ever known was the warmth and safety of my own home and a mother who loved me.

I don't know where Peter was that night. Already asleep, probably. Poor Peter. Never the same after that fall from the roundabout at the fairground. Stupid! One careless moment, stepping from the damned thing before it had fully stopped. And your life is changed for ever.

My mother had the darkest eyes, and the lamp on the bedside table was reflected in them. But I could see the light fading. She turned her head towards me. There was such sadness in them, and I knew the sadness was for me, not for herself. She reached her right hand over to her left above the covers, and drew the ring off her wedding finger. I've never seen a wedding ring like it. Silver, with two serpents intertwined. Some uncle of my father's had brought it back from overseas somewhere and it had been passed down through the family. My father had no money when they got married, so he gave it to my mum as her wedding ring.

She took my hand and placed it in my palm and folded my fingers over it. "I want you to look after Peter," she said to me. "He'll not survive this world on his own. I want you to promise me, Johnny. That you'll always take care of him."

Of course, I had no idea then what a responsibility that would be. But it was the last thing she asked of me, so I nodded solemnly and said I would. And she smiled then, and gave my hand a little squeeze.

I watched the light die in her eyes before they closed, and her hand relaxed and let go of mine. And the priest didn't arrive for another fifteen minutes.

What's that ringing sound? Dammit!

| TEN |

Marsaili fumbled in her handbag for her mobile phone. "Sorry," she said, flustered and embarrassed by the interruption. Not that her father had told them much, or was making any sense. But after revealing he had been with his mother when she died, big silent tears had run down his face, some highly charged emotional turmoil behind them. Which the ringing of her phone had interrupted.

"What the hell's that?" he was saying, clearly disturbed. "Can a man not get any peace in his own home?"

Fin leaned forward and put a hand on his arm. "It's all right, Mr. Macdonald. It's just Marsaili's mobile."

"One moment, please," Marsaili was saying into her phone. She put her hand over it and said, "I'll take this in the hall." And she rose and hurried away out of the big empty lounge. Most of the daycare patients had left in the minibus for a day out, so they had the place more or less to themselves.

Gunn nodded towards the door, and he and Fin stood up and moved away from Tormod, speaking in low voices. Gunn was perhaps six or seven years older than Fin, but there was not a grey hair on his head, and Fin wondered if he dyed it. He didn't seem the sort, though. There was barely a line on his face. Except for the frown of concern that creased it now. He said, "It's certain that they'll send someone over from the mainland, Mr. Macleod. They'll not entrust a murder investigation like this to an island cop. You know how it is."

Fin nodded.

"And whoever they send is likely to be a lot less sensitive in the handling of it than me. The only clue we have to the identity of the young man in the bog is that he is related in some way to Tormod Macdonald." He paused to purse his lips in what seemed to Fin to be something like an apology. "Which puts Tormod himself right in the frame for the murder."

Marsaili came back in from the hall, slipping her phone into her bag. "That was the social services," she said. "Apparently there's a bed available, at least temporarily, in the Alzheimer's unit right next door at Dun Eisdean."

| ELEVEN |

This is smaller than my room at home. But it looks as if it's been painted recently. There are no stains on the ceiling. Nice white walls. Double-glazing, too. Can't hear the wind, or the rain battering against the window. Just watching it running down the glass. Like tears. Tears in rain. Who would know? But if you're going to cry, do it on your own. It's embarrassing sitting there with tears on your face and folk watching you.

No tears now, although I do feel sort of sad. I'm not sure why. I wonder when Marsaili will come and take me home. I hope it'll be the good Mary when we get there. I like the good Mary. She looks at me and touches my face sometimes like she might once have liked me.

The door opens, and a kindly young lady looks in. She makes me think of someone, but I'm not sure who.

"Oh," she says. "You've still got your coat and hat on, Mr. Macdonald." She pauses. "Can I call you Tormod?"

"No!" I say. And I hear myself bark it, like a dog.

She seems startled. "Oh, now, Mr. Macdonald. We're all friends here together. Let me get that coat off you and we'll hang it up in the wardrobe. And we should unpack your bag, put your things in the drawers. You can decide what goes where."

She comes to the bed where I am sitting and tries to get me to stand. But I resist, shrugging her off. "My holiday's over," I say. "Marsaili's coming to take me home."

"No, Mr. Macdonald, she's not. Nobody's coming. This is your home now."

I sit there for a long time. What does she mean? What could she have meant?

And I do nothing to stop her now from taking off my cap, or lifting me to my feet to remove my coat. I can't believe it. This is not my home. Marsaili will be here soon. She'd never leave me here. Would she? Not my own flesh and blood.

I sit down again. The bed feels quite hard. Still no sign of Marsaili. And I feel . . . how do I feel? Betrayed. Tricked. They said I was going on holiday, and they put me in this place. Just like the day they brought me to The Dean. Inmates. That's what we called ourselves. Just like prisoners.

It was late October when we arrived at The Dean, me and Peter. You couldn't believe they would build a place like that for kids like us. It sat up on the hill, a long stone building on two levels with wings at either end, and two four-cornered bell towers at each side of the central elevation. Except that there were no bells in them. Just stone urns. There was a portico at the main entrance, with a triangular roof above it supported on four giant columns. Above that, an enormous clock. A clock whose golden hands seemed to tick away our time there as if they were going backwards. Or maybe it was just our age. When you are young a year is a big part of your life and seems to last for ever. When you are old, there have been too many of them gone before and they pass all too fast. We move so slowly away from birth, and rush so quickly to death.

We arrived in a big black car that day. I've no idea whose it was. It was cold and the sky was spitting sleet. Looking back, from the top of the steps, I could see the millworkers' tenements in the valley below, cold grey slate roofs and cobbled streets. And beyond that, the city skyline. We were surrounded by green here, trees, a huge kitchen garden, an orchard, and yet we were just a gob away from the centre of the city. In time I would learn that on a still night you could hear the traffic, and sometimes see red tail-lights distantly in the dark.

It was our last view of what I came to think of as the free world, because when we crossed that threshold we left all comfort and humanity behind, and entered a dismal place where the darkest side of human nature cast its shadow on us.

That dark side was made flesh by the governor. Mr. Anderson he was called, and a more brutal and cruel man you would be hard pushed to find. I have often asked myself what kind of man is it that would find fulfilment in abusing helpless children. Punishment, as he saw it. I often wished I could have met that man on equal terms, then we'd have seen how brave he was.

He kept a leather tawse in a drawer in his room. It measured about eighteen inches in length, had two tails, and was a good half-inch thick. And when he belted you with it, he would march you along the bottom corridor to the foot of the stairs leading to the boys' dorm and make you bend over. Your feet were on the first step, to elevate you a little, your hands supporting you on the third. And he would leather your arse till your legs buckled beneath you.

He was not a big man. Although he was to us. In fact, a giant in my memory. But actually he wasn't much taller than Matron. His hair was thin, the colour of ash, and oiled back across his narrow skull for all the world as if it had been painted on. A close-cropped black and silver moustache prickled his upper lip. He wore dark-grey suits that concertinaed around thick black shoes which squeaked on the tiles so that you always knew when he was coming, like the tick-tock of the crocodile in *Peter Pan*. There was a sour smell of stale tobacco that hung about him from the pipe he smoked, and spittle used to gather in the corners of his mouth, transferring from lower to upper lip and back again as he spoke, becoming thicker and creamier with every word.

He never referred to any of us by name. You were "boy," or "you, girl," and he was always using words we didn't understand. Like "comestibles" when he meant "sweeties."

I met him for the first time that day when the people who had brought us there took us into his office. He was all sweetness and light and full of assurances about how well we would be looked after here. Well, these people were barely out the door when we discovered what being well looked after actually meant. But first he delivered a short lecture.

We stood trembling on the linoleum in front of his big, polished desk, and he positioned himself, arms folded, on the other side of it, tall square windows rising to the ceiling behind him.

"First things first. You will refer to me at all times as sir. Is that understood?"

"Yes, sir," I said, and when Peter said nothing I dunted him with my elbow.

He glared at me. "What?"

I nodded towards Mr. Anderson. "Yes, sir," I said.

It took him a moment or two to understand. Then he smiled. "Yes, sir."

Mr. Anderson gave him a long, cold look. "We have no time for Catholics here. The Church of Rome is not welcome. You will not be invited to join us in hymn singing or Bible reading, and will stay in the dorm until morning prayers are over. Don't bother settling yourselves in, because with luck you won't be staying." He leaned forward, then, knuckles on the desk in front of him, glowing white in the gloom. "But for as long as you are here, be aware that there is only one rule." He paused for emphasis and enunciated each word. "Do. What. You. Are. Told." He stood up again. "If you break that rule you will suffer the consequences. Do you understand?"

Peter glanced at me for confirmation, and I gave him an almost imperceptible nod. "Yes, sir," we said in unison. We were nearly telepathic sometimes, Peter and me. As long as I did the thinking for both of us.

We were marched, then, along to Matron's room. She was an unmarried woman I think, in her middle years. I always remember her downturned mouth, and those shadowed eyes that seemed opaque somehow. You never knew what she was thinking, and her mood was always characterized by that sullen mouth. Even when she smiled, which was hardly ever.

We had to stand for ages in front of her desk while she opened a file on each of us and then told us to undress. It didn't seem to bother Peter. But I was embarrassed, and afraid I would get a hard-on. Not that there was anything remotely sexual about Matron. But you never knew when that damn thing would pop up on you.

She examined us both, I suppose for identifying marks, then went carefully through our hair searching for nits. Apparently she didn't find any, but told us that our hair was too long and that it would have to be shorn.

And then it was our teeth. Jaws prised apart, and stubby fingers that tasted bitter, like antiseptic, thrust in our mouths to poke around. As if we were animals being sized up for market.

I remember clearly the walk along to the bathroom. Stark naked, holding our folded clothes in front of us, prodded from the rear to hurry us along. I don't know where the other children were that day. At school probably. But I am glad there was no one there to see us. It was humiliating.

About six inches of lukewarm water were poured into a large zinc tub, and we sat in it together to work up a lather with rough lumps of carbolic soap and wash ourselves thoroughly under Matron's watchful eye. It was the last time at The Dean that I shared a bath with just one other person. Weekly bath night, it turned out, consisted of four to a bath, always in the same six inches of scummy water. So this was luxury.

The boys' dormitory occupied the first floor of the east wing. Rows of beds along facing walls of a long room. Tall arched windows stood at each end, and shorter rectangular windows lined the outside wall. In later days it was filled with spring sunshine, warm and bright, but today it breathed gloom and depression. Peter and

I were given beds side by side at the far end of the dorm. I had noticed, as we passed among them, that all the neatly made-up beds had small canvas sacks placed at the end of them, and when we reached ours I saw two empty sacks draped over our solitary case. There were no bedside cabinets, drawers or cupboards. We were, I soon found out, discouraged from accumulating personal belongings. And connections to the past were frowned upon.

Mr. Anderson came in behind us. "You can empty your case and place your belongings in the sacks provided," he said. "They will remain at all times at the foot of your beds. Understood?"

"Yes, sir."

Everything in the case had been systematically folded by somebody. I carefully separated my clothes from Peter's, and filled both our sacks. He sat for a while on the edge of his bed flicking through the only thing that remained of our father. A collection he had begun before the war of cigarette packets. Like a stamp album. Except that in place of the stamps, he had cut out the fronts of dozens of different cigarette packets and pasted them into the pages. Some of them had exotic names like *Joystick* or *Passing Cloud* or *Juleps*. All with colourful graphic illustrations, heads of young men and women seen puffing ecstatically at the tobacco-filled tubes that would later kill them.

Peter never tired of looking at them. I suppose the album was mine, really. But I was happy to let him have it. I never asked him, but it was as if those cigarette packets gave him a direct connection in some way to our father.

I felt a much stronger connection with our mother. And the ring she had given me was the symbolic memento of her that I guarded with my life. Not even Peter knew I had it. He couldn't be trusted with a secret. He was just as likely to open his mouth and blab to anyone. So I kept it hidden in a rolled-up pair of socks. It was just the sort of thing, I suspected, that would be confiscated or stolen.

The dining hall was on the ground floor, and that's when we met most of the other kids for the first time, after they got back from school. There were probably fifty or more of us at that time. Boys in the east wing, girls in the west. Of course we were a curiosity. Naïve newcomers. The others were blasé, experienced Dean kids. We were wet behind the ears, and worst of all, Catholics. I don't know how, but they all seemed to know that, and it separated us from the crowd. Nobody wanted to talk to us. Except for Catherine.

She was a real tomboy back then. Brown hair cut short, a white blouse beneath a dark-green pullover, a pleated grey skirt above grey socks gathered around her ankles, and heavy black shoes. I suppose I must have been about fifteen at that time, and she would have been a year or so younger than me, but I recall noticing that she already had sizeable breasts stretching her blouse. Though there really was nothing feminine about her. She liked to swear, and had the cheekiest grin I ever saw, and never took lip off anyone, even the bigger boys.

We were supposed to wear ties for going to school, but I noticed that first night that she had already discarded hers, and at the open neck of her blouse I saw a small Saint Christopher medallion hanging on a silver chain.

"You're papes, right?" she said, straight off.

"Catholics," I corrected her.

"That's what I said. Papes. I'm Catherine. Come on, I'll show you how this all works."

And we followed her to a table to retrieve wooden trays and queue up at the kitchen to be served our evening meal.

Catherine lowered her voice. "The food's shit. But don't worry about it. I've got an aunt somewhere that sends me food parcels. Keeps her from feeling guilty, I suppose. A lot of the kids aren't really orphans. Just from broken homes. Quite a few get food parcels. Got to get through them fast, though, before the fuckers in here confiscate them." She grinned conspiratorially and lowered her voice to a whisper. "Midnight feasts up on the roof."

She was right about the food. Catherine steered us to a table, and we sat among the hubbub of raised voices echoing around the high ceiling of the great hall, slurping at thin, flavourless vegetable soup and picking at green potatoes and tough meat swimming in grease. I found myself sinking into a depression. But Catherine just grinned.

"Don't worry about it. I'm a pape, too. They don't like Catholics here, so we won't be staying long." An echo of Mr. Anderson's words from earlier. "The priests'll be here for us any day now."

I don't know how long she had been deluding herself with that thought, but it would be another year before the incident on the bridge finally brought a visit from the priest.

They didn't like papes at school either. The school in the village was an austere grey granite and sandstone building pierced by tall arched windows set in stone dormers. Carved in the wall below the tower that held the bell which called us to lessons was a stone crest of the school board above a kindly lady in robes teaching a young student the wonders of the world. The student had short hair, and wore a skirt, and made me think of Catherine. Although I guess it was supposed to be a boy from classical times. It bore the date of 1875.

Being Catholics, we weren't allowed in to morning assembly, which was a Protestant affair. Not that I cared a hoot about missing the God stuff. I didn't find God till much later in my life. Strangely enough, a Protestant God. But we had to stand outside in the playground, in all weathers, until it was over. There was many a time that we would be let in, finally, soaked to the skin, to sit chittering at our desks in ice-cold classrooms. It's a wonder we didn't catch our deaths.

To make it worse, we were Dean kids. Which set us apart again. At the end of the school day, when all the other kids were free to escape into open streets, and homes with parents and siblings, we were made to line up in pairs, and suffer the barracking and cat-calls of the others. Then we were marched back up the hill to The Dean where we had to sit in silence for the next two hours doing our homework. Freedom came only at mealtimes, and in the short periods of free time before we were forced early to bed in cold, dark dorms.

During the winter months, those "free" periods were filled with Mr. Anderson's Highland dancing classes. Unlikely though it seemed, dancing was his passion, and he wanted us all perfectly drilled in the *pas-de-bas* and *drops of brandy* by the time the Christmas party came around.

In the summer months it was too light to sleep. By the time June came around, it stayed light until almost eleven, and restless soul that I was, I couldn't lie awake in my bed with the thought of a whole world of adventure out there.

I discovered very early a back staircase leading from the ground floor of the east wing down into the cellars. From there I was able to unbolt a door at the rear of the building, and escape out into the falling dusk. If I sprinted, I could very quickly reach the cover of shadows beneath the trees that lined the park. From there I was free to go where I would. Not that I ever went far. I was always alone. Peter never had trouble getting off to sleep, and if any of the others were ever aware of me leaving they gave no sign of it.

My solitary adventures, however, came to an abrupt end on the third or fourth outing. That was the night I discovered the cemetery.

It must have been quite late, because dusk had given way to darkness by the time I slipped out of the dormitory. I stopped at the door, listening to the breathing of the other boys. Someone was snoring gently, like a purring cat. And one of the younger ones was talking to himself. A voice unbroken, expressing hidden fears.

I could feel the cold of the stone steps rising as I descended into darkness. The cellar had a damp, sour smell, a place mired in shadow. I was always afraid to linger, and I never did know what it was they kept down there. The bolt protested a little as I eased it back across the door, and I was out. A quick glance in each direction, then legs pounding across asphalt to the trees. Usually I would head up over the hill, then down again towards the village. Street lights reflected on the water there, where the wheels of ten or more mills had once turned. Silent now. Abandoned. Lights twinkling in a few of the windows of the tenements built for the millworkers, trees and houses rising steeply on either side below the bridge that spanned the river a hundred feet above it.

But tonight, in search of something different, I turned the other way instead, and soon discovered a metal gate in the high wall that bounded the east side of the garden. I'd had no idea that there was a cemetery there, hidden as it was from the view of The Dean by tall trees. As I opened the gate I felt a little like Alice passing from one side of the looking glass to the other, except that I was passing from the world of the living into the world of the dead.

Avenues of tombstones led away left and right, almost lost in the shadow of willows that seemed to weep for those who had gone before. Immediately to my left lay Frances Jeffrey, who had died on January 26, 1850, at the age of seventy-seven. I don't know why, but those names are etched as clearly in my mind as they were in the stone that they lay beneath. Daniel John Cumming, his wife Elizabeth and their son Alan. How strangely comforting, it seemed to me, that they should all be together in death as they had been in life. I envied them. My father's bones lay at the bottom of an ocean, and I had no idea where my mother was buried.

One whole length of wall had tombstones set into it, with well-kept oblongs of grass in front of them, and ferns growing around the foot of the wall.

I am amazed that I was not afraid. A cemetery at night. A young lad in the dark. And yet, I must have felt that I had much more to fear from the living than from the dead. And I'm sure I was right.

I wandered off along a chalk path, headstones and crosses huddled darkly on either side. It was a clear sky and the moon was up, so I could see without difficulty. I was following the curve of the path around to the south when a noise made me stop in my tracks. It would be hard now to say what it was I heard. It was more like a thud that I felt. And then somewhere away to my left a rustling among the grass. Someone coughed.

I have heard it said that a fox makes a coughing sound that is almost human, so perhaps that is what I heard. But another cough, and a movement among the shadows of the trees, much bigger than any fox could have made, stilled my heart. Another thud and I was off. Running like the wind. In and out of the moon-dappled shade. Almost dazzled by the patches of bright silver light.

Maybe it was only my imagination, but I could have sworn I heard footsteps in pursuit. A sudden chill in the air. Sweat turning cold on my face.

I had no idea where I was, or how to get back to the gate. I stumbled and fell, skinning my knees, before scrambling to my feet and leaving the track, heading off among the shadows of brooding stones. To crouch now in the gloom, behind the shelter of a large tomb taller than myself, crowned by a stone cross.

I tried to hold my breath so as not to make any noise. But the pounding of my heart filled my ears, and bursting lungs forced me to suck in oxygen, before expelling it quickly to make room for more. My whole body was trembling.

I listened for the footsteps but heard nothing, and was just starting to relax and curse my overactive imagination, when I heard the soft, careful crunch of feet on gravel. It was all I could do to keep myself from crying out.

I peered out cautiously from behind the cross and saw, less than twenty feet away, the shadow of a man limping by on the path. He seemed to be dragging his left leg. A few more steps, and he emerged from the shadow of a huge copper beech into moonlight, and I saw his face for the first time. It was ghostly white, pale like my mother's the day she told us our father was dead. His eyes were lost in the darkness beneath prominent brows, almost as if the sockets were empty. His trousers were torn and he wore a ragged jacket and grey shirt open at the neck. A small sack of belongings hung from his left hand. A vagrant seeking a place to sleep among the dead? I didn't know. I didn't want to know.

I waited until he had shuffled off again to be swallowed up by the night, and I moved out from behind the tomb to see for the first time the name cut in the stone of it. And every hair on my body stood on end.

Mary Elizabeth McBride.

My mother's name. I knew, of course, that it wasn't her lying there beneath the ground. This Mary Elizabeth had been in residence for nearly two hundred years. But I couldn't shake off the sense that somehow it was my mother who had guided me to that place of concealment. She had charged me with looking after my brother, but had taken it upon herself to watch over me.

I turned and fled, back the way I had come, heart trying to crack open my ribs, until I saw the black-painted metal gate standing ajar. I was through it like a ghost, and sprinting across the asphalt to the door at the back of The Dean. The only time in my life, I think, that I was glad to be inside it.

Back in my bed I lay shivering for a long time before sleep took me. I'm not sure when it was that I was wakened by Peter. He was leaning over me, caught in the moonlight that angled in across the dorm in elongated rectangles. I could see the concern in his eyes, and he was touching my face.

"John," he was whispering. "Johnny. Why are you crying?"

It was Alex Curry's fault that the adventure on the roof ended in disaster. He was a brute of a boy, older than the rest of us, and had been there the longest. He was about as tall as Mr. Anderson, and probably stronger. He'd always been a rebel, the others said, and had his arse belted more often than anyone else at The Dean. But in three years he had developed to the point where his physical strength matched his rebellious nature. And that must have been pretty intimidating to Mr. Anderson. Lately he had refused to cut his thick, black hair and grown it into an Elvis quiff and duck's arse. I think that's probably the first time that Peter and I became aware of Elvis Presley. We had barely been conscious of the world outside of our own. The belting of Alex had tailed off, and it was rumoured that he was to be sent to a hostel. He was too old for The Dean now, and far too much for Mr. Anderson to handle.

Catherine had come to us the day before, with a wink and a smile and a conspiratorial tone. She and several of the other girls had received food parcels that week, and there was to be a midnight feast on the roof the following night.

"How do we get on to the roof?" I said.

She looked at me, eyes full of pity at my innocence, and shook her head. "There are stairs leading up to the roof from both wings," she said. "Go and take a look at your side. There's a door at the end of the landing, and behind it a narrow staircase. The door's never locked. The roof's flat, and perfectly safe if you stay away from the edge. It's the only time the boys and girls ever get to meet up without the bloody staff watching us." She grinned lasciviously. "It can get interesting."

I felt an immediate stirring somewhere deep in my loins. Like a worm turning over. I had long ago learned to masturbate, but I had never so much as kissed a girl. And there was no mistaking the look in Catherine's eyes.

I could hardly contain my excitement all the next day. School passed infuriatingly slowly, and at the end of the afternoon I couldn't remember a single thing that we'd been taught. No one ate much at dinner that night, conserving their appetites for the midnight feast. Of course, not everyone was going. Some of the kids were too young, and others too scared. But wild horses couldn't have kept me away. And Peter was fearless.

There were around ten of us who slipped out of the dorm on to the landing shortly before midnight that night. Alex Curry led the way. I don't know how he had managed it, but from somewhere he had acquired a couple of dozen bottles of pale ale which he shared out among us to carry on to the roof.

I'll never forget the feeling of emerging from that dark, narrow stairwell on to the wide open space of the roof, moonlight spilling freely across its tarred surface. It felt like escape. Even my later solitary outings never felt quite like that. I wanted to turn my face to the sky and shout out loud. But, of course, I didn't.

We all met up in the middle, behind the big clock and to one side of the huge skylight that lit the upper floor. The girls brought the food, the boys had the beer, and we sat around in a loose circle eating cheese and cake and biscuits, and dipping our fingers into jars of jam. At first we spoke in the faintest of whispers, but as the bottles of beer got passed around, we grew bold and careless. It was the first time I had ever drunk alcohol, and I loved the kick I got from that soft, bitter liquid foaming on my tongue and slipping over so easily to steal away inhibition.

I'm not sure how, but somehow I found myself sitting next to Catherine. We were side by side, shoulders and upper arms touching, legs drawn up. I could feel her warmth through her jumper, and I could have breathed in the smell of her for ever. I have no idea what that scent was. But it always hung around her. Faintly aromatic. I suppose it must have been a perfume of some kind, or the soap she used. Perhaps something sent by her aunt. It was always arousing.

I was already heady from the beer, and finding courage I never knew I had. I slipped my arm around her shoulder, and she leaned in against me.

"What happened to your folks?" I said. It was a question we hardly ever asked. We were never encouraged to dwell on the past. She took a long time to answer.

"My mum died."

"And your dad?"

"It didn't take him long to find someone else. Someone who would give him children, like a good Catholic. My mum had complications when I was born and couldn't have any more kids."

I was confused. "I don't understand. Why aren't you still at home?"

"*She* didn't want me."

I heard the pain in her voice, and felt it too. It was one thing to lose your parents to death, it was another to be turned away, unwanted. Especially by your own father. I sneaked a glance at her, and was shocked to see silvered tears run down her cheeks in the moonlight. Wee, tough Catherine. The arousal I'd felt earlier dissipated, and all I really wanted to do was hold her, and comfort her, so that she would know she was wanted by someone.

Which was when I became aware of a commotion on the far side of the skylight. Someone had taken Peter's bottle of beer off him, unopened, and several of the boys were throwing it from one to the other, tantalising him, making him run around in dizzying circles trying to catch it. It seemed that Alex Curry was the ringleader, bating and taunting, encouraging the others. Everyone knew Peter wasn't quite the full shilling, and without me to stand up for him he was an easy target.

Of course, I was no physical match for Alex Curry, but I had the mental strength to stand up to anyone when it came to Peter. I had promised my mother, and I wasn't about to renege on that.

I stood up immediately. "Oi!" I almost shouted, and immediately everyone went quiet. The bottle-throwing stopped, and one or two voices shushed me in the still night air. "Fucking leave off," I said, sounding much braver than I felt.

"You and whose army's going to make me?"

"I don't need an army to kick your arse, Curry."

I know whose arse would have got kicked that night if fate hadn't intervened. Before Curry could respond, Peter lunged at him to grab his beer, and the bottle spun away through the air, knocked from the bigger boy's grasp.

The silence of the night was shattered as the bottle broke through the glass of the skylight then fell through a moment of stillness to an explosion of glass and foam as it landed in the hall below. More glass showered down after it. It sounded as if a bomb had gone off.

"Holy Mary, mother of God" I heard Catherine whisper, and then everyone was up and running, shadows darting east and west across the roof in a panic, food and beer abandoned in haste and fear.

Bodies crammed together in the darkness of the stairwell, shoving and jostling in a rush to get down to the landing. Like rats we poured through the door of the dorm and fanned out towards our beds.

By the time the doors flew open and the lights came on, everyone was curled up beneath the sheets pretending to be asleep. Mr. Anderson, of course, wasn't fooled. He stood there, almost purple in the face, black eyes blazing. His voice, by comparison, was almost calm, controlled, and all the more intimidating because of it.

But it took him a moment or two to speak. He waited until pretend sleepy faces had emerged from their blankets, heads lifting from pillows, shoulders raised on crooked elbows.

"I know, of course, that not all of you will have been involved, and so I appeal to those of you who were not to speak up now, unless you want to share in the punishment of the others."

The janitor appeared at his shoulder, still in his dressing gown and slippers, hair tousled. Of all the staff, he was the one who treated the kids the best. But tonight his face was sickly pale, trepidation in darting brown eyes. Mr. Anderson leaned towards him as he whispered words too fast and soft for us to hear.

Mr. Anderson nodded, and as the janitor retreated said, "Food and alcohol on the roof. You stupid boys! An absolute recipe for disaster. Come on! Hands up those of you who *weren't* there." He folded his arms and waited. After just a few moments, hesitant hands lifted themselves into the air, identifying by omission those of us who were guilty. Mr. Anderson shook his head grimly. "And who was responsible for providing the alcohol?"

Dead silence this time.

"Come on!" His voice boomed now into the night. "If you don't all wish to suffer the same punishment, the innocent had better give up the guilty."

A lad called Tommy Jack, who must have been one of the youngest at The Dean, said, "Please, sir, it was Alex Curry." You could have heard a pin drop in England.

Mr. Anderson's eyes flickered towards the defiant Alex Curry, who was sitting up now in his bed, leaning his forearms on his knees. "So what are you going to do, Anderson? Belt me? Just fucking try it."

A mean little smile crept across Mr. Anderson's lips. "You'll see," was all he said. And he turned towards little Tommy, with the acid of contempt in his voice. "I don't admire boys who clype on their

friends. I'm sure that's a lesson you will have learned before this
night is out."

He flicked out the lights and pulled the doors shut, and there
was a long silence before Tommy's frightened voice trembled in the
dark. "I didn't mean it, honest."

And Alex Curry's growled response. "Ya wee fucker!"

Mr. Anderson was right. Wee Tommy learned that night, the
hardest way possible, that telling tales on your peers was not acceptable behaviour. And most, if not all, of those who had raised their
hands were taught similar lessons.

As for the rest of us, we could only await with trepidation whatever retribution Mr. Anderson had planned for us in the morning.

To our surprise nothing happened. The tension in The Dean was
palpable over breakfast, a strange muted dining room with inmates
and staff alike afraid, it seemed, to speak. By the time we left for
school, marching in pairs down the hill to the village, a little of the
anxiety had lifted. By the end of the day we had almost forgotten
about it.

We returned as usual, and nothing seemed out of the ordinary,
except that Alex Curry was gone. Left The Dean for good. And then
we got to the dorms. Which is when we realized that the sacks of
belongings which sat at the end of each bed were gone. All of them.
I panicked. My mother's ring was in my sack. I ran down the stairs
full of fire and indignation, only to bump into the janitor in the corridor below.

"Where's our stuff?" I shouted at him. "What's he done with it?"

His face was the colour of ashes, almost green around the eyes.
Eyes that were filled with anxiety and guilt. "I've never seen him
like that, Johnny," he said. "He came out of his apartment like a man
possessed after you'd all left for school. He went around the dorms
and collected all the sacks, making me and some of the others help
him." His words tumbled out of his mouth like apples spilling from
a barrel. "He gathered them all together down in the basement, and

got me to hold open the door of the central heating furnace while he threw them all in. One at a time. Every last one of them."

I felt anger blinding me. All that I had left of my mother was gone. Her ring with the intertwining serpents. Lost for ever. And Peter's album of cigarette packets. All ties to the past severed for eternity. Burned in petty revenge by Mr. Anderson.

Had I been able, I would have killed that man and never had a moment's regret.

| TWELVE |

Fin was a little uncomfortable. It felt strange to be back in this house, filled as it was with so many childhood memories. The house where he and Artair had been tutored by Mr. Macinnes. The house where they had played as children, best friends since the time they could first walk. A house filled with dark secrets that both had kept by unspoken assent.

To Marsaili it was just the house where she lived. Where she had spent twenty thankless years married to a man she didn't love, caring for his invalid mother, bringing up their son.

On their return from Stornoway she had invited Fin to eat with her and Fionnlagh, and he had accepted gratefully, spared from the can of soup he had planned to heat on his tiny gas camping stove.

Although it was still light outside, low black cloud had brought a premature end to the day. A fierce wind whistled around doors and windows, driving rain against the glass in unrelenting waves, blowing smoke down the chimney in the sitting room and filling the house with the stinging, toasted scent of peat.

Marsaili had prepared the meal in silence, and Fin had guessed that her whole conscious being was filled with something like guilt for having abandoned her father to a strange bed in a strange place where he knew no one.

"You're good with him," she said suddenly, without turning. She kept her focus on the pot on the hob.

Fin sat at the table with a glass of beer. "What do you mean?"

"With my dad. Like you were experienced in dealing with dementia."

Fin sipped at his beer. "Mona's mother suffered from early-onset Alzheimer's, Marsaili. A slow deterioration. Not too bad at first. But then she had a fall and broke her hip, and they hospital-ized her at the Victoria Infirmary in Glasgow, and put her in a geriatric ward."

Marsaili wrinkled her nose. "Bet that wasn't much fun for her."

"It was disgusting." The depth of feeling in his voice made her turn. "It was like something out of Dickens. The place stank of shit and urine, people crying out in the night. Staff who sat on her bed, blocking her view of the TV that *she* was paying for, watching soap operas while colostomy bags overflowed."

"Oh my God!" The horror was painted on Marsaili's face.

"There was no way we could leave her there. So we went with a bag one night, packed up her stuff and took her back to our place. I paid for a private nurse and she stayed with us for six months." He took another mouthful of beer, lost in the memory. "I got to know how to deal with her. To ignore the contradictions and never argue. To understand that it was frustration that caused her anger, and forgetfulness that made her cussed." He shook his head. "Her short-term memory was almost non-existent. But she could remember things from childhood with pin-sharp clarity, and we would spend hours talking about the past. I liked Mona's mum."

Marsaili was lost in silent thought for a while. Then, "Why did you and Mona split up?" And no sooner had she asked it, than she qualified her question. In case, perhaps, it was too direct. "Was it only because of the accident?"

Fin shook his head. "That was the breaking point . . . after years of living a comfortable lie. If it hadn't been for Robbie we'd probably have gone our separate ways a long time ago. We were friends, and I can't say I was unhappy, but I never really loved her."

"Why did you marry her, then?"

He met her eye and thought about it, forcing himself to confront the truth, perhaps for the very first time. "Probably because you married Artair."

She returned his gaze, and in the few feet that separated them lay all the wasted years they had let slip by. She turned back again to her pot, unable to face the thought. "You can't blame me for that. You were the one who drove me away."

The outside door flew open, and the wind and the rain blew in briefly with Fionnlagh. He shut it quickly behind him and stood pink-faced and dripping, his anorak soaked, his wellies caked with mud. He seemed surprised to see Fin sitting at the table.

"Get those things off you," Marsaili said, "and sit in. We're almost ready to eat."

The boy kicked off his boots and hung up his waterproofs, and brought a bottle of beer from the fridge to the table. "So what happened with Grampa?"

Marsaili swept back the hair from her face and served up three plates of chilli con carne scooped on to beds of rice. "Your gran won't have him at home any more. So he's in the care home at Dun Eisdean until I can figure out what to do about him."

Fionnlagh shovelled food into his mouth. "Why didn't you bring him here?"

Marsaili's eyes darted towards Fin and then away again, and he caught the guilt in them. He said, "Because he needs professional care now, Fionnlagh. Physically and mentally."

But Fionnlagh kept his focus on his mother. "You looked after Artair's mother for long enough. And she wasn't even your own flesh and blood."

Marsaili turned twenty years of resentment on her son. "Yes, well, maybe you'd like to change the bed every time he soils it, and go looking for him every time he wanders off. Maybe you'd like to feed him at every meal, and be there every time he's lost or forgotten something."

Fionnlagh didn't respond, except with the merest of shrugs, and kept forking chilli into his face.

Fin said, "There's a complication, Fionnlagh."

"Yes?" Fionnlagh barely glanced at him.

"They dug a body out of the peat bog near Siader a few days ago. A young man, about your age. As far as they can tell, he's been there since the late fifties."

Fionnlagh's fork paused midway between his plate and his mouth. "And?"

"He was murdered."

The fork went back down to the plate. "What's that got to do with us?"

"It seems he was related somehow to your grandfather. Which means he was also related to you and Marsaili."

Fionnlagh frowned. "How can they tell that?"

"DNA," Marsaili said.

He looked at her blankly for a moment, then realisation dawned. "The samples we gave last year."

She nodded.

"I fucking knew it! That should have been destroyed. I signed a form refusing to let them keep mine on the database."

"So did everyone else," Fin said. "Except, apparently, for your grandfather. He probably didn't understand."

"So they just put him on the computer, like some criminal?"

Marsaili said, "If you've got nothing to hide, what do you have to fear?"

"It's an invasion of privacy, Mum. Who knows who'll get access to that information, and what they might do with it?"

"It's a perfectly reasonable argument," Fin said. "But right now, that's not really the point."

"Well, what is?"

"Who the murdered man was, and how he was related to your grandfather."

Fionnlagh looked at his mother. "Well, he must have been a cousin or something."

She shook her head. "There's no one that we know of, Fionnlagh."

"Then there must be someone that you don't know of."

She shrugged. "Apparently."

"So, anyway, this guy was related to Grampa: so what?"

Fin said, "Well, from a police perspective it makes Tormod the most likely person to have killed him."

There was a shocked silence around the table. Marsaili looked at Fin. It was the first she had heard this. "Does it?"

Fin nodded slowly. "When the CIO arrives from the mainland to open the investigation, your father's going to be the prime suspect on a list of one." He took a pull at his beer. "So we'd better start trying to figure out who the dead man is."

Fionnlagh cleared the last of the chilli from his plate. "Well, you can do that. I've got other things to think about." He crossed the kitchen to retrieve his anorak and start pulling on boots that shed flakes of drying mud across the tiles.

"Where are you going?" Marsaili's forehead creased with concern.

"I'm meeting Donna at the Crobost Social."

"Oh, so her father's actually letting her out for the night?" Marsaili's tone was heavily sardonic.

"Don't start, Mum."

"If that girl had half an ounce of gumption in her, she'd tell her father where to go. I've told you a hundred times you can stay here. You, Donna *and* the baby."

"You don't know what her father's like." Fionnlagh almost spat the words at her.

"Oh, I think I do, Fionnlagh. We grew up together, remember?" Marsaili glanced quickly at Fin and then away again.

"Aye, but he didn't have God in those days, did he? You know what they're like, Mum, when they get the *curam*, these born-agains. There's no reasoning with them. Why would they listen to you or me when God has already spoken to them?"

Fin felt the strangest chill run through him. It was like hearing himself speaking. Since the death of his parents all those years before, his life had been a constant battle between belief and anger.

If he believed, then he could only feel anger at the God who had been responsible for the accident. So it was easier not to believe, and he had little patience for those who did.

"It's time you stood up to him." There was a weariness in Marsaili's voice, a lack of conviction that told Fin she didn't believe that Fionnlagh was ever likely to pit himself against Donald Murray.

Fionnlagh heard it too, and was defensive in return. "And tell him what? What great prospects I have? What a wonderful future I can offer his daughter and his granddaughter?" He turned away towards the door, and his last words were almost lost in the wind. "Gimme a fucking break!" He slammed the door shut behind him.

Marsaili flushed with embarrassment. "I'm sorry."

"Don't be. He's just a boy facing up too early to a responsibility he shouldn't have had. He needs to finish school and go to university. Then maybe he really could offer them a future."

Marsaili shook her head. "He won't do that. He's frightened he'll lose them. He wants to quit school at the end of term and get a job. Show Donald Murray that he takes his responsibilities seriously."

"By throwing away his only chance in life? Surely to God he doesn't want to end up like Artair."

The fire of resentment burned briefly in Marsaili's eyes, but she said nothing.

Fin said quickly, "And one thing's for sure. Donald Murray would never respect him if he did."

Marsaili lifted their plates away from the table. "Nice of you to come back after all this time and tell us how we should be running our lives." The plates clattered on to the counter top, and she laid her hands flat upon it, leaning forward to take her weight on them and letting her head fall. "I'm sick of it, Fin. Sick of everything. Sick of Donald Murray and his sanctimonious bullying. Sick of Fionnlagh's lack of backbone. I'm sick of fooling myself into studying for a future I'll probably never have." She drew a deep tremulous breath and forced herself to stand upright again. "And now this." She turned back to face Fin, and he saw that she was hanging on to control by a gossamer thread. "What am I going to do about my dad?"

It would have been easy for him to stand up and take her in his arms, and tell her everything was going to be all right. But it wasn't. And there was no point in pretending it was. He said, "Come and sit down and tell me what you know about him."

She pushed herself, laden with weariness, away from the counter and sat heavily in her chair. Her face was strained by tension and fatigue, pale and pinched in the harsh electric light. But he saw in it still the little girl who had first drawn him to her all those years before. The little girl with the blond pigtails who had sat next to him that first day at school and offered to translate for him, because for some reason inexplicable to the young Fin his parents had sent him to school speaking only Gaelic. He reached across the table and brushed the hair from her blue eyes, and for a moment she lifted a hand to touch his, a fleeting moment of recollection, of how it had once been long ago. She dropped her hand to the table again.

"Dad came up from Harris when he was still in his teens. About eighteen or nineteen, I think. He got a job as a labourer at Mealanais farm." She got up to take a half-empty bottle of red wine from the worktop and pour herself a glass. She held the bottle out towards Fin, but he shook his head. "It was sometime after that he met my mum. Her father was still the lighthouse keeper then, at the Butt, and that's where they lived. Apparently Dad used to walk to the lighthouse every night after work to see her, even just for a few minutes, and then back again. In all weathers. Four and a half miles each way." She took a large sip of her wine. "It must have been love."

Fin smiled. "It must have been."

"They went to all the dances at the social. And all the crofters' do's. They must have been going out steady for about four years when the farmer at Mealanais died, and the place came up for lease. Dad applied for it, and they said yes. On condition that he got himself married."

"That must have made for a romantic proposal."

Marsaili smiled in spite of herself. "I think my mum was just pleased that something had finally prompted him to ask. They were married in Crobost Church by Donald Murray's father, and spent the next God knows how many years eking a living off the land and raising me and my sister. In all my conscious life I can't remember my dad once having left this island. And that's all I know, really."

Fin finished the last of his beer. "Tomorrow we'll go and talk to your mum. She's bound to have a lot more information than you do."

Marsaili topped up her wine. "I wouldn't want to keep you from your work."

"What work?"

"Restoring your parents' croft."

His smile was touched by sadness. "It's lain derelict for thirty years, Marsaili. It can wait a little longer."

| THIRTEEN |

I can see a thin line of yellow light beneath the door. From time to time someone passes in the corridor and their shadow follows the light from one side to the other. I notice that I can't hear any footsteps. Maybe they wear rubber shoes so you won't know when they're coming. Not like Mr. Anderson with his tick-tock crocodile shoes. He wants you to know. He wants you to be afraid. And we were.

I'm not afraid now, though. I've waited all my life for this. Escape. From all those people who want to keep me in places I don't want to be. Well, fuck them!

Hah! It felt good to say that. Well, think it, anyway. "Fuck them!" I whisper it in the dark. And I hear it so loudly it makes me sit up straight.

If anyone comes in now, the game's up. They will see my hat and coat, and notice my bag sitting packed on the end of the bed. They'll probably call for Mr. Anderson, and I'll be in for a hell of a leathering. I wish they would hurry up and put the lights out. I'll need to be long gone by morning. I hope the others haven't forgotten.

I don't know how much time has passed. Did I fall asleep? There is no light beneath the door any more. I listen for a long time and hear nothing. So now I lift my bag from the bed and slowly open the door. Damn! I should have gone for a pee before now. Too late. Doesn't matter. No time to lose.

Old Eachan's room is next door. I saw him in the dining room earlier. And remembered him immediately. He used to lead the Gaelic psalm-singing in the church. I loved that sound. So different from the Catholic choirs of my childhood. More like tribal chanting. Primal. I open the door and slip inside, and immediately hear him snoring. I close the door behind me and switch on the light. There is a brown holdall bag sitting on the dresser and Eachan is curled up beneath the quilt, sleeping.

I want to whisper his name, but somehow it eludes me. Dammit, what's he called? I can still hear him singing those psalms. A strong clear voice, full of confidence and faith. I shake him by the shoulder, and as he rolls over I pull back the quilt.

Good. He's fully dressed, ready to go. Maybe he just got tired of waiting.

"Eachan," I hear myself say. Yes. That's his name. "Come on, man. Time to go."

He seems confused.

"What's happening?" he says.

"We're running away."

"Are we?"

"Yes, of course. We talked about it. Don't you remember? You're fully dressed, man."

Eachan sits up and looks at himself. "So I am." He swings his legs out of the bed, and his shoes leave dirty tracks on the sheets. "Where are we going?"

"Away from The Dean."

"What's that?"

"Shhh. Mr. Anderson might hear us." I take him by the arm and lead him to the door, opening it to peer out into the dark.

"Wait. My bag." Eachan lifts his holdall from the dresser and I turn off the light before we slip out into the corridor again.

At the far end I see a glow from the kitchen, and shadows moving around in the light that falls out into the hall. I wonder if one of the other boys has told. If so, we're done for. Trapped. I can feel old Eachan hanging on to the back of my coat as we shuffle closer, trying not to make a noise. I hear voices now. Men's voices, and I step smartly into the doorway to surprise them. Someone told me that once. Surprise is the best weapon when the numbers are against you.

But there are only two of them. Two old boys pacing around, all dressed with coats and hats, bags packed and sitting up on the counter.

One of them seems familiar. He is very agitated and glares at me. "You're late!"

How does he know I'm late?

"You said just after lights out. We've been waiting for ages."

I say, "We're making a run for it."

He is very irritated now. "I know that. You're late."

The other one just nods, eyes wide like a rabbit's in the headlights. I have no idea who he is.

Someone is pushing me from behind now. It is Eachan. What does he want?

"Go on, go on," he says.

"Me?"

"Yes, you," says the other one. "Your idea. You do it."

And the silent one nods and nods.

I look around, wondering what it is they want me to do. What are we doing here? Then I see the window. Escape! I remember now. The window leads out to the back. Over the wall and off across the bog. They'll never catch us. Run like the wind. Over the asphalt to the trees.

"Here, give me a hand," I say, and I pull a chair up to the sink. "Someone will have to hand my bag out after me. My mother's ring is in there. She gave it to me to keep safe."

Eachan and the nodding one hold me steady as I climb on to the chair and step into the sink. Now I can reach the catch. But it won't move, dammit! No matter how hard I try. I can see my fingers turning white from the pressure.

Suddenly there is a light in the corridor. I hear footsteps and voices, and I can feel panic rising in my chest. Someone's clyped on us. Oh God!

It's black on the other side of the window as I turn back to it. I can see the rain still running down the glass. I've got to get out. Freedom on the other side. I start pounding on it with my clenched fists. I can see the glass bending with each blow.

Someone's shouting, "Stop him! For heaven's sake stop him!"

Finally the glass breaks. Shatters. At last. I feel pain in my hands, and see blood running down my arms. The blast of wind and rain in my face nearly knocks me over.

A woman is screaming.

But all I can see is the blood. Staining the sand. Effervescent foaming brine turning crimson in the moonlight.

| FOURTEEN |

Fin drove them past the Crobost Social Club and the football pitch beyond it. Houses climbed the hill in sporadic groupings at Five Penny and Eòropaidh, facing south-west to brave the prevailing winds of spring and summer, and huddled low along the ridge with their backs to the icy Arctic blasts of winter. All along the ragged coastline, the sea sucked and frothed and growled, tireless legions of riderless white horses crashing up against the stubborn stone of unyielding black cliffs.

Sunlight flitted in and out of a sky grated by the wind, chaotic random patches of it chasing each other across the machair where headstones planted in the soft, sandy soil marked the passing of generations. A little way to the north, the top third of the lighthouse at the Butt was clearly visible. Fin supposed that in retirement Marsaili's mother had followed some basic instinct that took her back to childhood. Remembered moments of unexpectedly sunny days, or violent storms, the wildest of seas crashing all around the rocks below the lighthouse which had been her home.

From the kitchen window at the back of the modern bungalow that the Macdonalds had chosen as their retirement home, she could see quite plainly the collection of white and yellow buildings where she had once lived, and the red-brown brick of the tower that had weathered countless seasons of relentless assault to warn men at sea of hidden dangers.

Fin glanced from the window as Mrs. Macdonald made them tea, and saw a rainbow forming, vivid against a bank of black cloud off the point, a dazzle of sunlight burnishing the troubled surface of the ocean, from here like dimpled copper. The peat stack in the small patch of garden at the back was severely diminished, and he wondered who cut their peat for them now.

He was barely aware of the old lady's inconsequential babbling. She was excited to see him. So many years it had been since the last time, she said. He had been struck, the moment he entered the house, by the smell of roses that had always accompanied Marsaili's mother. It brought back a flood of memories. Home-made lemonade in the dark farmhouse kitchen with its stone-flagged floor. The games that he and Marsaili had played amongst the hay bales in the barn. Her mother's soft English cadences, alien to his ear then, and unchanged now, even after all these years.

"We need some background information about Dad," he heard Marsaili saying. "For the records at the care home." They had agreed that it might be better if they kept the truth from her for the moment. "And I'd like to take some of the old family photo albums to talk through with him. They say photographs help to stimulate memory."

Mrs. Macdonald was only too happy to dig out the family snapshots, and wanted to sit and go through the albums with them. It was so rarely these days that they had company, she said, speaking in the plural, as if the banishing of Tormod from her life had never happened. A kind of denial. Or a coded message. Subject not up for discussion.

There were nearly a dozen albums. The most recent were bound in garish floral covers. The older ones were a more sombre chequered green. The oldest had been inherited from her parents, and contained a collection of faded black and white prints of people long dead, dressed in fashions from another age.

"That's your grandfather," she told Marsaili, pointing at a picture of a tall man with a mop of curly dark hair behind the cracked glaze of a faded and over-exposed print. "And your grandmother." A small woman with long, fair hair and a slightly ironic smile. "What do you think, Fin? Marsaili's double, isn't she?" She was so like Marsaili it was uncanny.

She moved, then, on to her wedding photographs. Lurid sixties colours, flared trousers, tank-tops and floral shirts with absurdly long collars. Long hair, fringes and sideburns. Fin felt almost embarrassed for them, and wondered how future generations might view photographs of him in his youth. Whatever is à la mode today somehow seems ridiculous in retrospect.

Tormod himself would have been around twenty-five then, with a fine head of thick hair curling around his face. Fin might have had difficulty recognising him as the same man whose glasses he had fished out of the urinal only yesterday, if it hadn't been for the vivid memories he had from his childhood of a big, strong man in dark-blue overalls and a cloth cap permanently pushed back on his head.

"Do you have any older pictures of Tormod?" he said.

But Mrs. Macdonald just shook her head. "Nothing from before the wedding. We didn't have a camera when we were winching."

"What about photographs of his family, his childhood?"

She shrugged. "He didn't have any. Or, at least, never brought any with him from Harris."

"What happened to his parents?"

She refilled her cup from a pot kept warm in a knitted cosy, and offered refills to Fin and Marsaili.

"I'm fine, thanks, Mrs. Macdonald," Fin said.

"You were going to tell us about Dad's parents, Mum," Marsaili prompted her.

She blew air through loosely pursed lips. "Nothing to tell, darling. They were dead before I ever knew him."

"Was there no one from his side of the family at the wedding?" Fin asked.

Mrs. Macdonald shook her head. "Not a one. He was an only child, you see. And I think most, if not all, of his family had emigrated to Canada some time in the fifties. He never talked much about them." She paused and seemed lost for a moment as if searching through distant thoughts. They waited to see if she would come back to them with one. Eventually she said, "It's strange . . ." But didn't elucidate.

"What's strange, Mum?"

"He was a very religious man, your father. As you know. Church every Sunday morning. Bible reading in the afternoon. Grace before meals."

Marsaili glanced at Fin, offering him a rueful smile. "How could I forget?"

"A very fair man. Honest, and without prejudice in almost everything except . . ."

"I know." Marsaili grinned. "He hated Catholics. Papes and Fenians, he called them."

Her mother shook her head. "I never approved. My father was Church of England, which is not that different from Catholicism. Without the Pope, of course. But, still, it was an unreasonable hatred he had of them."

Marsaili shrugged. "I was never sure whether or not he was entirely serious."

"Oh, he was serious, all right."

"So what's strange, Mrs. Macdonald?" Fin tried to steer her back to her original thought.

She looked at him blankly for a moment before the memory returned. "Oh. Yes. I was going through some of his things last night. He's accumulated a lot of rubbish over the years. I don't know why he keeps the half of it. In old shoeboxes and cupboards and drawers in the spare room. He used to spend hours in there going through stuff. I have no idea why." She sipped her tea. "Anyway, I found something at the bottom of one of those shoeboxes that seemed . . . well, out of character somehow."

"What, Mum?" Marsaili was intrigued.

"Wait, I'll show you." She got up and left the room, returning less than half a minute later to sit down again between them on the settee. She opened her right hand over the coffee table in front of them, and a silver chain and small, round, tarnished medallion spilled on to the open pages of the wedding album.

Fin and Marsaili leaned closer to get a better look, and Marsaili picked it up, turning it over. "Saint Christopher," she said. "Patron saint of travellers."

Fin craned and tilted his head to see the worn figure of Saint Christopher leaning on his staff, as he carried the Christ child through storms and troubled waters. *Saint Christopher Protect Us* was engraved around the edge of it.

"Of course," said Mrs. Macdonald, "as I understand it, the Catholic Church removed his status as a saint about forty years ago, but it still belongs to a very Catholic tradition. What your father was doing with it is beyond me."

Fin reached out to take it from Marsaili. "Could we borrow this, Mrs. Macdonald? It might be interesting to see if it stimulates any memories."

Mrs. Macdonald waved a dismissive hand. "Of course. Take it. Keep it. Throw it away if you like. It's of no use to me."

Fin dropped a reluctant Marsaili off at the bungalow. He had persuaded her it might be better if she let him talk to Tormod on his own first. The old man would have so many memories associated with Marsaili that it might cloud his recollection. He didn't tell her that he had other business he wanted to attend to en route.

His car was barely out of sight of the cottage when he turned off the road, and up the narrow asphalt track and over the cattle grid to the sprawling car park in front of Crobost Church. It was a bleak, uncompromising building. No carved stonework or religious friezes, no stained-glass windows, no bell in the bell tower. This was God without distraction. A God who regarded entertainment as sin, art as religious effigy. There was no organ or piano inside. Only the plaintive chanting of the faithful rang around its rafters on the Sabbath.

He parked at the foot of the steps leading to the manse, and climbed to the front door. Sunlight was still washing across the patchwork green and brown of the machair, bog cotton ducking and diving among the scars left by the peat-cutters. It was exposed up here, closer to God, Fin supposed, a constant trial of faith against the elements.

It was almost a full minute after he had rung the bell that the door opened, and Donna's pale, bloodless face peered out at him from the darkness. He was as shocked now as he had been the first time he set eyes on her. Then, she hadn't looked old enough to be three months pregnant. She looked no older in motherhood. Her father's thick sandy hair was drawn back from a narrow face devoid of make-up. She seemed frail and tiny, like a child. Painfully thin in skin-tight jeans and a white T-shirt. But she looked at him with old eyes. Knowing, somehow, beyond her years.

For a moment she said nothing. Then, "Hello, Mr. Macleod."

"Hello Donna. Is your father in?"

A momentary disappointment flickered across her face. "Oh. I thought you might have come to see the baby."

And immediately he felt guilty. Of course, it would have been expected of him. But he felt, in a strange way, disconnected. Unemotional. "Another time."

Resignation settled like dust on her child's features. "My dad's in the church. Fixing a hole in the roof."

Fin was several steps down when he stopped and looked back to find her still watching him. "Do they know?" he said.

She shook her head.

He heard the hammering as he entered the vestibule, but it wasn't until he walked into the church itself that he found its source. Donald Murray was at the top of a ladder up on the balcony, perched precariously among the rafters, nailing replacement planking along the east elevation of the roof. He wore blue workman's overalls. His sandy hair was greyer, and thinning more rapidly now, it seemed. So concentrated was he on the job in hand that he didn't notice Fin standing among the pews watching him from below, and as Fin stood there looking up, a whole history spooled through his mind. Of adventures on bonfire night, parties on the beach, riding down the west coast on a fine summer's day in a red car with the roof down.

There was a pause in the hammering as Donald searched for more nails. "It seems you spend more time working as an odd-job man in this church than you do preaching the word of God," Fin called to him.

Donald was so startled he almost fell off his ladder, and had to steady himself with a hand on the nearest rafter. He looked down, but it was a moment before recognition came. "God's work takes many forms, Fin," he said when finally he realized who it was.

"I've heard it said that God makes work for idle hands, Donald. Perhaps he blew that hole in your roof to keep you out of mischief."

Donald couldn't resist a smile. "I don't think I've ever met any-one quite as cynical as you, Fin Macleod."

"And I've never met anyone quite as pig-headed as you, Donald Murray."

"Thanks, I'll take that as a compliment."

Fin found himself grinning. "You should. I could think of much worse things to say."

"I don't doubt it." Donald gazed down on his visitor with clear appraisal in his eyes. "Is this a personal visit or a professional one?"

"I don't have a profession any more. So I suppose it's personal."

Donald frowned, but didn't ask. He hung his hammer from a loop on his belt and started carefully down the ladder. By the time he had descended into the church Fin noticed that he was a little breathless. The lean figure of the once athletic young man, sports-man, rebel, and darling of all the girls, was beginning to go to seed. He looked older, too, around the eyes, where his flesh had lost its tautness and was shot through with lines like fine scars. He shook Fin's outstretched hand. "What can I do for you?"

"Your father married Marsaili's mum and dad." Fin could see the surprise in his face. Whatever he might have been expecting it wasn't that.

"I'll take your word for it. He probably married half the folk in Ness."

"What kind of proof of identity would he have required?"

Donald looked at him for several long seconds. "This sounds more professional than personal to me, Fin."

"Believe me, it's personal. I'm no longer in the force."

Donald nodded. "Okay. Let me show you." And he headed off up the aisle to the far end of the church and opened the door into the vestry. Fin followed him in and watched as he unlocked and opened a drawer in the desk there. He took out a printed form and waved it at Fin. "A marriage schedule. This one's for a couple I'm marrying next Saturday. It's provided by the registrar only after the couple have provided all the necessary documentation."

"Which is?"

"You're married, aren't you?"

"Was."

Donald's pause to absorb this information was almost imperceptible. He carried on as if he hadn't heard. "You should know, then."

"We had a quickie marriage in a registry office nearly seventeen years ago, Donald. To be honest, I remember very little about it."

"Okay, well you would have had to provide birth certificates for both of you, a decree absolute of divorce if you'd been married before, or the death certificate of your former spouse if you were a widower. The registrar won't issue the schedule unless all documentation has been provided and all forms completed. All the minister does is sign on the dotted line once the ceremony is over. Along with the happy couple and their witnesses."

"So your dad would have had no reason to doubt the identity of the people he was marrying."

Donald's eyes creased in bewilderment. "What's this about, Fin?"

But Fin just shook his head. "It's about nothing, Donald. A silly idea. Forget I ever asked."

Donald slipped the marriage schedule back into the drawer and locked it. He turned to face to Fin again. "Are you and Marsaili back together, then?"

Fin smiled. "Jealous?"

"Don't be stupid."

"No, we're not. I'm back to restore my parents' crofthouse. Pitched a tent on the croft, and roughing it till I get a roof on and some basic plumbing installed."

"So this *silly idea* that you had is all you called about?"

Fin gave him a long look, trying to subdue the flames of anger his own emotions were fanning somewhere deep inside him. He had not meant to embark on this. But it was an unequal struggle. "You know, Donald, I think you're a damned hypocrite."

Donald reacted as if he had been slapped in the face. He almost recoiled in shock. "What are you talking about?"

"You think I don't know that Catriona was pregnant when you got married?"

His face coloured. "Who told you that?"

"It's true, isn't it? The great Donald Murray, free spirit and lover of women, fucked up and got a girl pregnant."

"I'll not listen to language like that in the Lord's house."

"Why not! It's just words. I bet Jesus knew a few choice ones. You were pretty colourful yourself at one time."

Donald folded his arms. "What's your point, Fin?"

"My point is, it's all right for you to make a mistake. But God help that wee girl of yours, or Fionnlagh, if they do the same. You gave yourself a second chance because there was no one around to judge you back then. But you're not prepared to cut the same slack for your own daughter. What is it? Fionnlagh not good enough for her? I wonder what Catriona's parents thought about you."

Donald was almost white with anger. His mouth was pinched and drawn in tight. "You never get tired of judging others, do you?"

"No, that's your job." Fin jabbed a finger at the ceiling. "You and Him up there. I'm just an observer."

He turned to leave the vestry, but Donald grabbed him. Strong fingers biting into his upper arm. "What the hell's it to you anyway, Fin?"

Fin turned back and pulled his arm free. "Language, Donald. We're in the house of the Lord, remember? And you should know that *hell* is very real to some of us."

| FIFTEEN |

It was cold in here. A place suitable for the dead. The white-coated assistant slid open the drawer of the chill cabinet, and Fin found himself looking down on the remarkably well-preserved peat-stained face of a young man with boyish features who could not have been much older than Fionnlagh.

Gunn nodded to the assistant, who discreetly slipped away. He said, "This is between you and me, Mr. Macleod. Anyone finds out about this, I'm dead meat." And he flushed slightly. "If you'll pardon the pun."

Fin looked at him. "Don't think I underestimate the size of the favour, George."

"I know you don't. But it didn't stop you asking."

"You could have said no."

Gunn tilted his head in acknowledgement. "I could." Then, "Better be quick, Mr. Macleod. I'm led to believe that decomposition will progress rapidly."

Fin slipped a small digital camera from his pocket, and lined himself up to take a photograph of the young man's face. The flash reflected back off all the tiles around them. He took three or four, from different angles, then slipped the camera back in his pocket. "Anything else that might be useful for me to know?"

"He lay in a blanket of some sort, for several hours after death. It's left its pattern on his back, buttocks, his calves and the backs of his thighs. I'm waiting for the photographs from the pathologist, and we'll get an artist to make a sketch of it."

"But you've nothing to compare it with?"

"No. There was nothing found with the body. No blanket, no clothes . . ."

Gunn knocked on the door, and the assistant returned to slide the drawer shut, consigning the unknown young man they had pulled from the bog to an eternity of darkness.

Outside, the wind tugged at their jackets and trousers, spitting rain, but without serious intent. The sun was still breaking through in transient moments of illumination, quickly extinguished by an ever-changing sky. At the top of the hill they were building an extension to the hospital, the sound of drills and jackhammers carried on the wind, fluorescent orange vests and white hard hats catching fleeting fragments of sunshine.

There is always a moment of internal silence after being in the presence of death. A reminder of your own fragile mortality. The two men got back into Gunn's car without a word and sat for nearly a minute before finally Fin said, "Any chance you could slip me a copy of the post-mortem report, George?"

He heard Gunn's explosion of breath. "Jesus, Mr. Macleod!"

Fin turned his face towards him. "If you can't, just say no."

Gunn glared back at him, breathing through clenched teeth. "I'll see what I can do." He paused and then, in a voice laden with irony, "Anything else I can do for you?"

Fin smiled and held up his camera. "You can tell me where I can get prints made of these."

Malcolm J. Macleod's photography shop was in a whitewashed roughcast building in Point Street, or what they called The Narrows, where generations of island kids had gathered on Friday and Saturday nights to drink and fight, smoke dope and indulge teenage hormones. The smell of fat and fried fish carried on the breeze from the fish and chip shop two doors along.

When the photographs of the dead man had downloaded from Fin's camera and appeared on the computer screen, the shop assistant cast curious looks in their direction. But George Gunn's was a well-known face in the town, and so whatever questions there might have been remained unasked.

Fin looked carefully at the images. The flash of his camera had flattened the features a little, but the face was still perfectly recognisable to anyone who might have known him. He picked the best of them and tapped it with his finger. "That one, please."

"How many copies?"

"Just the one."

Fin was intercepted in the hallway as he entered the Dun Eisdean care home. An anxious young woman with dark hair drawn back in a ponytail. She ushered him into her office.

"You were with Tormod Macdonald's daughter when she brought him in yesterday, weren't you, Mr. er . . ."

"Macleod. Yes. I'm a friend of the family."

She nodded nervously. "I've been trying to get hold of her all morning, without any luck. There's been a bit of trouble."

Fin frowned. "What kind of trouble?"

"Mr. Macdonald . . . how can I put it . . . tried to escape."

Fin's eyebrows shot up in surprise. "Escape? This isn't a prison, is it?"

"No, of course not. Residents are free to come and go as they please. But this happened in the middle of the night. And, naturally, the doors were locked for reasons of security. It seems that Mr. Macdonald spent yesterday evening spreading discontent among some of the other residents, and there were four of them trying to get out."

Fin couldn't resist a smile. "A one-man escape committee?"

"It's no laughing matter, Mr. Macleod. Mr. Macdonald got up into the sink and smashed the kitchen window with his bare hands. He was quite badly cut."

Fin's amusement evaporated. "Is he all right?"

"We had to take him up to the emergency room at the hospital. They put stitches in one of his hands. He's back now, all bandaged up, and in his room. But he's been really quite aggressive, shouting at the staff, refusing to take off his hat and coat. He says he's waiting for his daughter to come and take him home." She sighed and moved away to her desk, opening up a beige folder. "We'd like to discuss medication with Miss Macdonald."

"What kind of medication?"

"I'm afraid I can only discuss that with the family."

"You want to drug him."

"It's not a question of drugging him, Mr. Macleod. He is in a very agitated state. We need to calm him down in case he does any more damage to himself. Or anyone else for that matter."

Fin ran the probable consequences of such medication through his mind. A memory already fragile and fragmented, dulled by tranquillisers. It could only inhibit their attempts to stimulate his recollection of past events and establish his relationship to the dead man. But they couldn't risk him doing further injury to himself. He said, "You'd better try calling Marsaili again and talk to her about it. But let me see what I can do to calm him down. I was going to take him out for a run in the car anyway, if that's all right?"

"Oh, I think that would be a good idea, Mr. Macleod. Anything to reinforce the idea in his mind that this is not a prison, and he is not a prisoner."

| SIXTEEN |

Who is it now? I'm not budging. They can all go to hell.

The door opens and there is a young man standing there. I've seen him before somewhere. Does he work here?

"Hello, Mr. Macdonald," he says, and there is something comforting in his voice. Familiar.

"Do I know you?"

"It's Fin."

Fin. Fin. Strange name. Shark's fin. Tail fin. French fin. "What kind of name's that?"

"Short for Finlay. I was Fionnlagh till I went to school, then they gave me my English name. Finlay. It was Marsaili who called me Fin." He sits down beside me on the bed.

I feel hope lifting me. "Marsaili? Is she here?"

"No, but she asked me if I would take you out for a wee run in the car. She said you would like that."

I am disappointed. But it would be nice to get out for a bit. I've been stuck in here for a while now. "I would."

"And I see you're all dressed up and ready to go."

"Always." I can feel a smile creeping up on me. "You're a good lad, Fin. You always were. But you shouldn't have been coming round the farm when your folks had forbidden it."

Fin is smiling, too, now. "You remember that, do you?"

"I do. Your mother was furious. Mary was scared she'd think we'd been encouraging it. How are your folks, by the way?"

He doesn't answer. He's looking at my hands, and lifts my right forearm. "They tell me you cut yourself, Mr. Macdonald."

"Did I?" I look at my hands and see white bandages wrapped around them. Oh! What the hell happened? I feel a spike of fear. "God," I say, quite shaken. "You'd think it would hurt. But I don't feel anything. Is it bad?"

"They gave you some stitches, apparently. Up at the hospital. You were trying to escape."

"Escape?" The very word lifts my spirits.

"Yes. But, you know, Mr. Macdonald, you're not locked in here. You can come and go when you like. Just like a hotel. As long as you let people know."

"I want to go home," I say.

"Well, you know what they say, Mr. Macdonald. Home is where your hat is."

"Do they?" Who the hell are *they*?

"Yes, they do."

"Well, where's my hat?"

Fin grins at me. "It's on your head."

I can feel my own surprise, and put my hand up to find my hat there right enough. I take it off and look at it. Good old hat. It's been with me for many a long year. I laugh now. "So it is. I didn't realize."

He helps me gently to my feet.

"Wait, I'll have to get my bag."

"No, you'd best leave it here, Mr. Macdonald. You'll need your things when you get back."

"I'm coming back?"

"Of course. You'll need to come back to hang up your hat. Remember? Home is where your hat is."

I look at the hat, still held in my bandaged hands, and laugh again. I put it firmly back on my head. "You're right. I'd almost forgotten."

I love to see the sun on the ocean, like this. You know that it's deep out there, because it's such a dark blue. It's only in the sandy shallows that it's green, or turquoise. None of that here, though. The sand shelves away almost immediately. It's the undertow that does it. You always hear stories of folk drowning here. Incomers or visitors, mostly. The sand fools them, because it's so soft, and fine, and yellow, and safe. The locals wouldn't dream of going in the water, except in a boat. Most of them can't swim, anyway. Dammit, what's the name of this beach again?

"Dalmore," Fin says.

I didn't realize I'd said that out loud. But, aye. Dalmore beach, that's right. I recognized it as soon as we turned down on the shore road, past the cottages and the wheelie bins to the cemetery. Poor souls laid to rest up there on the machair, the sea eating away at them.

These damn pebbles are big. Hard to walk on. But the sand's easier. Fin helps me take off my shoes and socks, and I feel the sand now between my toes. Soft, and warmed by the sun. "Makes me think of Charlie's beach," I say.

Fin stops and gives me an odd look. "Who's Charlie?"

"Oh, no one you'd know. He's a long time dead." And I laugh and laugh.

On the sand below the reinforcements at the cemetery wall, he spreads the travelling rug he took from the boot of the car, and we sit down. He has some bottles of beer. Cold, but not chilled. All right, though. He opens a couple and passes me one, and I enjoy that stuff foaming in my mouth, just like the very first time on the roof of The Dean.

The sea's a bit wild out there in the wind, breaking white all around those rock stacks. I can even feel a hint of spray on my face. Light, like the touch of a feather. Wind's blown all the clouds away now. There were days out on the moor I'd have killed for a piece of blue sky like that.

Fin's taking something out of his bag to show me. A photograph, he says. It's quite big. I bury the base of my beer bottle in the sand to keep it upright, and take the photograph. It's a bit awkward with my hands bandaged like this.

"Oh." I turn to Fin. "Is this a coloured man?"

"No, Mr. Macdonald. I thought it might be someone you know."

"Is he sleeping?"

"No, he's dead." He seems to wait, while I look at it. Expecting me to say something. "Is that Charlie, Mr. Macdonald?"

I look at him and laugh out loud. "No, it's not Charlie. How would I know what Charlie looks like? You daft *balach*!"

He smiles, but he looks a bit uncertain. I can't think why. "Take a good look at the face, Mr. Macdonald."

So I look at it, carefully, like he asks. And now that I see beyond the colour of the skin, there is something familiar about those features. Strange. That slight turn of the nose. Just like Peter's. And the tiny scar on his upper lip, at the right-hand corner of the mouth. Peter had a little scar like that. Cut himself on a chipped water glass once when he was about four. And, oh . . . that scar on his left temple. Didn't notice that before.

Suddenly it dawns on me who it is, and I lay the photo in my lap. I can't bear to look at it any more. I *promised*! I turn to Fin. "He's dead?"

Fin nods, looking at me so strangely. "Why are you crying, Mr. Macdonald?"

Peter asked me that same thing, too, once.

Saturdays were the best. Free of school, free of God, free of Mr. Anderson. If we had some money we could go up into the town to spend it. Not that we had money very often, but that wouldn't stop us going. Just a fifteen-minute walk and you were in another world.

The castle dominated the town, sitting up there on that big black rock, casting its shadow on the gardens below. And people all along the whole length of the street, in and out of shops and cafes, motor cars and buses belching great clouds of exhaust fumes into the air.

We had a wee scam going, me and Peter. We would sometimes go up into town on a Saturday morning, wearing our oldest clothes and our scruffiest shoes with the soles flapping away from the uppers, and we hung a little cardboard sign around Peter's neck, with the word BLIND scrawled on it. It's a good job we had a half-decent education and knew how to spell it. Of course, we had no idea then how hanging a cardboard notice around our necks would come back to haunt us.

Peter closed his eyes, and put his left hand on my right forearm, and we would move slowly among the weekend shoppers, Peter with his cap in his hand held out in front of him.

It was always the good ladies of the town who would take pity on us. "Awww, poor wee laddie," they would say, and if we were lucky drop a shilling in the cap. That's how we got enough money together to pay for Peter's tattoo. And it took all our ill-gotten weekend gains for a month or more to do it.

Peter was Elvis-daft. All the newspapers and magazines were full of him in those days. It was hard to miss the man, or the music. Everything back then, in the years after the war, had to be American, and before we started saving up for the tattoo, we used to go to the Manhattan Cafe next door to the Monseigneur News Theatre. It was long and narrow, with booths that you slid into, like an American diner. The walls were lined by mirrors etched with New York skylines. Considering how we spent the other six days of the week, it was like escape to paradise. A tantalising glimpse of how life might have been. A coffee or a Coke would use up all our cash, but we would make it last and sit listening to Elvis belting out on the jukebox.

Heartbreak Hotel. It conjured up such romantic images. New York city streets, flashing neon lights, steam rising from manhole covers. That slow walking bass, the jazz piano tinkling away in the background. And that moody, mouthy voice.

The tattoo shop was in Rose Street, next door to a working man's pub. It was a pretty seedy single room, with a space off the back separated by a vomit-green curtain with shredded hems. It smelled of ink and old blood. There were brittle and faded sketches and photographs pinned around the walls, of designs and tattooed arms and backs. The tattoo artist himself had tattoos on both forearms. A broken heart with an arrow through it, an anchor, Popeye. A girl's name, Angie, in fancy curlicued lettering.

He had a mean, underfed face, with fusewire sideburns. The last shreds of head hair were scraped back from a receded hairline across a shiny, almost bald, pate, to a luxuriant gathering of Brylcreemed curls around his neck. I noticed the dirt beneath his fingernails, and worried that Peter would catch some horrible infection. But perhaps it was just ink.

I don't know how much regulation there was in those days, or if it was even legal to tattoo a boy of Peter's age, but the Rose Street tattoo artist didn't care much about it if there was. He was taken aback when we said we wanted a tattoo of Elvis Presley. He'd never done one before, he said, and I think he saw it as a sort of challenge. He gave us a price: £2, which was a fortune in those days. I think he thought there was no way we could afford it, but if he was surprised when we turned up with the money nearly six weeks later he never showed it. He had prepared a sketch, from a photograph in a magazine, and worked the lettering below it, *Heartbreak Hotel*, into something like a banner blowing in the breeze.

It took hours, and a lot of blood, and Peter bore it without a single word of complaint. I could see in his face how painful it was, but he was never going to admit it. Stoic, he was. A martyr to his dream.

I sat with him the whole afternoon, listening to the whine of the tattoo gun, watching the needles engraving flesh, and admired my brother's fortitude as ink and blood got wiped away with every other stroke.

I would have done anything for Peter. I knew how frustrated he got sometimes, aware of his limitations. But he never got angry, or swore, or had a bad word for anyone. He was a good soul, my brother. Better than me. I never had any illusions about that. And he deserved better in life.

By the end of the afternoon, his arm was a mess. It was impossible to see the tattoo for the blood, which was already starting to dry in a patchwork of scabs. The tattoo man washed it with soapy water and dried it off with paper towels before wrapping it in a lint bandage which he fixed in place with a safety pin.

"Take this off in a couple of hours," he said, "and wash the tattoo regularly. Always pat it dry and don't rub it. You need air for the wound to heal properly, so don't cover it up." He handed me a small jar with a yellow lid. "Tattoo Goo. Rub this into the wound after every washing. Just enough to keep it moist. You don't want a scab to form. But if it does, don't peel it off, you'll pull the ink out. As the skin heals it will form a membrane. And eventually that will flake off. If you look after it carefully it should be fully healed in about two weeks."

He knew his stuff that man. It took about twelve days to heal, and it was only then that we saw what a good job he had done. There was no doubting that it was Elvis Presley on Peter's right forearm, and the way he'd worked in the banner lettering of *Heartbreak Hotel* it looked like the collar of his shirt. Very clever.

Of course, we had to go to some lengths to keep it hidden during that time. Peter always wore long sleeves around The Dean, and at school, even though it was still summer. On bath night he bandaged it up again and kept it out of the water. I told the other boys that he was suffering from psoriasis, a skin condition that I'd read about somewhere in a magazine, so the tattoo remained our secret.

Until that fateful day in late October.

Peter's problem was that just as a leaky bucket can't hold water, he couldn't keep a secret. So open was he, so incapable of dishonesty or concealment, that sooner or later he was bound to tell someone about the tattoo. If only for the pleasure he would derive from showing it off.

He used to sit sometimes just looking at it. Holding his arm in different positions, twisting his head this way and that to see it from various angles. The biggest kick he got was from gazing at his reflection in the mirror. Seeing it in full context, as if it were someone else, someone worthy of admiration and respect. There was a tiny broken heart between the *Heartbreak* and *Hotel*. Red. The only colour in the whole tattoo. He loved that tiny splash of crimson, and I sometimes found him touching it, almost stroking it. But most of all he loved the sense that, somehow, Elvis belonged to him, and would always be with him. A constant companion for the rest of what turned out to be his short life.

There was early snow that year. Not a lot of it. But it lay on the roofs, and in ledges along the walls, and dusted the branches of trees newly naked after unusually strong autumn winds. Everything else seemed darker, blacker, in contrast. The fast-flowing water of the river, the soot-blackened stone of the old mills, and the workers' tenements in the village. There was a leaden quality about the sky, but a glow in it, too. Like a natural lightbox diffusing sunshine. It cast no shadows. The air was crisp and cold and stung your nostrils. The snow had frozen and it crunched underfoot.

It was morning break at the school, and our voices rang out, sharp and brittle in the icy air, breath billowing about our heads like dragon smoke. I saw Peter at the centre of a small clutch of boys near the gate. But by the time I got there it was too late. He could hardly have chosen to show off Elvis in more dangerous company. They were the three Kelly brothers, and a couple of their friends. Equally unsavoury. We only ever hung out with the Kellys because they were Catholics, too, and we were all made to stand out in the cold waiting for the Proddies to finish their morning service. It bred a sort of camaraderie, even among enemies.

The Kellys were a bad lot. There were four boys. One much younger, who wasn't at our school yet. The two middle boys, Daniel and Thomas, were about my age, with a year between them. And Patrick was a year older. People said their father was involved with some notorious Edinburgh gang, and that he'd spent time in prison. He was rumoured to have a scar that ran in an arc from the left-hand corner of his mouth to the lobe of his left ear, like an extension of his lower lip. I never saw him, but the image conjured by that description always stayed with me.

Catherine got there before I did, because even then she'd become protective towards Peter. Although she was younger than me, and just about the same age as Peter, she fussed and mothered us both. Not in any sentimental kind of way. Hers was a bossy, almost brutal kind of mothering, perhaps born of experience. No gentle warnings, or loving pats on the head. A kick in the arse and a mouthful of abuse was much more Catherine's style.

I arrived among the group just in time to see her shock at the tattoo on Peter's arm. We had never told her about it, and the look she flashed me conveyed all the hurt she felt at not having been included.

Peter had his jacket off and his sleeve rolled up. Even the Kelly boys, who were not impressed by much, were wide-mouthed in admiration. But Patrick was the one to see mileage in the situation.

"You're going to be in trouble when they find out about that, Daftie," he said. "Who did it?"

"It's a secret," Peter said defensively. He started rolling down his sleeve. But Patrick grabbed his arm.

"That's a pro job, init? Bet that guy could be in big trouble for scarring a boy your age. What are you, fifteen? I'd say you'd need parents' permission for something like that." He laughed then, and there was a cruelty in his voice. "Course, since you don't have any, that would make it a wee bit difficult."

"Better to have no parents than a father who's been in the fucking jail." Catherine's voice cut through the laughter of the boys, and Patrick turned a dangerous look in her direction.

"You shut your mouth ya wee shite." He took a step towards her and I moved smartly between them.

"And you watch yours, Kelly."

Patrick Kelly's pale green eyes met mine. He had ginger hair and a face the colour of porridge. It was spattered with freckles. He was an ugly boy. I could see the calculation in his gaze. He was a big lad, but so was I. "What's it to you?"

"I'm a bit sensitive to bad language."

There was some laughter, and the eldest Kelly boy didn't like that. He glared at his brothers. "Shut the fuck up." Then he turned back to me. "So they let kids at The Dean get tattoos if they want, do they?" he said. And when I didn't reply, he grinned. "Why do I get the feeling that Daftie'll be in deep shit if they ever find out?"

"Why would they ever find out?"

"Someone might tell them." Patrick Kelly smiled disingenuously.

"Like who?"

His smile vanished and he leaned his face into mine. "Like me."

I stood my ground, flinching only from the stink of decaying teeth that he breathed in my face. "Only cowards tell tales."

"Are you calling me a fucking coward?"

"I'm not calling you anything. Cowards reveal themselves by their own actions."

The anger and humiliation of someone showing themselves to be smarter than him combined to make him brave. He stabbed my chest with his finger. "We'll see who's a fucking coward." He nodded his head towards the road bridge that soared overhead, connecting the city to the western suburbs. Thomas Telford's second-last, I would learn much later in life. "There's a ledge runs along the outside of the bridge, just below the parapet. It's about nine inches wide. Up there tonight. Midnight. You and me. We'll see who can walk it."

I glanced up at the bridge. Even from here I could see the snow crusted along the length of the ledge. "No way."

"Scared, are you?"

"He's a fucking coward," said one of the younger brothers.

"I'm not stupid," I said.

"Shame about your brother, then, eh? Guess they might even kick him out. Put him in a hostel. A load of shit like that on his arm. Guess you wouldn't be too happy about being separated."

It was a real possibility. I felt the net of inevitability closing around me. "And if I do it?"

"Elvis'll be our secret. Unless, of course, you chicken out halfway. In which case I'll tell."

"And you're going to do this walk, too?"

"Sure I am."

"And what do *I* get out of that?"

"The pleasure of calling me a coward if I chicken out."

"And if you don't?"

"I get the pleasure of proving you wrong."

"Don't do it." Catherine's voice came from behind me, low and laden with warning.

"Shut up, slag!"

I felt Kelly's spittle in my face and glanced towards Peter. I wasn't sure if he understood the gravity of his situation, or the trouble he'd got me into by showing off like this. "I'll come with you," he said earnestly.

"See? Even Daftie's got more balls than you." Kelly was gloating now. He knew he had me cornered.

I shrugged. Trying to be dead casual. "Okay. But let's make it a little more interesting. I'll go first. We'll time it. And whoever is slower has to do it again."

And for the first time I saw Patrick Kelly's confidence waver. It was his turn to be trapped. "No problem."

What stupid boys we were! As Catherine was quick enough to point out to me when I pulled Peter away across the playground to give him a piece of my mind.

"You're insane," she said. "It's about a hundred foot fucking high, that bridge. If you fall you're dead. Nothing surer."

"I won't fall."

"Well, I hope you don't. Cos if you do, I won't have the chance to say I told you so." She paused. "How are you going to get out of The Dean?"

I had never told anyone about my night-time jaunts to the village and the cemetery, and was a little reluctant now to reveal my secret. "Oh, there's a way," I said casually.

"Well, you'd better fucking tell me. Cos I'm coming, too."

"And me," Peter piped in.

I stopped and glared from one to the other. "No, you're not. Either of you."

"And who's going to fucking stop us?" Catherine said.

"Aye, who's going to fucking stop us?" Peter puffed up his chest defiantly. It was almost shocking to hear him swear like that. Catherine was a bad influence. But I knew I was beaten.

I said to Catherine, "Why would you want to come anyway?"

"Well, if you're going to do the walk against the clock, someone's got to keep the time." She paused and sighed. "Besides, if you do fall, someone needs to be there to make sure Peter gets safely back to The Dean."

I couldn't have slept at lights out, even if I had wanted to. Three hours to go and I was feeling sick. What on earth had possessed me to get sucked into this stupid dare? Even more annoying, Peter had fallen asleep almost immediately, with an absolute confidence that I would wake him when it was time to go. I toyed with the idea of sneaking out without him, but knew that the uncertain nature of his response if waking to find me gone would only make it dangerous for both of us.

And so I lay beneath the blankets, unable for some reason to get warm, and shivered from the cold and my own fear. Of course, word had spread like wildfire amongst the kids at school and everyone at The Dean that there was a dare between the Kellys and the McBrides. No one seemed to know why, but I knew it wouldn't be long before Peter's tattoo became public knowledge, and then only a matter of time before the powers that be got wind of it, too.

The future seemed a scary thing, then, obscured as it was by the darkness of unpredictability. I had the sense of my life, and Peter's, slipping out of our hands. And while we'd had no control over our incarceration in The Dean, the place had provided, in that last year, a degree of comfort, if only in the brutal certainty of its routine.

Time passed both slowly and quickly. Every time I checked my watch it seemed only five minutes later. And then suddenly it was fifteen minutes to midnight. I wondered if, at the last, I had somehow dozed off without realising it. But now my heart was hammering away, beating right up into my throat, nearly choking me. It was time to go.

I slipped out from between the sheets, fully dressed, and pulled on my shoes. They had thick rubber soles that I hoped would give me some grip. I tied my laces with trembling fingers and jiggled Peter by the shoulder. To my irritation it took him some time to wake up. When finally he had shaken himself free of sleep and some undeservedly happy dream, the memory of what we were to be about that night returned to him, and his eyes shone with anticipation. "Time to go?" he whispered loudly.

I put my finger to my lips and glared at him.

It wasn't until we reached the door of the dormitory that I realized just how many others were awake, too. Voices whispered in the dark.

"Good luck, Johnny."

"Show the fucker what the Dean boys are made of."

I felt like saying, "You fucking show him!"

Catherine was waiting for us at the foot of the cellar stairs. She had a torch with her, and shone it in our faces as we came down. It almost blinded me.

"For God's sake put that away!" I raised my hand to shade my eyes. And then, when the light went out, plunging us into darkness again, almost fell. "Jesus!"

"You're late!" she whispered. "It's scary as hell down here. Something keeps making strange clunking noises. And there are things scurrying about the floor. I'm sure it's rats."

I slid back the bolt to release the door, and felt the cold night air rush in as I opened it. There was a real smell of winter on its leading edge, and I could see stars, like pinholes in the black sheet that was the sky, revealing an imagined light that lay behind it. A light that was reflected in the frost that glistened all across the black of the tarmac. Heaven perfectly mirrored on earth. Or hell perfectly reflected above.

By the time we got down into the village we could hear a clock somewhere striking midnight. It pealed through the cold, clear night air, like a bell ringing for the dead, sonorous and deep and filled with a dreadful prescience. The hike up Bell's Brae in the dark, past the silent mews houses, was slow and treacherous. Snow had fallen, then melted where the sun had touched it, then frozen. By the time we reached Kirkbrae House at the top of the hill we were, all three of us, sweating from the effort. They had told us at school that the turreted and step-gabled Kirkbrae House, half of which disappeared down below the bridge, had been a tavern in the seventeenth century. I'd have given anything right then for a glass of the fine fizzing ale they had drunk back in those days. Something to stop my tongue from sticking to the roof of my mouth, and restore the courage I felt deserting me as the bridge approached.

The Kelly boys were waiting for us where the first arch of the bridge began, huddled in the shadow of Kirkbrae House. The town was deserted and as silent as Dean Cemetery. There wasn't a car on the road, or a light in any of the windows of the stone terraces that marched up Queensferry Street towards the west-end. But the moon reflected off every snow-covered surface of the village below. Only the black waters of the river itself were completely lost in darkness.

"You're late!" Patrick Kelly hissed from the shadows. "We've been waiting here for ages. And it's fucking freezing!"

I could hear him stamping and clapping his gloved hands together, trying to keep warm, and I wished I had gloves, too.

"Well, we're here now," I said. "And we might as well get started. Me first." I moved towards the parapet, but felt Patrick's big open hand pushing into my chest.

"No. Me first. I've been hanging around here long enough. Who's going to time it?"

"I am." Catherine stepped forward into the pale yellow glow of an electric street lamp and opened her hand to reveal an engraved silver stopwatch with a pink ribbon attached to it.

One of the other Kelly boys grabbed her wrist to get a better look, and you could hear the envy in his voice. "Where'd you steal that?"

Catherine pulled her wrist free and closed protective fingers around it again. "I didn't steal it. My dad gave me it."

Patrick said, "Okay, Danny, you check she disnae cheat." And he reached up to grasp the wrought-iron spikes that ran along the curve of the parapet, to pull himself up and over, feet sliding and scraping on the ice, till he had lowered himself down to the ledge below.

I had crossed the bridge on many occasions, but it was the first time I had really examined the parapet. I learned later that they had raised it about fifty years before to stop people throwing themselves off. What is it about bridges that lures folk to kill themselves by jumping off them? Whatever it is, the only thing that concerned me then was not falling off.

The bridge was carried on four arches from Kirkbrae House at the south end to the towering Gothic presence of the Holy Trinity Church at the other. It was one hundred and six feet above the river at its highest point, and maybe one hundred and fifty yards across. The ledge was wide enough to walk on. Just. If you didn't look down, or think too much about it. The problem came when it circumvented each of the vertical supports for the three columns. These were angled, and took you away from the safety of the parapet, where it was always possible to grab on to one of the spikes.

I felt my stomach flip over. It was madness. What in God's name was I doing here? I could hardly breathe.

I could see from Patrick's face that he was scared, too. But he was doing his best to hide it. "Okay, start the watch," he called, and we all leaned over as Catherine depressed the starter button, and Patrick Kelly set off across the bridge.

I was amazed at how quickly he moved, spreading himself wide, facing the parapet and moving sideways along the ledge, leaning in to let his hands guide him. He embraced each arch support, almost lying across the top of it, as he shuffled his feet around the ledge. Danny stayed at the Kirkbrae end, watching the stopwatch with Catherine, and me and Peter and Patrick's other brother, Tam, followed him from the safety of the pavement.

I could hear Patrick's breathing, laboured, from fear and effort. His breath exploded around him in the moonlight. I could just see the top of his head, and the concentration in his eyes. Peter hung on to my arm, absolutely focused on Patrick's progress. Even though this was the boy who was threatening to give away the secret of his Elvis tattoo, Peter genuinely feared for his safety. Such was his empathy. Tam called out constant encouragement to his brother, and when finally Patrick reached the church and hauled himself back on to the road side with trembling arms, he let out loud whoops of triumphant joy.

Catherine and Danny came running across to join us.

"Well?" Patrick said, his face positively glowing now with jubilation.

"Two minutes, twenty-three seconds," Danny said. "Straight up, Paddy."

Patrick turned his jubilation on me. "Your turn."

I glanced at Catherine and could see apprehension burning in her dark eyes. "How's the ice on that side?" I said to Patrick.

He grinned. "Slippy as fuck."

I felt my heart sinking into my boots. Two minutes, twenty-three seconds seemed very fast. And I knew that if I couldn't beat that time, then I would have to do it again. And Patrick's whole demeanour oozed confidence. He didn't believe for one moment that I would be faster than him. And, to be honest, neither did I. But there was no point in dwelling on it, to be defeated by my own fear.

I climbed up on to the parapet, and holding on to the top spikes, slid my feet down the other side of it until they reached the ledge. The iron of the spikes was icy cold, biting into already frozen hands. But I held on to them, testing the frosted snow beneath my feet. To my surprise, my rubber soles provided an amazing amount of grip. And I finally let go to find myself balanced on the curve of the ledge, with almost four hundred feet of it stretching ahead of me. If I crossed it using the same technique as Patrick, then whether or not I bettered his time was in the lap of the gods. But if I used my outstretched arms for balance and walked straight, as along a line of kerbstones, I was sure I could do it faster. As long as I didn't slip.

Only when I reached the arch supports would I have to resort to Patrick's method of getting around them.

I drew a deep breath, resisting the temptation to look down, and called out, "All right, start the watch." And I set off with my eyes firmly fixed on Kirkbrae House at the other end. I could feel the frozen snow creaking beneath my feet, my left arm raised higher than my right to avoid touching the parapet. The slightest miscalculation, even the smallest nudge of the parapet wall, would likely send me spinning off into space.

I reached the first arch support and flung my arms around it, sliding my feet sideways along the ledge, as I had seen Patrick do. Then steadied myself at the far side of it for the next length. I was filled with a strange sense of elation, feeling as if I could almost break into a run. Of course, that would have been impossible, but confidence surged through me now and I increased my speed, one careful foot in front of the other. From the far side of the parapet I could hear Tam's voice. "Jesus, Paddy, he's fast!"

And Peter. "Go, Johnny, go!"

By the time I reached Kirkbrae House, and pulled myself over the parapet to safety, I knew I'd done it faster. Patrick knew it too, and I could already see his apprehension growing as we waited for Catherine and Danny to run across the bridge to join us.

Danny's face was a mask of trepidation. Catherine's split by a triumphant smile.

"Two minutes, five seconds," Danny said, his voice barely a whisper.

I didn't care any more. I'd won the dare. And if Patrick Kelly was a boy of his word, then Peter's secret was safe, at least for a while. "Let's call it quits."

Patrick's mouth tightened into a bleak line. He shook his head. "No fucking way. Whoever was slower had to do it again. That was the deal."

"It doesn't matter," I said.

I saw the jut of the older boy's jaw. "It does to me." And he grabbed the spikes and pulled himself back on to the parapet.

Tam said, "Come on, Paddy, let's just go home."

Patrick dropped down on to the ledge. "Just start the fucking watch, will you?"

Danny looked at me as if there might be something I could do about it. I shrugged. I'd done my best. Catherine started the watch. "Go!" she shouted, and Patrick set off, adopting my technique this time. But even from the start I could see that it wasn't going to work for him. His shoes didn't appear to be providing the same grip as mine. He stopped several times during the span of the first arch, fighting to regain his balance. Tam and Peter and I ran along beside him, jumping up every few feet to get a clearer view.

I could see the sweat beading across his forehead, catching the light of the moon, his freckles a dark splatter across the whiteness of his face. The fear in his eyes was clear, but displaced by his own desperate need for self-esteem. To prove himself not only to us, but to himself. I heard him gasp as he lost his footing, saw his hand grasping at fresh air, and thought for one awful moment that he was gone. But his hand found the curve of the parapet, and he steadied himself.

We were about halfway across when I heard Danny's voice shouting from the Kirkbrae end. "Police!" And almost at the same time I heard the sound of a car's engine approaching from the direction of Randolph Place. He and Catherine ducked into the shadow of Kirkbrae House, but we were totally exposed out there on the bridge, me and Peter and Tam, with nowhere to hide.

"Down!" I shouted, and crouched against the wall, pulling Peter down with me. Tam dropped to his hunkers beside us. We could only hope that somehow the black patrol car would pass by without seeing us. For a moment we seemed caught in its headlights, before it appeared to accelerate past. I felt a huge wave of relief wash over me. And then there was a squeal of brakes, and the sound of tyres skidding on frosted tarmac. "Shit!"

"Run for it!" Tam shouted.

I could hear the whine of a car's motor turning in reverse and didn't need a second telling. I was on my feet in an instant and sprinting hard for Kirkbrae House and the escape route of Bell's Brae. We hadn't covered ten yards when I realized that Peter wasn't with us. I heard Danny shouting from the far side. "What the fuck's he doing?" And Tam grabbed my arm.

We turned to see Peter crouched up on the parapet, hanging on to a spike with one hand, his other stretched out towards the panicked figure of Patrick Kelly, almost as if he had pushed him. Kelly's arms were windmilling in a desperate attempt to retain his balance.

But it was already a lost cause. And without a sound he toppled into darkness. It was the silence of that moment that lives with me still. The boy never called out. Never cried, never screamed. Just fell soundlessly into the shadow of the bridge. Every fibre of me wanted to believe that somehow he would survive the fall. But I knew, beyond question, that he wouldn't.

"Fuck!" I could feel Tam's breath on my face. "He fucking pushed him!"

"No!" I knew how it looked. But I knew, too, that there was no way that Peter had done that.

Two uniformed police officers had jumped out of the patrol car now, and were running along the bridge towards us. I sprinted back to grab my brother and half drag him with me towards the others waiting at the south end. He was whimpering, desperate. His face wet and shining with tears. "He called for help," he said, gulping great lungfuls of air to feed his distress. "I tried to grab him, Johnny, honest I did."

"Hey!" the voice of one of the police officers called out in the dark. "You boys! Stop! What are you doing out here on the bridge?"

It was the signal for us to scatter. I don't know where the Kelly boys went, but me and Peter and Catherine went pell-mell down Bell's Brae, stumbling and sliding dangerously on the cobbles, hardly daring to look back. The darkness of the night, along with the shadows of buildings and trees, swallowed us into obscurity, and without a word spoken we climbed the hill at the other side towards the twin towers of The Dean.

I don't know how, but everyone at The Dean seemed to know about Patrick Kelly's fall from the bridge first thing the following morning. And then, when someone telephoned from the village to say that school had been cancelled for the day, everyone knew the worst. A boy had died falling from the bridge late the night before. None of the staff knew yet who it was. But there wasn't a boy or girl at The Dean who didn't.

Oddly, none of the others asked us what had happened. It was as if we were contaminated somehow, and no one wanted to catch what we had. All the inmates fell into their usual cliques, but gave Catherine, Peter and me a very wide berth.

We sat around in the dining room, the three of us, waiting for the inevitable. And it came just before midday.

A police car roared up the drive and pulled in at the foot of the steps. Two uniformed officers entered The Dean and were shown into Mr. Anderson's office. Only about ten minutes had passed before the janitor was sent to find us. He looked at us, concerned. "What have you kids been up to?" he whispered.

Being the oldest, the others looked to me, but I just shrugged. "No idea," I said.

He marched us along the bottom corridor to Mr. Anderson's room, and we felt the eyes of all our peers upon us. It was as if time had stopped, standing still, like all the kids gathered in groups to watch the condemned going to meet their maker. Each and every one of them, no doubt, thanking the Lord that it wasn't them.

Mr. Anderson was standing behind his desk, his face as ashen as his hair. The jacket of his dark suit was all buttoned up, and he had his arms folded across his chest. The two officers, helmets in hand, stood to one side, Matron on the other. The three of us lined up in front of the desk. Mr. Anderson glared at us. "I want one of you to speak for all of you."

Catherine and Peter both looked at me.

"All right, you, McBride." It was the first and only time I ever heard him call me by my name. He looked at the others. "If either of you disagree with anything he says, then speak up. Your silence will be taken as agreement." He drew a deep breath, then placed his fingertips on the desk in front of him, leaning slightly forward to let them take his weight. "You're here because a boy died last night falling from the Dean Bridge. One Patrick Kelly. You know him?"

I nodded. "Yes, sir."

"It seems there were some shenanigans on the bridge around midnight. Several boys and a girl involved." He looked pointedly at Catherine. "And there are reports of two boys and a girl from The Dean being seen in the village shortly beforehand." He pulled himself up to his full height. "I don't suppose you would have any idea who that was?"

"No, sir." I knew there was no way they could prove it, unless they had eyewitnesses to come forward and identify us. And if they had, then surely they would have been there in Mr. Anderson's office to point their fingers.

So I just denied everything. No, we hadn't left The Dean. We had been in our beds all night. No, we hadn't heard anything about Patrick Kelly's fall until this morning. And no, we had no clue as to what he or anyone else might have been doing on the bridge at that time of night.

Of course, they knew I was lying. Someone must have told them something. One of the Kelly boys, perhaps. Or one of their friends.

Mr. Anderson leaned forward on his knuckles now, and they glowed white, just like that first day almost a year before. "There is," he said, glancing at the two police officers, "some doubt about whether the boy fell, or was pushed. There will be an investigation, and anyone found guilty of pushing this boy to his death will be charged with murder. Manslaughter at the very least. This is a very, very grave matter indeed. And a dreadful blight on the reputation of The Dean, if any of its children are found to be involved. Do you understand?"

"Yes, sir."

Neither Peter nor Catherine had opened their mouths during the entire interview. Mr. Anderson looked at them now. "Does either of you have anything to add?"

"No, sir."

It was half an hour after we had been ushered from the room that the police officers finally left, and Mr. Anderson's voice could be heard booming along the corridor. "Damned Catholics! I want them out of here."

And finally Catherine's prediction came true. The priest arrived to take us away the very next morning.

| SEVENTEEN |

Fin watched the old man carefully. Sunlight caught the silver bristles on his face and on the loose flesh of his neck, and they stood out sharp against his pale, leathery skin. His eyes, by contrast, were almost opaque, obscured by memories he couldn't, or wouldn't, share. He had been quiet for a long time, and the tears had dried in salty tracks on his cheeks. His knees were pulled up to his chest, and he sat hugging them, staring out to sea with eyes that saw things Fin could not.

Fin lifted the photograph from the travelling rug, where Tormod had let it fall, and slipped it back into his bag. He took Tormod by the elbow to try to encourage him gently to his feet.

"Come on, Mr. Macdonald, let's take a walk along the water's edge."

His voice seemed to wake the old man from his reverie, and Tormod turned a look of surprise towards Fin, as if noticing him for the first time. "He didn't do it," he said, resisting Fin's attempt to get him to stand.

"Who didn't do what, Mr. Macdonald?"

But Tormod just shook his head. "Maybe he wasn't the full shilling, but he learned the Gaelic a lot faster than I did."

Fin frowned, his thoughts tossed around in a sea of confusion. On the islands, you grew up speaking Gaelic. In Tormod's day, you wouldn't have spoken English until you went to school. "You mean, he learned the *English* faster?" He had no idea who *he* was.

Tormod shook his head vigorously. "No, the *Gaelic*. Took to it like a native."

"Charlie?"

Tormod grinned, shaking his head at Fin's stupidity. "No, no, no. It would be the Italian *he* spoke." He put out a hand for Fin to help him to his feet now and stood up into the wind. "Let's get our feet wet, just like we always used to at Charlie's beach." He looked at Fin's boots. "Come on, lad, get those off you." He bent forward and began rolling up his trouser legs.

Fin kicked off his boots and pulled his socks from his feet, hoisting his trouser legs to his knees as he stood up, and the two men walked arm in arm across soft, deep sand, to where the outgoing tide had left it compacted and wet. The wind blew Tormod's coat around his legs and filled Fin's jacket. It was strong in their faces, and soft, laced with spray, blown uninterrupted across three thousand miles of Atlantic ocean.

The first foaming water broke over their feet, racing up across the slope of the sand, shockingly cold, and old Tormod laughed, exhilarated, lifting his feet quickly to step away as it receded. His cap blew off, and by some miracle Fin caught it, seeing it lift from his forehead in the moment before the wind whipped it away. Tormod laughed again, like a child, as if it were a game. He wanted to put it back on his head, but Fin folded it into his coat pocket so that they wouldn't lose it.

Fin, too, enjoyed the feel of the icy water washing over his feet, and he led them back into the last tame surge of a once towering ocean as it splashed around their ankles and calves. Both of them laughed and cried out at the shock of it.

Tormod seemed invigorated, free, at least for these few moments, of the chains of dementia that shackled his mind, and diminished his life. Happy, as in childhood, to delight in the simplest of pleasures.

They walked in and out of the brine for four or five hundred yards, towards the cluster of shining black rocks at the far end of the beach where the water broke in frothing white fury. The sound of the wind and the sea filled their ears, drowning out everything else. Pain, memory, sadness. Until finally Fin stopped and turned them around for the walk back.

They had only gone a few feet when he slipped his hand in his pocket to bring out the Saint Christopher medal on its silver chain that Marsaili's mother had given him a few hours earlier. He passed it to Tormod. "Do you remember this, Mr. Macdonald?" He had to shout above the elemental roar.

Tormod seemed surprised to see it. He stopped and took it from Fin, gazing at it lying in the palm of his hand before making a fist to close around it. Fin was shocked to see sudden tears following the tracks of their predecessors. "She gave it to me," he said, his voice almost inaudible above the din that crashed around them.

"Who?"

"Ceit."

Fin thought for a moment. Was Ceit the cause of his unreasonable hatred of Catholics. "And she was a Catholic?"

Tormod looked at him as if he were insane. "Of course. We all were." He started walking briskly along the line of the outgoing tide, wading through the water as it rushed up the sand, oblivious to it splashing around his legs and soaking his rolled-up trousers. Fin was taken by surprise and it took him several moments to catch him up. This made no sense.

"*You* were a Catholic?"

Tormod flicked him a dismissive look. "Mass every Sunday in the big church on the hill."

"At Seilebost?"

"The church the fishermen built. The one with the boat inside it."

"There was a boat in the church?"

"Beneath the altar." Tormod stopped as suddenly as he had started, standing ankle-deep in the water that broke against them, and gazed out at the horizon where the dark smudge of a distant tanker broke the line between sea and sky. "You could see Charlie's beach from up there. Beyond the cemetery. Like a line of silver painted along the shore between the purple of the machair and the turquoise of the sea." He turned and looked at Fin. "And all the dead in between wanting you to stop on the way. Some human company in the world beyond the grave."

He turned away again, and before Fin could stop him he had hurled the Saint Christopher medal into the rush of incoming water. It vanished into the swirl of sand and foam, to be sucked out by the undertow and laid to rest somewhere in the deep. Lost for ever.

"No need for papish things now," he said. "The journey's nearly over."

| EIGHTEEN |

Fin took the call from Gunn on his mobile as he left the Dun Eisdean care home. Tormod had been strangely subdued on the drive
back from Dalmore and went meekly to his room, where he allowed
staff to take off his coat without a word of protest, and lead him to
the dining room. Having eaten almost nothing the previous day he
had now, it seemed, rediscovered his appetite. And as he wolfed into
a plate of spring lamb and boiled potatoes, Fin slipped quietly out
into the midday sunshine.

He parked his car now at the top of Church Street and walked
down to where Gunn was waiting for him on the steps of the police
station. The wind was blustery and cooler here on the east coast,
rippling the water in the bay, rustling the first leaves in the trees on
the far side of it below the dark decay of Lews Castle. The two men
fell in step on the walk down to Bayhead, and saw the fishing boats
at high tide towering above the quays. Nets and creels and empty
fish boxes lay strewn across the cobbles, and the good people of
Stornoway leaned into the wind as they made their way towards the
centre of town.

As they passed a cafe with picture windows looking out on to the boats at dock, Gunn said, "Isn't that young Fionnlagh?"

Fin turned, and through the shadow of his own reflection he saw Fionnlagh and Donna together at a table on the other side of the glass. A carrycot sat on the floor between them, and Fionnlagh held his baby daughter in his arms, gazing with unglazed love into her tiny, round blue eyes. She gazed back adoringly at her father, impossibly small fingers grasping his thumb. Just as Robbie had once held Fin's.

Fin had only a moment to feel the regrets of a lifetime press down on him before Donna turned and saw him. Her face flushed with the first colour he had ever seen in it, and she turned away, speaking quickly to Fionnlagh. The boy looked up, startled. And Fin saw something strange in his eyes. Guilt? Fear? It was impossible to tell, evaporating in a moment to be replaced by a bashful smile. He nodded at Fin, who nodded back. An awkward moment, a silent exchange, the glass of the window a much easier barrier to breach than all the things left unsaid between them.

"You want to go in?" Gunn said.

Fin shook his head. "No." He gave the young couple a small half-wave, and turned away along Bayhead, making Gunn scurry to catch him up. He wondered only fleetingly why Fionnlagh wasn't at school.

They found a dark corner in The Hebridean, and Gunn ordered them a couple of half-pints of heavy. When he sat down again with their glasses, he drew an A4 manila envelope from inside his anorak and slipped it across the table. "You never got this from me."

Fin slid it into his bag. "Got what?"

Gunn grinned and they sipped in silence at their beers for a while. Then Gunn laid his glass carefully down on the beer mat in front of him and said, "I got a call about half an hour ago. The Northern Constabulary are sending a DCI from Inverness to open the murder investigation."

Fin inclined his head. "As expected."

"He probably won't be here for another week or so. It seems the powers that be don't think there's much urgency in the solving of a fifty-odd-year-old murder." He lifted his glass for another sip, then replaced it exactly on the ring it had left on the mat. "When he comes, I'll not be able to confide in you any more, Mr. Macleod. Which is a shame. Because I know you were a good cop. But the fact that you are no longer in the force is more likely to work against you than for you. I've no doubt you'll be told to keep your nose out of things."

Fin smiled. "No doubt." He took a sip from his own glass. "Where's this leading, George?"

"Well, Mr. Macleod, it seems to me we have a wee period of grace. And maybe it would be an idea to make hay while the sun shines."

"What did you have in mind?"

"Well, sir, it's in my mind to go down to Harris in the morning, to Seilebost, to check up on old Tormod Macdonald's family, and see if I can come up with any idea of who it was we took out of the peat. It would be nice to show these mainlanders that we're not all hick cops out here in the islands."

"And?"

"My motor's been playing up something terrible this last wee while. At least, that's the official story. I thought maybe you might like to give me a lift."

"Oh, did you?"

"Aye." Gunn took a longer draught of beer this time. "What do you think?"

Fin shrugged. "I think Marsaili's quite anxious for me to get to the bottom of all this."

"Aye, well, that would make sense. You being a former polis and all." He lifted his glass to his lips again, but hesitated. "Is there . . . a relationship between you two these days?"

Fin shook his head, avoiding Gunn's eye. "A lot of history, George. But no relationship." He drained his glass. "What time would you like to leave?"

As he drove back up the west coast, from Barvas through Siader and Dell, he watched the dark legions of yet another weather front assembling out on the horizon. In his rearview mirror he could still see the sun slanting across the purple-hued mountains of Harris to the south. The sky to the north remained clear, each successive village standing hard in silhouette against the light, old whitehouses, and the architecturally challenged standard homes issued in the twentieth century by the former Department of Agriculture and Fisheries. The DAF houses, as they were called, with their harled walls and steeply pitched slate roofs and tall dormers. Hopelessly inadequate, by modern standards, to withstand the ravages of the island climate.

Sun slanting across the bog to the east spun gold in the dead grass, and he saw huddled groups of villagers gathered among the trenches, wielding the long-handled *tarasgeir* to take advantage of the dry afternoon to cut and stack peat.

The dark shadow of the bleak and forbidding church at Cross signalled that he was nearly home.

Home? Was this really his home now, he wondered. This wind-ravaged corner of the earth where warring factions of an unforgiving Protestant religion dominated life. Where men and women struggled all their lives to make a living from the land, or the sea, turning in times of unemployment to the industries that came, and went again when subsidies ran out, leaving the rusting detritus of failure in their wake.

It seemed, if anything, more depressed than it had in his youth, entering again a period of decline after a brief renaissance fuelled by politicians courting votes by the spending of millions on a dying language.

But if here wasn't home, where was? Where else on God's earth did he feel such an affinity with the land, the elements, the people? And he found himself regretting that he had never brought Robbie here, to the land of his forefathers.

There was no one at Marsaili's bungalow when he stopped there, and he drove on up past his parents' croft, over the ridge, and saw the whole northern coastline stretch out ahead of him. He took a left on the road that ran down to the old Crobost harbour, where a steep concrete slipway below the winch house led to a tiny quay in the shadow of the cliffs. Coiled rope and orange buoys lay draped over piles of rusted chain. Creels for crab and lobster stood piled up against the wall. Tiny fishing dinghies lay canted at odd angles, secured to loops of rusted iron. Among them, still, the peeling remains of the boat his father had once restored, and painted purple like the house, and named after his mother. All these years later, the traces of lost lives remained.

His own among them. Sad and bittersweet memories lingered still within the decaying walls of the old whitehouse that sat up on the hill overlooking the harbour. The house where he had done most of his growing up, tolerated by an aunt who had reluctantly taken on the responsibility of her dead sister's orphan. A house empty of warmth or love.

There was still glass in the windows, and the doors were locked. But once-white walls ran black with damp, and door and window frames were rusted or rotten. Below it, on the stretch of grass along the clifftops, the deserted stone house where he had played forlornly at happy families as a boy still stood as it had then, two gable ends, two walls. No roof. No doors. No windows. Whoever had once called it home had built it for its view, but abandoned it long ago to the cruel arctic gales that assaulted this coast in winter. Long, hard winters that he remembered well.

A grassy path led down to a shingle beach. The black rocks around the cliffs had turned orange, crusted with the tiny shells of long-dead sea creatures, stained by the seaweed that rotted all along the shore. On the far headland stood three solitary cairns that had been there for as long as Fin could remember.

Nothing changed really, except for the people who came and went and left their evanescent traces.

He heard the rumbling of a car's engine above the roar of the wind, and turned to see Marsaili pulling in at the side of the road in Artair's old Astra. She got out and slammed the door, thrust hands deep into her jacket pockets, and walked slowly along the path to join him. They stood in a comfortable silence for some moments, looking at the DAF houses strung out along the cliffs on the west side of the bay, before she turned to look at the abandoned house above the harbour.

"Why don't you restore your aunt's house? It's in much better condition than your parents' place."

"Because I don't own it." Fin cast sad eyes over the neglected building. "She left it to some animal charity. Typical of her, really. They couldn't sell it, so they just left it to rot." He turned his gaze back out over the ocean. "Anyway, I wouldn't set foot in it again, even if it was mine."

"Why not?"

"Because it's haunted, Marsaili." He turned to see her frowning.

"Haunted?"

"By the young Fin, and all his unhappiness. The night before my aunt's funeral was the last time I slept in the place. And I swore I never would again."

She raised a hand to touch his cheek with feather-light fingertips. "The young Fin," she said. "I remember him. I loved him from the first moment I set eyes on him. And never forgave him for breaking my heart."

He met her eye, Gunn's question still ringing in his ears. The wind pulled her hair back from her face in long silken strands, flying out behind her like a flag of freedom. It coloured her skin pink, fine features hardened a little by time and pain, but still strong, attractive. The little girl of his childhood, the burgeoning woman of his adolescence, both still there in this cynical, funny, intelligent woman he had hurt so carelessly. But you could never go back.

"I showed your dad a photograph of the man they took from the bog," he said. "I'm pretty certain he recognized him."

She took her hand away, as if from an electric shock. "So it's true."

"Seems like it."

"I kept hoping they had made a mistake. Mixed up the DNA samples or something. Your parents are the rock you build your life on. It's a bit of a shock to find that rock is just an illusion."

"I showed him the Saint Christopher's medal and he threw it in the sea." Her consternation was apparent in the creasing of her eyes. "He said someone called Ceit had given it to him, and that they were all Catholics."

Now disbelief pushed her eyebrows up on her forehead. "He's demented, Fin. Literally. He doesn't know what he's saying."

Fin shrugged, not so sure. But he kept his misgivings to himself. He said, "George Gunn is going down to Harris tomorrow to check out your dad's family. He said I could go along. Should I?"

She nodded. "Yes." Then added quickly, "But only if you want to, Fin. If you feel you can spare the time. I have to go back to Glasgow for a few days. Exams to sit. Although, God knows, I'm hardly in the right frame of mind for it." She hesitated. "I'd appreciate it if you would keep an eye on Fionnlagh for me."

He nodded, and the wind filled the silence between them. It blew among the grasses, forced the sea against the rocks all along the northern cliffs, carried the cries of distant seagulls as they fought to master its gusts and currents. Fin and Marsaili were mercilessly battered by it as they stood on the clifftop, feeling it drag at their clothes, rushing into their mouths when they spoke, snatching their words away. Marsaili put an arm on his to steady herself, and he reached out to slip his fingers through her hair, feeling the soft, cool skin of her neck. She took an almost imperceptible step closer. He could very nearly feel her warmth. How easy it would be to kiss her.

A car horn sounded in the distance, and they turned to see a hand waving from the driver's window. Marsaili waved back. "Mrs. Macritchie," she said, and the moment was gone, carried off in the wind with their words.

| NINETEEN |

Although they are called the Isle of Lewis and the Isle of Harris, the two are in fact one island separated by a mountain range and a narrow neck of land.

The drive south, across the flat boglands of the northern half of the island, quickly becomes tortuous, a single-track road winding down among the lochs carved out of the rock by the last retreating ice sheets.

Fin and Gunn drove through the gloom of gathering storm clouds, wind and rain sweeping down off the ragged mountain slopes, and crossed into Harris just before Ardvourlie, where a solitary house stands out on the broken shores of Loch Seaforth.

From there the road rose steeply, carved out of the mountainside, a spectacular view opening out below them of the black, scattered waters of the loch. Snowpoles lined the road, and the mountains folded around them, swooping and soaring on all sides, peaks lost in cloud that tumbled down the scree slopes like lava.

The wipers on Fin's car could barely handle the rain that blew across the windscreen obscuring the road ahead. Sheep huddled in silent groups at the roadside, picking desultorily at the thin patches of grass and heather that somehow survived among the rocks.

And then, suddenly, as they squeezed through a narrow mountain pass, a line of golden light somewhere far below dimpled the underside of the purple-black clouds that surrounded them. A tattered demarcation between one weather front and another. The grim gathering of cloud among the peaks fell away as the road descended south, and the southern uplands of Harris opened out ahead.

The road skirted the port of Tarbert, where the ferries came in from the Isle of Skye and Lochmaddy, and climbed again to crest the cliffs that overlooked Loch Tarbert and the tiny clutch of houses huddled around the harbour. Sheltered from the prevailing westerlies, the water here was like glass, darkly reflecting the masts of sailing boats at anchor in the bay. Further out, sunlight coruscated across silvered waters to the east, and it was impossible to say where the sky ended and the sea began.

As they reached the summit of Uabhal Beag, the landscape changed again. Granite rock broke up green-covered hills that swooped down in folds and gullies through a wash of pale spring sunlight to the fabulous golden sands and turquoise sea of Luskentyre. The storm-gripped, glowering mountain ranges of the north had receded out of sight and mind, and their spirits lifted.

The road circumnavigated the beach, curving around a length of causeway, towards the collection of houses and crofts that made up the tiny community of Seilebost. Fin turned right on to the narrow school road, past the decaying remains of a red truck that had once belonged to Wm Mackenzie (contrs) Ltd. of Laxay. A flaking wooden sign propped between two decaying fenceposts warned that no dogs were allowed on the common grazing.

The pothole-pitted tarmac wound up over a grassy rise, to open out on a panorama across the machair towards the beach. Spring flowers bowed in the wind, and clouds hovered around the distant mountains that ringed the sands. No matter how often Fin had seen it, this was always a sight that took his breath away.

The school sat out on its own, a tiny collection of grey and yellow buildings and a football field a stone's throw from the beach. It would be hard to imagine a more idyllic setting for a childhood education.

As Fin drew his car into the little car park in front of the main building, half a dozen kids in crash helmets were receiving road-safety lessons on their bikes, weaving in and out of red traffic cones laid along the road by their teacher.

Gunn called to her as he stepped from the car. "We're looking for the headmaster."

"Headmistress," she called back. "The building to your right."

The building to their right was yellow-painted roughcast, with a mural of an underwater seascape painted on the gable end. Inside it smelled of chalk dust and sour milk, and took Fin tumbling back through time to his own childhood.

The headmistress left her class trying to solve an arithmetic puzzle and took the two men into the staffroom. She was delighted to be able to tell them that her predecessors had taken great pride in preserving an archive of the school, a tradition that she herself was anxious to perpetuate, and that they had a record of school registers going back to before the Second World War.

An attractive woman in her middle thirties, she fussed over her appearance, constantly sweeping a stray strand of chestnut hair behind her ear where the rest of it was drawn back in a bun. She wore jeans and tennis shoes, and an open cardigan over a T-shirt. A marked contrast with the severe middle-aged ladies who had taught Fin at that age. It didn't take her long, searching through boxes of old registers, to retrieve those spanning the time when Tormod would have been there.

She flipped back and forth across a period covering the mid forties to early fifties. "Yes," she said at last, stabbing a finger at the yellowed pages of the old school records. "Here he is. Tormod Macdonald. He was a pupil at Seilebost Primary from 1944 to 1951." She ran a pink-painted nail down the faded entries that recorded daily attendance. "A good attender, too."

"Might he have had any brothers or cousins at the school?" Gunn asked, and she laughed.

"He may well have done, Detective Sergeant, but there have been so many Macdonalds here over the years it would be almost impossible to tell."

"And what school would he have gone to from here?" Fin wondered.

"Most likely it would have been the secondary at Tarbert." She smiled and gave him strong eye contact, and he remembered Marsaili once telling him how all the girls had had a crush on him at school. He'd never even been aware of it.

"Do you have an address for him?"

"I can find out." She smiled again and disappeared into another room.

Gunn turned to Fin, a half-smile playing about his lips. Envy maybe, or regret. "Never works like that for me," he said.

The Macdonald croft sat about half a mile back from the shore, in an elevated position with views across the sands of Luskentyre and Scarista. A long, narrow strip of land ran all the way down from the crofthouse to the roadside, delineated now only by the stumped remains of decayed fenceposts, and the barely discernible texture of the land, altered by years of cultivation and grazing.

But there was no cultivation or grazing any more. The land had gone to seed, long abandoned and reclaimed by nature. The crofthouse itself was a shell. The roof had collapsed years before, the chimney at the north gable reduced to a pile of blackened rubble. Long grasses and thistles grew where once the floor had been. A floor of beaten earth, covered with sand that would have been changed daily by Tormod's mother.

Gunn thrust his hands deep in his pockets, gazing out across the expanse of golden sand below, to the streaks of turquoise and emerald that marked out the distant shallows. "It's a dead end."

But Fin was looking across the hillside towards the figure of a man stacking peats beside a freshly whitewashed cottage. "Come on," he said. "Let's see what the neighbour knows." And he set off, striding through the long grasses, fresh green pushing up through winter dead, flowers of purple and yellow reaching for the sky to herald the start of the spring season. The grass moved like water in the wind, ebbing and flowing in waves and eddies, and Gunn waded through it almost at a run in an effort to keep up with the younger man.

Everything about the neighbouring croft seemed to have been renewed. The paint, the roof, the fencing. Doors and windows were double-glazed. A shiny red SUV sat parked in the drive, and a man with a thatch of thick greying hair turned from his task at the peats as they arrived. He had the weathered face of someone who spent time out of doors, but his wasn't an island accent. He replied to Fin's Gaelic greeting in English. "I'm sorry, I don't speak the Gaelic myself."

Fin reached out to shake his hand. "No problem. Fin Macleod," he said, turning as the breathless Gunn finally caught up. "And Detective Sergeant George Gunn."

The man seemed a little more wary now as he shook their hands in turn. "What does the polis want up here?"

"We're looking for information about the family who used to live next door."

"Oh." The man relaxed a little. "The Macdonalds."

"Yes. Did you know them?"

He laughed. "I'm afraid not. I'm Glasgow born and bred. This is my folks' place. They moved to the mainland in the late fifties and had me just after they got there. I might even have been conceived in this house, though I couldn't swear to it."

"They would have known the neighbours, though," Fin said.

"Oh, aye, of course. They knew everyone around here. I heard a lot of stories when I was a boy, and we used to come up for the summer holidays. But we stopped in the late sixties after my dad died. My mum passed away five years ago, and I only decided to come back and restore the place last year after I got made redundant. To see if I could make a go of it as a crofter."

Fin looked around and nodded approvingly. "You're doing a good job so far."

The man laughed again. "A little redundancy money goes a long way."

Gunn asked, "Do you know anything at all about the Macdonalds?"

The man sucked in a long breath through clenched teeth. "Not first-hand, no. Though they were still here the first year or two we came on holiday. There was a family tragedy of some sort, I don't know what. One year we came back and they'd upped sticks and gone."

Gunn scratched his chin thoughtfully. "You don't know where?"

"Who knows? A lot of folk followed their ancestors from the days of the Clearances, over to Canada."

Fin felt a chill now on the edge of the wind, and zipped up his jacket. "They wouldn't have been Catholics, would they? The Macdonalds."

This time the man roared his mirth above the howl of the wind. "Catholics? Here? You must be kidding, man. This is Presbyterian country."

Fin nodded. It had seemed an unlikely scenario. "Where's the nearest church?"

"That would be the Church of Scotland at Scarista." He turned and pointed south. "Just five minutes away."

"What are we doing here, Mr. Macleod?" Gunn stood disconsolately in the metalled parking area at the top of the hill, huddled in his quilted jacket, nose red from the cold. Although the sun rode in patches like untamed horses across the hill and the beach below, there was little warmth in it. The wind had turned around to the north, breathing unpitying arctic air into their frozen faces.

The church at Scarista stood proud on the hill above a strip of mown grass peppered with headstones marking the final resting place of generations of worshippers. A hell of a view, Fin thought, to take with you to eternity: the smudged and shadowed blue of distant mountains beyond the yellow of the Scarista sands; the ever-changing light from a never-resting sky; the constant refrain of the wind, like the voices of the faithful raised in praise of the Lord.

Fin looked up at the church building. As plain and unadorned as the church at Crobost. "I want to see if there's a boat inside," he said.

Gunn scowled. "A boat? In the church?"

"Aye, a boat." Fin tried the door and it opened in. He passed through the vestibule into the body of the church, Gunn at his heels, and of course there was no boat. Just a plain beechwood altar draped in purple, a pulpit raised high above it from which the minister, in his exalted and privileged position closer to heaven than the masses to whom he preached, would deliver the word of God.

"What in heaven's name made you think there would be a boat in the church, Mr. Macleod?"

"Tormod Macdonald spoke of a boat in the church, George. A church built by fishermen."

"He must have made it up."

But Fin shook his head. "I don't think so. I think Marsaili's dad is confused and frustrated; he has trouble with words, and memories, and how to communicate them. And maybe he's even hiding something. Consciously or otherwise. But I don't think he's lying."

Outside the wind had, if anything, grown stronger and less forgiving. They felt the blast of it as they stepped from the church.

"The whole of Harris is pretty much a Protestant island, George, isn't it?"

"It certainly is, Mr. Macleod. I suppose there might be one or two Catholics around, like sheep who've strayed from the fank, but for the most part they're all in the southern isles." He grinned. "Better weather and more fun." He lowered his voice. "I hear the supermarkets even sell you booze on a Sunday."

Fin smiled. "I think hell will freeze over before we ever see that on Lewis, George." He opened the car door. "Where to now?"

"Back to Tarbert, I think. I'd like a copy of Tormod's birth certificate from the registrar."

The office of the registrar was to be found in council offices occu-
pying the former school hostel in West Tarbert, a drab, flat-roofed
building erected in the late 1940s to provide accommodation for
pupils from far-flung corners of the island attending the town's secondary school. The house opposite hid in seclusion behind a profusion of trees and shrubs, almost certainly cultivated to hide the
ugliness of the building on the other side of the road.

An elderly lady looked up from her desk as Fin and Gunn
brought the cold in with them.

"Shut the door!" she said. "It's bad enough that the wind blows in
through every ill-fitting window in the place, without folk leaving
the doors wide open!"

A chastened George Gunn quickly closed the door behind them,
then fought to retrieve his warrant card from the depths of his
anorak. The old lady examined it through half-moon spectacles,
then looked over the top of them to conduct a thorough examination of the two men on the other side of the counter. "And how can
I help you gentlemen?"

"I'd like an extract from the register of births," Gunn told her.

"Well, you needn't think you'll get it for free just because you're a
police officer. It'll cost £14."

Gunn and Fin exchanged the hint of a smile.

Fin tilted his head to read the nameplate on her desk. "Have you
been here a long time, Mrs. Macaulay?"

"Donkey's years," she said. "But retired for the last five. I'm only
standing in for a few days on holiday relief. Whose is the extract you
would like?"

"Tormod Macdonald," Gunn said. "From Seilebost. Born around
1939, I believe."

"Oh, aye . . ." Old Mrs. Macaulay nodded sagely and peered at her
computer screen as she started rattling age-spattered fingers across
her keyboard. "Here it is: August 2, 1939." She looked up. "Would
you like a copy of the death certificate as well?"

In the silence that followed, the wind seemed to increase in
strength and volume, moaning as it squeezed through every space
left unsealed, like a dirge for the dead.

Mrs. Macaulay was oblivious of the effect of her words. "A terrible thing it was, Mr. Gunn. I remember it well. Just a teenager he was at the time. A real tragedy." Her fingers spidered across the keyboard again. "Here we are. Died March 18, 1958. Would you like a copy? It'll be another £14."

It took just fifteen minutes for Fin to drive them back down to the church at Scarista, and less than ten walking among the graves on the lower slopes to find Tormod's headstone. *Tormod Macdonald, born August 2nd 1939, beloved son of Donald and Margaret, accidentally drowned in the Bagh Steinigidh on March 18th, 1958.*

Gunn sat down in the grass beside the lichen-covered slab of granite and leaned forward on his knees. Fin stood staring at the headstone, as if perhaps it might rewrite itself if he watched it long enough. Tormod Macdonald had been in the ground for fifty-four years, and just eighteen years old when he died.

Not a word had passed between the two men on the drive from the registry office. But Gunn looked up now and gave voice to the thought which had occupied them both since Mrs. Macaulay had asked if they would like a copy of the death certificate. "If Marsaili's dad is not Tormod Macdonald, Mr. Macleod, then who the hell is he?"

| TWENTY |

I'll just sit here for a while. The ladies are all in the activity room knitting. No kind of job for a man, that. The old boy in the chair opposite looks like a bit of an old woman to me. He should be in there knitting, too!

There's a square of garden out there through the glass doors that would be nice to sit in. I see a bench. Better than having to put up with that old bastard staring at me all the time. I'll just go out.

Oh! It's colder than it looks. And the bench is wet. Dammit! Too late. But everything will dry in time. I see a square of sky up there. Clouds blowing across it at a fair old lick. But it's sort of sheltered here, even if it is cold.

"Hello, Dad."

Her voice startles me. I didn't hear her coming. Was I sleeping? It's so cold.

"What are you doing sitting out here in the rain?"

"It's not raining," I tell her. "It's just seaspray."

"Come on, we'd better go inside and get you dried off."

She wants me to go in off the deck. But I don't want to go back to the Smoke Room. It's even worse than steerage. All these men smoking, and the stink of stale beer. I'll throw up again if I have to sit in there on those worn old leather benches with no air to breathe.

Oh, there's a bed here. I didn't realize they had cabins on board. She wants to take off my wet trousers, but I'm not having any of it. I push her away. "Stop that!" It's not the done thing. A man has a right to his dignity.

"Oh, Dad, you can't sit here in wet clothes. You'll catch your death."

I shake my head and feel the rolling of the boat beneath me. "How long have we been at sea now, Catherine?"

She looks at me so strangely.

"What boat is it we're on, Dad?"

"The RMS *Claymore*. Not a name I'm ever likely to forget. First boat I ever was on."

"And where are we sailing to?"

Who knows? It's almost dark now, and we left the mainland behind us so long ago. I never knew Scotland was so big. We've been travelling for days. "I heard someone in the Saloon talking about Big Kenneth."

"Is that someone you know?"

"No. Never heard of him."

She sits down beside me now and takes my hand. I don't know why she's crying. I'll look after her. I'll look after both of them. I'm the eldest, so it's my responsibility.

"Oh, Dad . . ." she says.

It was on the second day after Patrick's fall that the priest came. Matron told us to pack up our things, not that we had much. We were waiting for him at the top of the steps when the big black car drew up. Me, Peter and Catherine. The place was deserted, because all the other kids were back at school again. There was no sign of Mr. Anderson, and we never did see him again. Which didn't break my heart.

The priest was a small man, an inch or so shorter than me, and almost completely bald on the top of his head. But he had grown his remaining hair long at one side and combed it over to the other, plastering it down with oil or Brylcreem or something of that sort. I suppose he imagined it hid the fact that he was bald, but really it just looked silly. I have since learned never to trust men with comb-overs. They have absolutely no judgement.

He wasn't very impressive, and seemed a little nervous. Much more daunting were the two nuns who accompanied him. Both were taller than him, eagle-eyed, unsmiling, middle-aged ladies in black skirts and severe white coifs. One sat in the front with the priest, who was driving, and the other was squeezed into the back with us, right next to me. So intimidated by her was I, and so anxious not to press against her bony body, that I barely noticed The Dean disappearing behind us. It was only at the last that I turned, and saw its empty bell towers for the last time before it vanished behind the trees.

The priest's car bumped and rattled its way over the cobbles, around tree-filled circuses, and broad avenues lined by smoke-stained tenements. Snow still lay in patches, blackened by the traffic where it had piled up at the sides of the road. None of us dared speak, sitting silently among God's representatives on earth, watching an alien world pass by us in a wintry blur.

I have no idea where they took us. Somewhere on the south side of the city, I think. We arrived at a large house set back behind naked trees, and a lawn where leaves lay in drifts among the snow. Inside it was warmer, more welcoming than The Dean. I had never been in a house like this in my life. Polished wood panelling and chandeliers, flock wallpaper and shiny tiled floors. We were led up carpeted stairs to where Peter and I were put in one room, and Catherine in another. Silk sheets and the scent of rosewater.

"Where are we going, Johnny?" Peter had asked me several times, but I had no answer for him. We had, it seemed, no rights, human or otherwise. We were goods and chattels. Just kids with no parents, and no place to call home. You'd think we would have been used to it by now. But you never are. You only have to look around you, and life will always remind you that you are not like others. I'd have given anything right then for the touch of my mother's fingers on my face, her warm gentle lips on my forehead, her voice breathing softly in my ear to tell me that everything was going to be all right. But she was long gone, and in my heart of hearts I knew that everything would not be all right. Not that I was going to tell Peter that.

"We'll see," I said to him on the umpteenth time of asking. "Don't worry, I'll look after us."

We were kept in those rooms for the rest of the day and only allowed out to go to the toilet. That night we were led downstairs to a large dining room where the walls were lined with many coloured books, and a long, shiny dining table ran from a bay window at one end to double doors at the other.

There were three places set at one end, and the nun who had brought us down said, "Keep your fingers off the table. If I find a single mark on it you will all be beaten."

I was almost frightened to eat my soup in case it spilled or splashed on the table top. We had one slice of buttered bread each with our soup, and afterwards a slice of ham with cold boiled potatoes. Water was provided in heavy-bottomed glasses, and when we were finished we were marched back upstairs.

It was a long, restless night, Peter and I curled up together in one bed. He slept within minutes of us slipping beneath the covers. But I lay awake for a long, long time. There was a light beneath our door, and occasionally I heard the sound of distant voices, low and conspiratorial, talking somewhere deep in the house, before finally I drifted off into a shallow slumber.

The next morning we were up at first light, and bundled back into the big black car. No breakfast, no time to wash. This time we took a different route through town, and I had no idea where we were until I saw the castle away to our right, and the houses that piled up high above The Mound. We drove down a steep ramp on to a large concourse lit by a glass roof supported on an elaborate framework of metal struts. Steam trains stood chuffing impatiently at platforms along the far side of the concourse, and the nuns led us hurriedly through the crowds, almost running, to show our tickets to the guard at the gate before climbing aboard to find our seats in a six-person compartment off a long corridor. We were joined by a man in a dark suit and bowler hat, who seemed ill at ease in the presence of the nuns, and sat uncomfortably with his hat on his knees.

It was the first time I had been on a train, and in spite of everything, I felt quite excited. I could see that Peter was, too. We were glued to the window for the whole journey, watching the city give way to rolling green countryside, stopping at smaller stations with exotic names like Linlithgow and Falkirk, before another city grew up out of the earth. An altogether different city. Black with industrial pollution. Factory chimneys belching bile into a sulphurous sky. A long, dark tunnel, then the roar of the steam engine in the confined space of the station as we pulled into the platform at Queen Street in Glasgow, the screech of metal on metal ringing in our ears.

Several times I had glanced at Catherine, trying to catch her eye, but she had steadfastly refused to meet mine, staring at her hands in her lap in front of her, never once glancing from the window. I had no way to read what was going on in her head, but sensed her fear. Even at that age I knew that girls had much more to be afraid of in this world than boys.

We sat waiting for nearly two hours at Queen Street before boarding another train. A train that took us north this time and further west, through the most spectacular countryside I had ever seen. Snow-capped mountains, and bridges spanning crystal-clear tumbling waters, vast forests and viaducts over gorges and lochs. I can remember seeing one tiny whitewashed cottage in the middle of nowhere, mountain peaks rising up all around it. And I wondered who on earth lived in a place like that. It might as well have been on the moon.

It was getting dark by the time we arrived in the west coast port of Oban. It was a pretty town, with the houses painted in different colours, and a huge fishing fleet berthed at the quayside. The first time I'd seen the sea. The bay was ringed by hills, and a vast stone cathedral stood on the shore looking out over waters turned blood-red by the setting sun.

We spent the night in a house not far from the cathedral. There was another priest there. But he didn't speak to us. A housekeeper led us to two rooms up in the attic. Tiny rooms with dormer windows in the slope of the roof. All we'd had to eat all day were sandwiches on the train, and a bowl of soup when we arrived. I could hear my stomach growling as I lay in bed, keeping me awake. If Peter heard me, it didn't affect him. He slept like a baby, as he always did. But I couldn't get Catherine out of my mind.

I waited until after midnight, when all the lights went off in the house, before getting quietly out of bed. For a long time I stood at the door, straining to hear the slightest sound, before opening it and slipping out into the hall. Catherine's room was just a few paces away. I hesitated outside her door, listening to what sounded awfully like stifled sobs coming from the other side of it, and I had a feeling of sick anticipation rising from my stomach. She was a real hard case, was wee Catherine. If something had reduced her to tears then it had to be bad. I had never seen her cry once in the year I'd known her, except for that time in the moonlight on the roof of The Dean. But I'm sure she didn't know I'd noticed that.

I turned the handle and ducked quickly inside. Almost immediately the bedside light came on. Catherine was sitting up in the bed, her back against the headboard, knees drawn up to her chest, and a hand mirror from the dresser raised up in her right hand like a weapon. Her eyes were black with fear, her face the colour of the sheets.

"For God's sake, Catherine, what are you doing?"

Her relief at seeing me almost overwhelmed her. She allowed her hand to fall to the bed again and let go of the mirror. I could see her lower lip trembling, her tear-stained cheeks catching the light from the lamp. I crossed the room and slipped on to the bed beside her, and she turned her face into my shoulder to choke off her sobs, her arm across my chest, holding on to me like a child. I slipped my arm around her shoulder.

"Hey girl. It's okay. I'm here. What can be so bad?"

It took a long time for her to find her voice and trust herself to speak. "That dirty fucking priest!"

I frowned, not yet understanding. How naïve I was. "The one with the comb-over?"

She nodded, her face still pushed into my shoulder. "He came into my room last night. He said he thought I might need a little comfort . . . given the circumstances."

"And?"

"And what?"

"What happened?"

She turned her head up to look at me now in disbelief. "What the fuck do you think?"

And it dawned on me.

At first I was shocked, that a priest of all people might do something like that. Then incensed that he had. And then almost overcome by the most powerful physical and mental urge to kick the living shit out of him. And I think, had he been there I would, and could, have killed him.

"Oh shit, Cathy," was all I could say.

She buried her face in my shoulder again. "I thought the other one was coming for the same thing. I'm scared, Johnny. I don't want anyone to touch me again, ever."

"No one will," I said. And all I could feel was anger and outrage.

I sat with her all night that night. There was no more talking. I felt her finally drift off to sleep after about an hour, and her body became a dead weight against mine.

We never ever spoke of it again.

The RMS *Claymore* left from the big pier the next morning. The nuns walked us through the town to the waiting room at the ferry terminal. Peter and I had one small cardboard suitcase between us, which I carried. Catherine had a tashed canvas holdall that she slung carelessly over her shoulder, as if train rides and ferries were everyday fare.

It wasn't until we got to the pier that I realized we were going on the boat, and that the nuns weren't coming with us. That came as a bit of a shock. The presence of the nuns these last two days, cold black shadows though they'd been, had provided a sense of safety and purpose. The thought of setting sail on this big boat that smelled of oil and salt water, all alone and with no idea of where we were going, filled me with an unaccountable dread.

While one of them stood aloof and silent, the other lined us up in the terminal and knelt down in front of us. Her face seemed softer, somehow, than at any time since they had picked us up from The Dean. She almost smiled, and I saw something that looked close to sympathy in her eyes. From somewhere beneath her skirts she drew out three pieces of card, about nine inches by six. They each had a loop of string hanging from the top edge, just like the notice we'd fashioned to hang around Peter's neck when we were pretending he was blind. The ones she gave to me and Peter had the name GILLIES scrawled on them in bold black letters. Catherine's read O'HENLEY.

"When you get off the boat," she said, "put these around your necks and wait on the quayside. Someone will be there to meet you."

Finally I summoned the courage to ask the question that Peter had been demanding of me for the last two days. "Where are we going?"

Her face darkened, as if a cloud had passed overhead and cast a shadow on it. "It doesn't matter. Just stay off the deck. The sea can get rough out there."

She gave us our tickets then, and stood up, and we were shepherded through crowds of people on to the pier and up a steep gangplank to the deck. The *Claymore* had one big red funnel with a strip of black around the top, and lifeboats mounted on winches on either side of the stern. Folk gathered at the rail, pressing and pushing, to wave goodbye to friends and relatives as the ship's horn sounded and the thump of her motors came up through the deck, vibrating through our bodies. But the nuns didn't wait to wave us off. I saw their black skirts and white headgear as they walked back towards the terminal building. I've often wondered if they turned their backs to us because they couldn't bear to face us, afraid that somewhere deep inside of them, some long-buried spark of humanity might have pricked their conscience.

Desolate is how I felt in that first hour as the boat slid out across the grey waters of the bay, leaving a pale emerald trail in its wake, seagulls wheeling and cawing all around the masts like so many scraps of white paper flung into the wind. We became aware for the first time of the swell of the ocean, and watched the mainland retreating behind us. Until, in time, the green of the hills became smudged and distant, before vanishing altogether. And all that we saw around us was the sea rising and falling, with no idea of where we were going or when we would get there. Or what might be waiting for us when we arrived.

In the years to come I learned about the Clearances. How, in the eighteenth and nineteenth centuries, absentee landlords, encouraged by the government in London, cleared the people off the land to make way for sheep. Tens of thousands of crofters evicted from their homes and forced aboard boats that took them off to the new world where many had been pre-sold, almost as slaves. I know now how they must have felt as they saw their homes and their country vanish in the haze, with nothing ahead of them but mounting seas and a hopeless uncertainty.

I looked then at my little brother, clinging on to the rail and staring back, the salt-filled wind dragging at his clothes and raking through his hair, and I almost envied him his innocence, his lack of awareness. There was a look in his face almost like exhilaration. He had nothing to fear, because he knew beyond any shadow of a doubt that his big brother would look after him. For the first time I felt almost crushed by the weight of that responsibility.

Maybe Catherine saw it, too. I caught her looking at me, and a little half-smile stretched her lips before her hand slipped into mine, and I cannot begin to describe the comfort and warmth of that little hand in mine.

The nuns had given us a box of sandwiches which we ate quite quickly, and within an hour had thrown up again. As all trace of land vanished, so the wind had whipped itself into a fury, and the sea with it. The big black-and-white painted tub that was the *Claymore* ploughed through white-topped waves, spray breaking over her bow to carry on the wind and soak anyone who ventured out on deck.

And so we took it in turns to throw up in the toilet off the non-smoking lounge where we had managed to bag ourselves some seats by a rain-streaked window, and where people smoked anyway, and drank beer, and in a language we didn't understand shouted to be heard above the thud of the motors.

Sometimes in the distance we would see the blurry outline of some island come briefly into focus before vanishing again beyond the waves. Each time wondering if that was where we were headed. Hoping beyond hope that this nightmare was coming to an end. But it never did. Or so it seemed. Hour after hour we endured it. Wind and rain and sea, stomachs retching, with nothing more to give up but green bile. I am not sure that I have ever felt quite so miserable in my life.

We had left early that morning. And by now, late afternoon, it was starting to get dark. Mercifully the sea had calmed a little, and the approach of night offered the promise of smoother passage. Which was when I heard someone shouting, in English this time, that they could see Ben Kenneth, and everyone rushed on to the deck amid great excitement.

We went too, expecting to see someone called Kenneth, but if he was there among the crowd it was impossible to tell. It was only much later that I learned that Kenneth, or Coinneach in the Gaelic, was the name of the mountain that sheltered the harbour whose twinkling lights we saw for the first time emerging from the dusk.

The land rose darkly all around the town, and along the horizon lay a single line of bright silver light. The last of the day. Wherever we were, it was where we were going, and there was a great sense of anticipation among the other passengers.

A voice came over the Tannoy. "Will those passengers who are disembarking and have not yet purchased a ticket please make their way to the purser's office." There was a clanging of bells, and the deep, sonorous moan of the ship's horn, as she came in to dock at the pier. Deckhands with mops and buckets were sloshing water over salt-caked planking as families gathered with suitcases to watch as a gangplank was manoeuvred into place.

It was a mix of hunger, relief and trepidation that made my legs tremble as I made my way down the steep incline, Peter ahead of me, Catherine at my back, to find unaccustomed solid ground beneath my feet. My body was still moving to the rhythm of the boat.

As the crowd thinned, heading for buses and cars, and darkness fell across the hills, we took out our little rectangles of cardboard and hung them around our necks, just as the nuns had instructed. And we waited. And waited. The lights started to go out on the ferry behind us, and the long shadows we had cast across the pier vanished. One or two people threw curious glances in our direction but hurried on. Now there was almost no one left on the pier, and all we could hear were the voices of the sailors on the ferry as they prepared her to spend the night at dock.

A feeling of such despondency fell over me as we stood there alone in the dark, the black waters inside the protective arms of the harbour slopping against the stanchions of the pier. The lights of a hotel beyond the harbour wall looked warm and welcoming, but not for us.

I could see Catherine's pale face peering up at me out of the darkness. "What do you think we should do?"

"Wait," I said. "Like the nuns said. Someone will come."

I don't know where I found the faith to believe in that. But it was all there was to hold on to. Why would they have sent us all this way across the sea, and told us there would be someone there to meet us, if it wasn't true?

Then out of the darkness a figure emerged, hurrying along the pier towards us, and I wasn't sure whether to be relieved or afraid. It was a woman, and as she got closer I could see that she was in her late forties or early fifties. Her hair was piled up beneath a dark-green hat pinned to her head, and her long woollen coat was buttoned up tight to the neck. She wore dark gloves and wellington boots, and carried a shiny handbag.

She slowed as she reached us, a look of consternation on her face, and she bent to peer at the cards around our necks. Her frown vanished as she read the name O'Henley on Catherine's, and she gave her a good looking over. A hand came up to grip her jaw and turn her face one way, then the other. And then she examined both her hands. She gave us barely a glance. "Aye, you'll do," she said, and took Catherine's hand to lead her away.

Catherine didn't want to go, pulling back against her.

"Come on," the O'Henley woman barked. "You're mine now. And you'll do what you're told or suffer the consequences." She yanked hard on Catherine's arm, and I'll never forget the desperate look on wee Cathy's face as she glanced back at Peter and me. I really thought, then, that I would never seen her again, and I suppose that was the first time I realized that I was in love with her.

"Where's Catherine going?" Peter said. But I just shook my head, not trusting myself to speak.

I don't know how long we stood there then, waiting, growing colder, till I couldn't stop my jaw from chittering. I could see figures moving around inside the lounge bar of the hotel, shadows in the light, people in another world. One that we didn't inhabit. And then, suddenly, the lights of a vehicle raked across the pier, and a van drove right on to it, stopping just yards away, trapping us in the beam of its headlights like rabbits.

A door slammed and a man moved into the light, casting a giant shadow towards us. I could barely see him with the light behind him. But I could tell that he was a big man. He wore blue overalls and boots, and a cloth cap pulled down on his forehead. He took two steps towards us and peered down at the cards around our necks and grunted. I could smell alcohol and stale tobacco on his breath.

"In the van," was all he said, and we followed him around to the side of the van where he slid open a door to let us in. "Hurry up, I'm late enough as it is." Inside were ropes and fishing nets and orange buoys, old wooden crates stinking of rotten fish, creels and a toolkit, and the carcass of a dead sheep. It took me a moment to realize what it was, before recoiling in horror. For some reason it didn't seem to trouble Peter.

"It's dead," he said, and put a hand on its belly. "And still warm."

So we sat on the floor in the back of that van with the dead sheep and the fishing stuff, and had our bones shaken, breathing exhaust fumes, while he drove us over dark, single-track roads, flat bogland silvered by the moon shimmering away into a black distance.

Until we saw and smelled the sea again, almost dazzling in the glow of the moon, occasional lights rising up the hillside, burning in the windows of unseen cottages.

The long finger of a stone jetty reached out into still waters, and a small boat rose gently on the swell. A man we would come to know later as Neil Campbell sat smoking in the wheelhouse, and came out to greet us while the big man with the cap parked his van. When he'd done, he told us to get out.

The two men spoke and there was an exchange of laughter. But I had no idea what it was they said. We were ushered, then, down into the boat which chugged across the moonlit strait towards the ragged shape of an island rising up out of the sea, odd lights dotted around its looming hillsides. It took only ten minutes or so to reach it, and we climbed up on to a crumbling stone jetty at one side of a narrow neck of water leading into a small bay. I could see houses on both sides of it. Strange, squat, stone dwellings with grass for roofs that I later learned was called thatch. The tide was out, and the bay was ringed with black and gold seaweed.

The boat headed off, back across the strait. "Follow me," the big man said, and we trotted after him along a beaten track that circled the bay, and then up the hill on a stony, rutted path to one of those thatched cottages we had seen from the harbour. There I encountered my first-ever smell of peat smoke as the wooden door squeaked open into a dingy inner room, half filled with the stuff. A faint yellow light spilled from a Tilley lamp hanging low from the rafters, and a bank of peats glowed red in the open door of a black, cast-iron stove set against the end wall. An earthen floor was strewn with sand. This was the kitchen, living room and dining room all in one, a large table sitting in the middle of it, a dresser against the back wall, two small deep windows set on either side of the door. A tongue-and-groove wood-lined passage hung with coats and tools led off to what I would discover were three bedrooms. There was no toilet, no running water, no electricity. It was as if we had travelled back in time from the twentieth century to some medieval past. Sad little orphaned time-travellers.

A woman in a dark-blue patterned print dress and long white apron turned from the stove as we came in. It was hard to say what age she was. Her hair was like brushed steel, dragged back from her face and held by combs. But it wasn't an old face. Certainly not lined. Though she wasn't young. She gave us a long, appraising look and said, "Sit in at the table. You'll be hungry." And we were.

The man sat down, too, and took off his cap, so that I saw his face for the first time. A lean, hard face, with a big crooked nose on it. He had hands like shovels, with hair growing on his knuckles, and more of it poking out from beneath his sleeves. What little hair he had left on his head was plastered to it in swirls from the sweat of his cap.

The woman delivered four steaming plates to the table. Some kind of meat in a gravy swimming with grease, and potatoes boiled to the point of disintegration. The man closed his eyes and muttered something in a language I didn't understand, then as he started to eat he said to us in English, "My name is Donald Seamus. This is my sister, Mary-Anne. Mr. and Miss Gillies to you. This is our house, and this is your home now. Forget wherever it is you came from. That's history. From now on you'll be Donald John and Donald Peter Gillies, and if you don't do what you're told, so help me you'll regret the day you were born." He shoved a forkful of food into his mouth and glanced at his sister as he chewed on it. She remained silent and passive the whole time. He looked back at us. "We speak Gaelic in this house, so you'd better learn it bloody fast. Just like the poor souls who speak Gaelic in the English court, if you utter a word of English in my presence you'll be deemed not to have spoken. Is that understood?"

I nodded, and Peter glanced at me for confirmation before nodding too. I had no idea what Gaelic was, or how it would be possible for me to speak it. But I didn't say so.

When we had finished eating, he handed me a shovel and said, "You'll be needing to relieve yourselves before you go to bed. You can just water the heather. But if you need anything more you can dig a hole for it. Not too near the house, mind."

And so we were tipped out into the night to do our toilet. The wind had risen, and clouds scurried across the vast expanse of sky overhead, moonlight flitting in sporadic bursts across the hillside. I led Peter away from the house to where we had an uninterrupted view back across the water, and I began to dig, wondering what on earth we would do if it was raining.

"Hiya!" The little voice, caught on the wind, startled us both, and I turned in amazement to find Catherine standing there grinning at us in the dark.

I could barely formulate the question. "How . . . ?"

"I saw you come across in the wee boat, about half an hour after me." She turned and pointed across the hillside. "I'm just over there, with Mrs. O'Henley. She says I've to be called Ceit now. Funny spelling. C - E - I - T. But pronounced Kate. It's Gaelic."

"Ceit," I said. And I liked the sound of it.

"It seems we're what they call *homers*. Kids that the fucking Church has dumped here from the mainland. There's dozens of us on this wee island." Her face clouded for a moment. "I thought I'd lost you."

I grinned. "You cannae get rid of me that easy." And I couldn't have been happier that I'd found her again.

"Dad, you've got to take your trousers off. They're still wet."

So they are! They must have got soaked on the boat. I stand up and I can't seem to get the zip down. She helps me open them up and I step out of them as they fall to the floor. Now she's pulling my jersey up over my head. Easier just to let her do it. But I can manage the shirt buttons myself. I don't know why, but my fingers feel so stiff and clumsy these days.

I watch her as she crosses to the wardrobe to get fresh trousers and a neatly pressed white shirt. She's a lovely-looking girl.

"Here, Dad." She holds out the shirt towards me. "Do you want to put it on yourself?"

I reach out and stroke her face, and feel such tenderness for her. "I don't know what I'd have done if they hadn't taken you to the island, too, Ceit. I really thought I'd lost you for good."

I see such confusion in her eyes. Doesn't she realize how I feel about her?

"Well, I'm here now," she says, and I beam at her. So many memories, so much emotion.

"Remember how we used to haul the seaweed up from the shore?" I say. "In those big panniers on the little horses. To fertilize the *feannagan*. And I would help you dig yours."

Why is she frowning? Maybe she doesn't remember.

"*Feannagan*?" she says. "Crows?" Switching to English now. "How can you fertilize crows, Dad?"

Silly girl! I can hear myself laughing. "That's what they called them, of course. Grand tatties they gave us, too."

She's shaking her head again. And sighs, "Oh, Dad."

I want to shake her, dammit! Why doesn't she remember?

"Dad, I came to tell you that I have to go to Glasgow to sit some exams. So I won't be here for a couple of days. But Fionnlagh'll come and see you. And Fin."

I don't know who she's talking about. But I don't want visitors. I don't want her to leave. She's buttoning up my shirt now, her face very close. So I just lean in to kiss her softly on the lips. She seems startled and jumps back. I hope I haven't upset her. "I'm so glad I found you again, Ceit," I tell her, wanting to give her reassurance. "I'll never forget those days at The Dean. Never. And the turrets of Danny's place that we could see from the roof." It makes me laugh to remember it. "Just to remind us of our place in the world." And I lower my voice, proud of what we've become. "Still and all, we didn't do too bad for a couple of orphan waifs."

| TWENTY-ONE |

It was dark when Fin dropped George Gunn in Stornoway and headed across the Barvas moor to the west coast. It was a black, wet night, the Atlantic hissing its fury into his face as he drove west. Just like the night his parents were killed on this very road. He knew the dip in it like the back of his hand. He had passed it every week on the bus that took him to the school hostel in Stornoway on Monday, and then back again on Friday. Although he couldn't see it now, he knew that the green-roofed shieling was only a hundred yards or so away to his right, and that it was just about here that the sheep had leapt suddenly up from the ditch, causing his father to swerve.

There were still sheep on the road now. Crofters had long ago given up trying to fence off the grazing. Only a few rotted posts remained to give witness to the fact that they had once tried. At night you saw the eyes of the sheep glowing in the dark. Two luminous points of light, like devil's eyes reflecting your headlights back at you. They were stupid beasts. You never knew the minute they would startle, and run out in front of you. On still days they would congregate on the road, leaving the bog to escape the tiny, biting midges that were the curse of the West Highlands. And you knew that if the sheep were troubled by them, then it must be bad.

Over the rise he saw the lights of Barvas flickering in the rain, a long string of them following the line of the coast before vanishing into darkness. Fin followed intermittent beads of them north until the scattered lights of Ness spread more densely across the headland, and he turned up towards Crobost. The ocean was hidden in obscurity, suffocated by the night, but he heard it breathing its anger all along the cliffs as he parked and got out of his car at Marsaili's bungalow.

Her car was not there, and he realized that she must already have left for Glasgow. But there was a light burning in the kitchen window, and he made a dash for the door through the rain. There was no one in the kitchen and he went through to the living room where the television was playing the evening news in the corner. But there was no one here either. He went out into the hall and called upstairs to Fionnlagh's bedroom.

"Anyone home?"

A line of light lay along the foot of the door and he started up the stairs. He was only halfway up when the door opened and Fionnlagh came out on to the top landing, shutting it quickly behind him. "Fin!" He seemed startled, surprised, oddly hesitant, before hurrying down the stairs and squeezing past Fin on the way. "I thought you were in Harris."

Fin turned and followed him down to the living room, where he could see in the light that Fionnlagh was slightly flushed, self-conscious, almost embarrassed. "Well, I'm back."

"So I see."

"Your mum said I could use the plumbing whenever I needed to. Until I get things fixed up at the croft."

"Sure. Feel free." He was clearly uncomfortable, and moved now through to the kitchen. Fin followed in time to see him opening the fridge. "Beer?" Fionnlagh turned, holding out a bottle.

"Thanks." Fin took it, twisting off the cap, and sat down at the table. Fionnlagh hesitated before taking one himself. He stood leaning back against the fridge and threw the cap across the kitchen into the sink before taking a long pull at the bottle.

"So what did you find out about Grampa?"

"Nothing," Fin said. "Except that he's not Tormod Macdonald."

Fionnlagh stared at him, a look of vacant incomprehension on his face. "What do you mean?"

"Tormod Macdonald died at the age of eighteen in a boating accident. I've seen his death certificate and his grave."

"It must be some other Tormod Macdonald then."

Fin shook his head. "It's the Tormod Macdonald your grandfather claims to be."

Fionnlagh took several swigs of beer, trying to digest this. "Well, if he's not Tormod Macdonald, who is he?"

"Good question. But not one he's likely to give us an answer to any time soon."

Fionnlagh was silent, then, for a long time, staring into his half-empty beer bottle. "Do you think he killed that man they found in the peat bog?"

"I have no idea. But he was related to him, that's for sure. And if we can establish the identity of one, then that'll probably tell us who the other is, and maybe what happened."

"You sound like a cop."

Fin smiled. "It's what I was for most of my adult life. The mindset doesn't change overnight just because you quit your job."

"Why did you?"

Fin sighed. "Most people spend their lives never knowing what lies beneath the stones they walk on. Cops spend theirs lifting those stones and having to deal with what they find." He drained his bottle. "I was sick of spending my life in the shadows, Fionnlagh. When all you know is the darkest side of human nature, you start to find the darkness in yourself. And that's a scary thing."

Fionnlagh tossed his empty bottle into a box of them by the door, and the dull clunk of glass on glass filled the silence in the kitchen. He still appeared ill at ease.

Fin said, "I hope I haven't interrupted anything."

Quick eyes flashed towards him, then away again. "You haven't."
Then, "Mum went to see Grampa this afternoon."

"Any joy?"

The boy shook his head. "No. He was sitting out in the rain,
apparently, but seemed to think he was on a boat. Then he started
wittering on about collecting seaweed to fertilize the crows."

Fin scowled. "Crows?"

"Aye. He used the Gaelic word, *feannagan*. Crows."

"That doesn't make any sense."

"No, it doesn't."

Fin hesitated. "Fionnlagh . . ." The boy looked at him expectantly. "Better let me tell your mum about your grandfather." And
Fionnlagh nodded, only too happy, it seemed, to be relieved of the
responsibility.

The wind whipped and tugged at the outer shell of his tent, straining at the guys, while the inner tent inhaled and exhaled partially
and erratically, like a failing lung. The rain driving against the thin
plastic exterior skin was almost deafening. The glow of Fin's battery-
powered fluorescent filled it with a strange blue light, by which he
sat wrapped in his sleeping bag reading Gunn's illicit autopsy report
on the body in the bog.

He was fascinated by the description of the Elvis tattoo on the
left forearm, and the legend, *Heartbreak Hotel*, although it had been
the headplate which had definitively established death as being
some time in the late fifties. Here was a young man with a passion
for the world's first rock star, whose intellectual powers had been
diminished by some accident that had left him brain-damaged.
Related, in some way, to Marsaili's father, whose own identity was
now shrouded in mystery.

It had been a brutal murder. Tied up, stabbed, throat slit. Fin
tried to imagine Marsaili's dad as his killer, but simply couldn't. Tormod, or whoever he was, had always been a gentle sort of man. A
big man, yes. Powerful in his day. But a man with such an even

temperament that Fin could not recall a single occasion when he had even heard him raise his voice.

He laid the report to one side, and picked up the open folder containing the details of Robbie's hit and run. He had spent nearly an hour going through it once more when he got back to the tent from Marsaili's. Futile, of course. He had lost count of the number of times he had read it. Every statement, the smallest measurement of every tyre track on the road. The description of the car, the driver. The police photographs he had photocopied in Edinburgh. He knew every detail by heart, and yet every time he read it hoped to stumble upon the one vital thing he had missed.

It was an obsession, he knew. An unreasonable, illogical, unviable obsession. And yet, like the addicted smoker, he was simply unable to put it aside. There couldn't be closure until the driver of the car had been brought to book. Until that day there would be no steering his life out of the rut, no getting it back on to the open road.

He cursed under his breath and tossed the folder away across the tent, before switching off the fluorescent, and throwing himself back to lie on his groundsheet, head sunk in the pillow, so anxious for sleep to take him that he knew it wouldn't.

He closed his eyes and listened to the wind and the rain, then opened them again. There was no difference. No light. Just absolute darkness. He doubted if he had ever felt quite so lonely in his life.

It was impossible for him to guess at how much time had passed. Half an hour, an hour? But at the end of it he was no closer to sleep than when he had first lain down. He sat up again and switched on the light, blinking in the harshness of its glare. There were some books in the car. He needed something to take him away from here, from who he was, who he had been, where he was going. Something to stop all the unresolved questions in his head endlessly repeating themselves.

He pulled his oilskin on over his vest and boxers and slipped bare feet into his boots, grabbing his sou'wester before unzipping the tent to face the rain and the wind. A twenty-second dash to the car, and he would be back in under a minute shedding dripping waterproofs in the outer tent, to slide back into the warmth of his sleeping bag. A book in his hand, escape in his heart.

Still, he hesitated to take the plunge. It was wild out there. It was why generations of his ancestors had built houses with walls two and three feet thick. How foolish was he to believe he could survive weeks, even months, in a flimsy little tent like this? He breathed out through clenched teeth, screwed up his eyes for a moment, then made the dash. Out into rain that stung his face, the force of the wind almost taking the legs away from him.

He reached his car, fumbling for keys with wet fingers, and a light came on in his peripheral vision. He paused, peering down the hill through the rain, to see that it was the light above Marsaili's kitchen door. It threw a feeble yellow glow up the path towards where Fionnlagh's car stood idling. He couldn't hear the engine, but he could see exhaust fumes belching from the rear of the old Mini to be whipped away into the night.

And then a figure with a suitcase dashing from the kitchen door to the car. Just a silhouette, but recognisably Fionnlagh. Fin called out his name, but the bungalow was a couple of hundred yards away, and his voice was lost in the storm.

Fin stood, hammered by rain that ran in sheets off his oilskin, blowing into his face, running down his neck, and watched as Fionnlagh opened the boot and jammed his case inside. He ran back to the house to turn off the light, and was the merest shadow as he dashed up the path again to the car. Fin saw his face caught for a moment in the courtesy light as the door opened and then closed again. The car pulled away from the side of the road and started off down the hill.

Fin turned to his own car, unlocked the door, and slid into the driver's seat. He started it up, slipped into first gear and released the handbrake. As long as he kept Fionnlagh's lights in sight, he could keep his own turned off. He rolled down the hill after the Mini.

Fin kept a good two hundred yards between the cars, and slowed to a stop as the Mini pulled up outside the Crobost stores at the foot of the hill. By the light of Fionnlagh's headlamps, he saw the tiny figure of Donna Murray dart out from the shelter of the shop doorway, hefting a carrycot in both hands. Fionnlagh jumped out to tip the driver's seat forward and she slid it inside before running back to fetch a small suitcase.

Which was when the headlamps of a third car flooded the scene with light. Fin could see the rain driving through them, and the figure of a man stepping out to interrupt their beam. He lifted his foot from the clutch and accelerated down the road towards them, turning on his headlights to throw this midnight drama into sharp relief. Three startled faces turned towards his car as he braked, skidding to a stop on the gravel. He let the door swing open and stepped out into the rain.

"What the hell are you doing here?" Donald Murray had to bellow to be heard over the roar of the storm. His face was liverish pale in the light of the cars, his eyes sunken in shadow.

"Maybe I should be asking you that," Fin shouted back.

Donald punched an angry fist through the air towards his daughter and her lover, a solitary finger pointed in accusation. "They're trying to run off with the baby."

"It's their baby."

A sneer curled Donald's mouth. "Are you in on this?"

"Hey!" Fionnlagh bellowed red-faced at the night. "It's none of your business! Either of you. She's our baby and it's our decision. So you can all go to hell."

"That's for God to decide," Donald Murray shouted back at him. "But you are going nowhere, son. Not with my grandchild, you're not."

"Try and fucking stop me!" Fionnlagh took Donna's bag and threw it into the car. "Come on," he said to her, and dropped into the driver's seat.

Donald was there in two strides to reach in and pull out the ignition key, turning to throw it into the teeth of the gale. He moved swiftly around the car to reach in and grab the carrycot.

Fionnlagh leapt out to stop him, but Fin got there first. His sou'wester blew off and vanished in the dark as he grabbed the

Reverend Murray by the shoulders and pulled him away from the car. Donald was still a powerfully built man, and he pushed back hard to try to break free of Fin's grip. Both men stumbled backwards and tumbled to the ground, rolling over on the gravel.

The fall expelled all the air from Fin's lungs, and he gasped for breath as Donald got back to his feet. He managed to rise to his knees, still fighting for air, and looked up as Donald reached out a hand to help him to stand. He caught a flash of white at Donald's neck. His dog collar. And for a moment the absurdity of their situation flashed through his head. He was fighting with the minister of Crobost Church, for God's sake! His boyhood friend. He grasped the hand and pulled himself up. The two men stood glaring at each other, both breathing hard, both faces wet with rain and shining in the light of the headlamps.

"Stop it!" Donna was screaming. "Stop it, both of you!"

But Donald kept his eyes fixed on Fin. "I found the ferry tickets in her room. The first sailing tomorrow for Ullapool. I knew they'd try and get away tonight."

"Donald, they're both adults. It's their baby. They can go where they like."

"I might have known you would take their side."

"I'm not taking anyone's side. You're the one who's driving them away. Refusing to let Fionnlagh come to the house to see his own daughter. You'd think we were still living in the Middle Ages!"

"He has no means of supporting them. He's still at school for God's sake!"

"Well, he's not going to make much of himself by dropping out and running away, is he? And that's what you're forcing him to do. Both of them."

Donald spat his contempt at the night. "This is a waste of time." He turned again to try and take the carrycot from the car. Fin grabbed his arm, and in that moment Donald swung around, his fist flying through the light to catch Fin a glancing blow on the cheek. The force of it knocked Fin off balance and he went sprawling backwards on the tarmac.

For several long moments, the scene was frozen, as if someone had flicked a switch and put the movie on pause. None of them could quite believe what Donald had just done. The wind howled its disapproval all around them. Then Fin struggled back to his feet and wiped a smear of blood from his lip. He glared at the minister. "For Christ's sake, man," he said. "Come to your senses." His voice was almost lost in the roar of the night.

Donald stood rubbing his knuckles, staring back at Fin, his eyes filled with disbelief, guilt, anger. As if it were somehow Fin's fault that Donald had struck him. "Why the hell would you care anyway?"

Fin shut his eyes and shook his head. "Because Fionnlagh's my son."

| TWENTY-TWO |

Catriona Murray's concern turned to confusion when she opened the door of the manse and found her husband and Fin Macleod standing on the top step like two drowned rats, bloodied and bruised. It wasn't who she had been expecting.

"Where's Donna and the baby?"

"Nice to see you, too, Catriona," Fin said.

Donald said, "They're at Marsaili's."

Catriona's dark eyes darted from one to the other. "What's to stop them heading for Stornoway first thing and catching the ferry?"

Fin said, "They won't do that."

"Why not?"

"Because they're afraid of what me and Donald might do to one another. Any chance we could come in out of the rain?"

She shook her head in confusion and frustration, and held the door wide for the two men to come, dripping, into the hallway. "You'd better get those wet things off you."

Fin smiled. "Better keep mine on, Catriona. I don't want to inflame your delicate sensibilities." He held open his oilskin to reveal his vest and boxer shorts. "I was only popping out to get a book from the car."

"I'll get you a dressing gown." She canted her head to take a closer look at him. "What happened to your face?"

"Your husband hit me."

Her eyes shot at once towards Donald, the slightest frown drawing creases between her brows. The guilt on his face, and his lack of a denial, deepened them.

Fifteen minutes later the two men sat around a peat fire in the living room, sipping on mugs of hot chocolate by the light of a table lamp and the glow of the peats. Donald wore a black silk dressing gown embroidered with Chinese dragons. Fin wore a thick white towelling robe. Both men were bare-foot and only just beginning to feel the circulation returning. On a nod from Donald, Catriona had retired to the kitchen, and the two men sat sipping in silence for some minutes.

"A splash of whisky would be good in this," Fin said at last, more in hope than expectation.

"Good idea." And to Fin's surprise Donald got up to retrieve a bottle of Balvenie Doublewood from the dresser. More than two-thirds of it had already gone. He uncorked it and poured generous measures into each of their mugs, and sat down again.

They sipped some more, and Fin nodded. "Better." He heard Donald sigh deeply.

"It sticks in my craw, Fin, but I owe you an apology."

Fin nodded. "Damn right you do."

"Whatever the provocation, I'd no right to hit you. It was wrong."

Fin turned to look at his one-time friend and saw genuine regret in his face. "Why? Why was it wrong?"

"Because Jesus taught us that violence is wrong. *Whoever shall strike thee on thy right cheek, turn to him also the other.*"

"Actually, I think it was me who turned the other cheek."

Donald threw him a dark look.

"Anyway, whatever happened to an eye for an eye?"

Donald took a mouthful of chocolate and whisky. "As Gandhi said, an eye for an eye and we'd all be blind."

"You really believe all this stuff, don't you?"

"Yes, I do. And the least you could do is respect that."

"I'll never respect what you believe, Donald. Only your right to believe it. Just as you should respect mine not to."

Donald turned a long, penetrating look upon him, the glow of the peats colouring one half of his pale face, the other in shadow. "You choose not to believe, Fin. Because of what happened to your parents. That's different from not actually believing."

"I'll tell you what I believe, Donald. I believe that the God of the Old Testament is not the same as the God of the New. How can you reconcile the cruelty and violence practised by one with the peace and love preached by the other? You pick and choose the bits you like, and ignore the bits you don't. That's how. It's why there are so many Christian factions. There are, what, five different Protestant sects on this island alone?"

Donald shook his head vigorously. "It is the weakness of men that they will always disagree, and fight over their differences, Fin. Faith is the key."

"Faith is the crutch of the weak. You use it to paper over all the contradictions. And you fall back on it to provide easy answers to impossible questions." Fin leaned forward. "When you hit me tonight, that came from the heart, not from your faith. It was the real you, Donald. You were following your instinct. However mis-guided, it came from a genuine desire to protect your daughter. And your granddaughter."

Donald's laugh was heavily ironic. "A real role-reversal. The believer doing the striking, the non-believer turning the other cheek. You must love that." There was no disguising the bitterness in his voice. "It was wrong, Fin, and I shouldn't have done it. It won't happen again."

"Damn right it won't. Because next time I'll hit you back. And let me tell you, I play dirty."

Donald couldn't resist a smile. He drained his mug and stared into it for several long moments as if the answers to all the questions of the universe might somehow be found at the bottom of it. "You want some more?"

"Chocolate or whisky?"

"Whisky, of course. I have another bottle."

Fin held out his mug. "You can put as much as you like in there."

Donald divided the rest of the bottle between them, and Fin felt the smooth malt, coloured and softened by the sherry in whose casks it had aged, slip easily down to warm his insides. "Whatever happened to us, Donald? We used to be friends. Everyone looked up to you when we were kids. You were almost heroic, a role model for the rest of us."

"A pretty bloody awful role model, then."

Fin shook his head. "No. You made mistakes, sure. Everyone does. But there was something different about you. You were a free spirit, Donald, raising two fingers to the world. God changed you. And not for the better."

"Don't start!"

"I keep hoping one day you'll turn around with that big infectious grin of yours and shout, *Only joking!*"

Donald laughed. "God did change me, Fin. But it *was* for the better. He taught me to control my baser instincts, to be a better person than I was. To do unto others only that which I would have them do unto me."

"Then why are you treating Fin and Donna so badly? It's wrong to keep them apart. I know you think you are protecting your daughter, but that baby is Fionnlagh's daughter, too. How would you feel if you were Fionnlagh?"

"I wouldn't have got her pregnant in the first place."

"Oh, come on! I bet you can't even remember how many girls you slept with at that age. You were just lucky that none of them got pregnant." He paused. "Until Catriona."

Donald glowered up at him from beneath a gathering of brows. "Fuck you, Fin!"

And Fin burst out laughing. "Now, *that's* the old Donald."

Donald shook his head, trying to hold back a smile. "You always were a bad influence on me." He got up and crossed to the dresser, finding and opening the fresh bottle. He returned to top up both their mugs and slumped again into his chair. "So after everything, we share a grandchild you and me, Fin Macleod. Grandparents!" He blew his disbelief through pursed lips. "When did you find out that Fionnlagh was your boy?"

"Last year. During the investigation into the Angel Macritchie murder."

Donald raised an eyebrow. "It's not generally known, is it?"

"No."

Donald fixed him with curious eyes. "What happened out on An Sgeir last August, Fin?"

But Fin just shook his head. "That's between me and my maker."

Donald nodded slowly. "And the reason for your visit to the church the other day . . . is that a secret, too?"

Fin thought about it, staring deep into the embers of the peats, and decided that there would be no harm in telling Donald the truth. "You probably heard about the body they found in the bog at Siader a couple of weeks ago."

Donald inclined his head in acknowledgement.

"It was the body of a young man of seventeen or eighteen, murdered some time in the late 1950s."

"Murdered?" The Reverend Murray was clearly shocked.

"Yes. And it turns out he's related in some way to Tormod Macdonald. Who turns out not to be Tormod Macdonald."

Donald's mug paused halfway to his mouth. "What?"

And Fin told him the story of his trip to Harris with DS Gunn, and what they had found there. Donald sipped thoughtfully on his whisky as he listened.

"The problem is," Fin said, "we'll probably never find out the truth. Tormod's dementia is well advanced and getting worse. It's hard to get any kind of sense out of him. Marsaili was there today and he was talking about using seaweed to fertilize crows."

Donald shrugged. "Well, that's not so daft."

Fin blinked in surprise. "It's not?"

"Sure, *feannagan* means *crows* here on Lewis, or Harris. But in the southern isles it's what they called the lazy beds."

"I have no idea what you're talking about, Donald."

Donald laughed. "You've probably never been to the Catholic south, Fin, have you? And I probably wouldn't either if it hadn't been for some ecumenical visits." He flashed him a look. "Maybe I'm not quite as narrow-minded as you would like to think?"

"What are lazy beds?"

"It's what the islanders developed to grow vegetables, mainly potatoes, when the soil was thin or poor in quality. Like you'll find in South Uist, or Eriskay. They use seaweed cut from the shore as fertilizer. They lay it in strips, about a foot wide, with another foot between them where they dig up the earth and turn it over on top of the seaweed. That creates drainage channels between the lines of soil and seaweed where they plant the tatties. Lazy beds, they call them. Or *feannagan.*"

Fin took a mouthful of whisky. "So it's really not that daft to talk about fertilising the crows."

"Not at all." Donald leaned forward on his knees, cradling his mug between his hands and gazing into the dying fire. "Maybe Marsaili's dad didn't come from Harris at all, Fin. Maybe he came from the south. South Uist, Eriskay, Barra. Who knows?" He paused to take another sip. "But here's a thought . . ." And he turned to look at Fin. "He'd never have got the marriage schedule from the registrar allowing my father to marry him if he hadn't been able to produce a birth certificate. So how would he have got that?"

"Not from the registrar on Harris," Fin said. "Because the dead boy was known there."

"Exactly. So he knew, or was related to, the family. Or someone close to him was. And he either stole the birth certificate, or was given it. All you need to do is find that connection."

A reluctant smile crept up on Fin, and he cocked one eyebrow towards the minister. "You know, Donald, you always were smarter than the rest of us. But a connection like that? It would be like searching for a speck of dust in the cosmos."

| TWENTY-THREE |

Catriona had given him a pair of Donald's trousers and a woollen jersey which he wore now under his oilskins as he braved the winds that swept unimpeded across the machair.

It had taken until the early hours for the two men to work themselves halfway down the second bottle. Fin had woken up on the settee some time after seven with the smell of bacon wafting through from the kitchen.

There had been no sign of Donald as Catriona served him a plate of bacon, egg, sausage and fried bread at the kitchen table. She had gone to bed long before they had finished with the whisky, and made no comment about the amount consumed. Neither Fin nor she had felt much like engaging in conversation. That she disapproved of him, and whatever had happened the night before, was evidenced by her silence.

The rain had stopped some time during the night, and already soft southern winds had dried the grasses, another change in the weather. The sun had rediscovered its warmth, and fought to take the edge off the wind.

Fin needed the air to clear a head still fuzzy and delicate from the words and whisky that he and Donald had spilled and consumed between them. He had not been back to his tent yet, dreading to think what state it might now be in, having left it open to the elements all night. There was a chance it might be gone altogether, and he wasn't sure that he was ready yet to face that possibility.

Whether drawn by his subconscious, or by pure chance, he found himself on the track leading to Crobost Cemetery, where headstones stood out on the rise of the hill like the spines of a porcupine. All the Macleods and Macdonalds and Macritchies, the Morrisons and Macraes, who had lived and died in this narrow neck of the world were buried here. Hard like rock, and carved out from the mass of humanity by the wind and the sea and the rain. Among them his own parents. He wished, now, he had brought Robbie back to put him in the ground here with his ancestors. But Mona would never have allowed it.

He stopped at the gate. It was here that Artair had told him all those years before that he and Marsaili were married. A part of him had died that day with the loss, finally, of the only woman he had ever loved. The woman he had driven from his life, by thoughtlessness and cruelty. A self-inflicted loss.

He thought about her now. Saw her in his mind's eye. Skin flushed by the wind, hair unravelling behind her. Pictured those cornflower-blue eyes piercing through all his protective armour, disarming him with her wit, breaking his heart with her smile. And he wondered if there was any way back. Or was it true what he had told Fionnlagh? That they hadn't been able to make it work all those years before, why would it be any different now? The pessimist in him knew that it probably was. And being consumed by pessimism, it was only the tiniest part of him that thought they had any chance at all. Was that why he had come back? In pursuit of that smallest of chances?

He didn't open the gate. He had revisited the past too often, and found only pain.

With alcohol still fogging his brain, he turned weary feet in the direction of the road home, past the school where he had so often walked with Artair and Marsaili. It hadn't changed much. Nor had the long straight road that led up to the Crobost stores, the silhouette of the church on the hill, and all the houses standing four-square to the wind along the ridge. Nothing grew here but the hardiest shrubs. Only man, and the homes he built, could stand up to the fury of the weather that swept in across the Atlantic. But only for so long. As the cemetery on the cliffs and the ruins of so many blackhouses could testify.

Fionnlagh's car still sat on the apron in front of the store, where it had been abandoned the night before, its ignition key lost somewhere in the bog. No doubt Fionnlagh would return some time later in the day to hotwire it and take it home. Fin's car stood proud near the summit of the hill, buffeted by the breeze at the top of the path leading down to Marsaili's bungalow. He had handed his keys to the boy and told him to take Donna and the child home with him, then driven back in Donald's car to the manse.

He knocked at the kitchen door before going in. Donna turned from the table where she had poured herself a bowl of cereal, her face a mask of apprehension. She relaxed only a little when she saw that it was Fin. Her features were devoid of all colour. Painfully pale. Shadows beneath frightened eyes. Her eyes flickered past him, as if she suspected he might not be alone.

"Where's my dad?"

"Sleeping off a hangover."

Her face creased in disbelief. "You're kidding."

And Fin realized that Donna knew only the Bible-thumping, God-fearing, self-righteous bully that Donald had become. She had no idea of the real man who hid behind the religious shell he had grown to conceal his vulnerability. The Donald Murray that Fin had known as a boy. The man he had glimpsed briefly once again in the small hours of this morning, when whisky had lowered his defences.

"Where's Fionnlagh?"

She nodded towards the living room. "He's feeding Eilidh."

Fin frowned. "Eilidh?"

"The baby."

And he realized it was the first time he had heard her name. She had only ever been referred to as "the baby" or "the child." And he had never thought to ask. He caught Donna looking at him with eyes that seemed to read him so easily, and he felt himself blushing. He nodded and went through to find Fionnlagh sitting in an armchair, cradling the baby in his left arm, holding a feeding bottle to her lips in his right hand. Wide eyes in a tiny face stared up at her father with absolute trust.

Fionnlagh seemed almost uncomfortable at his father finding him like this, but he was in no position to move. Fin sat down in the armchair opposite, and an uneasy silence settled on them. Finally Fin said, "Eilidh was my mother's name."

Fionnlagh nodded. "I know. That's who she's named after."

Fin had to blink hard to disperse the moisture that gathered suddenly in his eyes. "She'd have loved that."

A pale smile drifted across the boy's face. "Thanks, by the way."

"What for?"

"Stepping in last night. I don't know what would have happened if you hadn't showed up."

"Running away's not the answer, Fionnlagh."

The sudden fire of indignation flared in the young man. "Then what is? We can't go on like this."

"No, you can't. But you can't throw your lives away either. You can only do the best for your child by making the best of yourselves."

"And how do we do that?"

"For a start you need to make your peace with Donald."

Fionnlagh gasped and turned his head away.

"He's not the monster you think he is, Fionnlagh. Just a misguided man who thinks he's doing the best for his daughter and his granddaughter."

Fionnlagh started to protest, but Fin raised a hand to stop him.

"Talk to him, Fionnlagh. Tell him what it is you want to do with your life, and how you intend to do it. Show him that you mean to support Donna and Eilidh when you can, and marry his daughter when you're able to offer her a future."

"I don't *know* what I want to do with my life!" Fionnlagh's frustration caused his voice to crack.

"Hardly anyone does at your age. But you're bright, Fionnlagh. You need to finish school, go to university. Donna, too, if that's what she wants to do."

"And in the meantime?"

"Stay here. The three of you."

"The Reverend Murray'll never accept that!"

"You don't know what he'll accept until you talk to him. I mean, think about it. You've got much more in common than you know. He only wants the best for Donna and Eilidh. And so do you. All you have to do is convince him of that."

Fionnlagh closed his eyes and took a deep breath. "Easier said than done."

The rubber teat slipped from Eilidh's mouth, and she burbled her protest. Fionnlagh refocused his attention on her and slipped it back between tiny milky lips.

Fin recognized Donald's car parked where his own should have been, on the curve of the road above the derelict croft and his wind-battered tent. Heavy low cloud scraped and grazed itself against the rise and fall of the land, pregnant with rain, but holding it still as if in realisation that the ground below was already beyond saturation.

Fin reached the car and looked around. But there was no sign of Donald. At least his tent was still there, beat up and bedraggled, guys slack and vibrating crazily in the wind, but still clinging to their pegs. He slithered down the slope towards it, and through the open flap saw that there was someone inside. He knelt down and crawled in to find a tousled-looking Donald Murray sitting cross-legged on the sleeping bag, the hit-and-run folder open on his knees.

Anger spiked through Fin and he grabbed the folder away. "What the fuck do you think you're doing?"

Donald was startled. And seemed embarrassed. "I'm sorry, Fin. I didn't mean to pry, honestly. I came down looking for you and found the tent open, and the contents of your folder blowing all over the place. I just gathered up the sheets, and . . ." He paused. "I couldn't help seeing what it was."

Fin couldn't meet his eye.

"I had no idea."

Fin tossed the folder towards the back of the tent. "It's old news." He backed out of the tent and stood up into the wind. The great rolling banks of cloud seemed to be just above his head, pressing down on him, and he felt the odd spit in his face. Donald clambered out after him, and the two men stood side by side, looking down the slope of the croft towards the cliffs and the beach below. It was some minutes before they spoke.

"You ever lost a child, Donald?"

"No, I haven't."

"It's gut-wrenching. As if your life no longer has any meaning. You just want to curl up and die." He turned quickly towards the minister. "And don't give me any shit about God, and some higher purpose. That would only make me more mad at Him than I already am."

"Do you want to tell me about it?"

Fin shrugged and pushed his hands into the pockets of his oilskins and started off down the slope towards the cliffs. Donald hurried to catch him up. Fin said, "He was just eight years old, Donald. We didn't have a great marriage, Mona and me, but we'd made Robbie, and in a way that made some kind of sense of us."

They could see now, below them, the sea rolling in off the Minch in great slow-motion waves that smashed in white, frothing fury on the rocks all along the coast, sending spray thirty feet in the air.

"She was out with him one day. They'd been shopping. She had bags in one hand, Robbie's hand in the other. It was a pelican crossing. Go for pedestrians. And this car just came straight through the lights. Bang. She went up in the air, he went under the wheels. She survived, he died." He briefly closed his eyes. "And we died, too. Our marriage, I mean. Robbie had been the only reason for staying together. Without him we simply fell apart."

They had almost reached the edge of the cliffs now, where weather erosion had made the soil unstable and it was unsafe to get any closer. Fin squatted down suddenly, and plucked the soft wet bloom from a single head of white bog cotton, rolling it gently between thumb and forefinger. Donald squatted down beside him, the ocean growling and snarling beneath them, as if hoping to pluck them from the cliff's edge and suck them down into the deep. It spat its spray in their faces.

"What happened to the driver?"

"Nothing. He didn't stop. They never got him."

"Do you think they ever will?"

Fin turned his head to look at him. "I don't know that there's any way I can move forward with my life until they do."

"And if they found him?"

"I'd kill him." Fin twisted the bog cotton between his fingers and threw it into the wind.

"No you wouldn't."

"Trust me, Donald. Given the chance, that's just what I'd do."

But Donald shook his head. "You wouldn't, Fin. You don't know anything about him. Who he is, why he didn't stop that day, what kind of hell he's been through since."

"Tell it to someone who gives a damn." Fin stood up. "I saw you last night, Donald. The look in your eyes, when you thought you were losing your baby girl. And all she was doing was catching a ferry. Think how you'd feel if someone laid hands on her, hurt her, killed her. You wouldn't be turning the other cheek. It would be an eye for an eye, and fuck what Gandhi said."

"No, Fin." Donald stood up too. "I can imagine I would feel many things. Rage, pain, a desire for revenge. But it wouldn't be my place. Vengeance is mine sayeth the Lord. I would have to believe that somehow, somewhere, justice would be done. Even if it was in the next life."

Fin looked at him for a long time, lost somewhere in myriad thoughts. At length he said, "There are times, Donald, I wish I had your faith."

Donald smiled. "Then maybe there's hope for you yet."

And Fin laughed. "Not a chance. Souls don't come any more lost than this one." He turned quickly away. "Come on. I know a path down to the rocks." And he headed off along the cliffs, too perilously close to the edge for Donald's comfort as he chased after him.

After about fifty yards, the land dipped down, cliff giving way to crumbling peat and shale, sheltered from the sea's assault by a towering cluster of rocks that stacked up from the shore. A ragged path led down at an angle to a protected shingle beach, almost hidden from the sea itself and nearly impossible to reach from either side. Only a matter of feet away, the ocean vented its anger all along the rocky shallows, the roar of it muffled by the stacks that kept it at bay. The clearest of water gathered in pools among the rocks below them, and the spray blew high over their heads.

"This was my secret place when I was a kid," Fin said. "I used to come down here when I didn't want to talk to anyone. I never came back after my parents were killed and I went to live with my aunt."

Donald looked around this tiny oasis of calm, the sound of the sea echoing around it, so close and yet so far away. Even the wind barely made it down here.

"I've been a couple of times since I got back." Fin smiled sadly. "Maybe I thought I'd find the old me still here. A ghost from an age of innocence. Nothing but pebbles and crabs, though, and a very distant echo of the past. But I think that's probably only in my head." He grinned and planted one foot on a ledge of rock. "What did you come to see me about?"

"I woke up thinking about Tormod, and his stolen identity." Donald laughed. "Well, after I'd drunk about a pint of water and swallowed two paracetamol, that is. I haven't had that much whisky in a long time."

"Catriona will be banning me from the manse."

Donald grinned. "She already has."

Fin laughed, and it felt good to laugh with Donald again after all these years. "So what was it you thought about Tormod?"

"There was an article in the *Gazette* a couple of months ago, Fin. About a genealogy centre down at the south end of Harris. Seallam, it's called. One man's hobby that became an obsession. And now it's just about the most comprehensive record of family relationships in the Outer Hebrides. Better than any church or government records. This guy's traced tens of thousands of family connections from the islands as far as North America and Australia. If anyone has a record of the Macdonald family and all its branches, it would be him." He raised his eyebrows. "What do you think?"

Fin nodded thoughtfully. "I think it would be worth a look."

| TWENTY-FOUR |

The drive south took Fin past Luskentyre and Scarista where he had gone the day before with George Gunn. He had been on the road nearly two hours when the bare green hills of South Harris rose up from the valley to dwarf the tiny settlements that clung tenaciously to the banks of the small lochs that flooded the gorges.

Beyond the single-storey white building with its pitched roofs that housed the Seallam visitor centre, cream-coloured cloud flowed down the sides of a conical hill like an erupting volcano. Unusually, the wind had dropped, and an unnatural still hung in the valley with the mist.

Dwarf pines crowded around the few houses that made up the village of Northton—An Taobh Tuath in the Gaelic. Yellow irises and the pink bloom of flowering azaleas lined the road, rare colour in a monotone landscape. A sign read: *SEALLAM! Exhibitions, Genealogy, Teas/Coffees.*

Fin parked in a gravel area on the far side of a stream that wound its way down between the hills, and he followed a rough path to the small wooden bridge that took him over it and across to the centre. A big man with a fuzz of white hair fringing an otherwise bald head introduced himself as Seallam's consultant genealogist, Bill Lawson. He pushed enormous seventies teardrop glasses back up on to the bridge of a long nose and confessed to being the man whose hobby had become the obsession described by the *Stornoway Gazette*.

He was only too happy to show Fin the huge wall maps of North America and Australia that comprised a part of the centre's public exhibition. Clusters of black-headed pins identified settlements of Hebridean families who had gone in search of new lives in California, the eastern seaboard of the United States, Nova Scotia, southeastern Australia.

"What exactly is it you're looking for?" he asked Fin.

"It's one particular family. The Macdonalds of Seilebost. Murdo and Peggy. They had a son called Tormod who drowned in a boating accident in 1958. They left their croft some time in the early sixties, and may have gone abroad. It's now lying derelict."

"That should be simple enough," the genealogist said, and Fin followed him through to a small sales and reception area where shelves groaned with coffee-table tomes, and hard-cover tourist guides to the islands. Bill Lawson stooped to recover a volume from a pile of buff-coloured publications on the bottom shelf. "These are our croft histories of Harris," he said. "We do it by village and croft. Who lived there, when and where they went. Everything else changes, but the land itself stays in the same place." He flipped through the pages of the spiral-bound book. "Prior to civil registration in 1855 information was thin on the ground. What information was kept was all in a foreign language. English." He smiled. "So you got what the registrar thought the name should be. Wrong in many cases. And often they just weren't interested. Same as the church records. Some ministers kept a faithful register. Others couldn't be bothered. We've combined word-of-mouth with the official records kept since 1855, and when the two match up you can be pretty sure it's accurate."

"So you think you can tell me what happened to the Macdonalds?"

He grinned. "Yes, I do. We have research on virtually every household in the Western Isles over the last two hundred years. More than 27,500 family trees."

It took him about fifteen minutes searching through record books and his computer database to track down the croft and its history, and the ancestral lineage of all those who had lived on it and worked the land over generations.

"Yes, here we are." He stabbed a finger at the pages of one of his books. "Murdo and Peggy Macdonald emigrated to Canada in 1962. New Glasgow, Nova Scotia."

"Were there any branches of the family who stayed on in the islands?"

"Let me see . . ." He ran his finger down a list of names. "There's Peggy's cousin, Marion. Married a Catholic lad just before the war. Donald Angus O'Henley." He chuckled. "I bet that caused a bit of a stir."

"And any surviving members of that family?"

But the old genealogist shook his head as he examined the records. "Looks like he was killed some time during the war. There were no children. She died in 1991."

Fin breathed his frustration through his teeth. It seemed as if he had made his journey in vain. "I don't suppose there would be any neighbours around who might still remember them?"

"Well, you'd have to go down to Eriskay for that."

"Eriskay?"

"Oh, aye. That's where Donald Angus came from. And there's no way a Catholic lad was ever going to settle down among the fun-hating Presbyterians of Harris." He laughed at his own joke. "When they got married she went to live with him on his family croft at Haunn on the Isle of Eriskay."

The little ferry and fishing port of An t-Òb was renamed Leverburgh by William Hesketh Lever, later Lord Leverhulme, who bought the town, along with most of South Harris, just after the First World War.

Very little evidence remained now of the half a million pounds he had spent to develop it into a major fishing port, designed to supply the more than four hundred fish shops he had purchased throughout Britain. Piers were built, curing sheds, smoke houses. Plans had been made to blast a channel through to the inner loch, creating a harbour for up to two hundred boats.

But the best-laid schemes of mice and men gang aft agley, and when Leverhulme died of pneumonia in 1924, the plans were abandoned and the estate sold off.

Now, a dwindling population of little over two thousand lived in a scattering of houses around the pier and concrete ramp built to accommodate the roll-on roll-off ferries that plied back and forth among the islands peppering the waters between South Harris and North Uist. Dreams of a major fishing port were lost irretrievably in the mist.

Fin pulled in behind two lines of vehicles that sat on the tarmac waiting for the ferry. Beyond piles of discarded creels, and grazing sheep, a line of green-clad houses ran between hills that folded one upon the other down towards the shore. The wind had died completely, and water like glass reflected rocks strewn with amber seaweed. Out in the Sound of Harris, the ferry emerged distantly from the grey, like a ghost drifting among the shadows of the islands: Ensay, Killegray, Langaigh, Grodhaigh.

He sat and watched as the ferry approached the harbour, hearing at last the thud, thud of its engines. It would take an hour, perhaps an hour and a half, to drive south through the Uists, across the barren moonscape that was Benbecula, to the Sound of Eriskay, and the island itself at the southern end of the archipelago, the last stop before Barra.

The leads that drew him there were tenuous. A cousin of the dead Tormod Macdonald's mother who had moved to the island. The lazy beds of Eriskay, the *feannagan* of which Marsaili's father had spoken. And then, there had been the church on the hill that he had described, with its view over the cemetery to the silver sands beyond. It could have been the church at Scarista, except that there was no boat in that church, and the sands it overlooked were golden, not silver. Somehow he trusted the old man's scattered recollections, fragments of memory painting a picture not to be found on Harris, where the real Tormod Macdonald had lived and died. These were memories from another place, another time. Eriskay. Perhaps.

The warning sirens started up as the *Loch Portain* slipped into harbour, and began lowering her ramp to the concrete. A few cars and a handful of lorries spilled out from her belly, and the waiting lines of vehicles started down the slope one by one.

The one-hour crossing from Harris to Berneray drifted by like a dream. The ferry seemed almost to glide across the mirrored surface of the Sound, drifting past the spectral islets and rocks that emerged phantom-like from a silvered mist. Fin stood on the foredeck, grasping the rail, and watching clouds like brushstrokes leaving darker streaks against the palest of grey skies. He had rarely seen the islands in such splendid stillness, mysterious and ethereal, without the least sign that man had ever passed this way before.

Finally the dark outline of the island of Berneray loomed out of the gloom, and Fin returned to the car deck to disembark at the start of his long drive south. This disparate collection of islands, which had once been miscalled the Long Island, was now largely connected by a network of causeways bridging fords where once vehicles could only pass at low tide. Only between Harris and Berneray, and Eriskay and Barra, was it still necessary to cross by boat.

North Uist presented a dark, primal landscape. Soaring mountains shrouded in cloud that poured down their slopes to spread tendrils of mist across the moor. The skeletons of long-abandoned homes, gable ends standing stark and black against a brooding sky. Hostile and inhospitable bogland, shredded by scraps of loch and ragged inlets. The ruins of all the failed attempts by men and women to tame it were everywhere in evidence, and those who remained were huddled together in a handful of small, sheltered townships.

Further south, over yet more causeways, the island of Benbecula, flat and featureless, passed in a blur. Then somehow the sky seemed to open up, the oppression lifted, and South Uist spread itself out before him, mountains to the east, the fertile plains of the machair to the west, stretching all the way to the sea.

The cloud was higher now, broken by a rising wind, and sun-light broke through to spill itself in rivers and pools across the land. Yellow and purple flowers bent and bowed in the breeze, and Fin felt his spirits lifting. He drove past the turn-off to the east coast ferry port of Lochboisdale, and away off to the west he could see the abandoned sheds of the old seaweed factory at Orasaigh, beyond a walled Protestant cemetery. Even in death, it seemed, there was segregation between Catholics and Protestants.

Finally he turned east on the road to Ludagh, and across the shimmering Sound of Eriskay he caught his first glimpse of the island itself. It was smaller than he had imagined, dwarfed somehow by the island of Barra and its ring of islets lingering darkly beyond the watercolour wash of sea behind it.

A stone jetty extended out across the mouth of the bay at Ludagh, and a few isolated houses stood up on the hill facing south across the Sound. The tide was out, and a handful of boats at anchor in the bay lay tipped over on their keels in the sand. The concrete stanchions of a disused pier extended out beyond the slip-way where once a ferry must have carried people and goods back and forth.

Fin parked his car on the jetty and stepped out into a stiffening breeze that blew warm into his face from the south. He breathed in the smell of the sea and raised his hand to shade his eyes from the glare of sunlight on water as he gazed across to Eriskay. He could not have said why, but he was almost overtaken by the strangest sense of destiny, something like déjà vu, as he looked upon the island.

An elderly man in jeans and a knitted jumper was working on the hull of an upturned dinghy. He had a face like leather beneath a thatch of spun silver. He nodded, and Fin said, "I thought there was a causeway over to Eriskay now."

The man stood up and pointed east. "Aye, there is. Just carry on round the road to the point there."

And Fin strained against the glare to see the causeway spanning the Sound along the horizon. "Thanks." He got back into his car and followed the road to where it curved around to the point, and he found himself crossing a cattle grid on to the long, straight stretch of road built atop the thousands of tons of boulders that had been dumped to create the causeway between the islands.

As he approached it, Eriskay filled his field of vision, treeless and barren, a single mountain pushing up into the sky. The road turned up between the folds of rising hills to lift him on to the island proper. It reached a T-junction, and he turned left on a narrow ribbon of tarmac that took him down to the old harbour at Haunn, where Bill Lawson had told him the O'Henley family croft was to be found.

An old stone jetty in a state of considerable disrepair reached out into a narrow, sheltered bay. A couple of derelict houses stood up among the rocks on the far side where a concrete quay looked all but abandoned. A handful of other houses stood around the bay, some inhabited, others in ruins. He parked at the end of the old jetty and walked over the rise, past piles of creels and nets laid out to dry, and found himself looking down the length of a concrete ramp, and back across the Sound to South Uist.

"That's where the car ferry used to come in." An old man with a quilted jacket and cloth cap stopped at his side, his wire-haired fox terrier pulling and twisting at the end of a long lead. "The old passenger boat used to come in at the other quay." He chuckled. "There was no call for a car ferry till they built the roads. And they didn't do that till the fifties. Even then, there wasn't many folk had cars."

"I take it you're a local, then," Fin said.

"Born and bred. But I can tell from your Gaelic you're not from around here yourself."

"I'm a Leodhasach," Fin said. "From Crobost in Ness."

"Never been that far north myself," the old man said. "What brings you all the way down here?"

"I'm looking for the old O'Henley croft."

"Oh, well, you're not far off the mark. Come with me."

And he turned and headed back over the rise towards the old jetty, his dog running on ahead, leaping and barking at the wind. Fin followed him until he stopped by the quayside, the little bay stretched out ahead of them.

"That yellow building over there on the left, the one without a roof—that used to be the village store and post office. Run by a chap called Nicholson, I think it was. The only Protestant on the island." He grinned. "Can you imagine?"

Fin couldn't.

"Just up beyond that, to the right, you'll see the remains of an old stone cottage. Not much left of it now. That's the O'Henley place. But she's long dead. Widowed quite young, too. She had a wee lassie that stayed with her. Ceit, if my memory serves me well. But I'm not sure that she was her daughter."

"What happened to her?"

"Oh, heaven knows. Gone long before the old lady died. Like all the young ones. They just couldn't wait to get off the island in those days." His smile was touched by sadness. "Then and now."

Fin's eyes strayed beyond the ruin towards a large white house built on the rocks above it. What looked like a brand-new driveway snaked up the hill to a levelled garden area at the front, and a wooden deck accessed by French windows from the house. Above it, a balcony was glassed in against the elements, and on the wall above that a neon star. "Who lives in the big white house?" he said.

The old man grinned. "Oh, that's Morag MacEwan's house. Retired to the island of her birth nigh on sixty years after she left it. I don't remember her at all, but she's a character, that one. You'll maybe know her yourself."

"Me?" Fin was taken aback.

"If you watched much telly, that is. She was a big star on one of those soap operas. Not short of a bob or two, I'll tell you. Keeps her Christmas lights up all year round, and drives a pink, open-topped Mercedes." He laughed. "They say her house is like Aladdin's cave inside, though I've never been in it myself."

Fin said, "How many people are there still living on Eriskay these days?"

"Och, not many. About a hundred and thirty now. Even when I was a lad there was only about five hundred or so. The island's only two and a half miles long, you see. One and a half at its widest point. There's not much of a living to be made here. Not from the land, and not from the sea now either."

Fin let his gaze wander over the desolate, rocky hillsides and wondered how folk had ever managed to survive here. His eyes came to rest on a dark building sitting high up on the hill to his right, dominating the island. "What's that place?"

The old man followed his gaze. "That's the church," he said. "St. Michael's."

Fin drove up the hill towards the little settlement of houses known as Rubha Ban which was built around the primary school and the health centre. A sign for *Eaglais Naomh Mhicheil* led him up a narrow track to a stone-built church with steeply pitched roofs and tall windows delineated in white. An arched doorway topped by a white cross and the logo *Quis ut Deus*—Who is like God?—opened into the church at its south end. Outside its walls a black ship's bell was mounted on a stand, and Fin wondered if that is what they rang to call the faithful to worship. The name, painted on it in white, was SMS *Derfflinger*.

He parked his car and looked back down the hill towards the jetty at Haunn, and across the Sound to South Uist. The sea shimmered and sparkled and moved as if it were alive, and sunlight streamed across the hills beyond it, the shadows of clouds tracking across their contours at speed. The wind was powerful up here, filling Fin's jacket, and blowing through the tight curls of his hair as if trying to straighten them.

A very elderly lady in a red cardigan and dark-grey skirt was washing the floor in the entrance hall. She wore elbow-length green rubber gloves and sloshed soapy water from a bright red bucket. She wore a silk headscarf around cotton-wool hair, and nodded acknowledgement to him as she moved aside to let him past.

For just a moment time stopped for Fin. Light poured in through arched windows. Colourful statues of the Virgin Mary and baby

Jesus, and winged angels bowed in prayer, cast long shadows across narrow wooden pews. Stars shone in a blue firmament painted in the dome above the altar, and the white-draped table itself was supported on the bows of a small boat.

Every hair on his arms, and the back of his neck, stood on end. For here was the church with the boat in it that Tormod had spoken of. He turned back towards the entrance.

"Excuse me."

The old lady straightened up from her bucket. "Yes?"

"What's the story of the boat beneath the altar? Do you know?"

She placed both hands behind her hips and arched herself backwards. "Aye," she said. "It's a wonderful tale. The church was built by the people themselves, you see. Quarried and dressed the stone, and carried the sand and all the materials up here on their backs. Devout souls they were. Every last one of them with a place in Heaven. No doubt of that." She thrust her mop back into the bucket and leaned on its handle. "But it was the fishermen who paid for it. Offered to give the proceeds of one night's catch towards the building of the church. Everyone prayed that night, and they came back with a record catch. £200, it was. A lot of money away back then. So the boat's a kind of homage to those brave souls who risked the wrath of the sea for the Lord."

Outside, Fin followed the gravel path around to the west side of the church and saw how the land fell away to the shore. Past the houses on the rise, and the headstones on the machair below, to a strip of beach glowing silver against the shallow turquoise waters of the bay. Just as Tormod had said.

Fin remembered a paragraph from the post-mortem report, which he had read only the night before in the flickering fluorescent light of his tent.

There is an oval, dark brown-black, apparent abraded contusion, measuring 5 x 2.5 centimetres, over the inferior aspect of the right patellar area. The surface skin is vaguely roughened and there are fine grains of silver sand in the superficial skin.

The pathologist had found fine silver sand in all the abrasions and contusions of the lower body. Not golden sand, as found on the beaches of Harris. But silver sand, as found here, down there, on what Tormod had called Charlie's beach.

Fin focused on the crescent of silver that led the eye around the bay to a new breakwater at the south end, and wondered why he had called it *Charlie's* beach.

| TWENTY-FIVE |

"Who's this?"

"It's your grandson, Mr. Macdonald. Fionnlagh."

He doesn't seem at all familiar to me. I see some of the other inmates sitting in their armchairs like Lord and Lady Muck, eyeing up this young boy with his odd, spiky hair who's come to see me. They seem curious. How does he make it stand up like that? And why?

The nurse pulls up a chair and the boy sits down beside me. He looks uncomfortable. I can't help it if I don't know who the hell he is. "I don't know you," I tell him. How could I have a grandson? I'm hardly old enough to be a father. "What do you want?"

"I'm Marsaili's boy," he says, and I feel my heart skip a beat.

"Marsaili? Is she here?"

"She's gone to Glasgow, Grampa, to sit some exams. She'll be back in a day or so."

This news comes to me like a slap in the face. "She promised to take me home. I'm sick of this hotel." All I do all day is sit in some damned chair and look out the window. I see the children across the street leave for school in the morning, and I see them come home at night. And I can't remember anything that's happened in between. I suppose I must have had lunch, because I'm not hungry. But I don't remember that either.

"Do you remember, Grampa, how I used to help with the gathering? When we brought the sheep in for the shearing."

"Oh, God, aye! The shearing. Back-breaking that was."

"I used to help out from when I was just four or five."

"Aye, you were a bonny wee laddie, Fin. Marsaili thought the world of you, you know."

"No, I'm Fionnlagh, Grampa. Fin's my dad."

He gives me one of those smiles I see people give me all the time these days. Sort of embarrassed, as if they think I'm daft.

"I've been helping out Murdo Morrison for a bit of extra pocket money. Gave him a hand with the lambing too, this year."

I remember the lambing well. That first year on the island. You never got snow, but it could be bloody cold, and the wind on a wet March night would cut you in two. I'd never seen a lamb born before, and was very nearly sick the first time. All that blood and afterbirth. But what an amazing thing it was to see that skinny wee thing, like a drowned rat, breathing its first breath, and taking its first wobbling steps. Life in the raw.

I learned a lot of things that winter. I learned that however hard I thought my existence had been at The Dean, there were much worse things in life. Not that anyone treated us badly. Not really. But survival was brutal work, and you weren't spared it because you were a kid.

There were daily chores. Up in the pitch-black, long before we left for school, to climb the hill and fill our buckets from the spring. There was cutting the seaweed from the shore. So much a ton Donald Seamus got for it from Alginate Industries at the seaweed factory over at Orasaigh. Killer work it was, slipping and sliding over the black rocks at low tide, bent double with a blunt sickle hacking away at the kelp, crusted shells, like razors, shredding your fingers. I think they burned the seaweed and used the ashes for fertilizer. Someone once told me they made explosives and toothpaste and ice cream from it too. But I never believed that. They must have thought I was as simple as Peter.

After the lambing there was the peat-cutting, up over the other side of Beinn Sciathan, lifting the peats as Donald Seamus cut them with the *tarasgeir*, stacking them in groups of three. We would turn them around from time to time till they were dried hard in the wind, then fetch them in big wicker baskets. We shared our pony with a neighbour, so it wasn't always available, and then we had to carry those baskets on our own backs.

After that there would be the hay, hand-cut with a scythe into long swathes. You took out the rough shaws and laid it out to dry, praying that it wouldn't rain. It had to be turned, shaken and dried again, or it would rot in the stack. So you needed fine weather. Back at the stackyard it would be made into bales, and it wasn't until the stackyard was full that Donald Seamus would be satisfied that there was enough to feed the beasts through the winter.

You wouldn't think there was much time for school, but Peter and me were sent over with the other kids every morning on the boat to be picked up by the bus and taken to the corrugated-iron building by Daliburgh crossroads that was the secondary school. There was another building, the technical school, about a quarter of a mile down the road. But I only went until the incident at New Year. After that Donald Seamus refused to send me back, and Peter had to go on his own.

They weren't bad folks, Donald Seamus and Mary-Anne, but there was no love in them. I knew some homers that got terrible abuse. That wasn't us.

Mary-Anne hardly ever spoke. Barely acknowledged our existence, except to feed us and wash the few clothes we had. Most of her time was spent spinning, dyeing and weaving wool, and joining with the other women in the waulking of the cloth, all sitting around a long wooden table out front and turning and beating the weave until it was thickened and fully waterproof. As they waulked they sang to the rhythm of it. Endless songs to make bearable the mindless repetition. I've never heard women sing so much as I did during my time on the island.

Donald Seamus was hard but fair. If he took his belt to me it was usually because I deserved it. But I never let him lay a hand on Peter. Whatever wrong the boy might have done, it wasn't his fault, and it took a confrontation between me and Donald Seamus to establish that.

I can't remember what it was now that Peter had done. Dropped the eggs on the way from the henhouse and broken the lot, maybe. I remember he did that several times before they stopped asking him.

But whatever it was he'd done, Donald Seamus was in a fury. He grabbed Peter by the scruff of the neck and dragged him into the shed where we kept the animals. It was always warm in there and smelled of shit.

By the time I got there my brother's trousers were already down around his ankles. Donald Seamus had him bent over a trestle and was in the process of slipping his belt out of its loops, ready to give him a leathering. He looked around as I came in and told me in no uncertain terms to get the hell out. But I stood my ground and looked around me. There were two brand-new axe handles leaning up against the wall in the corner of the shed, and I lifted one, feeling the cool, smooth wood in my palm as I wrapped my fingers tightly around it and tested its weight.

Donald Seamus paused, and I met his eye, unblinking, the axe handle dangling at my side. He was a big man was Donald Seamus, and I have no doubt that in a fight he could have given me a good hiding. But I was a sturdy kid by then, almost a young man, and with a stout axe haft in my hand, there was no doubt in either of our minds that I could do him a lot of damage.

Neither of us said a word, but a line was drawn. If he laid a hand on my brother he would answer to me. He buckled up his belt and told Peter to clear off, and I laid the axe handle back in the corner.

I never resisted when it came my turn to feel his belt on my arse, and I think maybe that he belted me twice as much as he might otherwise have done. Like I was taking the punishment for both of us. But I didn't mind. A sore arse passed, and I kept my word to my mother.

It was during our second lambing that I rescued one of them from certain death. It was a feeble wee thing, barely able to stand, and for some reason its mother took against it, refusing it the teat. Donald Seamus gave me a bottle with a rubber teat and told me to feed it.

I spent nearly two weeks feeding that wee beast, and there was no doubt she thought I was her mother. Morag I called her, and she followed me everywhere, like a dog. She would come down to the shore with me when I went to cut the kelp, and when I sat among the rocks at midday eating the rough sandwiches Mary-Ann had wrapped up for me in an oiled paper parcel, she would coorie in beside me, sharing her warmth and soaking up mine. I could stroke her head, and she would look up at me with adoring big eyes. I loved that wee lamb. First loving relationship I'd had with any other living creature since my mother died. Except, perhaps, for Peter. But that was different.

Funny thing is, I think it was the lamb that brought about my first sexual experience with Ceit. Or, at least, her jealousy of it. Seems daft to think of someone being jealous of a lamb, but it's hard to overestimate my emotional attachment to that wee thing.

I'd never had sex of any kind, and some part of me figured that it was probably just for other people, and that I would likely spend the rest of my life beating the meat below the sheets.

Until Ceit took me in hand. So to speak.

She'd complained on several occasions about the amount of time I was spending with the lamb. I had always been at the jetty to meet her and Peter off the boat after school, and we'd go skimming pebbles in the bay, or cross the hill and make our way down to what she always called Charlie's beach on the west side of the island. There was never anyone there, and we aye had great fun playing hide-and-seek among the grasses and the ruined crofts, or racing each other along the compacted sand at low tide. But since Morag came along, I'd been a bit preoccupied.

"You and that bloody lamb," Ceit said to me one day. "I'm sick of it. Nobody has a pet lamb! A dog, maybe, but a lamb?" It was well past the point where it needed me to feed it, but I was reluctant to let it go. We walked in silence up the track that led past Nicholson's store. It was a fine spring day, a soft breeze blowing out of the south-west, the sky streaked with high cloud, like wisps of teased wool. The sun was warm on our skin, and winter seemed at last to have retreated to crouch in the dark, quietly awaiting the autumn equinox, when it would send word of its imminent return on the edge of savage equinoctial gales. But all that seemed a long way away during those optimistic days of late spring and early summer.

Most of the women were out on their doorsteps spinning and weaving. Most of the men were away at sea. The sound of voices raised in song drifted across the hills on the breeze, strangely affecting. It raised goose pimples all across my shoulders every time I heard it.

Ceit lowered her voice as if someone might overhear us. "Meet me tonight," she said. "I've got something I want to give you."

"Tonight?" I was surprised. "When? After dinner?"

"No. When it's dark. When everyone else is sleeping. You can sneak out of your window at the back, can't you?"

I was nonplussed. "Well, I could, I suppose. But why? Whatever it is, why can't you just give me it now?"

"Because I can't, stupid!"

We stopped at the brow of the hill, looking down over the little bay, and out across the Sound, back towards Ludagh.

"Meet me down at the quayside at eleven. The Gillies will be in bed by that time, won't they?"

"Of course."

"Good. No problem, then."

"I'm not sure that Peter'll be up for it," I said.

"For fuck's sake, Johnny, can you not do something without Peter for once!" Her face was flushed, and she had the strangest look in her eyes.

I was taken aback by her sudden passion. We always did things together, me and Ceit and Peter. "Of course I can." I was a bit defensive.

"Good, just you and me, then. Eleven o'clock at the jetty." And she stomped off across the hill towards the O'Henley croft.

I don't know why, but I was strangely excited by the idea of sneaking out at night in the dark to meet Ceit. And as evening fell, and the wind dropped, I could barely contain my impatience. Peter and I completed our evening chores and then ate with Mary-Anne and Donald Seamus in the silence that always followed grace. It wasn't that they didn't talk to us on purpose. They never had a word for each other either. In truth, none of us had anything to say to one another. What was there to talk about? The cycle of life hardly changed from day to day. From season to season, yes. But one thing followed another quite naturally and never required discussion. It wasn't from Donald Seamus Gillies or his sister that we learned the Gaelic. Peter picked it up from the other kids at school. In the playground, of course, not in the classroom where only English was spoken. I picked it up from the other crofters, some of whom hardly spoke any English at all. Or if they did, they weren't going to speak it to me.

Donald Seamus smoked his pipe for a while by the stove, reading the paper while Mary-Anne washed the dishes and I helped Peter do his homework. Then at ten on the dot it was off to bed. The fire was tamped down for the night, lamps extinguished, and we went to our rooms with the smell of peat smoke, tobacco and oilwick in our nostrils.

Peter and I shared a double bed in the back room. There was a wardrobe and a dresser, and hardly enough room to get the door open. Peter was asleep in minutes, as he always was, and I had no fears about disturbing him by getting dressed again and climbing out of the window. But I had no idea how well or badly Donald Seamus or Mary-Anne slept. And so just before the clock struck eleven and I had committed myself, I opened the door a crack and listened carefully in the dark of the hallway. Someone was snoring

fit to register on the Richter Scale. Whether it was brother or sister
I didn't know, but after a while I became aware of another, higher-
pitched, intermittent snoring that came from the throat rather than
the nose. So, both were asleep.

I closed the door again and crossed to the window, drawing the
curtain aside to unsnib the sash and slide it up as quietly as I could.
Peter grunted and turned over, but didn't wake. I saw his lips moving as if he were talking to himself, perhaps using up the words that
were never required of him at mealtimes. I sat on the ledge, swing-
ing my legs over to the other side, and dropped down into the grass.

It was still surprisingly light out, a faint glow dying in the west,
the moon already spilling its colourless light across the hills. The
sky was a dark blue rather than black. In full summer it would still
be light at midnight and later, but we had some weeks to go before
then. I reached back in to pull the curtains shut, and slid the window closed.

And then I was off down the hillside like a greyhound out of the
trap, sprinting through the long grass, feet squelching in the bog,
exhilarated by an extraordinary sense of freedom. I was out, and the
night was mine. And Ceit's.

She was waiting for me down at the jetty, nervous I thought,
and a bit impatient. "What took you so long?" Her whisper seemed
excessively loud, and I realized that there was no wind, just the slow,
steady breathing of the sea.

"It must be all of five past," I said. But she just tutted and took
my arm and led me up the track towards Rubha Ban. There wasn't a
single light burning in any of the crofts across the hillside, an entire
island asleep, or so it appeared. Visibility was no problem in the
wash of moonlight, but it made us feel vulnerable, too. If anyone
should venture out we would be clearly visible.

"Where are we going?" I asked her.

"Charlie's beach."

"Why?"

"You'll see."

There was only one moment when it might all have gone wrong. Ceit yanked suddenly on my sleeve, and we flattened ourselves into the long grass at the side of the track as a light flared in an open doorway, and we saw an old man stepping out into the moonlight with a shovel and a newspaper in his hand. Most folk used a chanty during the night, which got emptied in the morning. But old Mr. MacGinty must have thought it was a fine night to relieve himself out on the moor. And so we had to lie there, giggling in the grass, while he dug himself a shallow hole and crouched over it, with his nightgown up around his neck, grunting and groaning.

Ceit put a hand over my mouth to shut me up, but she could barely contain her own mirth, air escaping through tightly pressed lips in tiny explosions. So I put my hand over hers, and we lay like that, pressed together, for nearly ten minutes while Mr. MacGinty did his business.

I suppose that must have been the first time I became aware of her body in a sexual way. Her warmth, the softness of her breasts pressed against my chest, one leg crooked over mine. And I felt the first stirrings of arousal, both surprising and scary. She was wearing a sort of pale print dress with a V-neck that showed her cleavage. And I remember she was barefoot that night. There was something sensuous and tempting in those bare legs exposed in the moonlight.

She wore her hair a lot longer now than she had at The Dean, and it fell in soft, chestnut curls over her shoulders, a too-long fringe constantly in her eyes.

I noticed, too, as we lay in the grass a faint smell of flowers about her, aromatic, with a low, musky note, different from the smell she'd had at The Dean. When Mr. MacGinty had finally gone back to his bed and we took our hands from each other's mouths, I sniffed and asked her what the scent was.

She giggled. "It's Mrs. O'Henley's eau de cologne," she said.

"What's that?"

"Perfume, silly. I sprayed a couple of puffs of it on my neck. Do you like it?"

I did. I don't know what it was about it, but it set butterflies free in my stomach. Her eyes seemed very dark as we lay there in the moonlight. Her lips full, with an almost irresistible allure. I found myself so much wanting to kiss them. But before I could succumb to the temptation, she was on her feet, holding out her hand and urging me to get up quick.

I scrambled to my feet and she took my hand, and we ran then up over the hill, past the primary school and along the road above the beach. We stopped, breathless, to take in the view. The sea simmered in a shimmering silence around the curve of the bay below us, rolling gently in to break in soft silver foam along the sand. The reflection of moon on water stretched away into a never-ending distance, the horizon broken only by a handful of dark islets and the brooding shadow of Barra.

I had never seen the island like this. Benign, seductive, almost as if it were colluding in Ceit's grand plan.

"Come on," she said, and led me down a narrow path through the heather to where the remains of an old ruined cottage looked out across the sands, and we picked our way through the stones to its grassy interior. She promptly sat herself down in the grass and patted a place beside her. I sat down, immediately aware of the warmth of her body, the soft sighing of the sea, the vast firmament overhead, the sky black now and crusted with stars. I was full of breathless anticipation as she turned those dark eyes on me, and I felt her fingertips on my face like tiny electric shocks.

I have no idea where we learn how to do these things, but before I knew it I had my arms around her and we were kissing. Lips soft and warm, parting to let our tongues meet. Shocking, thrilling. I felt her hand between my legs, where I was already straining at my trousers, and mine slid beneath the cotton of her dress to find it filled by a soft, pendulous breast, a nipple as hard as a nut grazing my palm.

I felt intoxicated. Drunk. Swept away on a sea of hormones. Completely out of control. We undressed in a kind of frenzy, clothes discarded in haste, and then we were skin to skin. Soft, warm, hot, wet. I had no idea what I was doing. Boys never do. They just follow some crude instinct. Ceit was much more controlled. Taking me in her hand, guiding me gently inside her. Gasping, almost crying out. I wasn't sure if it was from pain or pleasure. Then all my primal instincts took over, and I performed as I suppose I was programmed to do. Her cries only aroused me more, driving me on towards the inevitable, which of course came far too soon.

But Ceit was ready for it, forcing me away so that my seed spilled itself silver in the moonlight across the soft curve of her belly. "Don't want me getting pregnant now, do we," she said, and she put my hand down between her legs. "Finish me off."

I had no idea what she meant, but with her guidance my clumsy fingers quickly learned how to elicit a response from between the wet softness of her lips, and I was filled with such a desire to please as her body arched and arched beneath me before she cried out to the night and lay panting in the grass, her face flushed and smiling.

She reached up, taking my head between her hands, and pulled me down to kiss me. A long, lingering kiss, her tongue turning slowly around mine, again and again. And then she was on her feet, grabbing my hand. "Come on, Johnny." And we ran naked among the stones and down on to the beach, helter-skelter across the sand and into the sea.

The shock of it very nearly took my breath away completely. Freezing cold water on hot skin. Both of us called out involuntarily, and it was a good thing that there were no inhabited crofts close to the beach or we would certainly have been heard. As it is, I am amazed we weren't. Our cries must have carried right across the island.

"Fuck me!" Ceit shouted out in the dark

And I grinned and said, "I think I just did."

We ran, splashing, back on to the beach, and up the sand to the old cottage where we rolled in the grass to dry ourselves off and slip quickly back into our clothes. Now the cold gave way to burning skin as we lay wrapped up in each other's arms, lying there and looking up at the stars, breathless, enthralled, as if we had somehow discovered sex for the first time in human history.

Neither of us spoke for a long time, till I said, finally, "What was it you wanted to give me?"

And she laughed so long and hard.

I lifted myself up on my elbow and looked at her, perplexed. "What's so funny?"

Still laughing, she said, "One day you'll work it out, big boy."

I lay back down beside her, and the sense of being on the wrong side of a joke quickly passed, overcome, nearly overwhelmed, by feelings of love, and the desire to hold and protect her, to keep her safe and secure. She wrapped herself around me, her face nuzzled into my neck, an arm across my chest, a leg thrown over mine, and I just gazed at the stars, filled with a new sense of joy in being alive. I kissed the top of her head. "Why do you call this Charlie's beach?" I asked.

"Cos this is where Bonnie Prince Charlie first landed when he came to raise an army to march against the English in the Jacobite uprising of 1745," she said. "They taught us that at school."

We met several times in the weeks that followed, to find our way to that old ruined cottage and make love. The fine spring weather continued, and you could feel how the ocean was warming, the conveyor belt of the Gulf Stream invading the cold winter waters of the North Atlantic. Until the night of the storm, when it all went wrong.

I had arranged to meet Ceit as usual that night. But some time during the late afternoon the wind changed, and great dark clouds bubbled up on the horizon, sweeping in as darkness fell. The wind rose, and must have been Force 8 or 9, driving the rain that came with the cloud almost horizontally across the island. Blow-backs from the chimney filled our living room with smoke that night, in the end driving us early to our beds, even although it wasn't yet dark.

I lay for a long time staring at the ceiling wondering what to do. I had made the arrangement with Ceit, and there had been no chance to call it off. Although it would have been impossible for us to make love that night, there was no way I could not go, just in case she did. I couldn't leave her to brave the weather on her own, standing exposed down at the jetty waiting for me to show up.

So I bided my time, checking frequently with my watch, its luminous hands glowing in the dark, until it was time to go. I slipped out from between the sheets and got dressed, and pulled out my oilskins from where I had concealed them earlier beneath the bed. I was just sliding the window up when Peter's voice came out of the dark, raised a little to be heard above the howl of the wind outside.

"Where are you going?"

My heart stopped, and I turned, an unreasonable anger welling up in my chest. "Never bloody mind where I'm going! Go back to sleep."

"But Johnny, you never go anywhere without me."

"Keep your voice down, for Christ's sake. Just turn over and pretend I'm still in bed. I'll be back before you know it."

I pushed the window all the way up and swung my legs out to jump down into the rain. As I turned to draw the window down again, I saw Peter's bloodless face as he sat up in bed watching me go, a look of both fear and incomprehension etched all over it. I pulled the window shut and turned my hood up against the rain.

There was no racing down the hill tonight. It was pitch-black, and I had to pick my way carefully through the rock and long grass, bracing myself against the wind and the rain that it drove into my face. Finally I reached the track that led down to the jetty, and was able to move a little faster.

When I reached it, there was no sign of Ceit. It looked as if the tide was in, and neither the quay nor the lie of the land afforded much protection against the sea. It drove in, wave after wave breaking on the rocks all around the shore. The roar of it was deafening. The spray thrown up by the sea thrashing against the stone of the jetty combined with the rain to soak me through. I could feel my clothes wet beneath my oilskins. I peered around me in the dark, wondering how long I should stay. It was madness to have come out at all. I should have known that Ceit would not have expected me on a night like tonight.

And then I saw a tiny figure darting from the shadow of the hill. Ceit, in floppy green wellies, sizes too big for her, and wrapped in a coat that must have belonged to Mrs. O'Henley. I took her into my arms and crushed her against me. "I didn't want to not come in case you did," I shouted above the roar of the night.

"Me too." She grinned up at me, and I kissed her. "But I'm glad you did. Even if it was just to tell me that you couldn't come."

I grinned back at her. "No pun intended, I guess."

She laughed. "One-track mind, you have."

We kissed again, and I held her tight against the battering of the wind and the rain, the storm crashing all around us. Then she broke away.

"I'd better go. God knows how I'm going to explain all this wet stuff."

She gave me one last quick kiss, and then she was off, swallowed up by the storm and disappearing into the night. I stood for a moment catching my breath, then found my way back on to the track, to head up the hill towards the Gillies croft. I hadn't gone more than ten yards when a figure emerged out of the dark. I got one hell of a fright, and nearly cried out, before I realized it was Peter. He was wearing no waterproofs, just his dungarees and his worn old tweed jacket, a hand-me-down from Donald Seamus. He was soaked through already, his hair smeared over his face, his expression of abject misery visible to me even in the darkness. He must have got up and dressed himself and come after me as soon as I had gone.

"For God's sake, Peter, what are you doing?"

"You were with Ceit," he said.

I couldn't deny it. He had obviously seen us. "Yes."

"Behind my back."

"No, Peter."

"Yes, Johnny. It's always you, me and Ceit. Always. The three of us, ever since The Dean." His eyes burned with a strange intensity. "I saw you kissing her."

I took his arm. "Come on, Peter, let's just go home."

But he pulled himself free. "No!" He stared at me out of the storm. "You've been lying to me."

"No, I haven't." I was starting to get angry now. "For fuck's sake, Peter, Ceit and I are in love, okay? It's got nothing to do with you."

He stood for a moment staring at me, and I'll never forget the look of complete betrayal in his eyes. Then he was off, into the night at a run. I was so surprised it took me several seconds to react, in which time he had already vanished from sight.

"Peter!" I shouted after him. He had run off in the opposite direction from the croft, towards the shore. I gasped in frustration and ran after him.

Mountainous seas were breaking all along the jagged northern coastline, where giant rocks lay in blocks and shards all along the foot of the low-rise cliffs. I could see Peter now, the merest shadow of a dark figure, scrambling over them. It was insanity. Any moment the sea could reach in and take him, dragging him out into the Sound and certain death. I cursed the day he'd ever been born, and started off over the rocks in pursuit.

I shouted after him several times, but my voice was drowned by the sound of the sea and whipped away by the angry bellow of the wind. All I could do was try to keep him in my sights and endeavour to catch him up. I got to within fifteen or twenty feet of him when he started to climb. In normal circumstances not a difficult climb, but tonight in these impossible conditions it was nothing short of madness. The machair dipped down to within twenty feet or so of the shore before dropping sheer to the rocks below, and a deep crack ran back from it, for all the world as if someone had taken a giant wedge and a big mell and split it open.

Peter was almost at the top when he fell. If he called out, I never heard it. He just vanished into the black chasm of that crack in the earth. I abandoned all caution and climbed up the rock in a panic to where I had last seen him. The darkness below me, as I peered into the chasm, was absolute.

"Peter!" I screamed his name and heard it echoing back at me out of the ground. And to my relief I heard a faint call in return.

"Johnny! Johnny, help me!"

It was lunacy what I did. If I had stopped to think, I would have run back to the croft and roused Donald Seamus. No matter how much trouble we would have been in, I should have gone for help. But I didn't stop, and I didn't think, and within moments I was as much in need of help as Peter.

I started to climb down into the crack, attempting to brace myself between the two walls of it, when the rock simply crumbled away beneath my left foot, and I fell into the blackness.

At some point during my fall I struck my head, and I lost consciousness even before I reached the bottom. I have no idea how long I was out, but the first thing I became aware of was Peter's voice, very close to my ear, repeating my name again and again, like some mindless mantra.

And then awareness brought pain. A searing pain in my left arm that took my breath away. I was lying spreadeagled on a bed of rock and shingle, my arm twisted under me in an unnatural way. I knew at once that it was broken. It cost me dear to turn myself over and haul myself into a sitting position against the rock, and I yelled my imprecations at the night, cursing God and the Holy Mother, and Peter and anyone else who came to mind. I couldn't see a thing, but the roar of the ocean was quite deafening. The shingle beneath me was wet with seaweed and sand, and I realized that the only reason we were not under water was that the tide must have turned.

At high tide, in a storm like this, the sea would rush into this crack in the earth in a fury of boiling, foaming water, and we would both have been drowned. Peter was wailing, and I could hear his teeth chattering. He pressed himself up against me, and now I could feel his shivering.

"You've got to go and get help," I shouted.

"I'm not leaving you, Johnny." I felt his breath in my face.

"Peter, if you've got nothing broken, you've got to climb out of here and go get Donald Seamus. My arm's broken."

But he just clung on to me all the more tightly, sobbing and shaking, and I let my head fall back against the rock and closed my eyes.

When I opened them again, the first grey light of dawn was angling into the crevice from above. Peter was curled up beside me on the shingle, and he wasn't moving. I panicked and started shouting for help. Crazy! Who was going to hear me?

I was hoarse and had all but given up, when a shadow leaned over the opening fifteen feet above us, and a familiar voice called down. "Holy Mary Mother of God, what are you doing down there, boys?" It was our neighbour, Roderick MacIntyre. I discovered later that he had found sheep missing first thing after the storm, and had come down along the cliffs looking for them. Had it not been for that serendipitous piece of good luck, we might both have died down there. As it was, I still feared for Peter's life. He hadn't moved since I regained consciousness.

The men who weren't away with the fishing fleet assembled on the clifftop and one of them was lowered down on a rope to pull us up. The storm had abated by now, but there was still a strong wind, and I'll never forget the look on Donald Seamus's face in that yellow-grey dawn light as they brought me up. He never said a word, but lifted me into his arms and carried me down to the jetty where a boat was waiting to take us over to Ludagh. Peter was still unconscious, and in the crowd of men huddled around us at the boat I heard someone say he was suffering from exposure. "Hypothermia," someone else said. "He'll be lucky if he survives." And I felt a terrible pang of guilt. None of this would have happened if it hadn't been for me sneaking out to meet Ceit. How could I ever face my mother in the next life if I let anything happen to Peter? I had *promised* her!

I don't remember much about the next day or so. I know that they put us in the back of Donald Seamus's van at Ludagh, and we were driven to the cottage hospital at Daliburgh. The Sacred Heart. I must have been suffering from exposure, too, because I don't even remember them putting the plaster on my arm. A big, heavy white stookie from my wrist to my elbow, with just my fingers and thumb sticking out the end of it. I remember nuns leaning over my bed. Scary they were, in their black robes and white coifs, like harbingers of death. And I remember sweating a lot, a bit delirious, burning up one minute, then shivering with cold the next.

It was dark outside when I finally recovered my senses. I couldn't have told you whether one day had passed, or two. There was a light burning at my bedside, and it seemed shocking to have electric light again, as if I had been transported back to my former life.

I was in a ward with six beds in it. A couple of them were occupied, but Peter was in neither of them, and I began to get a bad feeling. Where was he? I slipped out of the bed, bare feet on cold linoleum, trembling legs that would hardly hold me up, and padded to the door. On the other side of it was a short corridor. Light spilled out from an open doorway. I could hear the hushed voices of the nuns, and a man's voice. The doctor maybe. "Tonight will be critical," he said. "If he makes it through, then he should be okay. But it'll be touch and go. At least he has youth on his side."

I walked in something like a trance along that corridor and found myself standing at the open door. Three heads turned towards me, and one of the nuns was on her feet immediately, coming to grab me by the shoulders. "What on earth are you doing out of bed, young man?"

"Where's Peter?" was all I could say, and I saw them all exchanging looks.

The doctor was an older man, in his fifties. Wearing a dark suit. He said, "Your brother has pneumonia." Which meant nothing to me then. But I knew from his grave demeanour that it was serious.

"Where is he?"

"He's in a special room down the hall," one of the nurses said. "You can see him tomorrow."

But I'd already heard them say that there might be no tomorrow. I felt sick to my stomach.

"Come on, now, let's get you back into bed." The nun who had me by the shoulders guided me back up the hall and into the ward. When I was safely tucked up in bed, she told me not to worry and to try to get some sleep. She turned out the light and slipped back out into the hall in a whisper of skirts.

In the darkness I heard a man's voice coming from one of the other beds. "Pneumonia's a killer, son. Better pray for your wee brother."

I lay for a long time, listening to the beat of my own heart, the blood pulsing in my ears, until I heard the gentle purring of my fellow patients as they finally succumbed to sleep. But I knew there was no way that I was going to sleep that night. I waited, and waited, until finally the light in the hall outside was doused and a blanket of silence descended on the little cottage hospital.

At length I summoned the courage to slip from the bed and cross once more to the door. I opened it a crack and peered down the hall. There was a line of light beneath the closed door to the nun's station, and a little further down, light seeped out from beneath another door, also closed. I squeezed out into the corridor and drifted past the nun's station till I reached the second door and very slowly turned the handle to ease it open.

The light in here was subdued. It had a strange yellow-orange quality. Warm, almost seductive. The air was suffocatingly hot. There was a single bed with electrical equipment along one side, cables and tubes trailing across the covers to the prone figure of Peter lying beneath the sheets. I closed the door behind me and hurried over to his bedside.

He was a terrible colour. Paler than white, with penumbrous shadows beneath his eyes, his face glistening with sweat. His mouth hung open, and I could see that the sheets that covered him were soaked through. I touched his forehead with the backs of my fingers and almost recoiled from the heat. He was burning up, unnaturally hot. His eyes were moving beneath his eyelids, and his breathing was shallow and rapid.

My sense of guilt very nearly overwhelmed me then. I pulled up a chair to his bedside and perched myself on the edge of it, taking his hand in mine and holding on to it for dear life. If I could have given my life for his I would.

I don't know how long I sat there. Some hours, I think. But at some point I fell asleep, and the next thing I knew I was being wakened by one of the nuns who took me by the arm and led me back to the ward, without a single word of admonition. Back in my own bed I dozed fitfully, never far from the surface, troubled by strange dreams of storms and sex, until the light of the dawn began creeping in around the edges of the curtains. And then sudden sunlight laid itself down across the linoleum in narrow burned-out strips.

The door opened, and the nuns wheeled in a trolley with break-fast. One of them helped me to sit up and said, "Your brother's fine. His fever broke during the night. He's going to be all right. You can go along and see him after breakfast."

I could hardly get my porridge and toast and tea down me fast enough.

Peter was still prone in his bed when I went in. But there was colour in his face now, his eyes a little less shadowed. He turned his head to look at me as I pulled up the chair beside his bed. His smile was pale, but he seemed genuinely happy to see me. I had feared that I would never be forgiven. He said, "I'm sorry, Johnny."

I felt tears prick my eyes. "What for? You've nothing to be sorry about, Peter."

"It's all my fault."

I shook my head. "Nothing's your fault, Peter. If anyone's to blame it's me."

He smiled. "There was a woman who came and sat with me all night."

I laughed. "No. That was me, Peter."

He shook his head. "No, Johnny. It was a woman. She sat right there in that chair."

"One of the nuns then."

"No. It wasn't a nun. I couldn't really see her face, but she was wearing a sort of short green jacket, and a black skirt. She held my hand all night."

I knew enough, even then, to know that a fever can make you delirious. That you can see things which aren't there. It had been me holding his hand, and no doubt the nuns had been in and out. It had all merged together in his mind.

"She had beautiful hands, Johnny. Such long white fingers. Married, too. So it couldn't have been a nun."

"How do you know she was married?"

"She was wearing a ring on her wedding finger. Not like any ring I've ever seen before. Sort of twisted silver, like snakes wrapped around each other."

I think, then, every hair on my body stood on end. He had never known about our mother giving me her ring. Never knew how I hid it in a sock in the sack at the end of my bed. Never knew how it had gone into the furnace along with everything else that Mr. Anderson had thrown into the flames that day.

I suppose it is always possible that some childhood memory of it had remained in his mind, of seeing it on my mother's hand. But I believe that what he saw that night had nothing to do with lost memories or delirium. I believe that my mother sat with him through all the critical hours of his pneumonia, willing him to live from the other side of the grave. Stepping in to fill the vacuum left by my failed promise to always look out for him.

And I will carry the guilt of that with me to my grave.

It was some days before they let us go home, my arm still in plaster, of course. I was dreading it, afraid of the certain retribution that would be awaiting us at the hands of Donald Seamus. The look on his face when they pulled us out of the crevice was still vivid in my memory.

He turned up at the Sacred Heart in his old van and slid open the side door to let us climb in the back. We drove the twenty minutes down to Ludagh in silence. At the ferry, Neil Campbell asked after us both, and he and Donald Seamus passed a few words, but still he never spoke to us. When we climbed on to the jetty at Haunn, I could see Ceit watching from the door of the O'Henley croft, a tiny figure in blue on the hillside. She waved, but I didn't dare wave back.

Donald Seamus marched us up the hill to the croft, where Mary-Anne was waiting for us inside, our dinner cooking on the stove, the room filled with the smell of good things to eat. She turned as we came in the door, and gave us a good looking over, but she too said nothing, turning instead back to the pots on her hotplate.

The first words spoken were the grace said in thanks to the Lord for the food on our plates, and then Mary-Anne served us up a meal fit for a king. I wasn't big on the Bible then, but I was minded of the story of the prodigal son, and how his father had welcomed him home as if nothing had happened. We gulped down thick, hot vegetable soup and cleaned our plates with hunks of soft bread torn from a fresh loaf. We had a meat stew and boiled tatties, and bread and butter pudding to finish. I am not sure if I have ever enjoyed a meal so much in my life.

Afterwards, I changed into my dungarees and my wellies and went out to feed the animals, the hens and the pony. Not so easy with your left forearm in plaster. But it felt good to be back. And maybe, for the first time in a year and a half of being there, it felt like home. I went down the croft then, looking for Morag. I was sure she must have missed me, though perhaps a part of me was half afraid that she had forgotten me in my absence. But I couldn't find her anywhere, and after nearly half an hour of searching I went back up to the house.

Donald Seamus was in his chair by the stove, smoking his pipe. He turned around as the door opened.

"Where's Morag?" I said.

There was an odd dull look in his eyes. "You just ate her, son."

I never let him see how his cruelty affected me, or gave any hint of the tears I cried silently under the covers that night. But he wasn't finished with me.

The next day he took me up to the shed where they kill the sheep. I'm not sure what it was about that old hut with its rusted tin roof, but you knew the minute you went into it that it was a place of death. I'd never seen a sheep slaughtered before, but Donald Seamus was determined that it was time that I did. "Animals are for eating," he said. "Not for affection."

He pulled a young sheep into the shed and hauled it up on to its hind legs. He got me to hold it by the horns, struggling while he placed a bucket beneath it, and then he slid out a long, sharp knife that flashed as it caught the light from the tiny window. In one quick, short movement, he drew it across the major artery in the neck and blood spurted out of it into the bucket.

I thought the beast would struggle more, but it gave up on its life almost immediately, big hopeless eyes looking up at me till the blood had all been spilled and the light went out of them.

The same look I saw in Peter's eyes that night on Charlie's beach when his throat was cut, too.

The boy's sitting staring at me now, as if he expects me to say something. In a strange way, I see me in his eyes, and I reach across to take his hand in mine. Damned tears! They blur everything. I feel him squeeze my hand and everything my life is, and has been, seems black with despair.

"I'm sorry, Peter," I say. "I'm so sorry."

| TWENTY-SIX |

The old cemetery was full to overflowing behind its lichen-covered stone walls, spilling over now into a new one dug into the machair as it rose up the hillside towards the church.

Fin parked his car and walked among the headstones in this extended home for the dead. Death was a crowd, even on a tiny island like this. Crosses growing out of the ground, brutally stark in such a treeless place. So many souls passed from one life to another. All in the shadow of the church where once they had worshipped. A church paid for by fishermen. A church with the bow of a boat beneath its altar table.

On the far side of the fence stood a modern, single-storey bungalow with a conservatory at the back overlooking the Sound. But this was no private dwelling. A red board fixed to the gable end, and an oval sign on the wall of the ramp that led to its side door, revealed it to be a pub, *Am Politician*. A handy watering hole for the dead, Fin thought, en route from the church to the graveyard, or for their mourners at least. A place to drown their sorrows.

There was a pink, soft-top Mercedes in the car park. A yappy Yorkie dog barked at him from the other side of the glass as he passed it.

It was quiet in the pub, only a handful of customers nursing drinks on this late afternoon. Fin ordered a beer from a garrulous young woman behind the bar who was anxious to explain to him that the pub was named after the boat, *The Politician*, which had foundered in the Sound en route to the Caribbean during the war.

"Of course," she said, "anyone who has read Compton Mackenzie's *Whisky Galore* will know that its cargo included 28,000 cases of fine malt whisky. And that the islanders spent most of the next six months 'rescuing' it and hiding it from the excise man."

As she produced three bottles reputed to have come from the wreck, still with whisky in them, Fin wondered how many times she had told the story.

He sipped on his pint and changed the subject. "That beach on the west side of the island," he said. "Beyond the cemetery."

"Yes?"

"Why would anyone call it Charlie's beach?"

The girl shrugged. "I've never heard it called that." She turned and called over to an older woman who was sitting alone in the conservatory gazing out over the Sound while toying with her gin and tonic. "Morag, have you ever heard the beach down by called Charlie's beach?"

Morag turned, and Fin saw that she must have been a striking woman in her day. She had strong features and smooth, tanned skin beneath a chaotic pile of thick, dyed blond hair, giving perhaps the impression of a woman in her fifties, although he could see that she was probably nearer seventy. Both wrists dangled with silver and gold, fingers crusted with rings, and she took a sip of her G & T, holding her glass in an elegant hand adorned with long, fuchsia-pink nails. She wore a patterned bolero jacket over a white blouse above diaphanous blue skirts. She was not at all someone you would expect to find in a place like this.

She directed a beatific smile towards them. "I have no idea, *a ghràidh*," she said speaking in English, but using the Gaelic term of endearment. "But if I were to take a guess, I'd say it would probably be because that's where the French frigate, the *Du Teillay*, landed

Bonnie Prince Charlie and the Seven Men of Moidart to raise an army for the '45 Jacobite rebellion against the English."

"I didn't know that," the girl said.

Morag shook her head. "They teach you children nothing in school these days. Charlie reputedly sheltered in a cove down there called *Coilleag a' Phrionnsa*. The Prince's Dell." She turned rich, brown eyes on Fin. "Who wants to know?"

Fin lifted his pint and crossed into the conservatory to shake her hand. "Fin Macleod. I'm trying to trace the family who used to live on the croft just below your house."

She raised her eyebrows in surprise. "Oh. You know who I am, then?"

He smiled. "Not before I got to the island, no. But it didn't take long for someone to tell me. I'm making a wild guess here, and it's nothing to do with the pink Merc in the car park. You're the actress, Morag McEwan?"

She beamed. "A good guess, *a ghràidh*. You should have been a policeman."

"I was." He grinned. "Apparently I should know you from television."

"Not everyone's a slave to the box." She sipped at her gin. "You *were* a policeman?"

"Just plain old Fin Macleod now."

"Well, *a ghràidh*, I grew up here in the days when all the crofts were still occupied. So if anyone can tell you what you want to know, it's me." She drained her glass and stood up stiffly, her hand shooting out suddenly to support herself on his arm. "Damned rheumatics! Come back to my place, Mr. Fin Macleod, former policeman, and I'll pour you a drink or three while I tell you." She leaned confidentially towards him, although her voice remained well above the level of a stage whisper. "The booze is cheaper there."

Outside she said, "Leave your car here and come with me. You can always walk back for it." She slipped into her pink Mercedes to an ecstatic welcome from the Yorkie. And as Fin slid into the passenger seat she said, "This is Dino. Dino meet Fin." The dog looked at him then jumped into her lap as she started the car and lowered the roof. "He loves the wind in his face. And on those rare days when the sun shines, it seems a shame not to have the roof down, don't you agree?"

"Absolutely."

She lit a cigarette. "Damned government laws. Can't enjoy a good smoke over a drink any more, except in your own house." She sucked smoke deeply into her lungs and breathed out again with satisfaction. "That's better."

She crunched the car into first gear and kangarooed towards the gate, narrowly missing the gatepost as she swung the wheel to turn them on to the road up the hill. Dino had draped himself over her right arm, face pushed out of the open window into the wind, and she juggled her cigarette and the gear lever to propel them at speed up towards the primary school and the road leading off to the church. Fin found his hands moving down to either side of his seat and gripping it with white knuckles at the end of arms stiff with tension. Morag was oblivious, veering left, and sometimes right, each time she changed gear. Her cigarette ash, and the smoke from her mouth, were whipped away in the rush of air.

"The Mercedes dealer said they didn't do pink, when I told them what colour I wanted," she said. "I told them, of course you do. I showed them my nails, and left them a bottle of the nail varnish so they could get the match just right. When they delivered the car I said, you see, anything's possible." She laughed, and Fin wished she would keep her eye on the road rather than looking at him as she spoke.

They crested the hill, then accelerated down towards the harbour at Haunn, veering right at the last moment around the small bay, and turning up on the new driveway towards Morag's big white house. They rattled over a cattle grid and crunched across granite chippings interspersed with coloured glass beads.

"They glow at night when the lights are on," Morag said as she and Dino got out of the driver's side. "It's like walking on light."

Plaster statues of naked ladies guarded the steps to the deck, while life-sized deer stood or lay in the garden, and a bronze mermaid draped herself over rocks around a small pool. Fin saw tubular neon lighting strung along the fencewire, and blocks of terracotta tiling among clumps of heather and a few hardy flowering shrubs that seemed somehow to have survived the wind. Windchimes sounded all around the house, a constant cacophony of bamboo and steel.

"Come away in."

Fin followed Morag and Dino into a hallway where thick-piled tartan carpet led up a broad staircase to the first floor. The walls were covered with prints of Mayflowers and Madonnas, sailboats and saints. Chintzy ornaments stood on Greek columns, and a sleek, full-sized silver cheetah stretched itself out just inside the doorway to the living room and bar, a room lined by picture windows on both sides, and French windows out to the patio. Every available laying space, shelves and tables and bar top, was covered in china statuettes and mirrored jewellery boxes, lamps and lions. The tiled floor was polished to an almost reflective gleam.

Morag tossed her jacket on to a leather recliner and slipped behind the bar to pour their drinks. "Beer, whisky? Something more exotic?"

"A beer would be fine." Fin had drunk less than half of his pint at *Am Politician*. He took his foaming glass from her and wandered through the bric-a-brac to the French windows and their view north across the Sound towards South Uist. Immediately below was the little bay with its tiny stone harbour from which the boat had come and gone across the water to Ludagh in the days before the building of roads had required the car ferry. "You were born here?"

"No. But I did most of my growing up here."

Fin turned to see her taking a stiff pull at her gin and tonic. The ice in her glass sounded like the windchimes outside. "And how does a girl from Eriskay come to be a famous actress?"

She laughed uproariously. "I don't know about famous," she said, "but the first step for an Eriskay girl to being almost anything other than an Eriskay girl, is to leave the damned place."

"What age were you when you left?"

"Seventeen. I went to the Royal Scottish Academy of Music and Drama in Glasgow. Always wanted to be an actress, you see. Ever since they showed a film of Eriskay in the church hall. Not that it was a drama. It was a documentary made by some German chap in the thirties. But there was something about seeing those folk up on the big screen. Something glamorous. And, I don't know, it gave them a kind of immortality. I wanted that." She chuckled and moved out from behind the bar to drape herself on the settee. Dino immediately jumped up on to her knee. "I got very excited once when a teacher on the island let the kids know that he would be showing films at his house. It was just after the electricity came, and everyone squeezed into his sitting room to see them. Charged us a penny each, he did, then projected slides of his holiday in Inverness. Imagine!" She roared with laughter, and Dino raised his head and barked twice.

Fin smiled. "Did you come back for visits?"

She shook her head vigorously. "No, never. Spent years working in theatre in Glasgow and Edinburgh, and pantos around Scotland. Then I got offered my first part in TV by Robert Love at Scottish Television and never looked back. Went down to London, then. Went to a lot of castings, got a few parts, worked as a waitress to fill the gaps in between. I did all right, I suppose. But never was a great success." Another mouthful of gin induced a moment of reflection. "Until, that is, I got offered a part in *The Street*. It came kind of late in life, but I was an overnight success. I don't know why. Folk just loved my character." She cackled. "I became what you might call a household name. And the twenty years of fame that it brought, and the marvellous earnings that went with it, have paid for all this." She waved an arm around her empire. "A very comfortable retirement."

Fin gazed at her thoughtfully. "What made you come back?"

She looked at him. "You're an islander, aren't you?"

"I am. From Lewis."

"Then you know why. There's something about the islands, *a ghràidh*, that always brings you back in the end. I've already got my place booked in the cemetery over the hill."

"Were you ever married?"

Her smile carried a sadness in it. "In love once, but never married."

Fin turned to the side windows looking back out across the hill. "So you knew the people who lived on the croft below here?"

"Aye, I did that. Old widow O'Henley it was who stayed there when I was a kid. Her and a young lassie called Ceit who was in my class at school. A homer."

Fin frowned. "A homer? What's that?"

"A boy or a girl from a home, *a ghràidh*. There were hundreds of them taken out of orphanages and local authority homes by the councils and the Catholic Church, and shipped out here to the islands. Just handed over to complete strangers, they were. No vetting in those days. Kids were dumped off the ferry at Lochboisdale to stand on the pier with family names tied around their necks, waiting to be claimed. The primary school up on the hill there was full of them. Nearly a hundred at one time."

Fin was shocked. "I had no idea."

Morag lit a cigarette and puffed away on it as she spoke. "Aye, they were at it right into the sixties. I once heard the priest saying it was good to have fresh blood in the islands after generations of inbreeding. I think that was the idea. Though they weren't all orphans, you know. Some came from broken homes. But there was no going back. Once you got sent out here all ties with the past were cut. You were forbidden contact with parents or family. Poor little bastards. Some of them got terribly abused. Beaten, or worse. Most were just treated like slave labour. A few were luckier, like me."

Fin raised an eyebrow. "You were a homer?"

"I was, Mr. Macleod. Boarded with a family at Parks, over on the other side of the island. All gone now, of course. No children of their own, you see. But unlike many, I have happy memories of my time here. Which is why I had no problems about coming back." She emptied her glass. "I need a wee top-up. How about you?"

"No thanks." Fin had barely touched his.

Morag moved Dino off her knee and eased herself out of the settee to pour another drink. "Of course, it wasn't just the locals who gave the kids a hard time. There were incomers, too. Mostly English. Like the headmaster at Daliburgh school." She smiled. "Thought he was coming here to civilize us, *a ghràidh*, and banned the Gillean Cullaig."

"What's that?"

"It's the name they gave to the Hogmanay tradition when gangs of boys went around the houses on New Year's Eve blessing each house with a poem, and being rewarded with bread and scones, and cake and fruit. All dropped into the white flour sacks they carried. They'd been doing it for centuries. But Mr. Bidgood thought it smacked of begging, and issued an edict forbidding any of his pupils to take part."

"And everyone obeyed?"

"Well, most did. But there was one boy in my class. Donald John. A homer. He boarded with the Gillies family, a brother and sister, over there on the other side the hill. He defied the ban and went out with the older boys. When Bidgood found out he gave that lad such a leathering with the tawse."

Fin shook his head. "He shouldn't have had the right to do that."

"Oh, they had the right to do what they pleased in those days. But Donald Seamus—that was the man that Donald John boarded with—he took exception. Went up to the school and beat the living shit out of that headmaster. Excuse my French. He took Donald John out of school that very day, too, and the boy never went back." She smiled. "Bidgood returned to England with his tail between his legs within the month." She smiled. "It was a colourful life we lived back then."

Fin looked around and thought that it was a colourful life that she was living still. "So do you have any idea what happened to Ceit?"

Morag shrugged and sipped again at her gin. "None at all, I'm afraid, *a ghràidh*. She left the island not long before myself, and for all I know never came back."

Another dead end.

By the time Fin came to leave, the cloud was gathering ominously all along the western bay, the wind had stiffened and carried the odd spot of rain. Somewhere much further to the west, beyond the cloud, the sun was drizzling liquid gold on the ocean as it dipped towards the horizon.

Morag said, "I'd better run you back over the hill, *a ghràidh*. It looks like you could get caught in a downpour. I'll just open the garage doors now, so that I can drive straight in when I get back."

She tapped a code into a controller at the side of the door, and it swung slowly upwards to fold flat into the roof. As they got into the car, Fin spotted an old spinning wheel at the back of the garage. "You don't spin wool, do you?" he said.

She laughed. "Good God, no. Never have, never will." Dino jumped up into her lap and she closed the door, but kept the roof down this time. He snuffled and yelped and rubbed his wet nose all over the window until she lowered it, and he draped himself in his habitual place over her arm to poke his face out into the wind. As she drove down the driveway she said, "It's an old one I'm having restored. It'll sit nicely in the dining room. A reminder of days gone by. All the women spun wool here when I was a girl. They would oil it and knit it into blankets and socks and jerseys for the menfolk. Most of the men were fishermen in those days, at sea five days a week, and the Eriskay jerseys knitted with that oiled wool were as good as waterproofs. They all wore them."

She swerved at the foot of the drive as she took a draw on her cigarette, and missed the fencepost by inches.

"Each of the women had her own pattern, you know. Usually handed down from mother to daughter. So distinctive that when a man's body was pulled from the sea, decayed beyond recognition, he could almost always be identified from the knitted pattern of his pullover. As good as a fingerprint, it was."

She waved at the old man and his dog to whom Fin had spoken earlier, and the Mercedes nearly went into a ditch. But Morag seemed oblivious.

"There's an old retired priest on the island who's a bit of a historian." She laughed. "Nothing much else for a celibate man to do on a long winter's night." She swung a mischievous smile Fin's way.

"Anyway, he's a bit of an expert on the knitted patterns of old Eriskay. Has a collection of photographs and drawings, I've heard. Goes back a hundred years and more, they say."

As they reached the top of the hill she glanced curiously across at her passenger. "You don't say much, Mr. Macleod."

And Fin thought it would have been difficult to get a word in edgeways. But all he said was, "I've enjoyed hearing your stories, Morag."

After a moment she said, "What's your interest in the folk who lived at the O'Henley croft?"

"It's not really the O'Henley woman herself that I'm interested in, Morag. I'm trying to trace the roots of an old man now living on Lewis. I think he might have come from Eriskay."

"Well, maybe I know him. What's his name?"

"Oh, it's not a name you would know. He calls himself Tormod Macdonald now. But that's not his real name."

"Then what is?"

"That's what I don't know."

The rain started as Fin drove north from Ludagh, sweeping across the machair from the open sea to the west. Big fat drops that came first in ones and twos, before reinforcements arrived and compelled him to put his wipers on at double speed. He turned off at Daliburgh on to the Lochboisdale road, his mind filled still with the thought that Morag's story of Eriskay knitting patterns was perhaps his last chance to track down the true identity of Marsaili's father. A very, very long shot indeed.

The Lochboisdale Hotel sat on the hill above the harbour, in the lee of Ben Kenneth. It was an old, traditional, whitewashed building with modern extensions, and a dining lounge with a view out over the bay. At a dark reception desk in the lobby, a girl in a tartan skirt gave him keys to a single room, and confirmed that they did, indeed, have a fax machine. Fin noted the number and climbed the staircase to his room.

From his dormer window, he looked down on the pier in the fading light as the CalMac ferry from Oban, with its red twin funnels, emerged from the rain to manoeuvre itself up to the ramp and lower the door of its car deck. Tiny figures in yellow oilskins braved the weather to wave the cars off. Fin wondered how it must have been for those poor bewildered kids, plucked from everything they had known and dumped here on the pier to face their fate. And he felt anger at the men whose religion and politics had dictated it.

Who had known about it then, apart from those involved? Why had it never been reported in the press, as it certainly would be today? How would people have reacted had they known what was going on? His own parents, he was sure, would have been outraged. Anger welled within him as he thought about it. The anger of a parent. And the hurt of an orphan. His ability to empathize with those wretched children was almost painful. He wanted to lash out and hit something, or someone, on their behalf.

And the rain ran down his window like tears spilled for all those poor lost souls.

He crossed his room to sit on the edge of the bed in the evening gloom, and as he turned on his bedside lamp felt depression descend on him like a shroud. From the address book on his mobile phone he tracked down George Gunn's home number and hit the dial key. Gunn's wife answered, and Fin recalled the invitations George had extended on more than one occasion to come and eat wild salmon with him and his wife. He had still never met her.

"Hello, Mrs. Gunn, it's Fin Macleod here. Is George there?"

"Oh, hello, Mr. Macleod," she said, as if they were old friends. "One moment. I'll go and get him."

After a few moments he heard Gunn's voice. "Where are you, Mr. Macleod?"

"Lochboisdale, George."

He heard the surprise in his voice. "What on earth are you doing down there?"

"I'm pretty certain that Marsaili's dad came from Eriskay. And I think there might be a way of identifying who he was. Or is. But I have to play a wild card, George, and I need your help."

There was a long silence. "In what way?"

"Did you ever get those drawings done of the blanket pattern bleached into the lividity of the body?"

More surprise. "I did. The artist was in today, actually." He paused. "Are you going to let me in on this?"

"I will, George, when I know for sure."

There was a sigh at the other end of the line. "You're stretching my patience, Mr. Macleod." Fin waited. Then, "What do you want me to do?"

"I want you to fax the drawings to me here at the Lochboisdale Hotel."

| TWENTY-SEVEN |

The damned dark again! It's always dark. I was dreaming. Something very clear to me. Damned if I can remember what it was now. Woke me up, though, I'm certain of that.

What time is it? Oh. Mary must have taken the bedside clock. But it must be time for the milking. I hope the rain's off by now. I pull back the curtain and see it running down the glass. Dammit!

It doesn't take me long to get dressed. And there's my good old cap sitting on the chair. Been with me for years that old hat. Kept me warm and dry in all weathers, and blown off a few times, too.

The light's on in the hall, but there's no sign of Mary. Maybe she's in the kitchen preparing my breakfast. I'll just sit at the table and wait. I can't remember what we had for dinner last night, but I'm hungry now.

Oh God! Suddenly it comes back to me. That damn dream. I was on a beach somewhere, walking with a young man, and he gave me a little medallion, like a coin, on a chain. And I reached back with it clutched in my fist and threw it into the ocean. It was only as I saw it vanish that I realized what it was. The Saint Christopher. Ceit gave it to me. I remember that as clear as day. Only it was dark, and I was in a terrible state.

Peter was in the back of Donald Seamus's van on the jetty at Ludagh, wrapped in an old knitted bedcover. Dead. A bloody mess. And I could barely control my emotions.

We had rowed him across the Sound from Haunn in the little rowing boat that Donald Seamus kept in the bay. It was a hellish night, too. I felt God's anger in the wind, and my mother's reproach in its voice. Thank heavens for the lights of the crofts on this side of the bay, or we'd never have made it. Pitch it was that night, and the boat got tossed about like a cork. There were times when I found it hard to dip the oars back in the water for the next pull.

The boat was tied up at the end of the jetty, rising and falling fiercely in the dark, and I knew that Ceit would have to take it back across on her own. I knew she didn't want to, and I will never forget the look in her eyes. She reached up to grasp my collar in both her hands.

"Don't go, Johnny."

"I have to."

"You don't! We can tell what happened."

But I shook my head. "No we can't." I took her by the shoulders, holding her too tightly. "You can't tell anyone, Ceit. Ever. Promise me." When she said nothing, I shook her. "Promise me!"

Her eyes dipped away, and she turned her head towards the ground. "I promise." Her words were cast away in the wind almost before I heard them. And I wrapped my arms around her and held her so tight I was afraid I might break her.

"There's no way to explain this to anyone," I said. "And there's things I have to do." I had let my mother down, and I knew that I couldn't live with myself until I had put things right. If they ever could be.

She looked up at me, and I saw the fear in her face. "Let it go, Johnny. Just let it go."

But I couldn't. And she knew it, too. She wriggled free of my arms and reached around behind her neck to unclasp the chain of her Saint Christopher medal. She held it out towards me, and it turned and twisted in the wind. "I want you to have this."

I shook my head. "I can't. You've had that ever since I've known you."

"Take it!" It was a tone I knew there could be no arguing with. "It'll keep you safe, Johnny. And every time you look at it I want you to think of me. To remember me."

Reluctantly, I took it from her and clasped it tightly in my hand. The little bit of Ceit that I would have with me all of my life. She reached up then and touched my face, the way she had done that first time, and kissed me. Such a soft, sweet kiss, full of love and sorrow.

It was the last time I ever saw her. And though I married, and fathered two wonderful girls, I have never loved anyone else since.

Oh God! What possessed me to throw it in the sea? Did I dream that, or did I really do it? Why? Why would I do something like that? Poor Ceit. Lost for ever.

The light comes on, and I blink in the harshness of its glare. A lady is looking at me as if I had two heads. "What are you doing sitting here in the dark, Mr. Macdonald? Fully dressed, too."

"It's time for the milking," I tell her. "I'm just waiting for Mary to bring me my breakfast."

"It's too early for breakfast, Mr. Macdonald. Come on, I'll help you back to bed."

Crazy! I'm up now. And the cows won't wait.

She has her hand under my arm helping me to my feet, and she is staring into my face. I can see that she's concerned about something.

"Oh, Mr. Macdonald . . . You've been crying."

Have I? I put my hand to my face and feel how wet it is.

| TWENTY-EIGHT |

The old priest's house sat up on the hill overlooking Charlie's beach, just before the curve of the road, where the single track led off to Parks and Acarsaid Mhor. He was a shrunken man, the priest, stooped and wizened by the years and the weather, though he had a fine head of white hair on him, and sharp blue eyes that betrayed a keen intelligence.

From the door of his old crofthouse you could see right along the length of Coilleag a' Phrionnsa and down to the new breakwater almost immediately below, with a fine view out across the Sound of Barra.

Fin had arrived mid-morning and stood on the doorstep taking in the view while he waited for the old man to answer his knock, sunshine cascading in waves across the crystal turquoise of the bay, the wind yanking at his trousers and his jacket.

"I can't imagine a better place on earth to pass your final years." The priest's voice had startled Fin, and he turned to find the old man gazing out over the Sound. "I watch the roll-on roll-off come and go from Barra every day, and I keep promising myself that one time

I'll get on it and make a wee trip across the water. Visit old friends before they die. It's a beautiful island, Barra. Do you know it?"

Fin shook his head.

"Then you should pay a visit yourself, and not be a procrastinator like me. Come away in."

He bent now over the dining table in the living room, where sketches and photographs lay strewn among open albums filled with cuttings and photocopies and handwritten lists. He had laid everything out immediately after the phone call from Fin. It was not often he got the chance to show off his collection. Beneath a buttoned-up green cardigan he wore a white shirt with a fine brown check, open at the neck. His grey flannel trousers gathered in folds over his brown slippers. Fin noticed that there was dirt beneath his fingernails, and that he had not shaved for perhaps two days, a fine silver stubble clinging to the loose flesh of his face.

"The Eriskay jersey is one of the rarest pieces of craftwork you'll find in Scotland today," he said.

Fin was surprised. "They are still made?"

"Aye. For the co-operative, the Co-Chomunn Eirisgeidh. There's only a few women still producing them. In the old days they were single-coloured. Navy blue. But they make them in cream now, too. It's a shame, but the single colour doesn't really show off the intricacy of the patterns."

He reached down into a carrier bag on the floor and drew out an example of the jersey to show to Fin. He flattened it out across the table, and Fin could see what the old priest meant. The pattern was incredibly fine, with row upon row of vertical, horizontal and angled ribs, some in diamond shapes, others in a zigzag motif. The old man ran his finger lightly over the ribbed blue wool.

"They use very fine needles and a tight stitch. As you can see, the jersey is seamless. Very warm and dry. It takes about two weeks to knit one."

"And every family had its own distinct pattern?"

"Aye, they did. Passed down through the generations. Used to be practised all over the Hebrides at one time, but only in Eriskay now. And no doubt it'll die out here, too, in the end. The young ones don't show much interest in taking it on. Takes too long, you see. The girls now want everything today. Or even yesterday." He smiled sadly and shook his head at Fin. "Which is why I thought it would be a shame for such a fine craft to pass into history unrecorded."

"And you have examples of every family pattern on the island?"

"Pretty much so. For about the last seventy years anyway. Can I get you something to drink? A wee dram, maybe."

Fin declined politely. "It's a bit early for me."

"Och, it's never too early for a sip of whisky, Mr. Macleod. I didn't get to be this age by waiting for a nip, or drinking milk." He grinned and crossed to an old bureau with a drop-down door that opened to reveal a collection of bottles. He selected one and poured himself a small measure. "Sure I can't tempt you?"

Fin smiled. "No thanks."

The old priest returned to the table and took a tiny sip. "Do you have an example of what it is you're looking for?"

"I do." Fin took Gunn's fax from his bag and smoothed it over the jersey on the table.

The old man peered at it. "Oh, aye. Definitely an Eriskay pattern," he said. "Where did you get this?"

Fin hesitated. "It was drawn from an impression left by a blanket, or a rug. Something knitted anyway."

The priest nodded. "Well, it'll take me some time to compare it with all my samples. If I can't tempt you to a wee dram, make yourself a cup of tea." He nodded towards the stove. "And sit in by the fire. I'd offer you a Bible to read." He smiled mischievously. "But it's maybe a bit early in the day for stuff that strong."

Fin sat by the fire, nursing a mug of dark, sweet tea, and gazed from the small, recessed window out across the beach below. All his instincts told him that he was looking down on the scene of the crime. That this was where the young man whose body had been taken from the peat bog in Lewis had actually been murdered. He still had no idea yet who that young man was, although if he held his breath and listened to the wind he could almost hear it whisper that he was within touching distance now.

"Mr. Macleod?"

Fin turned his head towards the table.

The old priest smiled. "I think I might have found who knitted this."

Fin stood up and crossed the room to join the priest at the table, and found himself looking down at an old black-and-white photograph of an Eriskay jersey. It was pin-sharp, and placed next to Gunn's fax of the artist's sketch it was possible—eyes flickering back and forth from one to the other—to make a direct comparison between the patterns. The old man indicated all the points of correlation. There were too many to be in any doubt that they had been knitted by the same hand. They were, to all intents and purposes, identical.

Fin stabbed the fax with his finger. "But this wasn't a jersey."

"No." The priest shook his head thoughtfully. "I think it was a bed cover of some kind. Knitted squares sewn together. It would have been wonderfully warm." He traced the faint outline of the right-angled corner of one of the squares, and Fin thought that a dead man would have had no need of warmth. "You still haven't told me where you got this."

"I'm afraid," Fin said, "that I'm not really at liberty to say just yet."

The old man nodded with the fatalistic acceptance of someone whose life had been built on faith.

But Fin couldn't contain his curiosity any longer. "Whose knitting pattern is it?"

The priest turned over the photograph, and written on the other side in a neat hand and faded ink was the name Mary-Ann Gillies. And the date 1949.

The ruin stood in an elevated position on the hillside, almost lost in long grass that bowed in the wind. The top half of the crofthouse had fallen down years before, the front door an opening between two crumbling walls. Small, deep-set windows on either side of it remained intact, although all wood and glass were long gone. Chimneys survived at each gable. One even had a tall, yellow ceramic pot still perched precariously on top of it. The foundations of other buildings around the house remained visible among the grasses: a shed where they no doubt kept the beasts; a barn for storing the hay for winter feed. The strip of land where it would have been grown extended down the hill to the road below. At the far side of the road, sunlight glistered all across the small bay and the Sound beyond it. Cloud fragments raced across the bluest of skies, chasing their own shadows across the hillside. In the tiny, wind-blasted garden of a white cottage at the roadside, tall spring flowers with vividly coloured red and yellow heads ducked and dived among the turbulent currents of air.

Clearly visible from here, on the hilltop opposite, stood the granite church built from the proceeds of a single night's catch. It had dominated the life of the island for more than a century, and physically loomed over it still.

Fin picked his way carefully through the interior of the crofthouse, a jumble of fallen walls half-hidden by grasses and nettles. This was the Gillies croft that Morag McEwan had pointed out to him yesterday. The home of the boy called Donald John, who had been belted for disobeying his headmaster at Daliburgh school. The home of Mary-Anne Gillies, who had knitted the blanket whose pattern was blanched into the body of a young man taken from a peat bog on the Isle of Lewis four hours north of here. More, Fin reflected. For in the days when the body had been buried, the roads would have been much poorer, there would have been few if any causeways, and the ferry crossings would have taken longer. To the folk living on Eriskay back then, the Isle of Lewis would have been a whole world away.

The blast of a car's horn was carried to him on the wind, and he stepped out of the ruin, knee-deep in spittle-grass and yellow flowers, to see Morag's pink Mercedes drawn up beside his own car at the foot of the hill. The roof was down, and she waved up at him.

He started off down the hill, treading cautiously through the patches of bog where the land squelched beneath his feet, until he reached the car. Dino barked a greeting from his accustomed place on his mistress's lap. "Good morning," Fin said.

"What are you doing up there, *a ghràidh*?"

"You told me yesterday that was the Gillies croft."

"Aye, that's right."

"And that a homer called Donald John Gillies lived there."

"Yes. With old Donald Seamus and his sister, Mary-Anne."

Fin nodded thoughtfully. "Just the three of them?"

"No, Donald John had a brother." Morag sheltered a fresh cigarette from the wind as she lit it. "Just trying to remember his name . . ." She got her cigarette going and blew out a long stream of smoke that vanished at the same moment it left her lips. "Peter," she said at last. "Donald Peter. That was his name." She laughed. "Everyone here's called Donald. It's your middle name that counts." Then she shook her head sadly. "Poor Peter. A lovely boy he was. But not all there, if you know what I mean."

And Fin knew then that he had found the place that Marsaili's father had come from, and whose body it was they had dug out of the bog at Siader.

| TWENTY-NINE |

A strange calm had settled across the northern half of the Isle of Lewis. In contrast to the confusion of chaotic thoughts which had filled Fin's mind on the long drive north.

He had not stopped once, except for the half-hour spent in Stornoway briefing George Gunn on what he had discovered. Gunn had listened in silence in the incident room. He had stood staring out over the roofs of the houses opposite, towards Lews Castle and the trees on the hill, the final sunshine of the day slanting down among the branches and lying in long pink strips across the slope. And he had said, "So the dead boy is Marsaili's father's brother."

"Donald Peter Gillies."

"Except that neither of them is really called Gillies. That's just their homer names."

Fin nodded acknowledgement.

"And we have no idea where they came from, or what their real names might be."

After leaving Stornoway, Fin had thought about that on the drive across the Barvas moor, and through all the villages of the west coast. Siader, Galson, Dell, Cross. A blur of churches, each one a different denomination. Of DAF 2s and 3s, whitehouses, blackhouses, modern harled bungalows, braced all along the coast for the next assault.

He had no idea what kind of record, if any, the Church might have kept of those poor children it had torn from homes on the mainland to transport to the islands. There was no guarantee that the local authorities would be any more forthcoming. It was all so long ago. And who had cared back then about the human detritus of failed families, or orphaned children without relatives to champion their rights? Fin's overwhelming emotion was one of shame that such things should have been so recently perpetrated by his fellow countrymen.

The biggest problem in trying to identify who Donald John and Donald Peter Gillies actually were, was that no one had any idea where they came from. They would have arrived, anonymous passengers off the ferry at Lochboisdale, with cards around their necks and their past erased. And now, with Peter dead and his brother John lost in a fog of dementia, who was there to remember? Who was there to testify as to who they had really been? Those boys were lost for ever, and the likelihood was that neither he, nor the police, would ever know who had killed Peter, or why.

The lights of Ness sparkled all across the headland in the gloom, like a reflection of the stars emerging in the clear, settled sky above. The wind that had buffeted his car on the unprotected drive up through the Uists had died to an unnatural stillness. In his rear-view mirror he could still see the clouds brooding in their habitual gathering place around the peaks of Harris, and away to the west on an ocean like glass, the reflected last light of the day was fading into night.

There were three cars parked on the gravel above Marsaili's bungalow. Fionnlagh's Mini, Marsaili's old Astra and Donald Murray's SUV.

Donald and Marsaili were sitting together at the kitchen table when Fin knocked and walked in. For a moment he felt a strangely unpleasant pang of jealousy. After all, it had been Donald Murray who had taken Marsaili's virginity all those years before.

But that had been in another life, when they had all been very different people.

Donald nodded. "Fin."

Marsaili said quickly, almost as if she wanted Fin to know straight away that there was no cause for jealousy, "Donald came with a proposition about Fionnlagh and Donna."

Fin turned to Donald. "Has Fionnlagh been to see you?"

"He came this morning."

"And?"

Donald's smile was wry, and laden with history. "He's his father's son." Fin couldn't resist a smile.

Marsaili said, "They've moved in here permanently, the two of them. And the baby. They're upstairs." She flicked an uncertain glance Donald's way. "Donald has suggested that he and I share the cost and responsibility of the baby to let Fionnlagh and Donna finish their studies. Even if it means one, or both of them, leaving the island to go to university. I mean, we all know how important it is not to throw away the opportunities life offers when you are young. You spend the rest of your life regretting it."

There was more than just a hint of bitterness in her voice. And Fin wondered if there was recrimination in it, too.

"Sounds like a plan."

Marsaili lowered her eyes to the table. "I'm just not sure I can afford it. Fionnlagh going to university, I mean. And the cost of the baby. I've been surviving on Artair's life policy, and was hoping it would see me through university, if I get in. I guess I'll have to postpone my degree and get a job in the meantime."

"That would be a shame," Fin said.

She shrugged. "Not much alternative."

"There could be."

She turned inquisitive eyes on him. "Like what?"

"Like you and I share the burden of your half." He smiled. "I am Eilidh's grandfather, after all. Maybe we can't stop our children making the same mistakes we did, but at least we can be around to pick up the pieces."

Donald's gaze alternated between them, discerning and interpreting everything that remained unspoken. He stood up then. "Well, I'll leave you two to talk about it." He hesitated before offering Fin his hand. Then, at length, held it out and they shook. He left without another word.

The kitchen was oddly silent in the wake of his departure, burned out, almost unreal in the flickering glare of the overhead fluorescent. Somewhere deep in the house they could hear the thump, thump of Fionnlagh's music.

Finally Marsaili said, "How can *you* afford it?"

Fin shrugged. "I have a bit put by. And it's not my intention to remain unemployed for ever."

More silence hung heavy between them. A silence born of regret. Of all their failures, individually and together.

Fin said, "How did your exams go?"

"Don't ask."

He nodded. "I guess you weren't exactly best prepared."

"No."

He drew a deep breath. "Marsaili, I have some news for you. About your dad." Blue eyes fixed him in their gaze, filled with naked curiosity. "Why don't we get out of here, get some fresh air. It's a beautiful night out there, and there won't be a soul on the beach."

The night was filled with the whispering sound of the sea. It sighed, as if relieved by the removal of its obligation to maintain an angry demeanour. A three-quarters moon rose into the blackness above it and cast its light upon the water and the sand, a light that threw shadows and obscured truths in half-lit faces. The air was soft, and pregnant with the prospect of coming summer, a poetry in the night, carried in the shallow waves that burst like bubbling Hippocrene all along the beach.

Fin and Marsaili walked close enough to feel each other's warmth, leaving tracks in virgin sand.

"There was a time," Fin said, "when I would have held your hand when we walked along a beach like this."

Marsaili turned a look of surprise towards him. "Can you read minds now?"

And Fin thought how completely natural it would have been, and how immediately embarrassing. He laughed. "Remember how I dropped that sack of crabs off the cliff on top of you girls sunbathing down here?"

"I remember slapping you so hard I hurt my hand."

Fin grinned ruefully. "I remember that, too. I also remember you were topless at the time."

"Damned peeping Tom!"

He smiled. "And I recall making love to you among the rocks back there, and skinny-dipping in the ocean afterwards to cool down." When she didn't react he turned to look at her and saw a distant look in her eyes, thoughts transporting her to some far-off place and time.

They were almost at the boat shed now. It loomed out of the darkness like a portent of past and future pain, and he put his hand lightly on her shoulder to turn her back the way they had come. Already the sea was washing up over their footprints, erasing any history of their ever having passed this way. He left his arm around her shoulder and felt her lean in to him as he steered her a little further up the beach, away from the water.

They walked in silence for almost half its length until they stopped, by some mutual unspoken consent, and he turned her towards him. Her face was in shadow, and he put a finger under her chin to turn it up to the light. At first she wouldn't meet his eye.

"I remember the little girl who took me in hand that first day at school," he said. "And walked me up the road to the Crobost stores and told me that her name was Marjorie, but that she preferred her Gaelic name of Marsaili. That same little girl who decided that my English name was ugly, and shortened it to Fin. Which is what everyone has called me for the rest of my life."

She smiled now, a smile touched by sadness, and finally met his eye. "And I remember how I used to love you, Fin Macleod." Moonlight shimmered in the tears that brimmed in her eyes. "Not sure I ever stopped."

He leaned in, then, until their lips touched. Warm, tentative, uncertain. And finally they kissed. A soft, sweet kiss full of everything they had once been, and everything they had since lost. His eyes closed, and the regrets and passions of a lifetime washed over him.

And then it was over. She stepped back, breaking free of his arms, and looked at him in the dark. Searching eyes full of fear and doubt. Then she turned and walked away towards the rocks. He stood for a moment watching her go, then had to run to catch her up. When he did she said, without breaking stride, "What did you find out about my dad?"

"I found out that he's not Tormod Macdonald."

She stopped dead and turned her frown towards him. "What do you mean?"

"I mean he borrowed, or stole, that identity off a dead boy from Harris. His name was actually Donald John Gillies, and he came from the Isle of Eriskay. The young man they took out of the bog was his brother, Donald Peter."

Marsaili gaped at him in disbelief.

"Only Donald John isn't his real name either." He saw her whole world falling apart in the look of pain that creased her eyes. All the certainties of her life shifting beneath her feet like the sand she stood on.

"I don't understand . . ."

And he told her everything that he had learned, and how he had learned it. She listened in silence, her face paler than the moon, and in the end put a hand on his arm to steady herself.

"My dad was a homer?"

Fin nodded. "An orphan in all probability. Or a child in care, shipped out to the islands with his brother by the Catholic Church."

She slumped down into the sand, sitting cross-legged, her face falling forward into open hands. At first he thought she was crying, but when she took her face out of her hands it was dry. Shock had blunted all other emotions. Fin sat down beside her. She gazed out over the transient benevolence of the sea and said, "It's strange. You think you know who you are, because you think you know who your parents are. Some things are just . . ." she searched for the word ". . . unquestioned, unquestionable." She shook her head. "And then suddenly you learn that your whole life has been based on a lie, and you've no idea who you are any more." She turned to look at him, eyes wide with disillusion. "Did my dad kill his brother?"

And Fin realized then that while for him it might be possible to accept the idea that her father's true origins and who murdered his brother might never be discovered, Marsaili could not rest until she knew the truth. "I don't know." He put an arm around her and she rested her head on his shoulder.

They sat like that for a long time, listening to the slow, steady pulse of the ocean, drenched in moonlight, until he felt her trembling with the cold. But she made no attempt to move. "I went to see him, just before I left for Glasgow, and found him sitting in the rain. He thought he was on a boat. The *Claymore*, he said it was, sailing from the mainland." She turned to look at Fin, her eyes clouded and sad. "I thought he was just rambling. Something he'd seen on television or read in a book. At first he called me Catherine, and then Ceit, like I was someone he knew. Not his daughter. And he talked about someone else called Big Kenneth."

"Beinn Ruigh Choinnich. It's the mountain that shelters the harbour at Lochboisdale. They would have seen it from the ferry, from a long way off." He reached out a hand to brush stray hairs from her eyes. "What else did he say, Marsaili?"

"Nothing that made much sense. At least, not then. He was talking to Ceit, not me. He said he would never forget their days at The Dean. Or the turrets at Danny's. Something like that. Reminding them of their place in the world." She looked at him with pain etched in every line of her face. "And something else, that takes on a whole different meaning now." She closed her eyes, trying to recall exactly. Then opened them wide. "He said, we didn't do too bad for a couple of orphan waifs."

There must have been light in Fin's eyes, because she frowned, canting her head, staring at him. "What is it?"

And if she had seen light, it was the light of revelation. He said, "Marsaili, I think maybe I know exactly what he meant when he talked about The Dean. And Danny's turrets. And it must mean that Ceit, the girl who boarded with the widow O'Henley, came with them on the boat." And he thought, *maybe there is someone after all who still knows the truth.* He stood, then, and offered Marsaili his hand. She pulled herself up to stand beside him. He said, "If we can get seats, we should try to be on the first flight to Edinburgh tomorrow."

The only light in the room came from the blue-tinged illumination of his laptop computer screen. He sat alone at the desk, in the dark, the stillness of the house pressing in all around him. The presence of others, in other rooms, seemed somehow only to increase his sense of isolation.

This was the room where he had spent so many hours tutored by Artair's dad. Where he and Artair had sat, individually or together, listening to long lectures on Hebridean history, or puzzling over mathematical equations. Where the years of his boyhood had passed in suffocating incarceration, freedom glimpsed only occasionally in stolen glances from the window. Marsaili had said he could spend the night on the fold-down settee. But there were too many memories here. The Cyprus-shaped coffee stain on the card table where they worked. The rows of books with their exotic titles, still there on the shelves. The smell of Artair's dad's pipe smoke, hanging in the still air in slow-moving blue strands. If he breathed deeply the scent of it remained, even if only in his memory.

Marsaili, fragile and fatigued, had gone to bed some time ago, telling him he could stay as long as he liked, to benefit from

Fionnlagh's wifi. The cursor on his screen winked over a webpage with the crest of the National Galleries of Scotland. Below it, a blue window with cotton-wool clouds announced *Another World. Dalí, Magritte, Miró and the Surrealists*. But he had long since stopped looking at it. It had taken him almost no time to confirm his suspicions, and immediately reserve their tickets on the morning flight. He had then spent much of the next hour in deep research.

He was tired. An ache behind his eyes. His body felt punched, bruised, his brain short-circuiting thoughts almost as soon as they appeared. He had no desire to go back to Edinburgh, a return to a painful past he had been unable to put behind him. The best he had been able to do was achieve a little distance. Now Fate was robbing him even of that. For Marsaili there would be no closure without it, while for him it would only serve to reopen old wounds.

He wondered, briefly, how she would receive him if he were to slip softly along the hall to her room and slide beneath the covers beside her. Not for sex, or even for love. But for comfort. The warmth of another human being.

But he knew he wouldn't. He closed the lid of his laptop and moved silently through the house, shutting the kitchen door gently behind him. He walked up the road in the night to where his tent awaited him. Moonlight reflecting on the still of the ocean was almost painfully bright, stars overhead like the white-hot tips of a billion needles pricking the universe. All that awaited him within the soulless confines of his tent were a cold sleeping bag, a few sheets of paper in a buff folder describing the death of his son, and all the sleepless hours he knew he would have to endure before morning.

| THIRTY |

It was milder in Edinburgh, a light wind blowing in off the Pentland
Hills, the sun dipping in and out from behind bubbles of cumu-
lus, splashing light and colour across this grey city of granite and
sandstone.

They had brought overnight bags in case of the need to stay,
although Fin was not optimistic that they would find anything
other than the places of which Marsaili's father had spoken. A visit
that would take them less than an hour. They took a taxi from the
airport, and as it approached Haymarket the driver set his indicator
going for a left turn into Magdala Crescent. Fin said to him, "Not
this way."

"It's a short-cut, mate."

"I don't care. Go up to Palmerston Place."

The driver shrugged. "You're paying."

Fin felt Marsaili's eyes on him. Without meeting them he said,
"When Padraig MacBean took me out to An Sgeir on his old trawler,
he told me the story of how he'd lost his father's brand-new boat in
the Minch. Barely escaped with his life." He turned to see her eyes
fixed upon him, wide with curiosity. "Even though there is nothing

to mark the spot where she went down, Padraig said he feels it every time he sails over it."

"Your son was killed in Magdala Crescent?"

"In a street off it."

"Do you want to tell me about it?"

He gazed past the driver, through the windscreen and the traffic stretching ahead of them along West Maitland Street. Finally he said, "No. I don't think I do."

The taxi turned into Palmerston Place, past smoke-blackened bay-windowed tenements, a park in early spring leaf, the Gothic grandeur of St. Mary's Episcopal Cathedral, and down the hill to where the red-sandstone church on the corner had been converted to a youth hostel with pillar-box red doors.

It swung up the hill, then, on Belford Road, to drop them in the forecourt of a Travelodge hotel opposite a stone gateway beneath a blue-and-white banner fluttering in the breeze.

"Dean Gallery," Marsaili read when they stepped out of the cab. Fin paid the driver and turned to face her confusion. "The Dean is an art gallery?"

Fin nodded. "It is now." He took her arm and they ran across the road between cars. Through a black, wrought-iron gate they followed a narrow cobbled path up the hill between a high privet hedge and a stone wall. The path opened up then, and curved its way through parkland shaded by tall chestnuts, where bronze statues stood on stone plinths planted on manicured lawns. "In the days before the welfare state," he said, "there was something in Scotland called the Poor Law. It was a kind of social security for the poorest in society, pretty much paid for by the Church. And where there were gaps, sometimes private charities stepped in. The Orphan Hospital of Edinburgh was set up in the early 1700s by the Society for Propagating Christian Knowledge to fill one of those gaps."

"This is what you were looking up on the internet last night?"

"Yes." They passed a tarnished sculpture of the Madonna and Child called *The Virgin of Alsace*. "In 1833 the hospital moved into a

new building, here on the Dean Estate, and it became known as the
Dean Orphanage." An Edinburgh lady of indeterminate age with
bob-cut silver hair and navy-blue skirts hurried by with a whiff of
floral scent that reminded Fin briefly of Marsaili's mother.

As they rounded the bend at the top of the hill, The Dean
swung into view in all its towering sandstone grandeur: porticos,
arched windows, four-cornered towers and stone balustrades.
Fin and Marsaili stopped to take it in. There was an odd sense
of destiny in finding it here at the top of the hill, hidden behind
hedges and trees, revealing itself suddenly like a glimpse into history, national and personal. The circle of fate whose first curve had
begun with the departure of Marsaili's father was completed now
by her arrival.

Her voice was hushed by awe. "This was an orphanage?"

"Apparently."

"My God. It's a wonderful building, Fin. But no place to bring up
orphaned children."

Fin thought that his aunt's house had been no place to bring up
an orphaned child either. He said, "I read last night that originally
they were fed on porridge and kale, and that the orphan girls had to
make clothes for all the children to wear. I guess things would have
been very different in the fifties." He paused. "But it's hard to picture
your dad here."

Marsaili turned to him. "Are you sure this is where he meant?"

He led her a little further up the hill, and pointed beyond The
Dean, to the twin towers of another impressive building in the valley
below. "Stewart's Melville," he said. "A private school. In the days your
dad would have been here it was called Daniel Stewart's College."

"Danny's place."

Fin nodded. "A terrible irony in it, not missed by your dad. The
poorest and most deprived children of his generation living cheek
by jowl with the most privileged. What was it he said? The turrets
at Danny's had always been a reminder of their place in the world?"

"Yes," Marsaili said. "At the bottom of the pile." She turned to Fin.
"I want to go in."

They followed the drive to the portico at the entrance, where steps led up between pillars to a rust-red door. A stone stairway to their left descended to an open green space that might once have been gardens. Fin watched Marsaili's face as they crossed a tiled vestibule into the main hallway that ran the length of the building. Impressively grand rooms led off either side of it, galleries hung with paintings, or filled with sculptures, a shop, a cafeteria. Light cascaded down at either end of it from windows in the stairwells of each wing. You could very nearly hear the distant echo of lost children.

The emotion in Marsaili's face was almost painful to watch as she reassessed everything about herself. Who she was, where she had come from, what dreadful kind of a life her father had endured as a boy. Something he had never shared with any of them. His lonely secret.

A uniformed security guard asked if he could help them.

Fin said, "This place used to be an orphanage."

"Yeah. Hard to believe." The guard tipped his head towards one end of the corridor. "The boys used to be in that wing, apparently. The girls in the other. The exhibition room along there on the left used to be the headmaster's office. Or whatever he was called."

"I want to go," Marsaili said suddenly, and Fin saw that there were silent tears reflecting light on her cheeks. He slipped his arm through hers and led her back out through the entrance, watched by a bemused guard wondering what it was he had said. She stood breathing deeply at the top of the steps for almost a minute. "We can find out from the records, can't we? Who he really was, I mean. Where his family came from."

Fin shook his head. "I checked online last night. The records are kept locked up for a hundred years. Only the children themselves have a right of access to them." He shrugged. "I guess it's designed to protect them. Though I suppose the courts could grant the police a warrant to gain access. This is a murder investigation, after all."

She turned teary eyes in his direction, wiping her cheeks dry with the backs of her hands. He saw in her face the same question he had been unable to answer on the beach the night before. Had her father killed his brother? Fin thought it unlikely they would ever know, unless by some miracle they were able to find the girl called Ceit, who had boarded at the O'Henley croft.

They walked in silence back down the cobbled path to Belford Road, the Dean Cemetery brooding in shaded tranquillity behind a high stone wall. As they arrived at the gate Fin's mobile phone alerted him to an incoming email. He scrolled through its menu with his finger and tapped to open it. When he took some time to read it, frowning thoughtfully, Marsaili said, "Something important?"

He waited until he had tapped in a response before replying. "When I was looking for references to the Dean Orphanage on the internet last night I came across a forum of former Dean orphans exchanging photographs and reminiscences. I suppose there must be some kind of bond between them all that they still feel, even if they didn't know one another at The Dean."

"Like family."

He looked at her. "Yes. Like the family they never had. You still feel a greater affinity to a second cousin you've never met than to some complete stranger." He pushed his hands deep into his pockets. "A lot of them seem to have emigrated. Australia the most popular destination."

"As far away from The Dean as they could get."

"A fresh start, I suppose. Putting a whole world between you and your childhood. Erasing the past." Every word he uttered had such resonance for Fin that he found himself almost too choked to speak. It was, after all, only what he had done himself. He felt Marsaili's hand on his arm. The merest touch that said more than anything she could have put into words. "Anyway, there was one of them still living here in Edinburgh. A man called Tommy Jack. He might well have been at The Dean around the same time as your dad. There was an email address. I wrote to him." He shrugged. "I very nearly didn't. It was a real afterthought."

"That was him replying?"

"Yes."

"And?"

"He sent his address and said he would be happy to talk to us this evening at his home."

| THIRTY-ONE |

Afternoon sunlight leaked in all around drawn curtains that breathed in and out in the breeze from the open window beyond them. The noise of passing traffic came with it, distant and unreal, along with the sound of falling water from the weir in the Water of Leith below.

Their room was up in the roof, with views across the river and the Dean Village. But Fin had drawn the curtain on it as soon as they entered the room. They needed the dark to find themselves.

There had been no discussion, no plan. The hotel was directly across the road from the gallery, and they required a place for the night. Fin was not quite sure why neither of them had corrected the receptionist's mistaken notion that they were a couple looking for a double room. There had been ample opportunity.

They had ascended to the top floor in a tiny elevator without a word passing between them, Fin's stomach alive with butterflies in collision. Neither had met the other's eye.

It had been easier, somehow, to undress in the dark, although there was a time when they had known each other's bodies intimately. Every curve, every surface, every softness.

And now, with the cool of the sheets on their skin, they rediscovered that intimacy. How bizarrely comfortable it was suddenly,
and familiar, as if no time had passed at all since the last time. Fin
found the same passion deep inside as she had aroused in him that
very first time. Fierce, trembling, all-consuming desire. He found
her face with his hands, all its well-known contours. Her neck, her
shoulders, the gentle swell of her breasts, the curve of her buttocks.

Their lips were like old friends rediscovering each other after so
many years, searching, exploring, as if not quite believing that nothing had really changed.

Their bodies rose and fell as one, breath coming in gasps, invol-
untary vocal punctuation. No words. No control. Lust, passion,
hunger, greed. Generating heat, sweat, total immersion. Fin felt
the blood of his island heritage pulsing in every stroke. The endless
windswept moors, the fury of the ocean as it smashed itself upon
the shore. The Gaelic voices of his ancestors raised in tribal chant.

And suddenly it was over. Like the first time. Sluice gates
opened, water released, after years of constraint behind emotional
dams built from anger and misunderstanding. All of it gone, in a
moment, washing away every last wasted minute of their lives.

They lay afterwards, wrapped in each other, lost in their
thoughts. And in a while Fin became aware that Marsaili's breathing had slowed, grown shallow, her head heavier on his chest, and
he wondered where in God's name they went from here.

| THIRTY-TWO |

Tommy Jack lived in a two-bedroomed tenement flat above a wine shop and a newsagent's in Broughton Street. The taxi dropped Fin and Marsaili in York Place and they walked slowly down the hill in the soft evening light, breathing in the strange smells of the city. Exhaust fumes, malt bins, curry. Nothing could have been further from the island experience. Fin had spent fifteen years of his life in this town, but just a matter of days back among the islands and already it seemed alien, impossibly claustrophobic. And dirty. Discarded chewing gum blackening the pavements, litter blowing in the gutters.

The entrance to the close was in Albany Street Lane, and as they turned into it Fin saw a van driving past up the hill. It was a vehicle belonging to Barnardo's, the children's charity, and carried the logo, *Giving children back their future*. And he wondered how you could give back what had already been destroyed.

Tommy was a short man with a round, shining face beneath a smooth, shiny head. His shirt collar was frayed. He wore a grey pullover with egg stains down the front, tucked into trousers a size too big that were held up high around his stomach by a belt tightened one notch too many. There were holes worn in the toes of his carpet slippers.

He ushered them into a narrow hallway with dark wallpaper, and a front room which probably trapped the sun during the day, but which was dingy now in the dying evening light. A smell of stale cooking fat permeated the flat, along with the faintly unpleasant perfume of body odour.

But Tommy was a man of cheerful disposition, with sharp dark eyes that shone at them through frameless glasses. Fin figured that he was probably in his mid to late late sixties. "Would you like a cup of tea?"

"That would be nice," Marsaili said, and he talked to them through the open door of the tiny kitchen scullery as he boiled a kettle and brought out cups and saucers and teabags.

"I'm on my own these days, ever since my missus died about eight years ago. More than thirty years we were married. Still can't get used to being without her."

And Fin thought that there was a certain tragic irony in both starting and finishing life all alone.

Marsaili said, "No children?"

He appeared at the door, smiling. But it was a smile laden with regret. "Afraid not. One of the big disappointments of my life. Never having children, and being able to give them the kind of childhood I would have wanted for myself." He turned back into the scullery. "Not that I could have given them that much on a bank clerk's salary." He chuckled. "Imagine, a lifetime spent counting money, and all of it belonging to someone else."

He brought their tea through in china cups, and they perched on the threadbare fabric of ancient armchairs dressed with grubby white antimacassars. A black-and-white framed photograph of Tommy and what had to be his wife stood on the mantelpiece above a tiled fireplace where a gas fire glowed dully in the gloom. The photographer had captured the mutual affection in their eyes, and Fin was moved to think that Tommy had, at least, found some happiness in his life. "When were you at The Dean, Tommy?"

He shook his head. "Couldn't give you exact dates. But I was there for a few years in the fifties. It was run by a brute of a man, then. Anderson, his name was. For someone in charge of a home supposed to provide comfort and refuge for orphans, he didn't like children very much. A foul temper, he had. I remember one time he took all our things and burned them in the central heating furnace. Retribution for having fun." He chuckled at the memory.

From somewhere he was able to find humour in the story, and Fin marvelled at the human capacity for making light of the worst that life could throw at you. An endless resilience. It was all about survival, he supposed. If you gave in, even for a moment, you would be dragged down into the dark.

"Of course, I wasn't only at The Dean. You got moved around quite a bit. It was hard to keep friends, so you just stopped making them. And you never let yourself hope there might be an end to it. Even when the grown-ups came to look at us, and pick out one or two for adoption." He laughed. "They wouldn't do it now, but in those days they used to give us a good scrubbing, get us all dressed up in our best togs, and stand us in a line while ladies smelling of French perfume and men that reeked of cigars came and examined us, like sheep at a market. Of course, it was always the girls they picked. Wee boys like me had no chance." He leaned forward. "Can I refill your cups?"

"No thanks." Marsaili put a hand over her still half-full cup. Fin shook his head.

Tommy stood. "I'll have another one myself. If I have to get up in the night, I might as well have something in the tank to empty." He returned to the scullery to bring the kettle back to the boil. He raised his voice to be heard above it. "There was one place I was in that got visited by Roy Rogers. Remember him? Famous cowboy he was, in films and TV. Came touring round Scotland with his horse, Trigger. Stopped off at our orphanage and picked out one of the lassies. Adopted her and took her back to America. Imagine! One minute you're a poor wee orphan lassie in a home in Scotland, the next you're a rich man's daughter in the wealthiest country in the world." He came back out with a fresh cup in his hand. "Of such things are dreams made, eh?" He sat down, then suddenly stood again. "What am I thinking? I never even offered you a biscuit."

Fin and Marsaili politely declined and he sat down once more.

"When I got too old for the orphanages they put me in a hostel in Collinton Road. They were still talking then about an older boy who'd come to stay for a short time about ten years before. Returning home from the navy, and his family had no room for him. Something like that. Big Tam, he was called. A handsome big fella by all accounts. One of the other boys had heard there were auditions in town for the chorus of *South Pacific* and suggested Big Tam put himself up for it." Tommy grinned. "You know what's coming."

Neither Fin nor Marsaili had any idea.

"Big Tam was Sean Connery." Tommy laughed. "Big star. And we shared the same hostel! He came back to Scotland for the opening of the Scottish Parliament. First time a parliament had sat in Edinburgh for nearly three hundred years. I went along, too. Historical moment, eh? Not to be missed. Anyway, I see Sean as he's going in. And I wave at him from the crowd and shout, 'How are you doing, Big Tam?'" Tommy smiled. "He didn't recognize me, of course."

Fin leaned forward. "Was The Dean a Catholic home, Tommy?"

Tommy's eyebrows shot up in surprise. "Christ, no! That Mr. Anderson hated Catholics. Hated everything and everyone, come to think of it."

Marsaili said, "Were there ever any Catholics in the home?"

"Oh, aye, but they never stayed. The priests would come and fetch them and take them away to some Catholic place. There was three of them once, I remember, got whipped off double quick after a boy died on the bridge."

"What bridge was that?" Fin asked, his interest suddenly piqued.

"The Dean Bridge. Crosses the Water of Leith just above the Dean Village. Must be a hundred-foot drop."

"What happened?"

"Oh, nobody knew for sure. There was lots of gossip and speculation, of course. Some bet, or dare, about walking across the ledge on the outside of the parapet. Something like that. Anyway, some of The Dean kids were involved. Sneaked out one night, and a village boy fell to his death. Two days later those three Catholic kids were gone. Taken away in a big black car by all accounts."

Fin felt a stillness in his heart, that sense of being close enough to the truth to touch it. "Do you remember their names?"

"Oh," Tommy shook his head. "It was a long time ago, Mr. Macleod. There was a lassie. Cathy, or Catherine, I think it was. And two brothers. One of them could have been John. Maybe Johnny." He paused, searching back in his mind. "I do remember quite clearly the name of the boy who died, though. Patrick Kelly. Everyone knew the Kelly boys, of course. They lived in the Dean Village, and their dad was involved in some kind of criminal gang. Been to prison, they said. The boys were right tough nuts. You stayed out of their way if you could." He tilted his head in a moment of lost reflection. "A bunch of them came up to the Dean a few days later looking for the daftie."

Marsaili frowned. "The daftie?"

"Aye, the brother. What was his name . . . ?" Recollection broke suddenly in his eyes, like dawn light. "Peter! That was it. Johnny's brother. Nice laddie, but not quite right in the head."

It was almost dark by the time they stepped back out into the street, earlier than it would have been up on the islands, and everything a little unreal, leached of colour by the pools of cold light that fell from the overhead streetlamps.

"So my dad and his brother really were John and Peter," Marsaili said, as if knowing their names in some way made them more real. "But how will we get to find out their family name?"

Fin looked thoughtful. "By talking to someone who knew them."

"Like who?"

"Like the Kellys."

She frowned. "How would we ever find *them*?"

"Well, if I were still a policeman I would have said, because they're known to us."

"I don't understand."

A young couple emerged from the blue frontage of the wine shop, bottles clunking in a paper bag. She slipped her arm through his, and their voices came like chattering birds in the twilight.

Fin said, "The Kellys are a well-known crime family in Edinburgh, Marsaili. Have been for years. Started out in what was then the slum village of Dean. Drugs, prostitution. They've even been implicated in a number of gangland killings, though nothing was ever proved."

"You know them?" Marsaili couldn't keep the incredulity out of her voice.

"I never had any dealings with them, no. But I do know that my old DCI did. He was my boss when I was first in the force. Jack Walker. Retired now." He took out his mobile. "He'd probably be happy to meet us for a drink."

Someone seemed to be going around Edinburgh painting shopfronts, bars and restaurants in primary colours. Vandals with a misplaced sense of civic pride. The Windsor Buffet at the top of Leith Walk was a virulent green, the former Scottish Television studios next door to it a shocking blue. Yellows and reds featured up and down the street, along with more greens and blues. All topped by drab sandstone tenements, some of which had been stone-cleaned, while others remained blackened by the years, like bad teeth in a brave smile.

The Windsor was nearly full, but Jack Walker had reserved them an alcove at the back. He looked curiously at Marsaili when they were introduced, but didn't ask. He ordered beers for Fin and himself, and a glass of white wine for Marsaili. He was a big man with wide shoulders, and an untidy shock of white Brillo-Pad hair. For all that he must have been in his mid-seventies, he was not a man you would choose to pick a fight with. He had a sunbed-tanned face and emerald eyes that never quite achieved the same apparent warmth as the sardonic smile that played constantly about his lips.

He shook his head gravely. "You don't want to mess with the Kellys, Fin. They're bad bastards."

"I don't doubt that they are, sir. And I have no intention of mess-
ing with them." Even as he said it, he was aware of addressing his
former boss as "sir." Old habits died hard. "I just want to talk to any
one of them who might have been around in the fifties when the
family lived in the Dean Village."

Walker cocked an eyebrow. His interest had been engaged,
but all his years in the force had taught him that sometimes there
were questions better left unasked. "The only one left from that
time would be Paul Kelly. He would just have been a kid, then. There
were two older brothers, but they were gunned down outside their
home well over fifty years ago. Tit-for-tat killings, we figured. There
were some pretty violent turf wars going on at that time. I was just
a young cop starting out. We never probed these gangland murders
too deeply, so no one ever got done for it. And then over the years
I watched as the young Paul Kelly took the reins. Built himself a
bloody empire on the back of other people's misery." He made a face
that masked a lot of pent-up anger and frustration. "We never were
able to lay a finger on him."

"So he's still the head honcho?"

"Getting on a bit now, Fin, but aye. No doubt likes to think of
himself as the Godfather. Came from the gutter, but lives in a big
fucking mansion in Morningside." He glanced at Marsaili, but there
was no apology for his language. "He has kids and grandkids now.
Sends them all to private school, while honest Joes like you and me
struggle to pay the heating. He's scum, Fin. Just scum. I wouldn't
give him the time of day."

They lay in silence for what seemed like an eternity in the darkness
of their hotel room. The only accompaniment to their breathing was
the sound of running water coming from the river below. The same
water that flowed under the Dean Bridge. Fin had taken them there
after they left the Windsor, and they had crossed to the middle of it,
looking down on the Dean Village, and the Water of Leith a hundred
feet beneath it. Marsaili's father and his brother had been here once.
Something had happened on this bridge and a boy had died.

Marsaili's voice seemed resoundingly loud coming out of the dark, crashing into his thoughts. "It was strange watching you tonight," she said. "With that policeman."

Fin turned his head towards her, even although he couldn't see her. "Why strange?"

"Because it was like looking at someone I didn't know. Not the Fin Macleod I went to school with, or the Fin Macleod who made love to me on the beach. Not even the Fin Macleod who treated me like shit in Glasgow."

He closed his eyes and remembered how it had been, that brief sojourn together at university in Glasgow. Sharing a flat. How badly he had treated her, incapable of dealing with his own pain, and taking it out on Marsaili. How often is it, he thought, that it's the people closest to us that we hurt the most?

"It was like looking at a stranger. The Fin Macleod you must have been all these years when I didn't know you. Married to someone else, raising a kid, being a policeman."

He was almost startled by the sudden touch of her hand on his face.

"I'm not sure I know you at all. Not any more."

And those few moments of passion they had shared that afternoon, pencil-thin lines of sunlight zigzagging across their frantic lovemaking, already seemed like a lifetime ago.

| THIRTY-THREE |

Paul Kelly lived in a detached yellow sandstone house built on three levels, with gables and dormers, an elaborate entrance porch, and a conservatory at the rear that extended right out into a mature, well-maintained garden.

A semicircular drive led up to the front door from Tipperlinn Road, with wrought-iron electronic gates at each end of it. Sunlight tipped down over azaleas in bloom, green-dappled by young beech leaves.

Their taxi dropped Fin and Marsaili at the south gate, and Fin asked the driver to wait. But he shook his head. "Naw. You'll pay me now. I'm no hanging around." It seemed that he knew the address and was anxious not to linger. They stood and watched as he drove off and swung into Morningside Place.

Fin turned to the intercom set in the stone gatepost and pressed the buzzer. After a moment a voice said, "What d'ye want?"

"My name's Fin Macleod. I used to be a cop. I'd like to speak to Paul Kelly."

"Mr. Kelly disnae speak tae anyone without an appointment."

"Tell him it's about something that happened on the Dean Bridge fifty-odd years ago."

"He'll no see you."

"Just tell him." There was an imperative quality to Fin's voice. A tone that brooked no argument.

The speaker went dead and Fin glanced self-consciously at Marsaili. He was again being that Fin Macleod she didn't know. And he had no idea how to bridge the gap between the two.

They seemed to wait an inordinately long time before the speaker crackled again and the voice returned. "Okay," was all it said, and the gates immediately began to swing open.

As they walked up the drive, Fin noticed the security lights and CCTV cameras mounted around the house and in the grounds. Paul Kelly was evidently keen to avoid unwanted visitors. The front door opened as they reached the entrance porch, and a young man in an open-necked white shirt and sharply creased grey trousers folding neatly over Italian shoes surveyed them with cautious eyes. His black hair was cut short, and gelled back from his forehead. An expensive haircut. Fin could smell his aftershave from six feet away.

"Need tae frisk you."

Without a word Fin moved forward, legs apart, arms raised to either side. The young man patted him down carefully, front and back, along each arm and down each leg.

"The woman, too."

Fin said, "She's clean."

"I need to check."

"Take my word for it."

The young man looked at him very directly. "More than my job's worth, pal."

"It's okay," Marsaili said. And she presented herself for the search.

Fin watched with a simmering anger as the man put his hands on her. Front and back, buttocks, legs. But he didn't linger where he didn't have to. Professional. Marsaili remained expressionless, although her face coloured slightly.

"Okay," the man said. "Follow me."

He took them through a cream and pale-peach hallway with a thick red carpet and a beechwood staircase rising through two floors.

Paul Kelly was lounging on a white leather settee in the conservatory at the rear of the house smoking a very large Havana cigar. Although a light breeze rustled through the spring leaves in the garden outside, Kelly's smoke hung in still strands, blue-grey where it was caught by the sunlight that angled through the trees. There was an impression here almost of being in the garden itself, although you could neither smell nor hear it. Red plush armchairs sat around a brushed steel table, and bright daylight reflected off a polished wooden floor.

Kelly stood as his flunky showed them in. He was a giant of a man, well over six feet tall, and although a little overweight still in good condition for someone in his mid to late sixties. His florid round face was shaved to a shine, steel-grey hair cropped to bristle. His starched pink shirt was stretched a little too tightly over an ample belly, his jeans ironed to an incongruous crease.

He smiled, a slight query in the tilt of his head, and he offered a large hand to each of them in turn. "An ex-cop and tales of the Dean Bridge. I must admit, you've aroused my curiosity." He waved the same big hand towards the red armchairs. "Take a seat. Can I offer you something to drink? Tea? Coffee?"

Fin shook his head, "No thanks." He and Marsaili perched uncomfortably on the edge of the armchairs. "We're trying to establish the identity of a man, now living on the Isle of Lewis, who was at the Dean Orphanage some time in the mid 1950s."

Kelly laughed. "Sure you're not still in the force? You don't sound like an *ex*-cop to me." He sank back into his white settee.

"I can assure you I am."

"Well, then, I'll take your word for it." He drew reflectively on his cigar. "What makes you think I can help?"

"Your family was living in old millworkers' tenements in the Dean Village at that time."

Kelly nodded. "We were." He chuckled. "Wouldn't recognize the place now, though. A yuppie paradise it is these days." He paused. "Why do you think I would know some boy from The Dean?"

"Because I believe he was involved in an incident on the Dean Bridge that affected your family."

There was the merest flicker of something in Kelly's eyes, the slightest heightening of the colour on his face. Fin wondered if it was pain he saw there. "What's his name?"

Marsaili said, "Tormod Macdonald." And Fin flicked her a look. He said quickly, "But you wouldn't know him by that name."

Kelly's eyes turned towards Marsaili. "What's he to you, this man?"

"He's my father."

The silence that ensued hung heavy in the air, like Kelly's cigar smoke, and lingered for longer than was comfortable. Finally, Kelly said, "I'm sorry. This is something I've spent a lifetime trying to forget. It's not easy to lose a big brother so young. Especially when he was your hero, too." He shook his head. "Patrick meant the world to me."

Fin nodded. He said, "We think the boy's first name was John. Something. That's what we're trying to find out."

Kelly took a long slow pull on his cigar and let the smoke leak from his nostrils and the corners of his mouth before blowing a grey stream of it into the pregnant atmosphere of the conservatory. "John McBride," he said at last.

Fin tried to control his breathing. "You knew him?"

"Not personally. I wasn't on the bridge that night. But three of my brothers were."

"When Patrick fell to his death?" Marsaili said.

Kelly turned his focus from Fin to Marsaili. His voice was barely audible. "Yes." He sucked in some more smoke, and Fin was shocked to see what looked almost like moisture gathering in his eyes. "But I haven't talked about that in more than fifty years. And I'm not sure I want to start now."

Marsaili nodded. "I'm sorry. I can understand that."

They walked in silence up Tipperlinn Road, stone villas brooding privately behind high walls and tall trees, past the old coach-house at Stable Lane to where the cobbled Albert Terrace ran off up the hill to their right in a profusion of green.

Eventually, Marsaili could no longer contain herself. "What do you think really happened on the Dean Bridge that night?"

Fin shook his head. "Impossible to know. Everyone who was there is dead. Except for your father. And maybe Ceit. Though we have no idea whether she's still alive or not."

"At least we know now who my father is. Or was."

Fin looked at her. "I wish you hadn't told him your dad's name."

The blood drained from her face immediately. "Why?"

He sighed deeply. "I don't know, Marsaili. I just wish you hadn't."

| THIRTY-FOUR |

Fin looked down out of the late afternoon at the ragged fingers of rock that reached out into the Minch, water breaking white all around them. Peat bog stretched away into the island's interior, scored and scarred by centuries of cutting. Loch a Tuath reflected the darkly ominous clouds gathering overhead, ridged by the wind through which the small British Airways plane fought bravely to achieve a smooth landing on the short runway at Stornoway airport. The same wind that whipped about them now in the car park as they threw their overnight bags in the boot and sought shelter in Fin's car from the first heavy drops of rain blowing across the moor from the west.

Fin started the engine and set the wipers going. It had taken them almost no time at the Scotlands People Centre of the National Archives of Scotland to track down John William and Peter Angus McBride, born 1940 and 1941 respectively, in the Slateford district of Edinburgh to Mary Elizabeth Rafferty and John Anthony McBride. John Anthony had died in 1944 while serving in the Royal Navy. Mary Elizabeth eleven years later from heart failure, the cause of which was not specified. Marsaili had paid for extracts of birth and death certificates for the entire family, and slipped them into a buff envelope that was tucked away now in the bag she held to her chest in the passenger seat.

Fin had no real idea how it was affecting her. She had said nothing throughout the flight back to the islands. He could only guess that she was reassessing everything she had ever known or thought about herself. She had just found out that although born and brought up on the Isle of Lewis she had, after all, no island blood in her. An English mother, a mainland father from a Catholic family in Edinburgh who had fabricated his entire life. It was a revelation.

He glanced at her. Complexion pasty-white, eyes shadowed, windblown hair lacklustre and limp. She looked crushed and small, and although all his instincts led him to want to put his arms around her, he felt a barrier between them. Something had happened to them in Edinburgh. In one moment, it seemed, they had rediscovered everything they had once been. In the next it was all gone, like smoke in the wind.

The process of discovering who her father really was had changed her. And the Marsaili he had known was lost now somewhere in a confusion of history and identity. Fin feared there was a chance that neither of them would find her again. Or that if they did, the change would be irrevocable.

He also knew that discovering the identity of her father, and his brother, had still failed to establish the events which had led to the murder of Peter McBride on Eriskay all those years before.

After a very long time of simply sitting there with the engine running, battered by the wind, lashed by the rain, wipers juddering across the windscreen, Marsaili finally turned to him. "Take me home, Fin."

But Fin made no move to shift into gear and reverse out of their space. Both hands gripped the wheel in front of him. Something had come into his head, out of nowhere it seemed. Something shockingly simple and blindingly obvious. He said, "I want to go to your mum's."

She sighed. "Why?"

"I want to look through your dad's stuff."

"For what?"

"I won't know for sure until I find it."

"What's the point, Fin?"

"The point is, Marsaili, that someone murdered Peter McBride. There is going to be an investigation. A senior officer will be arriving next week. And unless we have evidence to the contrary, your dad is still going to be the number one suspect."

She shrugged wearily. "Should I care?"

"Yes, you should. He's still your dad. Nothing we've learned about him changes that. He's still the same gentle giant who carried you on his shoulders out to the peat-cutting. The same man who kissed your forehead at night when he tucked you into bed. The same man who was there for you all of your life, from your first day at school to the day you got married. Now it's you who needs to be there for him."

She turned confusion-filled eyes towards him. "I don't know what to feel about him any more, Fin."

Fin nodded his understanding. "I'll bet though, that if he could, he would want to tell you everything, Marsaili. All the things he's kept inside all these years, all the things he's shared with no one. I can't imagine how hard that must have been." He ran a hand back through tight blond curls in frustrated empathy. Who could ever have guessed the truth behind the facade? "We walk into that nursing home, and all we see are a lot of old people sitting around. Vacant eyes, sad smiles. And we just dismiss them as . . . well, old. Spent, hardly worth bothering about. And yet behind those eyes every one of them has had a life, a story they could tell you. Of pain, love, hope, despair. All the things we feel, too. Getting old doesn't make them any less valid, or any less real. And it'll be us one day. Sitting there watching the young ones dismiss us as . . . well, old. And what's that going to feel like?"

Guilt burned hot in her eyes. "I've never stopped loving him."

"Then believe in him, too. And believe that whatever happened, whatever he did, he did it for a reason."

Visibility over the north-west corner of Lewis was almost zero. The rain blew off the ocean in obscuring sheets so fine it was like a fog. Only the vaguest hint of white breakers smashing over black gneiss could be seen beyond the machair. Even the powerful beam of light sent out into the dark by the lighthouse at the Butt was barely discernible.

Marsaili's mother was startled by their arrival, huddled together, sheltering under Fin's coat, already soaked through on the short dash from the car to the kitchen door.

"Where have you been?" she said. "Fionnlagh said you'd gone to Edinburgh."

"Then why are you asking?"

Mrs. Macdonald tutted her irritation. "You know what I mean."

"It was personal business, Mum." Marsaili and Fin had agreed on the drive up to Ness that they would say nothing to her mother of what they had learned about her father. It would all, no doubt, come out one day. But for the moment they had decided it would serve no useful purpose.

Fin said, "We'd like to look through Tormod's things if that's possible, Mrs. Macdonald."

Colour rose on her cheeks. "Why?"

"We just would, Mum." Marsaili headed off through the house to her father's old study, her mother trailing in her wake.

"There's no purpose to be served in that, Marsaili. That stuff's no more use to you or me than it is to him any more."

Marsaili stopped in the doorway and looked around the empty room. Pictures had been taken off the walls, the desktop cleared. She went to open its drawers. Empty. The filing cabinet. Empty. Old boxes filled with his bric-a-brac were gone. The place was sterile, disinfected, as if her father had been a disease. All trace of him removed. She turned to face her mother in disbelief. "What have you done?"

"He's not here any more." Guilt fed her defensiveness. "I'll not have my house cluttered with his old rubbish."

But the accusation in Marsaili's voice was unmistakable. "Mum, you were married to him for nearly fifty years, for God's sake! You loved him. Didn't you?"

"He's not the man I married."

"Which isn't his fault. He has dementia, Mum. It's an illness."

Fin said, "You've thrown everything out?"

"I wasn't going to put it out till bin day. It's all in boxes in the front hall."

Marsaili was pink-faced with indignation. She raised a solitary finger in her mother's face. "Don't you *dare* throw that stuff out! Do you hear? These are my dad's things. If you don't want them in the house, I'll take them."

"Take them then!" Guilt fuelled anger now. "Take the damned stuff. I don't want it! You can burn it for all I care!" And, close to breaking, she pushed past Fin, hurrying away down the hall.

Marsaili stood breathing hard, staring at Fin with fire still in her eyes. And he thought that at least she had rediscovered her feeling for her father. He said, "I'll put the back seat down and we'll load up the car."

Condensation steamed up the kitchen windows in Marsaili's bungalow. The cardboard boxes had got wet in the transfer from the house to the car and then the car to the bungalow. But their contents had been protected by the bin bags that Fin had taped over the top of them. There had been nothing to save Fin and Marsaili from a soaking, though. Fin had stripped off his wet jacket immediately, and Marsaili was still rubbing her hair vigorously with a large towel.

Fionnlagh stood watching as Fin opened up the boxes one by one. Some contained photograph albums, others old accounts. There were boxes of junk, tools and tins of nails, a magnifying glass, boxes of unused pens whose ink had all dried up, a broken stapler, cartons of paperclips.

Fionnlagh said, "I've sort of made my peace with the Reverend Murray."

Fin looked up. "He said you'd been to see him."

"Several times."

Fin and Marsaili exchanged glances. "And?"

"You know he's agreed to let Donna and Eilidh stay here."

Fin nodded. "Yes."

"Well, I told him I was going to quit school and try to get a job at Arnish. To make sure I could feed and clothe us all."

Marsaili was surprised. "What did he say?"

"He just about took my head off." Fionnlagh smiled wryly. "Told me if I didn't finish my studies and get a place at university he would personally beat the crap out of me."

Fin raised an eyebrow. "In those words?"

Fionnlagh grinned. "Pretty much. I thought ministers weren't supposed to use language like that."

Fin laughed. "Ministers have a special dispensation from God to swear their fucking heads off if they like. As long as it's in a good cause." He paused. "So you're going to go to university, then?"

"If I can get in."

Donna appeared at the door with the baby propped over her shoulder and supported on one arm. "Are you going to feed her or am I?"

Fionnlagh grinned at his daughter and brushed her cheek with the backs of his fingers. "I'll do it. Bottle in the warmer?"

"It is." Donna handed the baby over to him.

He turned in the doorway before he followed her out. "By the way, you were right, Fin. About Donna's dad. He's not so bad."

A moment passed between father and son, then Fin grinned. "Aye, there's hope for him yet."

When Fionnlagh had gone he turned to the next box and tore it open to reveal that it was full of books and jotters. He lifted out the top book, a green hardback. An anthology of twentieth-century poetry. "I didn't know your dad liked poetry."

"Neither did I." Marsaili crossed the kitchen to take a look.

Fin opened the book, and on the inside cover, written in an elegant hand, were the words, *Tormod Uilleam Macdonald. A happy birthday. Mum. August 12th 1976.* Fin frowned. "Mum?"

He heard the tremor in her voice as she said, "They always referred to one another as Mum and Dad."

As he flipped through the pages a folded sheet of lined paper fell out. He picked it up. It was covered in shaky handwriting, and titled, *Solas*.

"That's the daycare centre we took him to that day next to the care home," Marsaili said. "It's his handwriting. What does it say?" She took the sheet from Fin and he stood up to look at it with her. Every third or fourth word was scored out, sometimes several times, as he had tried to correct his misspellings. Her hand flew to her mouth to try to contain her distress. "He always prided himself on his spelling." Then she read, "*There were about anything up to twenty people while I was there. Most of them are very old.*" There were three attempts to write "old." "*Some are very weak and seem unable to speak. Others are unable to walk, but try to put their feet down on about one inch at a time. But there were a few who could step to a reasonable distance.*" Her voice choked off her words and she could read no further.

Fin took it from her and read aloud. "*When I am writing letters I cannot avoid making feeble mistakes in my words. My loss, of course, didn't come suddenly. It began about the end of the eleventh year, but it was hardly noticed at all at first. However, as time went on, and on, and on, I began to realize that I was more and more losing my ability to remember things. It is a dreadful thing, and I am very near the moment when I realise I am helpless.*"

Fin laid the sheet of paper on the table. Outside, the wind still howled around the door, rain pounding against the window. He ran his finger along the ragged edge, where the sheet had been torn from some jotter. Almost worse than the disease itself, he thought, must be the knowledge that it was taking you. That inch by inch you were losing your reason and your mind, your memories, everything that makes you who you are.

He glanced at Marsaili, who was breathing deeply, drying her cheeks with her palms. There was only so much crying you could do. She said, "I'll make us a cup of tea."

As she busied herself with the kettle and the mugs and teabags, Fin crouched down again to open more boxes. The next was full of ledgers, incomings and outgoings at the farm over all the years he had worked it. He lifted them out one by one, until at the bottom he found a large, soft-covered cuttings album bulging with articles taken from newspapers and magazines over many years. Fin placed it on top of the box next to him and opened it. At first the cuttings had been neatly stuck to the early pages, then later simply shoved, loose-leaf, between them. There were so many.

He heard the kettle coming to the boil, the weather at the door, music vibrating distantly through the floor from the kids' room, and Marsaili's voice. "What is it, Fin? What are all these cuttings?"

But at Fin's very centre all was still. His own voice came to him from a long way away. "I think we should take your dad back to Eriskay, Marsaili. That's the only place we're going to find the truth."

| THIRTY-FIVE |

Marsaili's here! I knew she'd come for me some day. And the young chap. I'm not sure who he is, but he is kind enough to help me pack some of my things into a bag. Socks and underpants. A couple of shirts. A pair of trousers. They are leaving a lot of stuff in the wardrobe and the drawers. But I suppose they'll come back for it later. It doesn't matter. I feel like singing! Good old Marsaili. I can't wait to get home, although I'm not quite sure now that I remember where exactly that is. But they'll know.

Everyone's sitting smiling at me as I leave, and I wave happily at them. The lady who is always trying to make me undress and get into that damned bath doesn't look too pleased. Like she squatted down on the moor for a pee and sat on a thistle. Ha! I want to say. Serves you right. But I'm not sure what came out in the end. Sounded like Donald Duck. Who said that?

It's cold outside, and that rain takes me back. All those solitary days out on the land with the beasts. I used to love that. The freedom of it. No more pretending. Just me and the rain in my face. The young man tells me to be sure and say if I need a pee. He'll stop anywhere, any time, he says. Well, of course, I say. I'm not likely to pee my pants, am I?

We seem to have been driving for a very long time now. I'm not sure if I maybe slept for a bit. I look at the land passing by the window. It hardly seems familiar at all. Not sure if it's the grass bursting through the rock, or the rock bursting through the grass. But that's all there is. Grass and rock over all the hillsides.

Oh, and now, down there in the distance, I see a beach. You wouldn't believe a beach could be that big, or the ocean that blue. I remember seeing a beach like that once. Biggest beach I ever saw. Much bigger than Charlie's beach. But I was filled with so much grief and guilt that I hardly noticed. I was driving Donald Seamus's old van. Peter was still in the back, wrapped in the blanket I took from the bedroom to carry him down to the boat.

Mary-Anne and Donald Seamus were dead to the world. It seemed that nothing would shake those two out of their sleep once they got their heads down. It's just as well, because I was in a panic that night, and still weeping. And I suppose I must have left blood everywhere. But I was hardly in a state to care.

By the time we got to Ludagh I was a little more controlled. I had to put a face on it for Ceit's sake. I can remember looking in the wing mirror of Donald Seamus's van, and seeing her standing there on the jetty in the dark, watching me go. And I knew, even then, that I would never see her again. But I had her Saint Christopher around my neck, so she would always be with me. One way or another.

I was lucky with the tides, able to cross at the fords without waiting. I knew I had to put as many miles between me and the island as possible before morning broke. It wouldn't take Donald Seamus long to realize that Peter and I were gone, with his gun and his money, and that his van was missing, too. Likelihood was that he would call the police straight away. I needed to put distance between us.

I was waiting at Berneray for the first ferry of the day when dawn came pale out of the mist across the Sound of Harris. Most of the other vehicles waiting there were commercial, and no one paid much attention to me. But I had my dead brother in the back of a stolen van, and I was nervous as hell. Here was where I would be most vulnerable, and at Leverburgh when the ferry berthed. But I tried to put myself in the shoes of the police. I had stolen a gun, some money and a van. They didn't know about Peter, of course. They would assume we were in it together. Where would we go? I was sure they'd think we would try to make it back to the mainland. In which case we would have driven to Lochmaddy to catch the ferry to Skye. Why would we head north to Harris, or Lewis? Well, that was my reasoning, although right then I didn't have that much faith in it.

The ferry crossed the Sound like a ghost that morning, just a gentle swell on a pewtery sea, the sun obscured by thick, low cloud. And then I was off up the ramp at Leverburgh and on the road again.

That's when I saw the beaches for the first time, at Scarista, and Luskentyre, and drove through the tiny village of Seilebost, realising that's the place I was supposed to come from. I stopped there for just a few minutes, following a track out on to the machair, and gazed over the golden sands that seemed to stretch all the way to eternity. I was Tormod Macdonald now. And this is where I grew up. So many people I had been, and was, and no doubt would be in the future. I got back in the van and drove without stopping, passing the outskirts of Stornoway, across the Barvas moor to the west coast road that led to Ness. I could hardly get much further away.

At Barvas I turned off on a bumpy dirt track that led out past a few houses dug in at the roadside, to a windswept loch almost entirely locked in by the land. I could see the sea breaking all along the shore in the distance, and sat there with Peter, waiting for dark.

It seemed to take forever to come. My stomach growled and snarled at me. I'd put nothing in it for nearly twenty-four hours, and I felt quite light-headed. At last, I watched the light dying into darkness along the western horizon, and Donald Seamus's old van coughed its fumes into the night. I bumped back along the track to the main road and turned north.

At Siader I spotted a track heading off into the dark, towards the sea, and I turned off on it, extinguishing my lights, and making my slow, painful way out towards the cliffs, navigating only by infrequent fleeting patches of moonlight. Within sight and sound of a sea that seemed to glow almost phosphorescent in the dark, I killed the motor and got out of the van. There was not a light anywhere to be seen, and I retrieved Donald Seamus's *tarasgeir* from the back of the vehicle.

Even though the bog was soft and wet, it took me nearly an hour to dig a hole in it big enough for Peter's final resting place. First I cut turfs off the top and laid them to one side, and then dug, and dug, deep enough that the water seeping into the hole would be displaced by the body. Deep enough that when I had filled it in, and replaced the turfs, no one would ever know it had been disturbed. And even if they did, would probably think it had been some abortive attempt to cut peat. But I knew the land would knit together in no time, sealing him in, folding him into its arms and holding him in its embrace for ever.

When I had finished, finally, I unwrapped my brother from his blanket and laid him carefully in his grave. I knelt at his head, and kissed him, and prayed for his soul, even although I was no longer certain that there was a God out there. Then I covered him over, so consumed by sorrow and guilt that I could hardly wield the spade. When I had replaced the last turf, I stood for ten minutes or more, letting the wind dry my sweat before lifting the bloody blanket and trudging over the moor and down across a jumble of rocks to a tiny, sandy inlet.

There I crouched in the sand to give shelter from the wind as I set light to the blanket, then sat upwind of it to watch its flames flare and dance briefly in the dark, carrying sparks and smoke off into the night. A symbolic cremation. My brother's blood returned to the earth.

I sat on the beach until the cold nearly took me, before walking stiffly back over the moor to the van and starting the motor. Back along the track to the road, and then south through Barvas, before turning off east on a narrow track somewhere near Arnol. A track that wound out through the bog towards a rising of hills. I had been going to set the van on fire, but always feared it would be seen, no matter how remote I went. And that's when I saw, in a moment of moonlight, the loch shimmering below me. I took my stuff out of the back and drove it to the edge of the drop. Then I cut the engine and jumped out into soft turf, my shoulder to the door, helping it the last few feet, till it took on its own momentum.

Off it went down the hill in the dark, and I heard more than saw it hit the water. In brief blinks of moonlight over the next hour, sitting up there on the hill, I saw a part of it still visible above the surface, and I thought perhaps I had made a terrible mistake. But by morning it was gone.

I used the hours of darkness to dismantle the shotgun that Donald Seamus had used to shoot rabbits, so that I could fit it into my bag. Then at first light I hoofed it back across the moor to the road. I had only been walking five minutes in the direction of Barvas when someone stopped to give me a lift. An old crofter on his way into Stornoway. He talked and talked, while I felt life slowly coming back to my limbs, warmed by the heater in his car. We were about halfway across the Barvas moor when he said, "It's a strange sort of Gaelic you speak, son. You're not from around here."

"No," I said. "I'm from Harris." And I reached across to shake his hand. "Tormod Macdonald." Which is who I have been all my life since.

"What's your business in Stornoway?"

"I'm taking the ferry to the mainland."

The old crofter grinned. "Good luck to you, then, boy. It's a rough crossing."

I had no idea, then, that I would come back when it was over. Drawn by the need, somehow, to be near to my brother, as if that could in some way make amends for my dismal failure to keep my promise to my mother.

"Where are we now?" I ask.

"This is Leverburgh, Dad. We're taking the ferry over to North Uist."

North Uist? I'm sure I don't live there. I scratch my head. "Why?"

"We're taking you home, Dad."

| THIRTY-SIX |

Marsaili and Fin had left Fionnlagh with no idea of how long they might be gone, so she had given him her phone in order that she could always reach him. And late that morning he had driven down to Crobost stores to stock up the larder for the next few days.

It was a filthy morning, the wind sweeping in explosive gusts across the point, bringing with it waves of fine wetting rain, and laying flat the new-growth spring grasses. But he didn't mind. He had grown up with this. It was normal. He loved to feel the rain stinging his face. He loved, too, the way the sky would open up at unexpected moments to let the light through. Flashes of cold, blinding sunlight on the surface of the ocean, like pools of mercury. They could last minutes or seconds.

Dark clouds lumbered across the landscape in folds so close to the earth it was almost possible to believe you could reach up and touch them. The top of the hill was nearly lost in cloud as Fionnlagh drove back up to the bungalow. Donna had promised to have lunch waiting for them. Nothing special. A bacon and egg salad, she had said. He was surprised to see a white Range Rover drawn up on the gravel above the house where he would normally park his Mini.

He didn't recognize the licence plate. On Lewis it was customary to look at the number of an approaching vehicle and wave if you recognized it. Faces were rarely seen through windscreens reflecting light, or smeared with rain. This wasn't an island number.

He drew up beside the Range Rover, and as he got out of his car saw a copy of the *Edinburgh Evening News* lying on the back seat. He grabbed his bags of provisions from the back of the Mini and made a dash through the rain to the kitchen door. He managed to stoop down and turn the handle without dropping the paper bag he was supporting in his right hand, and as the door swung in he saw Donna standing in the doorway to the hall. There was an alien smell of smoke in the house, and Donna was holding Eilidh to her as if she might fly away if she dared to let her go. Her face was the colour of the Range Rover parked at the top of the path, her pupils so dilated her eyes looked black. He knew at once that something was very wrong.

"What is it, Donna?"

Her frightened rabbit's eyes darted across the kitchen, and Fionnlagh turned to see a man sitting at the kitchen table. He was a big man with cropped silver-grey hair. He wore a white shirt open at the neck beneath a Barbour jacket, jeans and black Cesare Paciotti designer boots. He was smoking a very large cigar which had already burned halfway down to his nicotine-stained knuckles.

At the same moment, Donna was propelled forward into the kitchen from behind. She took two or three forced steps before steadying herself, and a man appeared behind her. He was much younger than the man sitting at the table. Thick black hair gelled to a shine was scraped back across his head. He was dressed casually in a blue shirt and charcoal trousers beneath a long, brown, waxed raincoat. Incongruously, Fionnlagh noticed that his fine black Italian shoes were caked with mud. But it was with a sense of shock and disbelief that he saw what looked very much like a sawn-off shotgun half-raised in his right hand.

"What?" The word was out of his mouth before he realized how foolish it sounded. His first thought was that this had to be some kind of a joke, but there didn't seem anything remotely funny about it. And it was real fear he saw in Donna's face. He stood, his arms full of shopping, wind and rain blowing about his legs in the open doorway, and had no idea what to do.

The man sitting at the table was leaning back in his chair watching him speculatively. He pulled gently at the wet end of his cigar. "Where's your grandfather?"

Fionnlagh turned consternation in his direction. "I have no idea."

"I think you do. Your mother and her friend took him out of the care home first thing this morning. Where did they go?"

Fionnlagh felt his hackles rising now. "I don't know." He hoped to sound defiant.

"Don't get cute with me, sonny." The cigar smoker's tone remained even, unruffled. His eyes slid towards Donna and the baby. "That your kid, is it? Old Tormod's great granddaughter?"

Fear spiked through Fionnlagh. "You lay a fucking finger on them . . . !"

"And you'll what? What'll you do, sonny? Tell me."

Fionnlagh glanced towards the man with the gun. His face was completely impassive. But something in his eyes counselled against foolishness.

"Just tell me where they took your grandfather. That's all you have to do."

"And if I don't?"

There was an imperceptible shaking of the cigar smoker's head before he drew another mouthful of smoke to let it escape with his smile. "You don't even want to know what I'll do to your girlfriend and your daughter."

At first Fionnlagh couldn't breathe, and he panicked. Before realising it was a dream. It had to be. He was at the bottom of the ocean. It was very dark and cold here, and he was aware that if he drew a breath his lungs would fill with water. So he kicked off for the surface. Somewhere very far above him he could see light filtering down. Slowly, too slowly, it grew brighter around him, but still the surface seemed a long way away. His lungs were bursting now. He kicked harder, all his focus on the light. Until suddenly he broke the surface in a blinding flash, and pain splintered all conscious thought.

His head was filled with it, and he could hear his own voice gasping from its sheer intensity. He rolled over, wondering why he couldn't move his arms and legs, eyes screwed up against the light until gradually the kitchen took shape around him. But his thoughts were still unfocused, confused. Clarity and recollection returned only slowly.

He lay still, controlling his breathing, trying to ignore the pain in his head, and forced himself to recall his return from the store: the white Range Rover, the man with the gun, the man with the cigar threatening harm to Donna and Eilidh if he didn't tell them where his mother and Fin had taken Tormod. But no matter how hard he tried, he had no memory of anything beyond that. Which is when he realized why he couldn't move.

He was lying on the floor, ankles bound, hands tied behind his back. There was blood on the tiles, and he panicked, shouting, "Donna!" as loudly as he could. His voice resounded in the empty kitchen and was met by a deep, troubling silence. Fear and panic nearly paralysed him. It was pure adrenalin that fuelled his frantic attempts to get himself up into a sitting position.

When finally he managed it, he saw that his feet were bound by a dishtowel, twisted and tied in a clumsy knot. With a huge effort, he succeeded in getting himself on to his knees, and then sat back on his feet, allowing his fingers access to the knotted dishtowel behind his back. It took a matter of minutes to untie it and struggle to his feet. He called out Donna's name again and followed his voice through the house. It resounded around empty rooms. There was no sign of either Donna or the baby. In the bedroom he caught a glimpse of himself in the mirror, blood trickling down his face from a head wound. The only comfort he took from it was the thought that the blood on the kitchen floor was his own and not Donna's or Eilidh's.

But where were they? Where in God's name had these people taken them?

He ran back to the kitchen and looked around in a frenzy. There were knives in a block on the worktop, but he didn't see how he could access them to cut the wrist bindings behind his back. He had to get help.

With difficulty, he managed to open the kitchen door, his back to it, fingers fumbling for the latch. And then he was out. Into the rain. Running through the long grass up the slope towards the road. As he reached the tarmac he stumbled and fell, landing heavily, and grazing his cheek on the metalled surface. The rain slapped his face as he staggered back to his feet and ran through it, into the teeth of the wind, down the road to where the turn-off led up to the church and the manse.

There was not a soul around anywhere. No one in their right mind would venture out in this unless they absolutely had to.

He felt his strength ebbing as he ran up the hill to the car park, picking his precarious way across the cattle grid rather than trying to negotiate the gate, then sprinting towards the steps leading to the manse. He took them two at a time. When he reached the front door he realized he could neither ring the bell nor knock on it. So he started kicking at it and shouting, tears and blood almost blinding him.

Until the door flew open, and Donald Murray stood there, staring at him in utter consternation. It took only a moment for that consternation to turn to fear, and Fionnlagh saw the colour drain from his face.

| THIRTY-SEVEN |

They had left the bad weather far behind, wind and rain driving down with them from the north-west, foundering finally on the mountains of North Uist. The further south they had come then, the more it had softened, rain retreating, the wind sinking into the ocean, the yellow sunlight of the late afternoon sending long shadows across the land.

Only when they stopped at a tea-room in Benbecula did Fin realize that his mobile phone was dead. Nights spent in hotel rooms and his tent had meant that it was several days since he had last charged it. When they got back to the car, he plugged it into the cigarette lighter and dropped it in the cup holder between the seats. An hour later, as they rounded the headland at East Kilbride, they saw the little jetty at Ludagh, and the island of Eriskay drenched in sunlight across the water.

It was a light wind that ruffled the clear blue surface of the Sound as they drove across the straight stretch of causeway to where it curved around and climbed gently between rising slopes. At the road end, Fin turned down towards the tiny bay and harbour at Haunn.

He watched Tormod in the rearview mirror as the old man gazed from the window, no sign of recognition in dull eyes. It had been a tiring drive down the spine of *the long island*. With the ferry crossing and stops for lunch and coffee, it had taken nearly five hours. The old man was weary and drowsy-eyed.

Where the single-track road curled around the head of the bay, Fin turned off on the gravelled drive that led up to the big white house on the hill. His car rattled over the cattle grid, and he drew it in beside the pink Mercedes. He and Marsaili helped Tormod out of the back seat. He had stiffened up during the long journey, and found it hard to move until he was out on the path and had straightened up to look around, feeling the cool breeze in his face, and breathing in the salt air. He seemed brighter now. His eyes clearer, but still without recognition as he gazed around the hillside and down towards the harbour.

"Where are we?" he said.

"Back where it all began, Mr. Macdonald." Fin glanced at Marsaili. But her eyes were fixed anxiously on her father. "Come on, there's someone I want you to meet."

They climbed the steps to the deck and the front door, and as Fin pressed the bell they heard the chimes of "Scotland the Brave" sound somewhere deep inside the house. After a short wait, the door opened wide, and Morag stood there, a gin and a cigarette in one hand, Dino barking around her ankles. She took in the three visitors standing on her doorstep, before a look of resignation crossed her face like a shadow. She said to Fin, "I had a funny feeling you'd be back."

"Hello, Ceit," he said.

A strange intensity burned for a moment in her dark eyes. "Long time since anyone's called me that, *a ghràidh*."

"John McBride might have been one of the last." Fin turned his head towards Tormod, and Ceit's mouth fell open as she looked at him.

"Oh, my God." She caught her breath. "Johnny?"

He looked at her blankly.

Fin said, "He has dementia, Ceit. And very little awareness of anything around him."

Ceit reached across more than half a century to touch a love lost irrevocably on a stormy spring night in another life, and her fingers lightly brushed his cheek. He looked at her curiously, as if to ask, Why are you touching me? But there was no recognition. She withdrew her hand and looked at Marsaili.

"I'm his daughter," Marsaili said.

Ceit laid her drink and her cigarette on the hall table and took Marsaili's hand in both of hers. "Oh, *a ghràidh*, you might have been mine, too, if things had turned out just a little different." She looked back towards Tormod. "I've spent a lifetime wondering what happened to poor Johnny."

Fin said, "Or Tormod Macdonald, as you would have known him last." He paused. "Did you steal the birth certificate?"

She flashed him a look. "You'd better come in." She let go of Marsaili's hand and lifted her gin and her cigarette, and they followed her and Dino through to the sitting room with its panoramic views across the hillside and the bay. "How did you know I was Ceit?"

Fin reached into his bag and drew out Tormod's book of cuttings. He opened it up on the table for her to take a look. He heard her sharp intake of breath as she realized that they were all media stories about her. Torn or cut from newspapers or magazines over more than twenty years, ever since she had achieved celebrity status through her part in *The Street*. Dozens of photographs, thousands of words. "You might not have known what became of Tormod, Ceit. But he certainly knew what had become of you."

Tormod took a step towards the table and looked down at them.

Fin said, "Do you remember these, Mr. Macdonald? Do you remember cutting them out and sticking them into this book? Cuttings about the actress Morag McEwan."

The old man stared at them for a long time. A word seemed to form several times on his lips before finally he spoke. "Ceit," he said. And he looked up at Morag. "Are you Ceit?"

It was clear that she couldn't find her voice, and simply nodded.

Tormod smiled. "Hello, Ceit. I haven't seen you for a long time."

Silent tears ran down her face. "No, Johnny, you haven't." She seemed on the verge of losing control and took a quick gulp of gin before moving quickly behind the bar. "Can I get anyone something to drink?"

"No thanks," Marsaili said.

Fin said, "You haven't told us about the birth certificate yet."

She refilled her own glass with a trembling hand and lit another cigarette. She took a stiff drink and a long pull on her cigarette before finding her words. "Johnny and I were in love," she said, and she looked at the old man standing now in her living room. "We used to meet at night down by the old jetty, then go over the hill to Charlie's beach. There was an old ruin there, with a view over the sea. It's where we used to make love." She glanced self-consciously at Marsaili. "Anyway, we talked often about running off together. Of course, he would never have gone without Peter. He would never go anywhere without Peter. He'd promised their mother, you see, on her deathbed, that he would look after his little brother. He'd had some kind of accident. A head injury. Wasn't all there."

She put her glass down on the bar and held on to it, as if she thought she might fall over if she let go. Then she looked again at Tormod.

"I'd have gone to the ends of the earth with you, Johnny," she said. When Tormod returned a blank stare she looked back to Fin. "The widow O'Henley used to take me with her when she went up to stay with her cousin Peggy on Harris during the holidays. Easter, summer, Christmas. And she took me to the funeral there when Peggy's boy was drowned in the bay. I'd met him a few times. He was a nice lad. Anyway, the house was full of relatives, and I slept on the floor of his room. Couldn't sleep at all that night. And someone, maybe his parents, had laid out his birth certificate on the dresser. I decided that with all the business of the funeral no one would miss it immediately. And when they did, they would never connect it with me."

"But why did you take it?" Marsaili asked.

"If we were going to run away together, me and Johnny, I thought maybe he would need a new identity. There's not much you can do without a birth certificate." She took a long reflective draw on her cigarette. "I never knew, when I took it, the circumstances in which it would be needed. Certainly not in the way I'd intended." She smiled then. A tiny smile tinged with bitterness and irony. "As it turned out, it was far easier for me to change my own name. Just register a new one with Equity and I was no longer Ceit anything. I was Morag McEwan, actress. And I could play any part I wanted, on or off the stage. No one would ever know I was just some poor abandoned orphan girl, shipped out to the islands to be a widow's slave."

A silence laden with unasked questions and unspoken answers settled on the room. It was Tormod who broke it. "Can we go home now?" he said.

"In a while, Dad."

Fin looked at Ceit. "Peter was murdered on Charlie's beach, wasn't he?"

Ceit pulled in her lower lip and bit on it as she nodded.

"Then I think it's time we all knew the truth about what happened."

"He made me promise never to tell a soul. And I never have."

"It was a long time ago now, Ceit. If he could tell us himself, I'm sure he would. But Peter's been found. Dug out of a peat bog on the Isle of Lewis. There's going to be a murder investigation. So it's important we know." He hesitated. "It wasn't Johnny was it?"

"Oh God, no!" Ceit seemed startled by the idea. "He would have died himself before touching a hair on that boy's head."

"Then who did?"

Ceit took several long moments to think about it, then stubbed out her cigarette. "Better if I take you over to Charlie's beach and tell you there. Easier for you to picture it."

Marsaili pulled her father's cap back on his head, and they followed Morag out into the hall, where she lifted a jacket from the coat stand. She stooped to scoop Dino up into her arms. "We can all go in the Merc."

Fin ducked quickly into his car to retrieve his mobile. It seemed to have stopped charging, and he turned it on. His screen showed that there were four messages. But he could listen to them later. He slammed the door shut and ran across the gravel to the waiting pink Mercedes.

The hood was down as Ceit accelerated up over the hill, Dino draped across her right arm, the soft air of this Hebridean spring evening blowing warm all around them. Tormod laughed with the exhilaration of it, holding his hat firmly on his head, and Dino barked by way of reply. Fin wondered if the church on the hill, or the primary school, or the old cemetery, would stir any memories somewhere in the mist that was Tormod's mind, but he seemed oblivious to his surroundings.

Ceit pulled up on a stretch of road overlooking Charlie's beach, immediately above an old ruined crofthouse set on the bank below.

"Here we are," she said. They all got out of the car and the little group picked its way carefully down through the grass to the ruin. The wind had stiffened a little, but was still soft. The sun was dipping towards the western horizon, spilling liquid copper across a simmering sea.

"It was just like this that night," Ceit said. "Or, at least, it had been earlier. By the time I got here it was almost dark, and there were storm clouds gathering out there beyond Lingeigh and Fuideigh. I knew it was just a matter of time before it would sweep in across the bay. But it was still douce, then, like the calm before the storm."

She leaned against the remaining wall at the gable end to steady herself and watch as Dino went scampering crazily across the beach, kicking up sand behind him.

"Like I said, at first we used to meet at the jetty at Haunn before crossing the hill together. But it was risky, and after a couple of times of nearly being caught we decided to meet up here instead, making our separate ways over the hill."

Dino was running in and out of the foam washing in with the tide, barking at the sunset.

"I was late that night. The widow O'Henley hadn't been well, and took much longer than usual to get off to sleep. So I was in a rush, and breathless when I got here. And disappointed when there was no sign of Johnny." She paused, lost in momentary reflection. "That's when I heard the voices coming from down below on the beach. I could hear them even above the beat of the sea, and the wind in the grass. And something in those voices put me on my guard straight away. I crouched down here behind the wall and looked across the sand."

Fin watched her face carefully. He could see from her eyes that she was there, crouched among the stone and the grass, looking down on the scene unfolding below her on the beach.

"I could see four figures. At first I didn't know who they were, and couldn't make any sense of what was going on. And then there was a parting of the sky, and moonlight washed over the beach, and it was all I could do not to cry out."

She took out a cigarette with fumbling fingers, and cupped her hand around its end to light it. Fin heard the tremor in her breath as she inhaled the smoke. Then his concentration was broken by the sound of his mobile ringing in his pocket. He searched for and found it, and saw that it was a call from Fionnlagh. Whatever it was it could wait. He didn't want to interrupt the telling of the story. He turned it off and slipped it back in his pocket.

"They were right at the water's edge," Ceit said. "Peter was naked. His hands tied behind him, his feet bound at the ankles. Two young men were dragging him along the sand by a length of rope tied around his neck. They stopped every couple of yards, kicking him till he got to his feet again, then pulling him till he fell. Johnny was there, too. And at first I couldn't understand why he wasn't doing something about it. Then I saw that his hands were tied in front of him, eighteen inches of rope strung between his ankles to limit his movement. He was limping along after them, imploring them to stop. I could hear his voice rising above the others."

Fin glanced at Marsaili. Her face was etched with concentration and horror. This was her father that Ceit was describing on the beach below them. Helpless and distressed, and pleading for his brother's life. And he realized that you can never tell, even when you think you know someone well, what they might have been through in their lives.

Ceit's voice was low and husky with emotion, and they could barely hear it now above the sea and the wind. "They had gone about thirty or forty yards, laughing and whooping, when suddenly they stopped and made poor Peter kneel there in the wet sand, the incoming tide washing around his legs. And I saw blades flashing in the moonlight." She turned to look at them, reliving every awful moment of what she had witnessed that night. "I couldn't believe what I was seeing. I kept thinking that maybe Johnny and me had met up after all, and made love, and that I was lying sleeping in the grass, and that this was all some dreadful nightmare. I saw Johnny trying to stop them, but one of them hit him, and he fell into the water. And then that man started stabbing Peter. From the front, while the other held him from behind. I saw that blade rise and fall, blood dripping from it each time, and I wanted to scream out loud. I had to stuff my hand in my mouth to stop myself."

She turned away again to look across the sand towards the water, the moment replaying itself in gut-wrenching detail.

"Then the one behind drew his blade right across Peter's throat. A single slashing movement, and I saw the blood spurt out of him. Johnny was on his knees in the water screaming. And Peter just knelt there, his head tipped back, until the life had drained out of him. It didn't take long. And they let him fall, face-first, into the water. Even from here, I could see the froth of the waves turn crimson as they broke. His killers just turned and walked away as if nothing had happened."

Fin said, "You recognized them?"

Ceit nodded. "The two surviving Kelly brothers from that terrible night on the Dean Bridge in Edinburgh." She looked at Fin. "You know about it?"

Fin tilted his head. "Not the whole story."

"The eldest brother fell to his death. Patrick. Danny and Tam blamed Peter. Thought he had pushed him." She shook her head in despair. "God knows how they found out where we were. But find out, they did. And came looking to avenge their dead brother." She gazed out across the beach.

Almost as if mirroring the moment, nature turned the sea the colour of blood as the sun sank on the horizon.

"When they had gone, I ran down the beach to where Johnny was kneeling over Peter's body. The tide was breaking all around them. Blood on the sand, foam still pink. And I knew then what an animal sounds like when it mourns for the dead. Johnny was inconsolable. I have never seen a grown man so distressed. Wouldn't even let me touch him. I told him I would go for help, and he was on his feet in a moment, grabbing me by the shoulders. I was scared." She glanced at Tormod. "It wasn't Johnny's face I saw looking into mine. He was possessed. Almost unrecognisable. He wanted me to swear on my soul that I would never breathe a word of this to anyone. I couldn't understand. These boys had just murdered his brother. I was almost hysterical. But he shook me hard, and slapped my face and said they'd made it clear that if he ever told what happened here they would come back for me."

She turned towards Fin and Marsaili.

"That's why he was going to do what they said. They'd told him to get rid of the body himself and never breathe a word of it to another living soul. Or they would kill me." She opened her palms in front of her in pure frustration. "Right then I couldn't have cared less. I just wanted him to go to the police. But he point-blank refused. He said he would bury Peter himself where no one would ever find him, and then there was something he had to do. He wouldn't say what. Just that he owed it to his mother for letting her down."

Fin looked across the ruin to where old Tormod had gone and sat on the remains of the front wall, staring vacantly out across Charlie's beach as the sun slipped, finally, from view, and the first stars began to emerge in a dusk-blue sky. He wondered if Ceit's words, so vividly recreating the events of that night, had penetrated his consciousness in any way. Or whether simply being here, all these years later, would in itself stir some distant memory. But he realized it was something they would almost certainly never know.

| THIRTY-EIGHT |

It is so hard to remember things. I know they are there. And some
times I can feel them, but I can't see them or reach them. I'm
so tired. Tired of all this travelling, and all this talk that I can't follow. I thought they were taking me home.

This is a nice beach, though. Not like those beaches on Harris.
But nice. A gentle crescent of silver.

Oh. Is that the moon now? See how the sand almost glows by
its light, as if lit from beneath. I think I was here once. I'm sure I
was, wherever the hell we are. It seems familiar somehow. With
Ceit. And Peter. Poor Peter. I can see him still. That look in his
eyes when he knew he was dying. Like the sheep in the shed that
time, when Donald Seamus slit its throat.

I still dream, sometimes, about anger. Anger turned cold. Anger
born of grief and guilt. I remember that anger. How it ate me up
inside, devoured every shred of the human being I had once been.
And I watch myself in my dream. Like watching some flickering old
movie, black-and-white or sepia-brown. Waiting. Waiting.

The air was warm on my skin that night, though I couldn't stop
shivering. The sounds of the city are so different. I had got used to

the islands. It was almost a shock to be back among tall buildings and motor cars and people. So many people. But not there, not that night. It was quiet, and the sound of traffic was far away.

I had waited maybe an hour by that time. Concealed in the bushes, crouched down on stiffening legs. But anger gives you patience, like lust delaying the moment of orgasm to make it all the sweeter. It makes you blind, too. To possibilities, and consequences. It dulls the imagination, reduces your focus to one single point, and obliterates all else.

A light came on, then, in the porch, and all my senses were on heightened awareness. I heard the latch scrape in the lock, and the squeal of the hinges before I saw them stepping out into the light. Both of them. One behind the other. Danny stopped to light a cigarette, and Tam was about to lean back to close the door.

And that's when I moved out on to the path. Into the light. I wanted to be sure they saw me. To know who I was, and what I was going to do. I didn't care who else might see me, as long as they knew.

The match flared at the end of Danny's cigarette, and I saw in the light it cast in his eyes that he knew I was going to kill him. Tam turned at that moment and saw me, too.

I waited.

I wanted him to realize.

And he did.

I raised my shotgun and fired the first barrel. It hit Danny full in the chest, and the force of it threw him back against the door. I'll never forget the look of sheer terror and certainty in Tam's eyes as I pulled again. A little off balance, but accurate enough to take half his head off.

And I turned and walked away. No need to run. Peter was dead, and I had done what I had to do. Hang the consequences! I was no longer shivering.

I don't know how many times I have dreamt that dream. Often enough that I am no longer sure if that's all it ever was. But no matter how many times I dream it, nothing changes. Peter is still dead.

And nothing can bring him back. I had promised my mother, and I had let her down.

"Come on, Dad. It's getting cold."

I turn to see Marsaili leaning down to slip her arm through mine and help me to my feet. I stand up and look at her in the moonlight as she straightens my cap. I smile and touch her face. "I'm so glad you're here," I tell her. "You know I love you, don't you? I really, really love you."

| THIRTY-NINE |

As they drove up the path to her house Ceit frowned and said, "There are no lights. The timer should have switched them on ages ago." But it wasn't until they clattered across the cattle grid that they saw the white Range Rover parked next to Fin's car.

Fin glanced at Ceit. "Looks like you've got visitors. Do you know the car?" Ceit shook her head.

They all got out of the Mercedes and Dino went running, barking, to the front door. As they climbed on to the deck in the dark, Fin felt glass crunching beneath his feet. Someone had smashed the light bulb above the door.

He said to Ceit, "Pick up the dog!" And something in his tone brought an immediate and unquestioning response. He was on full alert now. Tense and apprehensive. He moved cautiously towards the door, hand outstretched to grab the handle.

Ceit whispered, "It's not locked. It never is."

He turned it and pushed the door into darkness. He held his hand behind him to warn the others against following, and stepped carefully into the hall. More glass ground itself into the tartan carpet beneath his feet. The bulb in the hall had been smashed, too.

He stood listening, holding his breath. But he could hear nothing above the barking of Dino in the arms of Ceit on the deck outside. The door to the living room stood ajar. He could see the shadow of the silver panther cast by moonlight streaming in through the French windows. He stepped into the room and immediately sensed a presence, before a baby's muffled cry sounded in the dark.

A match flared, and by the light of its flame he saw the illuminated face of Paul Kelly. He was sitting in a chair by the window on the east side of the room. He puffed several times on his cigar until the end of it glowed red, then he reached across to turn on a glass standard lamp. Fin saw the sawn-off shotgun lying across his lap.

Directly opposite him, perched on the edge of the settee, Donna sat clutching her baby. The black-haired young man from the villa in Edinburgh stood beside her with another sawn-off shotgun extended towards her head. He looked nervous. Donna was like a ghost. Shrunken and shadow-eyed. Visibly shaking.

Fin heard the crunch of broken glass behind him, and Morag's gasp. The dog had gone silent, but Marsaili's whispered "Oh my God!" seemed almost deafening.

No one moved, and in the seconds of silence that followed, Fin's assessment of the situation was bleak. Kelly had not come all this way just to frighten them.

Kelly's voice was obversely calm. "I always figured it was John McBride who murdered my brothers," he said. "But by the time we got people up here he'd vanished without trace. Just like he never existed." He paused to draw on his cigar. "Until now." He lifted the shotgun from his lap and stood up. "So now he can watch his daughter and his granddaughter die, just the way I watched my brothers die in my arms." His mouth curled into a barely controlled grimace, ugly and threatening. "I was in the hallway behind them that night when they were gunned down and left bleeding to death on the steps. You've got to know what that feels like to know how I feel right now. I've waited a lifetime for this day."

Fin said, "If you kill one, you'll have to kill us all."

Paul Kelly smiled. His eyes creased with genuine amusement. "You don't say."

"You can't take us all at once. Shoot that girl and you're going to have to deal with me."

Kelly raised his shotgun and swung it towards Fin. "Not if I take you first."

"This is crazy!" Marsaili's voice pierced the still of the room. "My dad is in an advanced state of dementia. Killing people won't serve any purpose. It won't mean a thing to him."

Kelly's eyes turned cold. "It will to me. In the end, an eye for an eye'll suit me just fine."

Ceit stepped forward, Dino still clutched to her chest. "Only it won't be an eye for an eye, Mr. Kelly. It'll just be plain bloody murder. You weren't on the bridge that night. I was. And Peter McBride never pushed your brother. Patrick lost his balance in all the panic with the cops showing up. He was going to fall. Peter risked his life going up on the parapet to try and grab him. Your brothers killed an innocent man. A poor half-witted boy who would never have harmed a soul. And they got their just deserts. It's over! Let it go."

But Kelly just shook his head. "Three of my brothers are dead because of the McBrides. It's payback time." He half-turned towards Donna, shotgun levelled at the baby. And even as a desperate Fin started his lunge towards Kelly, he saw the younger man swing his shotgun to point straight at him.

The sound of the gun was ear-splitting in the confined space of the living room. The air seemed to fill with shattered glass. Fin felt it cut his face, and his hands as he raised them to protect himself. He felt warm blood splash across his face and neck, the smell of it filling his nostrils. He was only half aware of the bulk of Paul Kelly staggering backwards with the force of the blast, but was wholly confused by it. The big man crashed into the window at the far side of the room, turning it red, a gaping hole in the centre of his chest, a look of complete surprise frozen on his face as he slid to the floor. A woman was screaming, Dino was barking. Eilidh was sobbing. Fin felt the wind in his face and he saw Donald Murray standing on the far side of the window he had shattered with his shotgun. He held it still, levelled at Kelly's young protégé. The man looked shocked and dropped his weapon, quickly raising his hands.

Fin darted forward to grab it and throw it away across the room, and Donald lowered his weapon. Beyond him, in the dark, Fin saw a pale, wide-eyed Fionnlagh.

"He wouldn't let me call the police. He wouldn't." The boy was very nearly hysterical. "He said they would just make a mess of it. I called you, Fin, I called you. Why didn't you answer your phone?"

There was not a scrap of colour in Donald's face. Desperate eyes flickered towards Donna and the baby. His voice came in a whisper. "Are you all right?"

Donna couldn't bring herself to speak, her sobbing baby clutched tightly to her chest. She nodded, and her father's eyes briefly found Fin's, lingering for just a moment. Somewhere behind them was a recollection of all those beliefs asserted on a drunken night when they had fought in the rain, and again on the windblown cliffs in the cold light of the next morning. Blown away in the pulling of a trigger. Then they returned to the man he had shot dead, where he lay among shattered glass and ornaments in a pool of his own blood. He screwed his eyes closed to shut out the sight of him.

"God forgive me," he said.

| FORTY |

I don't know what's going on any more. My ears are still ringing and I can hardly hear a thing. Something terrible happened, I know that. They've sat me down here in the kitchen, out of the way. There's all sorts of people through there in the next room, and that damn dog just never stops barking.

There are blue lights and orange lights flashing out there in the dark. I heard a helicopter earlier. I've never seen so many policemen in my life. And that man who came to talk to me at Solas. I only remember him because of his widow's peak. Made me think of a boy at The Dean.

I wonder what the minister's doing here. I saw him earlier. He looked ill, not a well man. I feel sorry for him. Hasn't the gumption of his father. A fine, God-fearing man *he* was. Damned if I can remember his name, though.

That woman's coming into the kitchen now. I know I know her from somewhere. Just can't think where. Something about her makes me think of Ceit. Can't quite think what.

She pulls up a chair and sits down opposite me, leaning forward to take both of my hands in hers. I like her touch. She has fine, soft hands, and such lovely dark eyes looking into mine.

"Do you remember the Sacred Heart, Johnny?" she says. But I don't know what she means. "They took you and Peter there after that night you both got trapped at the cliffs. You broke your arm, remember? And Peter had pneumonia."

"There were nuns," I say. Strange, but I can see them in that yellow half-light of the ward. Black skirts, white coifs.

She smiles at me and squeezes my hand. "That's right. It's a care home now, Johnny. I'm going to ask Marsaili if she'll let you stay there. And I'll come and see you every day, and bring you back here to the house for lunch. And we can go for walks on Charlie's beach, and talk about The Dean, and the people we knew here on the island." She has such beautiful eyes, smiling at me like that. "Would you like that, Johnny? Would you?"

I squeeze her hands right back, returning her smile, and remember that night I saw her crying on the roof of The Dean.

"I would," I say.

ACKNOWLEDGMENTS

I would like to offer my grateful thanks to those who gave so generously of their time and expertise during my researches for *The Lewis Man*. In particular, I'd like to express my gratitude to pathologist **Steven C. Campman, M.D**, Medical Examiner, San Diego, California; **Donald Campbell Veale**, former "inmate" of The Dean; **Mary-Alex Kirkpatrick**, actress (Alyxis Daly), for her wonderful hospitality while I was in South Uist researching locations; **Derek (Pluto) Murray**, for his advice on the Gaelic language; **Marion Morrison**, Registrar at the Tarbert Registry Office; **Bill Lawson**, Seallam! Visitor Centre, Northton, Isle of Harris, who has been specialising in the family and social history of the Outer Hebrides of Scotland for over forty years.

Note: The actual Dean Orphanage closed its doors in the late 1940s, its children dispersed to other homes. For the purposes of my story I have extended its life by eight to ten years. Conditions at the home related in the book were, however, exactly as described by the last "inmate" to pass through its doors.

PETER MAY was an award-winning journalist at the age of just twenty-one. He left newspapers for television and screenwriting, creating three prime-time British drama series and accruing more than 1,000 television credits. Peter now lives in France where he focuses on writing novels.